PENGUIN BOOKS

THE MIDDLE AGE OF MRS ELIOT

Angus Wilson was born in the south of England in 1913. A part of his childhood was spent in South Africa, and he was then educated at his brother's school in Sussex, Westminster School and Oxford. He joined the staff of the British Museum Library in 1937. When the War came he helped towards the safe storage of the British Museum treasures before serving the rest of the War in Naval Intelligence. It was while trying to emerge from a period of depression and near-breakdown that he began to write short stories in 1946, a collection of which, *The Wrong Set*, was published in 1949. This met with immense critical acclaim and was followed a year later by a second collection, *Such Darling Dodos*. In 1952 his short critical study *Emile Zola* was published and was followed in 1953 by his first novel, *Hemlock and After*, one of his best known works. In 1955 he resigned from the Museum in order to devote his time to writing, and in 1963 became a part-time lecturer at the new University of East Anglia in Norwich, subsequently becoming Professor and Public Orator. He was made a CBE in 1968 and knighted in 1980.

His other novels are *Anglo-Saxon Attitudes* (1956), *The Old Men at the Zoo* (1961), *Late Call* (1964), *No Laughing Matter* (1967), *As If By Magic* (1973) and *Setting the World on Fire* (1980). His third volume of short stories, *A Bit Off the Map*, was published in 1957 and a critical autobiographical study, *The Wild Garden*, appeared in 1963. Many of his books, including his *Collected Stories*, are published by Penguin.

Angus Wilson died in 1991. Among the many people who paid tribute to him on his death were Malcolm Bradbury: 'He was brilliant in the real sense of the word. He shone and he was very theatrical. Lectures were packed'; Paul Bailey: 'He was the kindest of men. I am not the only younger writer who is indebted to him'; and Rose Tremain: 'Angus Wilson was a great novelist and a profoundly lovable man'.

ANGUS WILSON

THE MIDDLE AGE OF MRS ELIOT

PENGUIN BOOKS

PENGUIN BOOKS

Published by the Penguin Group
Penguin Books Ltd, 27 Wrights Lane, London W8 5TZ, England
Penguin Books USA Inc., 375 Hudson Street, New York, New York 10014, USA
Penguin Books Australia Ltd, Ringwood, Victoria, Australia
Penguin Books Canada Ltd, 10 Alcorn Avenue, Toronto, Ontario, Canada M4V 3B2
Penguin Books (NZ) Ltd, 182–190 Wairau Road, Auckland 10, New Zealand

Penguin Books Ltd, Registered Offices: Harmondsworth, Middlesex, England

First published by Martin Secker and Warburg Ltd 1958
Published in Penguin Books 1961
Reissued 1992
1 3 5 7 9 10 8 6 4 2

Printed in England by Clays Ltd, St Ives plc
Filmset in Bembo

TO
JOHN WITH GRATITUDE
AND TO
HELEN'S LOVED
MEMORY

BOOK ONE

HUMPTY DUMPTY

MEG ELIOT was well aware that in taking her place as Chairman of the Committee for the third time in succession she was acting in an unconstitutional way. The rules of 'Aid to the Elderly', as old Mr Purdyke had pointed out, were quite clear on this point. The chair was to be taken in rotation. As she sat once more at the centre of the table, with Lady Pirie on her left and old Mr Purdyke on her right, and with young Mr Darlington, the secretary, covering the end of the table with his neat files and card indexes, she wondered why exactly she set such store by getting her own way on this point. It seemed absurd on the face of it: Aid to the Elderly was only a medium-sized charitable organization and acting as chairman only brought more chores. In any case she had got her own way only because September with its holiday absences usually saw no more than the minimum statutory attendance of three. Had that ghastly old battleaxe Mrs Masters been there she would have fought tooth and nail to keep Meg in her place.

Meg felt a bit ashamed when she considered how she had persuaded them; she had made much of the fact that she would be playing truant for the next six months. She was much concerned that her superior financial position allowed her to take this jaunt round the world, so much beyond the purses of the other committee members; she had been anxious to atone for it. 'Do, for goodness' sake, work me to death while I'm still here,' she had said to them many times, yet the truth was that it was no atonement at all – at any rate not to her. She liked to be chairman, she liked to dominate any group of people with whom she worked. It had been the same with the Red Cross in the war. Other people make such stupid mistakes, she thought, and then she laughed at her own vanity. I may have been good for Aid to the Elderly, she thought, but I very much doubt if Aid to the Elderly has been good for me. They spoil me too much. They are easy game. A society which, despite its employment of trained social workers, was

7

still palpably a charity, an organization which for all its occasional government grants was so much an old-fashioned voluntary body of a now dying kind, did not expect that a woman like herself should choose to be on its committee at all. She was, she knew, better off than many of the committee members – than the 'new poor' like Lady Pirie. And even if there were some wealthy ones, they were people who 'lived quietly', whereas she and Bill spent as it came. It was not surprising that they thought her rich and an especially dazzling sort of rich – not at all of the stolid rich, but of the fashionable and lively rich. She knew exactly how they saw her when she heard Viola Pirie describe her as 'the younger hostess type, you know'. Her fluency in saying absurd or ironic things made them think her smartly 'irreverent', essentially worldly. And, as she well knew from the past, to conventional people her height and her irregular features qualified her as a 'striking woman'. Viola had told her that the committee were agreed in describing her as 'exotic looking'. She was very conscious of being forty-three, but since that was ten years less than any of the others, they no doubt thought of her as young. In any case, she thought, I don't seem my age and I don't believe, thank God, that I look as though I've 'kept going'.

It was hardly surprising that Aid to the Elderly should think of her as a 'catch'. It was more surprising that she should feel pleased that they did so. She had, of course, had to fight the few diehards who saw no need for 'catches', and who were suspicious of anyone from the smart world who wanted to meddle in the world of social service. She had, at any rate, forced them to feel that it was wiser to keep their doubts to themselves. Perhaps it was that victory, she decided, that made her pleased, but if so it wasn't really good enough – the victory was such an easy one. As old Mr Purdyke had said, 'Mrs Eliot's so quick, she rather leaves us standing. But I'm sure it's been very good for us all to be shaken up.' Viola Pirie, of course, in her mothering moods sometimes pulled her up sharply with a gruff, downright snub – but then Viola was happy to be known as a barker rather than a biter.

In gaining her mastery of the committee, however, Mr Darlington had been the greatest help to her, but then so had she been to him. When she found that he was a trained social worker brought in at the suggestion of the Ministry, she had immediately been on his side. She wondered for a moment if she was not too impressed by trained people; it was partly having missed the University herself, partly her brother David's academic training that had influenced her. Anyhow she'd been all for Darlington immediately.

The others, conscious that to refuse the Ministry's suggestion would be to lose the Ministry's occasional grants, had not been all for him. She hadn't really understood a lot of his modern university-trained methods, and when she had understood, she'd been a bit doubtful of some of them, but she had backed him against the others. He was obviously grateful and probably a bit affected by the paradox of having a fashionable woman for an ally. She was pretty sure that his idea of a useful world had not previously included fashionable women. Then, like her, he had a strong sense of the ridiculous, and she had encouraged him to think that, far from being a frivolity, it was in some way a necessary part of the 'modern' approach to the alleviation of human misery.

Meg came to from her reverie and felt a peculiar pleasure in realizing that she had been able to deal with three cases of aged hardship, and had used sense and humanity, while her mind had really been elsewhere. She felt, as in everything she did, a battle between this self-consciousness, between her histrionic enjoyment of it, and her certainty that she cared seriously and completely for the work itself. She had always to keep in check the self-mockery that would have persuaded her that her 'good', 'genuine' motives were only the protective product of a 'real', 'unworthy' desire to win applause. To strengthen her confidence in her own 'sincerity' she assumed a serious direct gaze and a frown, conscious at the same time that for her colleagues this only added to her charm – made her, for them, a child playing at 'hospitals' or at 'working in the office'. But as she went on dealing with the affairs of the afternoon meeting, absorption in immediate problems pushed the self-consciousness away into a remote corner of her mind, whence it issued only in momentary jabs of self-ridicule.

'Mrs Mountain's granddaughter has come along,' Mr Darlington said, as he filed away the draft of the letter they had decided to send to old Mr Runcorn's sharp-practising landlord. 'Miss Rank tells me she was somewhat unwilling. The bus journey from Brixton apparently brings on sickness. But,' he smiled, 'I understand that a reminder that the society might have to discontinue home-help to her grandmother, unless there was some family cooperation, lessened the dangers of this malady.' This was a familiar type of joke to the committee, but one which helped to ease the strain of their work and they were all smiles.

'I don't believe,' Meg said, 'that people are *ever* sick in buses. One hears about it a lot, but I've never seen it. However, I think, in view of this cooperation, we should see her immediately.' She looked at Lady Pirie and Mr Purdyke in turn, but without waiting for their verbal agreement, she said, 'Ask her to come in, Mr Darlington, will you, please?'

She anticipated with satisfaction a tarty girl, for she had found rather to her surprise that her own chic, instead of antagonizing, seemed to induce cooperation from the more showy daughters or granddaughters of Aid to the Elderly's protégés. The young woman who came in was neat, dowdy, and sullen looking. Meg felt immediately the challenge of producing a response that would not come easily.

'Thank you for coming here, Mrs Crowe,' she said, as the young woman sat down. There was no answer. Meg, elbows on the table, cupped her hands in front of her.

'We wanted so much to see you before the winter came on. You see, although your grandmother's a remarkable person and very independent, she is getting to the stage where she needs a lot of things done for her. Especially in the winter time.' She paused, but there was silence.

'We've been willing to do all we can,' she went on. 'Miss Rank does shopping and a lot of housework. But we have a great number of old people to help who have no family at all. We have to consider that.'

'It's a long bus journey down there,' Mrs Crowe said, 'and I get sick in buses. I told Miss Rank that.'

'Your grandmother's very lonely, you know,' Lady Pirie began, but Meg took it up.

'You've no idea, perhaps,' she said, 'how much she looks forward to seeing her family. You see she's very shy with strangers, even with Miss Rank. They fuss her. That's why we do so want to avoid an old people's home as long at any rate as we possibly can.'

'You want me to have her with us?' Mrs Crowe said, looking down at the table.

'Well,' Mr Purdyke said, 'if there is no other ...' But Meg smiled across at Mrs Crowe.

'You're quite right. We do,' she said, 'that's why we asked you here. As you know.' She caught the woman's eye and they both smiled.

'I *knew* it all right,' Mrs Crowe said, resuming her grim look. But she sat less stiffly.

'She'll ask very little, you know,' Meg said, 'and she goes to bed very early.'

'It'll mean going without the lodger's money,' Mrs Crowe announced.

Mr Purdyke stirred angrily. 'Your grandmother brought you up, didn't she?' he asked.

'Oh, she was good to me,' Mrs Crowe said, 'I'm not saying anything against that. But I'm not going to pretend I want her with us. I've got my husband and Cecil and the twins. We're happy as we are. But, of course, if it's our duty...'

'I think it is,' Lady Pirie said.

Meg leaned forward as though she were about to touch Mrs Crowe's sleeve. 'Oh, no,' she cried, 'that wouldn't work at all. I don't think you'd feel happy on that basis, and I'm sure Mrs Mountain wouldn't. But you must face the alternative. *We* can't do any more.'

'You want me to take her in out of pity,' Mrs Crowe said.

'I don't know that that's the word I'd choose,' Meg said, 'but that would be a beginning. What's most important is that you should make her as happy as you can.'

'Oh, we'd do our part by her all right if she came to us. But out of pity is what it would be.'

Meg stifled an impulse to carry the argument further.

'I'll talk to my husband about it,' Mrs Crowe said.

'Thank you. You know Mr Darlington and Miss Rank. If you want to discuss it further with them, they're always ready to help,' Meg said and brought the interview to an end with a handshake.

The others seemed most satisfied with the outcome of Mrs Crowe's visit.

Lady Pirie said, 'They'll shake down,' and Mr Purdyke, 'She was more frightened to take the first step than anything, I think. But with Mrs Eliot's able assistance ...'

Meg, silent, appeared to wait on a word from Mr Darlington, but when he said, 'From what Miss Rank tells me, the husband doesn't count, so I think we can hope to remove Mrs Mountain from our files. It's wonderful what a little faith will do,' she looked at her watch impatiently.

'Is there anything else?' she asked. 'It's after four.'

Mr Darlington said rather quickly, 'There is this business of Mrs Tucker's gin.'

'Mrs Tucker's gin!' Lady Pirie laughed. 'Surely that can wait until next time. Meg's obviously longing for her tea.'

Mr Darlington said, 'Well, I had hoped …' and he looked at Meg.

'Of course we'll deal with it,' she cried, 'but let's have a cup of tea while we're doing so.'

'If you remember,' said Mr Darlington, when the office caretaker had produced tea and ginger nuts, 'we had assigned Mrs Tucker to our new social visitor. We thought she was a good easy case for Miss Rogers to get her hand in on. She's not very mobile but perfectly clean and an easy-going person.'

'There's some contradiction there,' Mr Purdyke said, 'as to mobility, you know.'

Lady Pirie made a snorting noise. Someone, she felt, had always to mark Mr Purdyke's jokes. Mr Darlington accepted her snort as sufficient mark to allow him to continue.

'Everything seemed to be going very well from Miss Rogers' account. But I'm afraid that isn't altogether correct. Miss Rank went in to see Mrs Tucker last week and found her in a very upset state. It seems that Miss Rogers has refused to bring her her weekly nip of gin.'

Meg always approved the slight note of irony with which Mr Darlington gave his reports. She felt that it added to his sincerity, as any touch of moral earnestness would have removed from it.

'Refused?' Meg said. 'Well, you must tell Miss Rogers that we are not a temperance society. She's perfectly entitled to her own views about drink, but Mrs Tucker's equally entitled to her gin.'

'Oh, I should have done so in the ordinary way, but Miss Rogers tells me she referred the matter to a member of the committee and was told that she shouldn't encourage the old woman in drinking.'

'Oh dear,' Mr Purdyke said. He disliked all rows.

'You know,' Lady Pirie said gruffly, 'I think this had better hang over, Mr Darlington, until this member of the committee's present.'

'I don't agree,' Meg declared. 'Mrs Masters has absolutely no right …'

'We don't know that Mr Darlington's referring to Mrs Masters,' Mr Purdyke put in.

'I do,' said Meg. She lit a cigarette and drank some of the thick brown tea to relax her annoyance.

'I'm not going back over all this,' she said, 'don't worry. But it's one thing for Mrs Masters to bring in an untrained girl against the committee's advice ...'

'Against yours,' Mr Purdyke said. 'Be honest, Mrs Eliot.'

'I don't particularly want to be honest when the rest of the committee behaves so spinelessly.' She smiled at Mr Darlington.

'All right,' she amended, 'against *my* advice *and* Mr Darlington's.'

'Mr Darlington is not a member of the committee,' Lady Pirie said with a chuckle intended to appease the secretary.

'Mr Darlington has to manage the staff,' Meg declared. 'All right. The thing's done. We have Mrs Masters' old governess's great-niece or whatever other piece of family piety. An untrained social visitor. But she is responsible to Mr Darlington and through him to the committee as a whole. Not Mrs Masters' personal employee.'

'Now Meg,' Lady Pirie said. She remembered at times that she had after all brought Meg Eliot into the work of the Society. 'I do think we should wait until Mrs Masters is here.'

'I know you do, Viola, but I don't trust you all not to let Mr Darlington down. *He's* responsible for Miss Rogers' work.'

'I can't help thinking,' Mr Purdyke said, 'that it would not be fair to say anything before we've talked to Miss Rogers herself. I'm sure Darlington won't mind my saying so.'

'I think she may be in the office,' Mr Darlington said.

'Oh dear,' Mr Purdyke complained.

'You mean you know she is,' Lady Pirie declared.

'Mr Darlington's very efficient, Viola,' Meg smiled at him and he faintly smiled back.

'There are other words for it,' Lady Pirie said, laughing.

'Ask her to come in,' Meg requested. 'But before you do so, what do you think of her general work?'

Mr Darlington's rather cherubic face looked earnest, his small mouth set gravely.

He looks like a hockey-playing spinster when he's trying to be fair to people, Meg thought; he's a nice man and I'm all on his side, but how do women marry such unromantic little men?

'To be perfectly fair,' he began.

'You don't have to be *perfectly* fair,' Meg said. She could not bear him to look so solemn.

'Oh yes, he does,' Lady Pirie said.

'Well, don't fall over backwards doing it,' Meg amended.

Mr Darlington smiled. 'Shall I go on?' he asked and continued, 'I think she might be very good. Of course, she'd be better if she'd had some training. But she's hard working and sensible. Her manner's a bit unfortunate at times but I suspect' – he assumed his professional psychological air – 'that she's nervous at having got the job by unorthodox means.'

'I don't think that's a very *fortunate* phrase to use about any girl,' Meg commented, 'but you think the Society should try to keep her?'

'Yes,' said Mr Darlington, 'I do.'

'Well,' said Meg and she smiled at Lady Pirie, 'we must try, then, mustn't we?'

Miss Rogers' manner that afternoon was certainly most unfortunate. She was a heavy busted and broad hipped young woman and she scowled at the committee from beneath a fringe of black hair. Mr Darlington placed a chair for her which she ignored. Meg did not smile at her but she said:

'We just wanted to know how you were liking the work, Miss Rogers.'

'All right.'

'Good. I'm glad of that because Mr Darlington's given such a good report of you that we shouldn't want to lose you.'

Miss Rogers said nothing but she sat down.

'The Latimer Road area's not the nicest beginning,' Meg said. 'If she's survived that she'll survive anything, don't you think, Mr Purdyke?'

Mr Purdyke was vague about the area but he said: 'Yes. A very difficult district.'

Meg waited for Miss Rogers to register Mr Purdyke's vagueness; then she began to discuss the relative difficulties of the streets in Miss Rogers' area, asking her about her particular cases as she did so. At first the girl responded shortly, then with increasing eagerness; and then suddenly she said: 'Well, are you satisfied that I've done my work?'

'Yes,' said Meg, 'I am. But why do you ask?'

'Because you didn't want me to have the job.'

'Really,' said Lady Pirie, 'I don't think anyone should have told you that.'

'Oh, my dear Viola,' Meg laughed, 'committees always talk. You're quite right, Miss Rogers, I didn't. I prefer trained social workers. In principle I'm sure I'm right. Though in your case I was wrong.'

Miss Rogers smiled rather awkwardly.

'Thank you,' she said.

But Meg maintained her serious, straightforward manner. 'Oh, I've no doubt you can learn a lot still,' she declared. 'For instance refusing Mrs Tucker her gin. That seems to have been a mistake.'

Miss Rogers was confused.

'Mrs Masters agreed with me.'

Meg suppressed a smile.

'Yes,' she said dismissing this lightly, 'you should have gone to Mr Darlington about that, of course. But I'm more interested in *your* reasons. As a general rule we should never take such a thing on ourselves, should we, Viola?'

Lady Pirie, anxious to appease, said, 'No. But perhaps Miss Rogers had a special reason.'

'Yes, exactly,' Meg said casually, 'that's just what I was interested in.'

'Drink's a very dangerous thing for old people living on their own,' Miss Rogers declared.

Mr Purdyke seemed impressed by this answer, so she said directly to him, 'Mrs Tucker's very lonely.'

Meg smiled.

'That after all is why Aid to the Elderly is concerned with her, Miss Rogers. But because people are lonely and old we can't treat them like children. Not unless there's some urgent medical reason. There's no doctor's report in Mrs Tucker's case, is there, Mr Darlington?'

He shook his head.

'But if they're doing something harmful to themselves,' Miss Rogers said.

'Oh come,' Lady Pirie cried, 'a drop of gin isn't as bad as all that,' and she chuckled. But Meg took Miss Rogers' suggestion more seriously.

'Perhaps it may be. But we're out to help those old people to lead independent lives. The right to harm oneself a bit is surely the essence of independence. Why, one shouldn't even interfere where people are close to one, let alone with strangers.'

She paused for a moment; then to heighten the absurdity of the whole matter she produced an absurd example.

'My husband's an inveterate gambler. I'm sure it's frightfully bad for him to waste his money like that. But I would no more think of refusing to telephone to his bookmaker for him if he was ill ...' She left the absurdity in mid-air and then turned quietly to drawing the general conclusion.

'That really is the value of this training business I'm so keen on. It gives you at least a few basic rules in a job where, in the main, you're thrown back on personal decision all the time. Don't you agree, Mr Purdyke?'

'Oh, indeed,' Mr Purdyke said. He could hardly say less with Mr Darlington, all trained, sitting there; but he added, 'I think Miss Rogers was trying to use her initiative.'

Meg carefully mistook his intention.

'Yes,' she said, 'but you'll know better next time, won't you, Miss Rogers? You'll go to Mr Darlington if there's any query. But you're obviously cut out for this work.' She paused for a moment. 'I wish,' she said, 'you could take a social service course. Apart from this job, qualifications are so important in the modern world.'

'There is an evening course – a shortened one,' Mr Darlington began and Lady Pirie grunted to show that she was not out of touch.

'Why, that's a good idea, Viola,' Meg said, 'but do you think, Miss Rogers, you could do evening work as well as this? Lady Pirie suggests ...'

The girl's heavy body sagged a little.

'I don't know that I could afford the fees at the moment, to be honest.'

'Oh! I think the committee could do something about that,' Meg cried, 'surely. Unfortunately I shan't be here but you'll make it clear to the rest of them that it has my support, Viola, won't you? We haven't got Mr Purdyke's view yet, though.'

Mr Purdyke hastened to agree with Lady Pirie. Meg only just checked herself from saying something about Mrs Masters' undoubted support of the idea. Mr Darlington would like the joke, but such jokes often proved too costly pleasures. Miss Rogers' thanks she deflected on to Lady Pirie.

She could not avoid a small sigh of relief as the girl left the room. It's the thought of all that lumpy underwear that revolts me so, she decided.

As soon as Miss Rogers had gone, Mr Purdyke also took his leave. He found the meetings an increasing strain since Mr Darlington had introduced these little red American cloth chairs with metal legs, but he had to admit that the dirty cream distempered offices of the Society did need a note of brightness.

Mr Darlington, who hated disorder, would normally have escaped to his private office, leaving the slopped tea cups and overflowing ash-trays to tomorrow's cleaners. He wanted still more, however, to continue talking to Meg Eliot, and so he stayed, perched on the edge of the table and sucking at his empty pipe.

'If I may say so, Mrs Eliot,' he said, 'you handled that beautifully.'

Meg Eliot's dark eyes glittered. 'I hope I wasn't too fierce with the poor thing,' she said and by not waiting for his answer showed that her fears were a formality. 'But really,' she went on, and her tone became fierce and earnest, 'I can't let that moral bullying pass uncriticized. The paid social workers are here to administer the society's funds for the benefit of the old people. It's nothing to do with her whether old Mrs T. chooses to spend the little she gets on gin so long as the old creature doesn't let herself go downhill. It's her job to relieve the poor old thing's loneliness, not to moralize about the results of it. We're not a temperance society. I'm more and more convinced that we can't afford untrained people. It's a false economy. Indeed it would be a very good thing if the committee had to attend the course, though I'm sure very few of us would get our certificates or what have you.'

'Well, Meg dear, when you get back from your junketing in the East, you must enrol.' Lady Pirie checked Meg Eliot's enthusiasm by a dry mother-to-daughter manner, 'I'll suggest it to the committee while you're away.'

'I'll volunteer gladly if you will, Viola.' Meg winked at Mr Darlington.

'Splendid,' he said, 'now we're getting somewhere.'

'We all ought to be getting on with our work,' Lady Pirie said. 'I've got to feed a hungry son, Meg. I don't have Italians to do my housekeeping. And I've no doubt Mr Darlington's got plenty to do as well.'

'It's nice for Mr Darlington to do nothing for a change, I think.' Meg announced it simply as a fact.

Lady Pirie said, 'He'd probably like to choose his own place and time for that. Missing trains because of a lot of women's gossip ...'

Meg, laughing, interrupted. 'A *lot* of women's gossip perhaps, Viola, but not mine. You'd miss a train for me, wouldn't you, Mr Darlington?'

'I've plenty of trains, Mrs Eliot ...' he began, but Lady Pirie said, 'You may have, but I've got a lot of shopping to do and I'm relying on Mrs Eliot for a lift. Besides, she has a long and tiring journey ahead of her. I know you're an experienced traveller, Meg, but you don't fly about to the East and Australia every day. You're going to need all your energies. What on earth you're giving this party this evening for, I can't think.'

'We thought our old friends would like to say good-bye to us.' Meg assumed a mock pained expression, but Lady Pirie would not be teased.

'Good-byes,' she said. 'A lot of fudge.'

She sounded so cross that Mr Darlington, professionally conditioned to compose quarrels, called all his tact to the aid of the situation.

'We shall miss you very much, Mrs Eliot. A lot can happen in six months. There's this business of Mrs Chorley, for instance. I don't know what you think, but Aid to the Elderly's never contributed before where there's a rich family in the background.'

Meg Eliot shifted squarely in her seat. She seemed to mark the change to a more serious topic by her new posture.

'If she really wants to remain independent of her family then I think we must consider her eligible for help. But there can't be any of this preferential treatment for distressed gentlewomen if that's what she's after.'

'I think she's difficult,' Mr Darlington began.

Lady Pirie laid her huge bucket bag heavily down on the table.

'Mr Darlington,' she said, 'this is all coming up at the next committee meeting. It's quite improper to discuss it now. In the first place Mrs Eliot won't be here, so I'm afraid her opinions aren't going to help us. In the second place you know very well that many members of the committee have strong views on the subject. The secretary's job is to advise the committee, not to try to make up their minds for them.'

The rather sour smile with which she accompanied her rebuke was so patently the formal softening of an order to a subordinate that it only added to Mr Darlington's embarrassment. He seemed to look to Mrs Eliot for support, but such as she gave was indirect. Getting up from her seat, she held out her hand to him.

'Good-bye,' she said, 'I look to you to keep the flag of good sense flying here every month while I'm away.'

'Good-bye,' Mr Darlington answered. 'Six months seems a very long time.' Perhaps he remembered that he had said something very like this before, for he blushed as he had not done at Lady Pirie's rudeness. 'I hope you have a very good holiday indeed,' he added quickly.

'I expect I shall.' Meg's tone was casual. 'Malaya will be rather ghastly, I'm afraid, apparently we shall just hit the rainy season. But the company's paying Bill such an enormous fee to defend the case that we can't possibly refuse. Without it we couldn't afford the rest of the trip. And I *am* looking forward to Australia and the Pacific. Although I must say I have such a wonderful life anyway that I'm not as excited as I ought to be at the prospect of change.'

Clearly Lady Pirie felt the impropriety of this remark to Mr Darlington, but she only underlined it.

'We're not all rolling in money like you, Meg,' she announced.

Meg Eliot suggested the vulgarity she felt in the rebuke by slightly protruding the lower lip of her large sensual mouth.

'Oh, Bill and I don't *roll*,' she said. 'Far from it. No, I think the phrase for us is "spend as we get it". But if you mean should I like to be poor, the answer is no. I should loathe it.'

She smiled, even giggled at Mr Darlington. To Lady Pirie's evident annoyance he giggled with evident pleasure in return. He opened the door for them and watched them pass down the long stone corridor of the office building. He had hardly turned back into the disordered committee room, however, when Meg Eliot's head appeared round the door.

'Don't take any notice of her moods,' she said. 'She's always like that when she's got her Widow Twankey hat on.' She saw him laugh and was off again, delighted to have done the right thing.

Meg's pleasure at the good relationship she had made with Mr Darlington swelled into a vague general sense of well-being with the world as she ran down the broad stairs. The quick, light clicking of her high heels against the stone echoed gaily through the building, seeming indeed an echo of her light, gay, easy relationship with all the many different kinds of people she touched upon in her busy life. She was struck by her self-satisfaction and wanted to laugh at the absurdity of it, and yet her ever ready self-mockery only made her more content. This she acknowledged by permitting the laughter.

Pushing open the heavy door by its iron bar she came out into the drabness of Uxbridge Road, glaringly dusty in the bright August sunshine. She imagined herself, tall and graceful, as exotic as a flamingo against the dirty yellow London brick houses and the smut-coated privet hedges. But not exotic really, or rather no stranger here than anywhere else with her 'interesting' irregular shaped face, large brown eyes, and thick, greying straw-yellow hair. At once 'outside' and 'at home' anywhere. Laughing at her vanity, she crossed the road to where Viola Pirie was dressing down a group of children who were playing around the Humber.

'You children have got to realize,' she was saying, 'that you *must* not touch what doesn't belong to you. You've got plenty of things of your own nowadays. How would you like it if I came into your house and scratched your precious tele?'

Meg smiled, for the children's politeness and their awe of what was peculiar were clearly hardly sufficient to keep them from laughing in Viola's face.

'If you brats have written anything on my car!' she cried, still laughing. She surveyed the black surface rapidly. 'Not even a bad word,' she said and gave the tallest girl sixpence.

As she manoeuvred the Humber through the crowded traffic of Shepherd's Bush, she set herself to mollify Viola Pirie who was making bulldog snorts beside her.

'It's the fault of these cars,' Meg said, 'they have such huge, squat, shiny behinds that it's a constant temptation to write bad words on them. I feel it myself sometimes.'

But Lady Pirie seemed determined to be stern. She said nothing for some minutes, then, 'You trade on my being so fond of you, Meg. It really isn't good enough, my dear.'

'Oh, Viola, a few street children!'

'You know I'm not talking about the children. You're going well on the way to ruining a very good secretary in Mr Darlington. And he won't be the first.'

'Really, Viola, I don't think you've any right to imply such things. And Mr Darlington a respectable married man.' Meg spoke in imitated cockney. 'Besides,' she added, 'I don't seem to fancy gentlemen who smoke pipes.'

'No, Meg,' Lady Pirie said, 'I'm not going to laugh whatever Mr Darlington may do. You owe the committee some loyalty. And don't try to look serious when I say that, because you don't feel it.'

'Well, you were so awful to the poor man. I had to go back and say something. And you always are in a temper for some reason when you're wearing that Widow Twankey hat. It's psychosomatic.'

'So you *didn't* leave anything behind. Really!' Lady Pirie's square, grey face set in shocked maternal lines, then she saw reflected in the windscreen for a moment the green quills bobbing up and down above her russet felt cap.

'It is rather awful, isn't it?' she said, 'but I always get so fussed in shops.'

She laughed heartily on a deep, cracked note. She was silent, then at the traffic lights when they started again, she said: 'You're free to laugh at *me* as much as you like. You know that. But do you think it's fair to that man to undermine his respect for the committee?'

Meg controlled her rising annoyance, trying deliberately to remember that Viola's lecturing manner was a direct measure of her affection.

'And you're the person who's always fussing about the importance of a sense of humour for social work,' she said. 'The number of times that I've heard you ask those wretched applicants for home visiting jobs whether they can see a joke! Well, Mr Darlington can, and that's why I like him.'

'You like him to see *your* jokes,' Lady Pirie said gruffly. 'You don't consider that his job depends on getting on with the rest of the committee.'

Meg accelerated to pass two other cars, leaving barely sufficient time to avoid the oncoming traffic. The driver of one car hooted at her and she hooted back.

'I know what I'm doing,' she called out. In fact, she was trying to deflect her anger from Viola Pirie. Even so when she spoke it was in a drawling voice intended to provoke.

'Oh, I think Darlington's capable of fussing the committee when it's required.'

Lady Pirie seemed absorbed in the flower barrows at Notting Hill Gate.

'He understands us all much better than you think.'

Lady Pirie turned and looked at her. 'Nonsense,' she said. 'He understands even less about the sort of people we are than I had thought. Look at this afternoon! The way he rushed in with his uncalled for tact when you and I had got a little sharp with each other. The cheek of it! Anyone even a little sensitive would know that when people are such old friends as you and I are ...' Her voice tailed away. Her grey, wrinkled neck had turned pink. 'People like that have no shades of behaviour. For them a quarrel's a quarrel.'

Ordinarily Meg would have reacted strongly to 'people like that', but now she was aware only of compassion for Viola's loneliness; and as an older, more familiar pity, it clouded and obscured her feelings for Mr Darlington's dismal daily round.

She sought for an expression that was part of her regular communication with Viola Pirie. 'Oh, dear God!' she said – an oath that Viola always found peculiarly absurd and endearing when Meg used it – 'Dear God! I'm not proposing a friendship with him, Viola. I think he's frightfully efficient at the job. I agree with most of his ideas about the work, even though like all these trained people he's a bit solemn and absurd about it at times. And I like to protect him from all you old reactionaries on the committee. That's all.'

Lady Pirie even smiled a little now.

'Oh, he's excellent,' she said, 'and a nice person too. But he needs a bit of criticism to sharpen his wits on. So much of the work is routine.'

'Yes,' said Meg, 'and imagine how dreary his home life must be. He lives in North London, he told me. Merton or somewhere.'

'Kenton,' Lady Pirie corrected, 'Merton's in *South* London. I don't know why you should think it must be dreary,' she went on, 'I always think of his house as rather bright – each wall with a different coloured wallpaper, with those modern designs, you know.'

Meg was not in the imaginative habit of following the people she met back to their homes, so she made no comment.

'Not that I know much about how anybody lives nowadays.' Lady Pirie was quite mollified now. 'You're the one who goes about, Meg, and knows what life's like today, not me.'

They were in sight of the dismal converted mid-Victorian house in which Lady Pirie had her flat; looking at it, Meg could not bring herself to say, 'Well, yes, darling, that is so.' The teasing somehow seemed too cruel outside that decaying, genteel jail.

'You'll come early tonight, won't you, Viola?' she asked, as Lady Pirie got out.

'Of course. I'm looking forward to it. Though I still think you're very naughty to tire yourself like that.' Viola Pirie paused a moment and then added, 'You'll forgive Tom if he doesn't come, won't you?'

Meg said quickly, 'But of course. We know how he hates parties.'

'Oh, he probably will,' Viola rushed to get it in. 'You and Bill are such favourites.'

'Well, don't force the poor darling to come.' Meg pressed the starter and was gone.

As she made her slow way along Oxford Street, Meg contrasted her last errand with the next – Aid for the Elderly and Sczekely's. Few people were lucky enough to have such a range of interests. What would Mr Darlington make of a Meissen dish, or Miss Gorres of Sczekely's of modern methods in social case work? Detecting once more a note of cosy self-satisfaction in her thoughts, Meg applied the salt of irony – the Old and the Antique, that sort of journalistic phraseology was the price one paid for being under-educated, being brought up as a nice upper-middle-class girl.

She could not, however, help congratulating herself on her ability to cope with people as she trod the cushiony grey carpet that lined the passage to the showroom at Sczekely's. Most people found Miss Gorres difficult and abrupt; she conducted her business by successful bullying. But Meg, with her instinctive response to mood and shape of speech, had early adopted a casual yet direct manner with this chic and ageing refugee *gamine* that exactly fitted her shy, aggressive behaviour. Since she was a regular patroness at Sczekely's this adaptation had been no more than a convenience, had sprung in fact from her habitual desire to please; but today it promised to be of practical use.

She still found it strange that Bill should have asked her to cancel her purchase of the Nymphenburg figures. Two hundred pounds was not the sort of sum that he normally questioned; however, questioned he had, and Meg had been in a way pleased to have him deny her something; not only as a novelty, but as an expression of their relative positions in their devoted marriage. She loved Bill as much as anything for his conventional masculinity – or rather for the amalgam of qualities, sexual, emotional, and intellectual, which were implied in that term. His success had become for her a symbol of this masculine strength. She cherished his success and the way he used it – a way both generous and self-willed. A generosity that for her found expression in the allowance, growing as his success grew, that he automatically made to her; a self-will that showed itself in his unspoken demand that she should never inquire into the state of their finances, other than to know that he had been entrusted with this or this lucrative case.

It was an archaic position for a wife that most of her friends would have found intolerable, but, since it enabled her to lead the life she so exactly wanted, Meg had come to feel it almost an emancipation from the conventional feminine freedoms, certainly an advance over the starved lives that so many of her friends gained from their independent, mutually sharing marriages. When, then, Bill had said: 'Cancel the order for that bit of Nymphenburg nonsense, lovey, will you? This trip round the world, you know, means refusing a number of rather big cases,' she had been delighted to accept the request as an order. She had only wished that it had been more peremptory, unaccompanied by any reason.

So now she approached without concern the desk where Miss Gorres sat in a haze of cigarette smoke, once boyish but now a wrinkling monkey-boy.

'I've decided not to have the two pieces I ordered, Miss Gorres,' she said.

Miss Gorres' large brown eyes expressed only a perfunctory surprise; Meg's decision, they suggested, was so unlikely to be realized that surprise was hardly called for.

'The figures have been sent to you, Mrs Eliot,' she said patiently, 'and I believe your cheque has been paid into the bank.'

'I want to send them back,' Meg announced, 'and if you've paid in the cheque, you can refund the money to me.'

'I don't think,' said Miss Gorres, 'that there was any question of the objects being returned when you bought them.' Her accent became sterner and more foreign. 'I don't think Mr Sczekely will agree to it.'

'Oh,' said Meg, 'as to that, I'll talk to him if you like.'

'Those pieces are not everybody's taste, you know,' Miss Gorres observed.

Meg said nothing, and after a moment's silence, Miss Gorres remarked casually: 'We could try to find another buyer for you, if you like.' She began to sharpen a pencil.

Meg looked round at the room.

'I can't think why you show all this inferior late Chinese stuff,' she said. 'I'm leaving England for several months tomorrow morning so if you have my cheque, perhaps you'd return it to me now, otherwise you can make a refund. I'll arrange for the figures to be ready if you'll send someone to my house for them.'

For a moment Miss Gorres seemed on the point of arguing, then she asked, 'Shall I tell them to destroy the cheque?'

'Yes. That will do,' Meg answered. 'Maybe when I get back if they're still unsold ...'

'Oh, they won't be,' Miss Gorres said.

'No,' Meg picked on it, 'I didn't suppose for a moment that they would be.' And she laughed.

Miss Gorres accepted the friendly malice in the same spirit.

'You're giving us a lot of nuisance, Mrs Eliot,' she said, 'but so few people know as you do what they want and want what they should, so we must be indulgent for once.'

'Yes.' Meg took the compliment flatly. 'And then, of course, I buy a lot of objects from you.'

Now Miss Gorres too laughed. 'We shall miss you here, Mrs Eliot,' she said. 'Where are you going?'

'Oh, all over the place. Australia, South America, probably New York. My husband works so hard. This is a kind of treat for him. Only he's always so restless on holiday that it's no good trying to stay in one place.'

'If I had not travelled so much against my will,' said Miss Gorres, 'I should envy you. Even so I *do* envy you the collections you will see. Perhaps I can give you some introductions to collectors and galleries. Look,' she announced, 'have you time for a drink?'

Meg had no time at all to spare and had sworn to herself that she would not be cluttered up with introductions on the trip. To see Miss Gorres so relaxed, however, and to be offered a *tête-à-tête* that was surely given only to very few, and then only for the clearest business motives, was such a tribute to the easy terms she had established as she could not resist.

'Of course. Thank you,' she said.

Their heads were bowed almost conspiratorially over letters and visiting cards when a loud, flat drawl echoed through the small show-room.

'Meg! You're drinking. I do think you're clever to find drink here. You must be one of those people who get booze out of a stone.'

Meg turned, as indeed did the few other visitors to Sczekely's to see a dumpy figured, middle-aged woman in a grubby black suit smiling vaguely, moonily about the room. Moony, too, was perhaps the adjective to describe her face, for it was heavily made up in the Dutch doll manner – plump, smooth, and lifeless except for very bright blue eyes, so round that they gave an appearance of perpetual childish fright.

'Poll, how lovely to see you,' Meg said quietly.

Miss Gorres replaced the papers in her drawer and disposed of glasses and bottle in a cupboard, although Meg had not finished her drink.

'It isn't very lovely to see all the beautiful drink put away,' Poll said, more to the room than to Miss Gorres.

'Why are you going to all those filthy foreign places, Meg? Travelling in aeroplanes and never knowing where your things are. That's no life for a girl.'

'Bill's got an important case in Singapore, some big rubber company's interests. And we're going to blue the fees on a world trip. He so needs a rest, poor darling.'

'Oh, husbands!' said Poll, with a crushing emphasis on the first syllable of the word and in the tone of one who had enjoyed great numbers of husbands, which indeed she had.

'Not that Bill doesn't seem much more like one's favourite dish than a husband. But then they all do until you marry them. Have you got lots of lovely "mon" for me, Miss Garrish?' she asked without pausing.

Miss Gorres referred to a card index as the most appropriate place for Poll's affairs.

'I'm selling the two bits of Chelsea that my mum left me,' Poll explained to Meg. 'It's all against promises to the dying and so on. But I do think circumstances alter facts, don't you?'

To Meg it seemed that Poll was really asking for support. 'Of course they do, darling,' she said as warmly as possible.

Poll seemed to consider for a moment. 'I think,' she said with hesitation, 'I meant that facts altered circumstances. But thank you for agreeing with me.'

Miss Gorres meanwhile had taken one of the cards from the index drawer and laid it on her desk.

'No sale yet, I'm afraid, Mrs Robson,' she said.

Meg could not for the moment connect Poll with the name Robson, and Poll, seeing this, announced:

'You didn't know I'd gone back to Robson, did you, darling? Well, I have. Only not with everybody. I'm trying it out. But I think I shall, because although Robson was quite ghastly in a lot of ways, he was really better than my others. What do you mean "no sale"?' she continued, turning to Miss Gorres. 'I know for a fact that Mrs Chisholm was after one and Lord Morrington said he'd bought the other. *Mary* Chisholm, Meg,' she added in explanation, 'not the old one. I shouldn't think *she'd* buy porcelain, would you?' She burst into a loud laugh at the absurdity of the idea, completing the isolation of Miss Gorres whose tone of voice openly announced that she was not prepared to maintain patience with her as long as she would with most clients. 'You gave us a reserve price. None of the offers so far have reached that reserve.'

'What do you mean, reached that reserve?' Poll asked. She made Miss Gorres' phrase sound like the ultimate hypocritical evasion. 'I'm sure Lord Morrington would never have offered less than I asked. You don't seem very good at selling things.'

'You asked rather a high reserve,' Miss Gorres said.

I didn't ask more than I needed,' Poll said, and then laughed loudly at her own frankness. 'It's my bloody trustees,' she announced to the room.

Miss Gorres clearly found these personal revelations unpleasantly alien to the reticent decorum her own misfortunes had taught her. 'I think perhaps you should see Mr Sczekely himself about it.'

'I think I better had,' said Poll, 'where is he?'

'He's away this afternoon.'

'Well, really,' Poll cried. 'What was the good of saying I should see him?' To Meg she appeared to be about to stamp her foot in rage. Miss Gorres walked away ostentatiously to talk to another visitor to the gallery.

'I hope you're not going to be as cross as this at my party this evening,' Meg said.

'It isn't crossness. It's righteous anger. That beast must have known I wanted the money. I *always* hate little crop-haired women.'

'Poor thing,' Meg explained in a lowered voice, 'I know she's difficult. But she was in the worst of the concentration camps, Poll, for years.

'Well,' said Poll, 'suffering hasn't ennobled *her*, has it?' However, when Miss Gorres came back, she said, 'Mrs Eliot says I've been jolly cross. Forgive and put it down to aching feet, will you? But do get a good price for them. After all, seeing as how they've got the sentimental value, I wouldn't sell them unless I wanted the money pretty badly, would I?'

For a moment Meg thought that all Poll's little efforts to be nice, including the comic cockney of her last sentence, were not going to soften Miss Gorres, so she smiled herself and said, 'Well, I'm sure my friend couldn't say fairer than that, could she?'

It was unlikely that Meg's cockney appeased Miss Gorres as Poll's had not, but something did, for she said: 'I'll do my very best for you, Mrs Robson.'

Poll took no more notice of her. 'I promise I won't be cross at your party, Meg,' she said, 'but I expect I shall cry. I always do when people are going away. Even just for the weekend.'

After Poll's departure, Meg could not forbear completing the cordiality. 'Poor Poll,' she said. 'You were wonderful with her, Miss Gorres.' It was only when she saw that Miss Gorres was accepting the praise with a flush of pleasure that she realized where her mood had led her. She got up hurriedly and left the gallery with only a murmured good-bye.

She had passed Westminster Abbey and was nearing home, when she remembered that she had not called for the air-sickness pills Doctor Loundes had prescribed for her. And there in the chemist's shop in Victoria Street was Jill Stokes – poor Jill – her oldest friend whom at Bill's request she had *not* invited to the party. 'Oh, look here, not the Grim Grenadier, you know,' he had said, when he saw Jill's name on the list of prospective guests, 'at least not if my tastes are, being consulted.' And of course, they had been, for it was as much his party as Meg's.

Jill, standing so upright by the Toilet Requisites sign, did indeed look the Grenadier. Her red woollen suit was as simple as Meg's blue one, but the simplicity suggested drabness rather than chic. Meg reflected embarrassedly that this was merely the difference of cost. Jill's height, too, no greater than Meg's, seemed gawky rather than graceful; and her regular features – straight nose, high brow beneath swept-up grey hair – had the severity of a ward sister rather than of a Roman matron. Her smile, Meg thought, so perpetual, had become with years the frozen smile of death. Almost unconsciously Meg began to summon all the expressive pantomime of her own mobile irregular face. I do see what Mother meant by the advantages of being a *jolie laide*, she thought.

For a moment she was shocked at her instinctive pleasure at outshining poor Jill, but then remembering her youthful jealousy of her friend's classic looks she felt justified in her present little triumph. One can't always have kind thoughts, she decided.

'I'm buying some soap and maybe a hot water bottle,' Jill announced and added, 'I don't know why I should tell you. It can't be of any possible interest. But then, you know, I have no small talk these days.' She smiled even more brightly as she uttered the last words.

It was on the tip of Meg's tongue to say that she was quite up to any big talk in which Jill felt inclined to indulge – that was how she would have answered when they were girls. Then she remembered the significance that attached – had indeed now attached for fifteen years – to the words 'these days'. The greatest irony that she could permit herself nowadays without offending Jill was to parody her flatness. '*I'm* getting seasick pills for our little trip,' she said.

'*Little* trip! That's quite marvellous, isn't it?' Jill laughed. 'I thought you were going by air anyway,' she said.

'We are,' Meg admitted, 'but I think the pills are the same.'

'Are they? Well, I wouldn't know. I've never flown.' Jill paused and then added, 'I don't know why I say "never flown" as though I was always going by boat. I haven't been abroad since nineteen-thirty-nine.'

'I don't think you've missed much.'

'Haven't I? Well, that of course I can't tell, Meg.' She asked the price of the large sized cake of Sandalwood soap and then said, 'No, the small size will have to do. Isn't it appalling,' she remarked to the assistant, 'how everything goes up?' She turned to Meg, 'All this conversation about prices grows on one. It's one of the worst curses you avoid by not being poor.'

Meg, in retreat immediately, said the one thing she had determined not to. 'What have you been doing with yourself lately, Jill?' she asked.

'Oh, I seem to keep busy,' Jill began in the even, consciously boring voice that Meg had intended not to provoke. Or had she? Why else had she asked the pointless question?

'The flat's very small of course, but all the same ... I only have Mrs Davies once a week now, you know. So there are always a lot of chores to do when I get back from work. I actually went to a film last week. I must say one thing for going out so seldom, I enjoy it like a small child when I do. Evelyn came up on Thursday. She didn't bring the baby which was naturally a bit disappointing. But I do understand. London's hardly a pleasure to her if she has to lug babies around. Anyway grandmothers are always a pest. You're lucky not to be one,' she laughed. 'There you are,' she said, 'a dismal chronicle. But you asked for it. The truth is I'm just as jealous of the life you lead, Meg, as I sound to be. Beastly, isn't it? But there it is.'

Meg strove desperately to meet her friend's sincerity. 'I do wish,' she said, 'that we saw each other more often, Jill. It's idiotic to say this,

I know, when I'm just off to the ends of the earth. But I'll be back in the spring and then we'll meet regularly for lunch as we used to.'

'My dear Meg,' Jill announced maternally, but not with the gruff affectionate maternalism of Lady Pirie, rather as the mother deliberately carrying out a detachment of affection. 'Perhaps we may.' She smiled a little remotely and then added, 'And perhaps we won't. Let's be honest and add that.'

So it always was, Meg thought, their long friendship led her automatically to make advances only for Jill to cut them short when she felt them an intrusion. It was all very well for Jill to show that she had kept honesty and intelligence intact beneath her trivial grumblings and platitudes, but to be left holding the advances that had been forced from you – and they *were* forced by Jill's silent demand for commiseration – made the friendship seem so one-sided. Time and the instinctive sympathies bred of it made her prefer Jill to all her friends – to Viola Pirie or to Poll even – but instinct could after all prove a deceptive bore.

Meg moved away to a counter to ask for the pills, and Jill, with her usual informality, turned to leave the shop with no further goodbyes. So erect and dowdy and ungiving she seemed that Meg felt immediately how impossible it was for her ever to have any but a lonely 'plucky' life. And, after all, wasn't Jill's failure to give what her friends asked from her exactly the root of that independence which, however charmless, they all so applauded?

At once Meg called after her. 'Oh, Jill, we're having a few people in this evening. Just good-bye to old friends. Do come. About nine. I should be happy to see you.' And, fearing that her late invitation might only wound, she added, 'And Bill, too, will be so glad.'

When Jill did not even smile at the rider about Bill but said quite simply, 'Thank you, Meg. I should like that very much,' Meg felt for a moment that were Bill there to hear he *would* be glad that she had given the invitation, but the feeling was quickly gone. He would not be glad. He wanted no friendships for her that were centrifugal to her relationship with him. Such friends as he had who were not joint friends but nominally 'his own' – legal colleagues, poker or racing associates, a few limpetlike old school or university friends – he made nothing of, or, at any rate, no more than his social distractions demanded. And any surplus affection that such friends seemed to expect of him he warded off with easy chaffing generosity and 'a helping hand in time of trouble'. She needed her friends no more than he did his, for it was not as if she was without a balance to his absorption in his profession as some wives would have been. Social work, porcelain, books, etc. were not just fill ups for her, they were objects of real absorption. And, as the eighteenth-century red brick of Lord North Street came in sight through the windscreen, she added to them the house – for that was at the centre of all the life she had made for herself.

No, their need for friends was different only in kind. He complained of her friends as lame ducks, yet he saw all his own cronies as nice enough but faintly pathetic. It was a measure of their happiness together that they were bound to feel that most people had lost the main thing in life – except for the few happy couples they knew whose mutual absorption, as great as their own, kept them at a sensible and respected distance of intimacy. The difficulty was, she decided, as she brought the car to a halt, that Bill controlled his pity, either respected others too much or was too indifferent to them – she never really knew which – to release emotional demands that he could not satisfy. Whereas she ... Oh well, *she* allowed, even encouraged, her lame ducks to overrun the limits of her sympathy, to get themselves invited to parties when Bill didn't wish to see them. At least, she decided as she set her Yale key firmly in the front door lock, she would pay them the respect of not thinking of them as lame ducks. And when she came back in six months' time ...

Once inside the hall, however, Meg's thoughts ceased abruptly. They had been there fifteen years now, and though, in her determination to live consciously and fully, she fought a continuous battle against the grey ennui of habit, the house with its long familiarity had inevitably imposed certain rituals upon her. So now, as always when coming in, she called brightly 'Hello'. It was a greeting originally designed for old Mary at the time of the buzz bombs when they had bought the house so cheaply. It had kept the old thing's terror at bay; and, to be truthful, probably her own. But now there were no buzz bombs to provoke chumminess, and no old Mary to cry, 'Oh, thank goodness, you're back, Madam. Did you hear that one go over half an hour ago?' Only Bettina now answered or rather appeared from the kitchen bursting with smiles. With her and with Gino all communications seemed to be smiles, for their English did not increase and Meg's conscientious determination to improve her Italian had led only to her speaking the few phrases she needed with a convincingly native rapidity but had not materially added to her vocabulary. It was an easy relationship, but for Meg a source of dissatisfaction. She had voiced it to Bill.

'I simply can't believe they find life as easy as they seem to,' she had said. 'They're like two merry peasants.' And when he characteristically had mocked the banality of her views as he urged her to accept it – 'Well, that's what Italians are meant to be like isn't it? I shouldn't worry. They save you a great deal of trouble' – she had felt quite angry that his solicitude for her comfort should often so easily leave out of account consideration of her interests.

'But I don't want merry peasants about the house,' she had cried. And it was quite true; all her childhood there had been the vagaries of the servants' characters, her fuller comprehensions of them than her mother's or David's, and in the less affluent years of her early married life old Mary and Nanny and the succession of chars had always been central to her observation of people. And now there were these two efficient smiling dumplings.

She could not restrain her irritation as she gave the few orders that she knew would already have been anticipated. At such moments her rarely shown annoyance made her less like an exotic crane in flight, more like some greedy, pecking stork. In the distortion of the Empire mirror above the marquetry table she caught a glimpse of a long-nosed Pinocchio's face, dark eyes that were sharp rather than lively, lines formed by laughter that now seemed simply drawn and tired.

'I've had a terrible day, Bettina,' she cried. 'All my lame ducks in one afternoon.' If she hadn't said it then, it would have been said later to Bill. In breaking her promise only to Bettina's smiling incomprehension she had, after all, made no betrayal of her friends. She turned from the mirror and from Bettina's smoothness and ran up the stairs. Of late she had glimpsed such odious obverses too often to forget them easily. She had seen them first in Bill in moments of repose and now in herself at the rare times when she could find no way of enveloping life as she needed. What could you call them, she thought, but obverses – the other side of the medal you got for making some account of life? For it was this that was so frightening: that exactly those weapons one had used for victory seemed now to be turned against one, and since age was the enemy who could doubt that the end would be defeat? The offhand, easy indolence with which Bill had smoothed out the tearing, breaking grind of the hard work that had given him his success showed at these times as a drink-flushed, petulant, sensual coarseness, signalling red for thrombosis. And her own constant, hard-working eagerness to fill life with use and pleasure, to banish the spectre of her sex, class, and age – hypochondriac ennui – stared back at her as hungry, lean exhaustion and signalled red for nervous headaches, breakdown – all the boring paraphernalia of the sort of unfilled life she had so successfully avoided. Tails I win, heads you lose. It simply wasn't fair.

Meg pulled herself up sharply as she was about to light one cigarette from another, replaced the fresh one in the mother-of-pearl and ebony box, crushed out the used stub. When depression followed elation so closely, she knew that she must not deny her exhaustion for a moment longer. She might, of course, have guessed that she was over-tired when she had invited Jill like that and risked annoying the one person who really mattered in her life. Poor Bill! He too was often so tired now at the end of the day. She felt sure that the sudden fears that now attacked her visited him yet more fiercely. He looked sometimes possessed with more than the haggard anxiety of a difficult brief or an exhausting day in court; his blue eyes were glazed and his wide mouth loosely open with what seemed to her something very like plain fright.

This too would not do. She recited carefully to herself their personal beatitudes; and blessings they were indeed – good health, energy, a proper income, a decent social conscience, wide interests, humour shared, sufficient humour indeed to accept large parts of life unshared, and, through it all, complete happiness together. It was simply superstitious fear of hubris that threatened to gnaw through such a fabric; and for atavistic, puritan superstition there was no cure like the months of wonderful new interests, the days of lazy ease that now lay ahead of them. Meanwhile, however, it was clear that the fabric was not strong enough to withstand the gnawing, and she turned about the room for some distracting task.

It was now that her own energy and Bettina's competence seemed such mixed blessings. The packing had been completed two days before and the house made ready for the Copemans. There was little to do in any case, since Mrs Copeman thought everything 'quite beautiful' – especially the Louis XV buhl table and the Palladian secretaire; and, as she also thought Gino and Bettina 'quite wonderful people' and expressed her intention of leaving all the arrangements to them, there seemed nothing that Meg herself could do except to make the same act of trust. They had never before let the house, but then they had never before thought of being away for so long. No doubt

Bill's determination to find their American tenants so perfect, though intended simply to allay her qualms, was also a completely sensible one. Certainly the Copemans were perfect in one thing, their agreement to do without the porcelain collection. Mrs Copeman, having inquired if any pieces were Sèvres and having found that they were not, had been quite definite in her views.

'Well, they're certainly quite beautiful,' she had said. 'Trent and I don't care too much for things that can't be used as they were made to be, Mrs Eliot.'

Meg had said to Bill, 'I don't know whether she thought I was going to say she could use the Meissen plates or the Nymphenburg jug. And anyway what does she think the Derby Chinoiserie figures were meant to be used for?'

So the porcelain was to be stored. And Meg certainly felt that leaving the house was going to be the easier for it. She ought now, if friends' felicitations were any guide, to be giving herself up to wondrous imaginings of the six months ahead of her. Anticipation, they said, was the greater part of pleasure. But, of course, they were wrong. How could she, leaving Europe for the first time, suddenly imagine what she had never before thought of? She could delve up fragments of travel films ill attended to, and season them with the cautious reservation that the reality would probably prove far more commonplace, but such imaginings were hardly likely to be wondrous and would certainly not allay the pain in her stomach that always came when she contemplated the unknown. For this was it, of course – the cause and centre of all her recent unfamiliar depressions – simply what she had known so intensely in girlhood and adolescence, but had experienced decreasingly as the years passed, what, in their teens, she and David had christened 'The Horror in Between'. Every visit to the seaside, every return home had been a horror to them, a dreaded anticipation of what might lie at the other end. It was only in her twenties that she had been able to concentrate on books or scenery when travelling in trains, and, even later, as the destination approached, particularly on the return home, her mind would become clogged with a cotton wool of fright, and her stomach would heave in revolt against the inevitable.

She had decided later that it stemmed from a child's sense of the insecurity of her home, and from her father's sudden disappearance from the scene. She had declared it hysteria communicated by her mother. She had sometimes carried it further, to an equation with fear of death. But, of course, with Bill she was without these fears. With him, for all the aeroplane stoppings and startings of their coming journey, there could be no 'Horror in Between'.

Meanwhile until he returned to the house she was alone. There was nothing for it but to seek the escape she and David had found in the past. *Emma, The Mill on the Floss, The Small House at Allington, The Portrait of a Lady* lay together with the hand luggage. They were the basic necessities of the voyage, not on any account to be anticipated; there were rules of the game even in stressful times. She went to the bookcase and took down *Daisy Miller*, an old standby, familiar enough to take quick effect, short enough to anaesthetize only for the ugly hour or so until Bill's return, easily shaken off, leaving no after effects. Drawing her long legs up under her into the armchair, with cigarettes and matches on the table beside her, she felt herself suddenly the gawky, leggy girl of her past, who had obliterated dreary hotel bedrooms and hideous furnished flats with the subtleties of Daisy's innocence pitted against the guiles of Rome. It seemed absurd that there should be no David there also, very much the elder brother, legs stretched out, in the other armchair to match her absorption with an equal engrossment in the sad futilities of Emma Bovary's debts.

She saw her brother so seldom now, thought of him only rarely, so that his voice came to her imagination as it was in his most self-conscious, whimsical adolescence. 'My sister,' she could hear him saying, 'inclines to the native tongue. My taste is more for the French. But then what English lady can happily support the improprieties that our neighbours across the channel permit themselves in their so-called polite literature?' This parodying of early Victorian speech had, thank God, like all David's other affectations, lasted only a short while, but it came back to Meg now as clearly as if he were speaking in the room; and she found herself longing for a talk, a real gossip with him. Preferring not to dwell on the history of the distant though friendly relations that had grown up between them in the last years, she plunged headlong into *Daisy Miller*.

Some time later she was conscious of that muffled banging of the front door that meant that Bill had come home. He had never learned not to bang doors, yet he always remembered at the last minute, just in time to turn the knob and prevent the loudest reverberations. She did not go down to him. He liked to rush at the evening paper, to the stop press with his precious racing results; and then to read the letters that had come by the afternoon post. They were mostly bills or from bookmakers, anyway; she had seen them when she came in. He had got increasingly tetchy recently if anyone fussed him during this ritual. He took his racing so seriously nowadays, so differently from the time when a day at Kempton Park or Ascot had been a social occasion for them both. All his racing was by post nowadays. Silly ass, she thought with loving impatience. She could not stand people turning pleasures into fusses. He was just as keen on his bridge, but that had remained a game. Now he would bring with him an air of distraction simply because some wretched horse hadn't won. And the evening paper would be all muddled and unreadable.

She could just hear him move across the hall. He moved so deliberately, and yet, considering the extra weight the years had added to his tall, thickset body, surprisingly lightly. Really, she thought, at fifty-five, he's amazingly young, despite his flushed face and the way his hair is receding. One would take him for either a very mature young man or else an oddly youthful looking man for one who could accept such a position in life so easily. That was what she loved most – that look of a young man who'd succeeded gracefully. What at once stood out was that he *had* reached 'such a position', that he took it easily, and that he probably knew the advantages to be gained from appearing so to take it. And, of course, he *did* know them. He had always given people the impression of never acting without deliberation. She wished that so much consciousness of his own actions had not weighed upon him so greatly. It was this that made him look a little sad.

She could hear him talking with Gino and Bettina, giving last-minute orders about the drink probably. He seemed to be talking to them longer than usual this evening. He was always charming to them, but he had told her recently that Bettina was becoming a little too keen on him. He hated any involvement with people. Very well, she had laughed at him, ease up on the charm.

For some days now she had not heard his clear, very English Italian. They always understood him so much better than her. 'You try to be too Italian, darling,' he told her. But now he seemed to be having a full length conversation. Of course, they would not see Bettina and Gino again for six months.

Suddenly she could hear him striding the stairs two at a time. He was standing in the doorway watching her, but she pretended to be absorbed in her book. It was an absurd pretence, she knew; but she also knew that he liked to find her so. Treading carefully on the rugs only, he came behind her, bent over and kissed her mouth.

'Startled?' he asked, his hands on her shoulders.

'No,' she said. She laid *Daisy Miller* on the table, but did not uncurl in her chair. 'I expected it.' She did note with surprise, however, that the evening paper was in his pocket and that it had not been touched.

'And I suppose the anticipation spoiled your reading,' he said.

'Nothing really could spoil *Daisy Miller*,' she answered, 'not even you.' She pressed his hand.

'Is that the girl who didn't know that her parents were adulterous?'

'No,' said Meg, 'that was Maisie. Though it's a poor and vulgar description of the book.'

'Maisie, Daisy,' he remarked. 'Pretty poor and vulgar names. Did you cut your committee?'

'No. Certainly not. How could you think it of me?'

As her words came more quickly in mock indignation, her fingers moved more slowly rubbing his cheek.

'I thought it didn't end until six,' he announced.

'I know,' she said, 'you always do. But they still end at four.'

'I get it all wrong, don't I?'

'Yes, darling. But don't worry. You don't read the women's journals; if you did you'd know that every woman expects her husband to get it wrong but she still loves him to take an interest.'

He laughed. 'I don't think I care for you as every woman,' he said. 'I wish though you had cut it. You'll be tired out by the time we get on the plane. Committees! Parties!'

'That's what Viola Pirie said, darling.'

'Oh,' he left it. 'Has that son of hers got a job yet?'

'I don't think so. I didn't ask. She apologized for his probably not coming this evening.'

'Probably. That sounds threatening.'

'We're favourites of his, Viola says.'

Bill made a grimace of distaste.

'It's probably true, you know,' Meg told him.

'Oh, I daresay there are worse cases than Tom Pirie,' Bill admitted. 'If he'd only shave off that beard. And be a little less grubby. Grubby-minded, too, I suspect. All the same, I can't find him any more jobs. Poor old thing, she must have a life of it. But I still don't know how you put up with her.'

'Oh! She's the least of worries,' Meg cried, then as she saw him frown, she jumped up from her chair. 'I'm not feeling the faintest bit tired,' she said and kissed him. 'And *your* day?' she asked.

'Oh, winding things up at the office,' he said, 'whatever that may mean.'

'I don't think barristers say it, Bill, only business men. Whatever it means you look well on it. Something especially good has happened. What is it?'

He smiled. 'We don't go round the world every day, you know.'

'H'm,' she considered it, 'it's hit you all of a sudden in that case. You haven't shown any special excitement in the last weeks.'

'I probably didn't believe it until today.'

'I've believed it for a long time,' she told him and added quickly, 'Oh! I shall love every minute of it once we've started. I hate partings, that's all. We must go and dress.'

From Bill's boxlike dressing room across the large bedroom to the open-doored bathroom where Meg lay soaking, the talk went on. Shouting to each other in the morning and evening dressing hours had become over the years their most satisfactory, intimate form of conversation.

'There *is* another reason,' Bill called.

'I knew there was. What is it? Did you win a lot today? I saw it was Lingfield. You're always lucky there.'

There was a pause and Bill's voice came rather crossly. 'Nothing to do with racing. Anyway I never win at Lingfield.'

'Oh! Well there you are, *I* get things wrong too.' After a few minutes' silence she called, 'Well? What is it? You must tell me now.'

'I went to the doctor's.'

'Yes?' She failed to sound casual.

'I said that those T.A.B. inoculations were far more unpleasant than he'd warned us.'

'Oh, Bill, don't.'

'I've told you it's good news,' he said, laughing.

She wondered suddenly how much he savoured her anxiety over him.

'All right, then, darling, why can't you tell me straight away?'

'It seems a bit fatuous, that's why. The truth is I've been suffering from a sort of phobia about thrombosis for quite a while now. Putting on weight, high blood pressure, so many people we've known and so on.'

'Well?' She had come to the door of the bathroom now, water dripping from her body.

'*Very* well,' he called, invisible to her, 'nothing to worry about at all. Blood pressure quite normal. I was relieved because of the heat in the East.'

In her relief she considered for a moment going across to him as she was, wet and naked, but she turned back and plunged into her bath again.

'Oh, I should have spoken to you,' she cried, 'I could have discussed it and made you go to Loundes before. You need never have had all this anxiety. It's all your fault, Bill, for making me ashamed of hunches and intuitions. All these weeks I've been worrying about you and for just the same reason. I might have known that on anything so important we should be thinking the same. Any two people so close to one another are bound to.'

'Hunches only work for horses,' he shouted to her. She laughed but she said, 'You sound as though you'd hate us to have any intuitive communication.'

'Intuitive communication? Mind-reading the Victorians called it.'

'Well, would you hate it if I could read your mind?'

'Imagine,' he said, 'the social impossibility if such a thing became general. If Jill Stokes, for instance, could read what I was thinking.'

She decided to accept the evasion. 'She always knows you dislike her, Bill. You're so much more polite to her than to anyone else.'

'I could remedy that.'

She laughed and said quickly, 'Well, don't start tonight, darling.' She paused, ready with a glow of self-defence, but he only said, 'Oh, she's coming tonight, is she?'

Her defence, nevertheless, was too ready not to be given. 'Well, I couldn't do anything else, darling. I met her at the chemist's and she was so grumpy and pathetic.'

He made no answer, but a minute later she saw him in the bathroom doorway looking at her as she dried. He turned away.

'I wish you had a smaller store of pity,' he said, so peremptorily that she drew her towel around her tightly for a moment. They had argued the question so often that she had to ask, 'Bill, why suddenly now and so fiercely?'

'Oh, I don't know. Perhaps because you'll be so miserable in Malaya, and in Asia generally, if you're going to let pity ride you.'

She instinctively withdrew to the particular. 'I can't imagine it all, you know. Not even tomorrow night.'

'Oh, a hotel bedroom like most others, but with electric fans. And scorpions,' he added.

'My father chastised you with rods, I will chastise you with scorpions,' she said.

'What?'

'Rehoboam. In the Bible.'

'I don't know the Old Testament.'

She laughed to herself with pleasure and affection for him; it was what he always said, as though he were a devout practitioner of New Testament Christianity instead of a mild agnostic of fierce agnostic parents.

Later as she was combing her hair before the dressing table mirror, she said, 'I think pity's a sort of insurance with me. We're so much luckier than others. And anyway it's a very humble pity. I feel ashamed of having such good luck.'

'Well, you shouldn't be,' he said. 'And anyway all this talk about luck is nonsense. Luck works with cards or horses, and even there it's mainly intelligence and skill. But otherwise it's a destructive sort of sentimentalism which shouldn't be taken into account even in the rare cases where it operates. It's a destroyer of justice.'

She began to pencil in her eyebrows. 'I suppose you must think like that. You couldn't exist through the miseries of the courts if you didn't.'

'I've always felt like it. Ever since I was a boy.'

'Then perhaps it's why you chose the law. It seems very arrogant. And yet I know you want people to like you.'

'I don't care twopence,' he said, peering fiercely at her over the coils of the black tie he was knotting.

'Oh?' she questioned.

'I care for the respect of one or two people, yes. One or two of the judges and Donald Templeton. And when Aunt Hester was alive I wanted her to like me, but then she had been very good to me and she was the rich aunt.'

For a moment she accepted the pseudo-cynical note by which he was trying to drop the subject.

'Of course,' she said, 'and you did very well to persuade her to leave us the money for this house.' But she felt the need to defy his evasion, though she turned and smiled at him to take any sting from her words. 'And all the charm you use with people?'

'You speak as though I was a confidence trickster,' he laughed. 'As to that, I'm not sure that I don't think that the famous feminine interest in human beings, this intrusion, let's call it no more, let's say nothing about pity, isn't worse. You're bound to be giving blank cheques to all the lonely people and the misfits you come across, and you can't honour half of them. No, not only you,' he said, as she turned in protest. 'Nobody could. There isn't time if one's to make anything of one's life.'

She shaped in her mouth and then said rather ruefully, 'I try.'

'Oh, darling,' he came and clasping her arms from behind pressed her to him. 'I wouldn't have you any different to what you are.'

'I would,' she said, then looking at his reflection she added, 'we're popular and we're unpopular. At the same time and with the same people. Only I want to be liked and with no resentment. And you don't care. That's all the difference.'

'Maybe,' he said. She saw that he was determined now to be rid of the subject. 'But it doesn't matter,' he announced, 'we stand together against 'em all.' She rubbed the crown of her head against his chin. 'Yes, thank goodness. Together.' Then, getting up to break the mood for him, she said, 'There won't be much to eat for dinner. I hope you won't mind, before the party.'

Only as they were going downstairs she suddenly asked him, 'Do you think fear can be communicated in the womb?'

He stopped dead and held to the banister. She turned and, looking at him, was appalled that she could be so far from him as to have had no inkling of what issues, long dead for her, might still be brought to life in his mind by an idle word. She gave him release in words that came too casually quick to sound convincingly casual even to her own ear.

'I was thinking about Mother,' she said, 'and how I've always had irrational fears about journeys and homecomings. David had them too as a boy. It might so easily have been prenatal. Homecoming for her so often meant the discovery of some new exploit of Daddy's – an affair with the governess, even just that he'd gone away with no warning. Do you think that *could* be the reason?'

She saw that he could not easily throw off the first associations her question had aroused in him.

'I don't know, my dear,' he said, 'I'm no gynaecologist or pre-natal expert.'

She felt suddenly rebellious at having her communication, how-ever tactless, left on her hands. 'More likely really,' she went on, 'my early childhood. Daddy at the front and Mummy always apprehensive that she'd find a telegram when she got home. She could have communicated the fear to David too even though he was hardly born when the war ended. Don't you think so?' Bill did not answer.

But at dinner he asked her suddenly, 'Shouldn't you have invited David up here before we went off?'

'Oh, no darling. I've written to him and at this time of the year I imagine the nursery keeps him frightfully busy. Autumn's the time when all the big orders for next year come in.'

'Well, he's got Gordon Paget, hasn't he? To say nothing of Paget's capital. And that monstrous regiment of women in breeches. He could surely get up for one night.'

'Oh, he would have done, of course, if I'd asked him. But it would have meant asking Gordon too.'

He raised his eyebrows. 'When you're going away for six months?'

'Well, you know how David is if one doesn't ask Gordon.'

'It's so long since we've see him that I forget. In any case we could have stood Gordon for one night. I rather liked him the few times that I met him.'

She felt so annoyed at this continued implied rebuke of what was, after all, something entirely on her own conscience that she smiled and said, 'You're being very broad-minded.' How much in his turn he disliked her implication was clear to her from his remaining silent. Anxious to appease, she said, 'It would have meant inviting Else Bode too.'

He was clearly grateful for this release into more orthodox relation-ships. 'Oh well, in that case, of course, you couldn't. Not the whole caravanserai.' He laughed happily at Else Bode – a stock joke.

She felt it now due to him, her annoyance appeased, to express her grievance directly. 'Why should you think I ought to see David?' she asked.

'Oh – you mentioned partings,' he said, 'as the fly in your oint-ment of our holiday.'

'Oh, I didn't mean anyone in particular,' she cried, 'only leaving my regular life behind – the committee, the galleries, the theatres, and so on. It's just my love of tramlines. Once I've left them I shall adore it all.'

He smiled at her a little paternally. 'I think you will,' he said. 'But it might be different if we were leaving *people* behind as well.'

At first she was a little scornfully amused, thinking that he was jealous even of her threadbare tie with David, since he himself had no one at all in the world; but it then occurred to her that he was still brooding over her tactlessly sudden mention of childbirth. She sought for something that could please him out of his brooding thoughts but she could find nothing less trivial than, 'I've cancelled my order for the Nymphenburg figures.'

'Good girl,' he said, but his pleasure seemed tepid compared with the ardour he had shown in asking her to forgo the purchase.

It was not until a few moments before the first guest arrived, as they stood, tall, elegant, ready to please yet united to defend, that Bill suggested, 'I should have thought it was your mother's unreliability that was the trouble, if any. The constant moving from one place to another and the absurd enterprises that were bound to fail.'

Meg dismissed it instantly. 'Oh, no. That was only financial worry. Sordid if you like, but not that awful emotional chasm that Mummy faced or tried to. The person you loved simply not there. Think of it!' She shuddered and he put his arm round her waist. 'Oh, no,' she repeated, 'the tea-room and the bookshop and the curios came much later. When we were almost growing up and quite able to cope. Father had finally disappeared by then and I had David to go to.'

He was about to say something when the bell rang and he turned to opening a bottle of champagne – he would allow no one else to obscure his skill in such tasks.

At a little before eleven Meg felt free to stand apart from the party for a few minutes and observe. This time of withdrawal was perhaps the highest solemnity of the entertainment ritual for her – then, and, if Bill was in the mood, the inquest afterwards. Despite all her experience now as a hostess, she was still remained keyed up – as they said every good actress must – until this moment. It came then as a relaxation; but also as the time of judgement. She was very critical – the verdict was so nearly always 'success but' or 'success although'. Tonight it was very nearly plain 'success'. The lame ducks were less of a problem than she had expected, although poor Tom Pirie, anaemic and bearded, clearly needed watching. But then the lame ducks were closer to her affections than the other guests and she inevitably expected to be more on edge about them. Bill's ease had set the scene in the first quarter of an hour, until her own nervous tension was sufficiently relaxed to allow him to take three cronies into the small room for bridge. He would emerge only to dissolve it all with equal ease.

The word 'cronies' echoed in her head uncomfortably. It was not a word that she would ever *say*. It suggested a pseudo-Dickensian old lawyer and his friends. Bill was the least Dickensian person in existence, and not old. And he had no close friends. Perhaps she felt that his bridge playing marked the difference in their ages; if so it was very foolish indeed, lots of young people played cards. She turned from such unpleasing reflections about Bill's age impatiently. What was more absurd was this snobbish idea that there were things she didn't say! This too she rejected angrily. She was unashamed that they lived in a certain style. To be so would be the snobbery.

Suddenly she realized that she was standing there 'feeling like a successful hostess'. But if she was more self-conscious in this role than at other times it was a matter for amusement rather than for sharp self-censure. It was a part she had always so wished to play. She had hated the muddled, shabby gentility of the occasional parties her mother had given in the intervals of a plucky inefficient struggle to live. She had always made excuses, had been late at the secretarial college, or had hidden upstairs in her bedroom with a book – a book probably in which the part her mother muffed was played so splendidly by Glencora Palliser or Oriane de Guermantes or Clarissa Dalloway. It was not surprising, when at last she was able to assume the role herself, that her sense of it should have been a shade literary, a touch self-conscious.

She caught a look in young Tom Pirie's eye that suggested a disgusted rejection of the 'gracious living' around him – and no wonder, she thought, if she was playing Glencora Palliser, Oriane, and Mrs Dalloway all at the same time. Nevertheless if he wanted to be an angry young man he really should look less damp and dismal – and to suppose that a beard was going to help him! Vexed by his naïveté out of her abstraction, she reminded herself that a hostess exists only in fulfilling her hospitable functions. She saw Donald Templeton isolated in a corner. Over all the years of her marriage she had never succeeded in unbuttoning the urbane, slightly prim guise that Bill's nearest approach to a friend always presented to her; it was unlikely that she would ever succeed now. Yet on this last night before their long absence it would be not nice, but fitting, and therefore satisfactory, to go through the motions of trying once again to reach him. If by a wave of a hand, she thought, she could ever have transformed his sleek, waxy face and his plump body into something, well something less like a doctored tomcat, she would have been friends with him long ago.

For Bill, of course, a man's outward appearance hardly existed; men either shared his interests, in which case they were useful as friends, or they didn't. Donald had the best legal brain he knew and that was all there was to it. But she couldn't feel like that. Men shouldn't seem like doctored toms. Donald adopted the affectations of an eighteenth-century gentleman, but he was far more like an Edwardian drawing room tenor. She cut short the access of malice by going across to him.

'Well? Well?' he asked, thrusting his face a little too closely at her, 'so you're going to hold the gorgeous East in fee?'

It was ridiculous, she thought; he was less than Bill's age and he spoke to her as though she was a small girl.

'I hope it won't be too gorgeous,' she said. 'I imagine everything there to be in bright, eye-aching colours enough as it is.'

'So you think the Orient may be a bit of a sell, what?' He shouted this separated interrogative 'what' at intervals in his conversation, under the impression, she supposed, that he gave the effect of some portly Regency Admiral on the quarter deck.

If it was shyness, as no doubt she ought to think it was, she could only hope to reduce his affectation by answering on as simple a level as possible.

'The East isn't really the part I'm looking forward to,' she said. 'All the disease and the dirt and the teeming millions.' She spoke with an edge of irony, to set such a narrow Western point of view at a proper distance from herself. It annoyed her then when he ignored this separation.

'I don't imagine they see themselves like that.'

'Oh,' she cried, 'I know perfectly well that they're taking over tomorrow.' He did not answer and she asked almost angrily, 'Well, is that what you meant?'

'Yes,' he said doubtfully and he looked away from her, seeking an escape from the conversation, but finding none, he added, 'Yes. I suppose I did. But knowing's one thing, feeling's quite another. I imagine you'll *feel* it all when you're there. What?'

45

'You exaggerate my powers of comprehension. I'm far from the sort of person who apprehends history in a flash; not even a few weeks in Singapore will be able to do that for me.'

He laughed. 'Good,' he said and, although she could not be quite sure of what he was commending, she felt that he was accepting her a little for the first time.

'But as to having a point of view,' she said, 'how can I? I don't understand anything about *them*, and won't in such a short visit. As for regretting that *our* day is over, whatever would be the good of that?'

He made no comment and she felt the need to increase his sympathy at cost to herself.

'Bill,' she remarked, 'thinks my *compassion* will be strained.'

'By the teeming millions?' he asked and they shared for the first time a smile of affection for Bill; but he withdrew from any further intimacy.

'It'll do Bill the world of good. To take the holiday in Australia and America, don't you know?'

'If I can keep him from rushing back for some brief,' she said.

'Oh, for the Lord's sake, do,' he urged her.

She felt forced to admit to herself that he too might have been close enough to Bill to share in 'intuitive communications'. 'Have you been thinking that he was ill?' she asked curiously; and his genuine surprise restored her self-esteem.

'Ill?' he asked. 'No. Has he been?'

'He thought he was,' she said.

'Oh! Probably. He's thoroughly overworked. What?' This time he threw his interrogative at her as though he would do her violence.

'But he couldn't live without his work,' she cried, 'that's the trouble. I sometimes think he's in love with those damned courts.' As she spoke she asked herself why she was over-playing; and decided that she must assert to this waxy-faced man her closeness to Bill, even at the cost of appearing jealous.

'Every love affair can get a bit stale,' he said, 'what?'

She saw finally that she disliked him and his pretentious, knowing way of talking. 'Do you mean that you think Bill isn't any good at his job now?' she asked. She took his smile to imply pleasure at making her angry.

'Good heavens, no,' he cried. 'That's part of the trouble. A less brilliant man wouldn't have stayed the pace.'

'I just don't believe it. Bill adores his job. You should have heard him defending justice this evening.'

'Defending? Why? Don't you like justice?'

'Oh! I'm a sentimentalist. I should have thought that was all too apparent. My heart's always being wrung.' Really, she thought, anyone who is watching us must think we both have some nervous tic – all these smiles and gestures of frivolity to cover our hostility.

But immediately Donald spoke with a sudden uncovered fierceness. 'And you don't know whether Bill's is?' he asked. 'Justice isn't all Jehovah and thunderbolts, you know. It's righting the wrongs of the innocent.'

She answered now with a deliberate drawl to annoy.

'It must be absolutely ghastly in the *criminal* courts,' she said. 'I never rejoiced so much as the day that Bill gave it up for civil cases. Except when we were left the money for this house,' she added.

He looked round the room and finally fixed his eyes on the rather massive jewellery that covered the equally massive bosom of a Park Lane financier's wife.

'Big Company cases are a bit remote from the human heart,' he said. 'That's all I meant. But still Bill makes a lot of money, what?'

She would not be put on trial by a sentimental failure, for that's what he was – jealous of Bill's greater success; but if there was something he wanted to tell her about Bill, it was her duty to hear it, however little she liked him.

'Donald,' she said. She had only once or twice before ventured his Christian name and then only to please Bill. 'Do you really feel that Bill should …?' But her question had to remain unasked, for Lady Pirie was upon them.

'You're not tiring yourself too much, Meg, are you?' she asked. 'I'm sure we all ought to go.'

'I shouldn't be very pleased if you all did, Viola.' Meg hoped that the offhand answer would send her away, but it was clear she had come up to them with some purpose.

'This is Bill's friend Mr Templeton,' Meg said. 'Lady Pirie.' She suddenly felt exhausted and beckoned to one of the hired waiters for a glass of champagne.

'Meg never looks tired,' Lady Pirie announced, 'that's the trouble. But she's been bossing us around on the committee all the afternoon.'

'Bossing you for your own good, what?'

Even Lady Pirie seemed a little surprised by the booming fierceness of this fat little man's tone.

'Oh, we're always the better for Meg's advice,' she said, and she seemed about to pat Meg's arm, but finding it bare, ended with a vague gesture of protection.

'What other young woman with all this,' Lady Pirie waved her arm towards the room, 'would spend afternoons getting something done for derelict old people.'

'A great number much younger, my dear Viola,' Meg said, 'and with a great deal more than all this,' she imitated Lady Pirie's gesture. There seemed to be an absurd conspiracy, she reflected, to make her out a sort of millionairess.

'Wrung with pity? What?' Donald's ejaculation startled Lady Pirie. She looked at him as though he indeed belonged to the past century he affected. 'Pity! We shouldn't get very far if we approached our work in that state,' she said.

Meg could see that she felt him to be an opponent of Aid to the Elderly, but she was obviously not sure of the grounds of his opposition.

'There's still room for charity, you know. As long as it's efficient and not thought of as charity.'

Donald seemed to feel no wish to oppose this gruff, square lady so he merely smiled.

'How efficient we'll be when Meg's away, I don't know.'

'You'll do just what you want, Viola,' Meg said. If she could not get Lady Pirie to go, she would at least prevent her embarrassing maternal praises before Donald's cold fish eye.

'Mr Templeton pleads in the criminal courts. He has to be stern,' she added. She too could pat children on the head if she tried.

It was clear that Lady Pirie had something more important on her mind than Donald's profession, for she looked impatient. 'Ah! I daresay some of these wretched cases one reads of are enough to make anyone stern. Although I must say we find in *our* job that being tough is just a lazy way of avoiding the problem, don't we, Meg?' She looked up for approval at a modern lesson well learned. Meg smiled but Lady Pirie waited for no verbal agreement, she had seen her chance.

'You mustn't think I meant that Meg was hard when I said she was efficient, Mr Templeton. They don't go together at all you know, in the work we do. No, she's a model of *practical* kindness.' And now, as though she had prepared sufficient introduction to satisfy social politeness, she said in a lower voice to Meg, 'Go and be kind to my Tom, dear, will you? He's afraid that you're angry because he's come in those corduroys.'

Meg realized that she had so taken Tom Pirie's corduroys for granted that she had not noticed their incongruity with the rest of the company's dress. She believed that half Viola Pirie's trouble with her son came from treating him as a child, so she said, 'I'm sure he's not a bit afraid. Tom always has the courage of his beliefs. But I'd love to talk to him.'

Lady Pirie smiled happily and, her task done, resumed her social duty.

'You'd find it difficult to believe, Mr Templeton,' she said in her usual loud brusque tones, as Meg moved away, 'that our hostess of this evening was the same person as the efficient young woman ...'

Meg was glad to escape from Donald Templeton's eye as he listened. Besides, she reflected, it was only because Viola Pirie had felt so critical in the afternoon that she thought it necessary to be so praising in the evening; for all her honest gruffness she was a strangely up and down woman; no wonder that Tom Pirie fought with her as he did.

Meg thought of Bill's charge that Tom Pirie was dirty-minded as she advanced towards him. He *did* have what her mother would have called a very peculiar look in his eye. But it was impossible to associate anyone as feeble with sex. I feel sure, she thought, that he's never gone farther than pathetic masturbation fancies. She put the thought from her with disgust.

'Well,' he said as Meg sat down on the sofa beside him, 'you've got the establishment here tonight all right, haven't you?' His voice was solemn and funereal, making his beard seem to belong more to the ghost of Hamlet's father than to a young man in revolt.

It annoyed her that if he must try to keep up with his generation, he should get it all wrong.

'No,' she said, 'none of these people have anything to do with ruling the country. A few of them have a financial pull, I suppose, but that's their limit.'

'The money bags are the ruin of this country,' he said. He might have been one of his mother's ex-colonial friends instead of an angry young man. His ideas were in a sickening muddle.

'They seem to make you feel very superior,' Meg said and she looked at his glass of beer. It annoyed her that he alone had insisted on beer.

He disregarded her comment. 'It's the bottom, isn't it?' he said. 'What do you get out of it?'

She was hard put to it not to dry him up by being playful, but she had determined long ago on helping him, because of Viola and because of what she herself had felt at his age – keeping a lifeline to her youth had somehow become very important since she had turned forty.

'Partly pure pleasure. But not much, I agree,' she said. 'Partly it's something I can do well. Partly they're a lot of them important to Bill's career.'

'Ah,' he said, 'spending money to make money. Is it chargeable to expenses?'

Heaven knew, she thought, what absurd imaginings of brutal virility were going through his head when he spoke to her like that; and the folly of it was that if he shaved off that beard and dressed only a little more carefully he would be very attractive no doubt to some girl (although she'd have to be rather soulful to take those mournful dark eyes).

'I don't know,' she said, 'I don't do the income tax returns. Would you like me to ask Bill?' The introduction of Bill's name, even in so facetious a context, made Tom look as though he'd been 'threatened with the headmaster', so she went on hurriedly. 'A lot of them are old friends you know, like your mother.'

'You won't make much money out of her.'

'We're going away for six months. And so we asked our friends to a party. Does that satisfy you?' She put it to him simply.

He gazed round at the thirty or so guests. 'Friends!' he said, 'you must be big hearted.'

'What a sentimentalist you are!' she cried. 'Friend's a perfectly good conventional word covering a great number of people who don't touch one's heart deeply. Will you feel happier if I say "The Gang" is here?'

When he laughed, as now, he gave a high giggle even more out of keeping with his beard than was his hollow voice. 'All right, you win,' he said. 'Anyway, who are they?'

'Well, that's Alice Ripley, and that's a man called Turner who's head of some sort of big trust, and those are the Pargiters, they run that gallery off Brook Street ...'

'Oh! Blimey,' he said, 'not the names.'

Although the 'blimey' was an affectation there was a certain genuine youthfulness about his response that made Meg feel she was getting somewhere with him.

'Just the general lines of business will be enough,' he added. She had to laugh as she categorized, for his face showed how satisfied he was that the answer was as he expected.

'Architects, lots of lawyers, of course, some business men ...'

'But cultivated,' he interjected.

'I hope so,' she said, 'a civil servant or two, a couple of painters and their wives.'

'All at the top or on the way there,' he announced with naïve triumph, 'and what a glossy finish it's given them.'

'Now there you're just being silly,' she said. 'Glossy's quite the wrong word.'

'Oh, I don't mean vulgar. Not the least little bit,' he tried to imitate a mincing, ladylike voice, but he was no mimic, 'but glossy in the most gracious sort of way.'

'Oh! Gracious living!' she cried. 'Really, Tom, you live on catchwords. If you mean pretentious, they're not. And if you mean what you say, well why on earth shouldn't people lead decorative lives?' She chose the adjective to show that she had no intention of retreating.

'You judge so much by surfaces,' she went on. 'This is the social face. But most of these people are hard-working, married couples absorbed in each other and in their children. That's why,' she told him, 'we haven't that deep sincerity of friendship that you seem to feel is the only justification for knowing people. You don't, Tom, when you get to a certain age, if you've found any happiness. It's Bill and me,' she waved her hand, 'and Alec and Rosamund Turner and all the other couples. We're sufficient to ourselves. It doesn't mean we don't want to meet. But we *are* sufficient.'

'Very cosy,' he said.

'No. Just as happy as we can manage in a not very easy world. Oh! I wouldn't mind if you were complaining that we had no right to it because of others less fortunate, as I did when I was young. But you don't care about that. You're just jealous.'

'Of this?' he asked contemptuously.

She smiled and nodded; then, 'No,' she cried. 'I'm wrong. I judge everybody too much by myself. You may be more like my brother. I wish you could meet him. Not that you'd get on together, I expect. Generations are so different.'

'Generations?' he asked. 'Isn't *that* a catchword?'

But Meg, serious, was not to be deflected. She allowed herself a moment of feminine silliness to be rid of his intervention.

'Well, there it is. Some catchwords are true and some aren't,' she said.

'I only meant that I think I get on with you all right.' He stuttered as he said it and blushed as he saw that he had spat on her arm.

'Then you probably wouldn't get on with David,' she said, thinking how awful it was for him not to be able to be intimate without spitting, and how impossible it was for her to register the one without the other. 'David and I,' she said, warming to her reminiscence, 'reacted so differently to our background. We had a most impossible one, you know. Genteel penury.'

'It's my own,' Tom said.

'Nonsense,' she cried, 'or rather not nonsense, but how different the same things can be. Your father was a distinguished man and your mother's not only good but she has such marvellous good sense. My father was often called a very unsatisfactory man by people, or so Mother told us. He was certainly a very unsatisfactory husband and father. So unsatisfactory that in the end he just went away. To get away from the unsatisfactoriness, I suppose, but even that didn't work very well, because he'd hardly landed in America before he died of pneumonia. And then Mother buckled to – that was always her phrase – and coped. Unfortunately poor dear, unlike *your* mother, she hadn't the faintest idea how to cope. She had a little capital. Her father had been the headmaster of a successful private school. She tried her best to improve on it, but always with the rider that she should be known for a lady. I suppose she couldn't help that, it was her generation. But it was fatal for us. All along the South Coast – teashops in the South Downs without enough winter trade to survive, a curio shop tucked away in a part of Hove that no one went to. David and I loathed every minute of it, her pluckiness and her failures. And there's the difference between us. For all that, David now lives right on the middle of those ghastly Downs. And I can't even go down to see him; I hate the memory of it so.'

She looked up to see the Pargiters ready to depart. 'I must say good-bye to them, but I'll come back and finish my story. I think it's important to you,' she said, although by now she was not too certain how it affected him, only knew that she had found a ready vacuum to fill with a story she had long wanted to tell.

She made her good-byes to the Pargiters, spoke here and there, saw that drinks were replenished. She noted with amusement that Poll had found the only faintly disreputable man present and Jill the only completely dead one. Viola Pirie she saw was hard at it with Donald Templeton, telling him of the need for men to help in organized charity; and Donald oddly looked flattered but less smug. Under all this activity her story ran on in her mind. She brought two glasses of champagne to the sofa. 'No,' she said authoritatively to Tom, 'no more beer. You must drink champagne. Everyone needs a change now and again, dearie,' she added in a cockney accent.

And now having already constructed her story word for word in her mind, she started off again so quickly that Tom, who with difficulty pierced through a cloud of anxious self-absorption to hear any conversation, followed only with jolts and bumps.

'Neither David nor I were stupid,' she said. 'I don't know that Mother was really, but she had let her intelligence slide for the sake of the conventions she loved. And anyway she felt that being plucky was more appropriate, more correct for people of our class and time than being clever. She saw our bookishness as a sort of betrayal. And, of course, we were frightfully priggish at that age.'

Tom put on a face of humorous self-defence when he heard the word, but Meg was so concerned with her story that she hardly noticed it.

'David got all the university scholarships. It's easier for a man. But even so he was cleverer than me. Very clever, in fact, in his academic way. Just before the war he was elected to a junior fellowship at Magdalen. But when he came back he gave it all up and took the nursery garden that he runs down in Sussex.'

'*I* don't want to cultivate gardens,' Tom said, 'I want to cultivate myself. I suppose that's what you'd call the priggishness of youth.'

She couldn't quite let him get away with that. 'David and I were seventeen when we said that sort of thing,' she told him. 'You're – what is it, Tom? Twenty-four?' Conscious of the maternal, patronizing element in her remark, she tried to impart a more intimate note to her voice. 'I'm on your side,' she said. 'You know that. Neither Bill nor I were annoyed because you threw up the export job Bill found for you. I was only annoyed that you preferred to think we were. It was such a poor compliment to our friendship. If you want to go from job to job – selling vintage cars, serving in bookshops, all these other things – well and good. As long as you don't sponge on Viola, I'm with you.'

Below his beard his thin neck reddened. 'Of course you know that I am sponging,' he said defiantly.

'Well, it's disgraceful,' she cried, but there seemed nothing more to say about it.

She had wanted to tell him how David had chosen another path to hers; to suggest that if a man wanted to 'find himself' it might mean, as for David, isolation and hard manual work. But really there seemed no relation between the two cases – and anyhow to put David's decision in that light was complete falsification, for it omitted all mention of pacifism and of Gordon Paget. The truth was, she supposed, that she was anxious to clear her own conscience of the charge of narrow-mindedness, to show that she knew that there were other ways of living than the one she had chosen.

And her own way of living, of course, was what she really wanted to discuss, or rather expound – the life she and Bill had made, and why it had been worth making. Heaven knew why she would wish to extol it from the housetops and to poor Tom Pirie of all people, except that there was a strange feeling of judgement in the air, a sort of stocktaking. She saw for a moment her mother opening a long envelope at the breakfast table and heard her saying, 'Well, Meg, all very nice as usual. They place so much importance on success in exams nowadays, don't they? I wonder if that's quite right for girls. But then schoolmistresses live so much out of the world.' And what world do you live in? she had always wanted to cry, where success doesn't count? She had not felt that particular anger for many years. Viola Pirie was probably quite right – good-bye parties were all fudge. It was not as if they were going to the moon anyway.

She would have been well content to let the silence last until, her own remembered anger dissipated, she could leave Tom and make a very overdue round of her guests. Looking down, however, she saw that his long, thin and oddly hairy hands were trembling. For a moment she thought that his nervousness could not sustain a silence; then she remembered where this conversation had left him. She was not prepared to take back what she had said of his sponging; but she could at least ease his close hugged guilt, dissipate a little of that surrounding mist of gloom which she felt must make him 'wet' even to the touch.

'How did you find my suggestion for the start of the second act?' she asked. It was pandering to drug addiction where the real need was more like analysis; but at least the drug had the effect of benzedrine.

Tom's voice in reply sounded more buoyant than it had the whole evening – the wobbling, reedy note had gone from it. 'You were right,' he said, 'it does make the development more intelligible simply by making it more gradual. But I reject all your rules for neat play-making, you know.'

'This was nothing to do with rules,' she said. 'It's simply that no woman, certainly not your woman,' she ought to have remembered his heroine's name, 'who's supposed to be sensitive, would fail to de-tect a real unhappiness in the man she loved. Women are not all sensi-tive, and a lot of them are fools, but they're given a second sight when they're really in love.'

'I reject your woman's intuitive knowledge, too,' he said, 'along with all the other neat rules for explaining life. But,' he looked at her very earnestly, 'I do thank you very much for your interest, especially as I'm sure you must think the whole thing a bit of a fraud.'

If one had plumped for benzedrine, then one could not withdraw the supply, so she said, 'Why should you think that? I'm not the per-son to be bothered with it if it didn't interest me. I've always been fascinated by the theatre.' One general truth to one particular lie; there seemed to be rules for insincerity as for everything else.

'Yes, I know,' he said, 'I suppose it's because I've started so many things and scrapped them. I can't expect others to have the faith in my ability to write that I have.'

'Oh, I think you could be a writer,' she said.

'I don't think I *want* to be. I just want to write one good play – not one that succeeds, you know –'

'Oh, no, for heaven's sake. Not that. That would be terrible,' she cried. If her sarcasm sounded roguish it was in order to avoid showing anger.

But he said solemnly, 'Mind you, I'm pretty sure it will be a success if I can do it at all. But to have written one good thing that's all I care about. I should have proved something about myself and I should be quite happy if I never wrote again.'

She stifled her first impulse to dismiss what he said as posturing and considered carefully. 'I don't believe it ever works out like that,' she said. 'Do you see that woman over there? The one with the emerald green dress?'

'The one with the bathroom hair style?' he asked.

'Yes,' she cried. 'Poor Poll! She stuck about ten years ago as far as her appearance is concerned. And in other ways too. She's an old friend of mine. We were at the Slade together just before the war. Oh, yes, I've had my ambitions. I went there just after I married; but I hadn't got anything really, not even talent, so I stopped after a year. But Poll was good. She got so far as having an exhibition and quite a little réclame. And then it petered out. I don't know why. Perhaps because she had enough means not to go on when it became really difficult, perhaps because there wasn't anything more there.'

'Poor woman,' Tom said, 'she looks like an angry clown.'

'You *will* write,' Meg cried, 'or rather, you know something about people. It's always coming out in things you say. Proving that she could paint didn't make *her* happy.' Whether because Meg's compliment had put him on his mettle or whether from genuine curiosity, Tom stared fixedly at Poll with his huge, sad eyes.

'I'll take you over to introduce you,' Meg began. She could prevent him staring and be free of him in one move. But it was too late.

Poll abruptly left the man she had been talking to for so long. She walked towards them so carefully that Meg feared she was drunk; it was impossible to tell because her tight skirt might equally have been the cause. In any case, Poll always drank so much and showed so few signs of it that there was no cause for disquietude – or rather, would not have been in the old days, but people said nowadays that the extra drink or two made her quarrelsome.

'You'll know me when you see me next time,' she said to Tom, and to Meg, 'You were whispering about me with the beard. *That* wasn't very nice.'

Meg said, 'This is Tom Pirie, Poll. Mrs Robson.'

'Clever you,' Poll interjected.

'We've been discussing what's going to happen to Tom,' Meg announced.

'What *is* going to happen to you?' Poll asked.

'Nothing, really.'

'Well, that isn't very interesting, is it?' Poll declared. There was a moment's silence, then she added, 'But still you've got a beard. That might be a help. I thought at first it was a submarine one. But you're too young for that. Just after the war my house was filled with submarine beards. And duffle coats. But I don't allow duffle coats any more. They're always dirty and they smell. Meg doesn't have them here anyway. Everything's much too posh. By the way, Meg, I shouldn't have thought you would have had bottom-pinchers here. That man I've been talking to is rather a dish, but I'm sure he's a bottom-pincher. But then,' she came back to it in a low voice, 'I didn't think you'd whisper about me with beards.' Her blue eyes had such a fixed, staring look that Meg really could not tell whether she was angry or not.

She said, 'Tom thinks everybody here's rather glossy.'

'Oh does he? What does that mean?' Poll asked.

Tom decided to assert himself. 'I meant successful but not knowing anything worth knowing,' he said savagely.

Poll looked for a moment at his spittle that had settled on the sleeve of his coat, then, 'You're quite wrong,' she said, 'Meg knows an awful lot. And what she doesn't know Bill tells her. He's in with all the high ups.'

Tom, it was clear, could make nothing of her and he looked even more uncomfortable when, as though she was confiding a tremendous secret to him, she said, 'Do you know that they knew when the war was coming? Yes, they did. Meg left the Slade even before that old Chamberlain went to Munich and she joined the Red Cross.'

'It was one part patriotism,' Meg said, 'three parts good sense.'

'Well, anyway, it meant you had a good war. I didn't. I had no idea it was coming and in the end they sent me to the country just because I'd been taught languages properly as a girl. It was awful. We had to listen to the wireless all day. But I know when the *next* war's coming,' she announced, 'that bottom-pinching man told me. But I shouldn't think anyone would have a good war next time, would you?' She gave a loud laugh that blared through the babble of conversation.

Meg thought, whenever Poll laughs it's at something frightening or depressing, and she makes the noise others use to greet a coarseness that touches their fancy.

'I wish you weren't going away, Meg.' Poll sounded truly for a moment as though she were being abandoned on a desert island; then resuming her customary dead-pan manner she said, 'I shan't have anyone to borrow money from when those damned people don't send my cheques in time. Do you borrow from Meg?' she asked Tom.

That Tom had once done so was not a matter of great embarrassment to him, but his lack of embarrassment embarrassed Meg greatly, so she deflected wildly. 'Look at Jill talking to that boring architect. She looks as though she were sharing the funeral baked meats.'

Poll looked round for a moment. 'That Stokes woman of yours? But she always looks like grim death. I can't see why you mentioned *her*, Meg. I can't borrow any money from *her*. She hasn't got any, has she? If *I* knew all these high ups I wouldn't ask people like the Stokes woman and me and the beard here at all.' She gave Tom a questioning look to see how he reacted to her talk, and finding that he was still puzzled, she suddenly took his hand. 'I think I *like* the beard, Meg,' she announced.

This softening into whimsy embarrassed Tom, but he smiled a little nervously. Meg, however, was suddenly concerned for herself. Innuendo, direct attack, or friendly teasing, she had had enough of any sort of criticism for today. True, except for Donald, they would not voice it if they did not like her; true that for all of them it was a kindly office to let them ease their pinched feelings; but if there was a place to kick off tight shoes, it was not under her dinner table; and in any case they should all, even Tom, have provided themselves with shoes of the right size years ago. Had she not been tired she would not have let it go on for so long; but if she did not exert herself now, her fatigue would turn into anger, and then all her patience would have been wasted.

She sought for a tone that would at once be light and final. 'My guests can't live by bread alone, Poll,' she said. 'They expect me to provide a circus too.' But Poll met the emotion before she replied to the words.

'You're all right, Meg,' she said. 'It's bliss to see someone who's got what they want. I'm willing to jump through any number of hoops for you, darling. If the beard's been saying you aren't any good, he's wrong.'

'Oh,' Tom said, 'I've been behaving like a bear and Meg's been good enough not to bait me. Even to entertain her guests.'

'Yes. Well, we won't go on with Meg's little whatever it's called about the circus,' Poll told him. 'I'd have pushed too, you know,' she said, parodying whatever was wistful in her tone, 'if I'd had a husband like Bill. But if I'd pushed any of mine they'd have fallen flat on their faces.'

'Oh, I don't think *I* should do that,' Tom said, 'if I married a wife like Meg, that is.'

Meg wondered what sympathy he had found with Poll that he could say such a thing without spluttering.

'All the same,' he added, 'it must be a bit of a strain to be kept on the move.'

Here Meg felt it reasonable to snub a little. 'It would be for anyone without Bill's stamina. That and his knowing all the time where he's going.' She saw what she had accepted and laughed. 'In any case, I don't have a chance to push,' she cried. 'In fact I'm always out of breath keeping up with Bill.'

'Our mothers,' Poll said, 'would have thought all this talk about pushing very vulgar. Or at least mine would.'

'Our mothers,' Meg replied, 'were stupid snobs. Or at least mine was. Tom's mother is an angel.'

'Well, don't rub it in,' Tom said, 'anyhow she's always saying what an angel you are.'

'Yes,' said Poll. 'Well, we've all been saying that for the last ten minutes. Now I'm going to talk about *myself*.'

'Do that, Poll,' Meg said, 'I must go and talk to all these people. Anyway I know the story. But Tom wants to be a writer. You listen to Poll, Tom. Her life's as good as any book.'

As she moved away she saw that Poll had relaxed her square little body and was weighing in with relish.

'I'd better begin at the beginning,' she was saying. 'Well, my father was an awful old swine really. I can't find any other word for it. But a very rich one ...'

And Tom sat impressed and on his mettle to be amused as though Grock or some great clown had favoured him with a special interview.

It surprised Meg to see Bill and his cronies abandoning their game of bridge so early. One, at least, she noted, was no crony at all but a visiting American lawyer. It meant that the party would soon be over, for Bill's social gifts were used either to settle guests in or to prise them out. She would have gone to his help, for overstaying guests were an annoyance to him that she had always made it her duty to prevent, but Gino came with the news that David was on the telephone. Her absence would delay the guests' departure and she could detect a very slight over-hearty note in Bill's voice which gave meaning to the early end of bridge: the American perhaps had not been up to standard. The antithesis of her husband and her brother seemed determined to assert itself this evening. It was absurd that one moment of largely forgotten history should suddenly come alive again. Nevertheless she could not suppress her irritation as, picking up the telephone, she said, 'Yes, David?' in a voice which suggested that his call was one of a series of regular, unnecessary interruptions rather than a recall to past intimacy that he made at the most five or six times a year.

'Only to wish you a pleasant trip.' His voice, as always over the telephone, disturbed her by its nasal sound. She felt immediately guilty that she had forced him into apology for a call which no doubt he had already deferred as either obtrusively intimate or meaninglessly conventional.

'That's very sweet of you, David,' she said, 'I didn't expect it, my dear. I knew how busy you must be.'

'Well, we are. I should have come up to see you before you left, but Gordon hasn't been well.'

'Oh dear,' she cried. It was more distress that she had not been the first to pronounce Gordon's name in order to please David. 'What's wrong with him?'

'Some sort of stomach ulcers, we think.' There was a pause and then he said, 'Gordon says to tell you that *he* doesn't think anything of the kind. He says that between Else fussing with his soma and me with his psyche, all he really wants is a complete rest and he wishes he were travelling with you.'

She couldn't really reciprocate the wish, so she said, 'Tell him I would gladly give him my ticket. An infinity of aeroplanes and hotels fills me with horror at the moment.' Here there need be no fear of arousing envy in David; indeed he immediately said,

'Yes, awful. But I suppose there will be *some* things to see that will make up for it. There usually *are* moments. And you know how *I* hate foreign travel.'

His words suddenly gave her a sense of calm, smoothed out the strain that had been mounting all day, so that she cried, 'Oh, David, do let's meet more often when I come back.'

She heard him chuckle. 'You can't come to Sussex and I can never get to London. But we'll contrive, Meg, somehow. Clapham Junction refreshment room perhaps. But we *will* meet,' he said it with assurance. She longed to return from abroad the very next day just to set about showing that they could do it. And then the pips sounded and the spell was broken, for he immediately said, 'There. I must ring off. My good wishes to Bill.' His calm was no proof against his parsimony. She remembered all his cooperation with Mother over genteel cheeseparing. No wonder he had said 'contrive' – it was a key word to David and made all the peace he had found in life seem to her to narrow to a pinhead of petty isolation. She called almost spitefully, '*And* my regards to Miss Bode,' but he had hung up.

To her surprise when she returned to the room Bill seemed to be talking happily with Donald, the American and, of all people, Jill. She set about releasing him from his own good nature, however – making good-byes to those who were prepared to leave and drawing into the atmosphere of their departure those who showed no signs of going. It amused her to hear Bill detach himself from his group, saying, 'Meg's pushing people off. It's just as well, I'm afraid, because she's given herself no rest before our journey tomorrow.' He was probably paying her out for not having been on the spot when she was needed. She decided to say nothing about David as the cause of her absence. To Donald, as he put on his coat in the hall, however, she remarked as casually as she could, 'You see how you impress me. I've already decided that Bill has to be coddled. *All* my guests got rid of before midnight's finished sounding!'

He stared at her intently for a second, then, 'You both of you keep it up a bit too much. What?' he said.

Meg had been mistaken in her boast, as she saw on turning back into the drawing room. Jill stood in the corner of the room looking into the china cabinet. It was odd enough that Jill should bother with the Meissen or the Nymphenburg, it was odder still to Meg when she saw that Jill was smiling at her own reflection. And yet she had every reason to smile, for she had lost her grey grimness and, in her dress of silver and pink brocade – heaven knew how old and now almost fancy dress – she was for a moment the rather deadly beautiful, but quite perfectly beautiful person who had set such an impossible standard in their youth. She turned as Meg moved and came towards her.

'You're quite flushed, Meg,' she said. 'What is it with? Triumph, I suppose.'

'Oh, Jill,' Meg felt she could not stand it. 'Don't go on, for God's sake. It's been a ghastly evening, as you know.'

To her amazement, tears appeared at Jill's lashes. 'Meg, my dear. I was quite awful this afternoon. I had no right to speak to you like that. You know the reason. I said it quite honestly – jealousy. But I had no right to be jealous. None at all. Look at all the pleasure you give to people. To me. I've had a wonderful evening. That man Anderson knew the Barkers and the Crossthwaites. All the people that were our friends when Andrew was stationed at Malta.'

It was at once so absurd and so touching that Meg could find no answer; but she had no need, for as Bill came back into the room, Jill went up to him.

'Have a lovely holiday, Bill,' she said. 'You spoil Meg. But go on doing so, she has a right to it.'

Bill looked at her quizzically. 'Thank you,' he said, 'I shall do my best.'

'What's she bellyaching about now?' he asked, when Jill had gone. 'What the hell's it got to do with her?'

Meg said, 'No, Bill. She wasn't being critical. She was being sentimental about me, I'm afraid.'

'That's a change. I'm glad though, because she was rather nice this evening. What's put her in that soft mood?'

'She met someone who'd known people who'd known Andrew.'

'Andrew?' he asked, turning from the preparation of their whiskies.

'Andrew. Really, Bill. Her husband.'

'Oh! Andrew.' He paused. 'It's a pity, isn't it?' he added. 'Talk about spoiling *you*. She's spoilt herself with this hallowed memories stunt. Don't you do that, Meg, when I die. It suggests such a lot that she should have done when he was alive, and didn't. Much better take to drink like old Poll.'

Meg laughed. 'You know I honestly don't think, darling, that she was drunk. You can never tell with her now. She keeps up that line of hers so.'

'Well, why not? It amuses a lot of people, I suppose. Young Pirie'd become quite human. He told me just why the job I got him at Carthews stank.'

She sat swilling her whisky in its glass, letting it slop to the brim but never spill. Then a drop splashed on her dress and it brought her to life again.

'You liked the evening?' she asked.

'Yes. I was a bit worried about your overtiring yourself. But it went very well, I thought. Bessemer played an appalling game of bridge. You can never tell with Americans what their standard's going to be. But he's a pleasant and interesting person.'

She said, speaking each word with deliberation, 'I *am* looking forward to the holiday, Bill.' Then she added, 'You're a much nicer person than I am, you know.'

He came over and kissed her. 'You must go to bed,' he told her.

Sexual satisfaction, adding to her exhaustion, yet lent her a wakeful ease. She felt as though she were floating above the bed in the cool darkness of the room. She shut her eyes. Colours and shapes turned to unwilled scenes and faces from the past – absurdly dominating them, her mother's with her neck scrawny and yellow against her pearls and her large brown timid eyes. It had always been her mother's neck and eyes that in her last years had been the focus of Meg's exasperation in their mute demand for pity. She tried to will the image away, to summon others, but all that came were hideous, distorted versions of the same wretched appeal. Bill, in his sleep, moved his arm from under her and turned on his side. She opened her eyes and said, 'David rang me up, darling. He would have done so before, but Gordon has been ill.'

He was too far gone in sleep to understand her. 'That's all right,' he mumbled. 'We'll keep going.'

The phrase returned to Meg many times as Bill slept beside her in the aeroplane on the night after they left Paris. A whisky, a glance at the stockmarkets in the air-flown *Times*, a few pages of *The Portrait of a Lady* – he had insisted that he had better 'give all these Maisies and Daisies a second trial' since she found so much in them – and he had fallen asleep even before the beastly, dormitory-like semi-darkness, which was all that the air company allowed to encourage sleep, had transformed the cabin from two double rows of human beings carefully preserving their privacy and individuality in absorbed, petty occupations into a frightening, passive, ghostlike assemblage of contrasted breathings. It was not alone the irritating pilot light, nor the scrabblings and whispers of Miss Vines, the stewardess, and of Mr C. T. Colman, the steward, nor even the sense of Greece and Turkey and the sea so many thousand feet below them, that kept Meg desperately awake, absurdly fighting the effects of a sleeping pill while pretending to welcome them; it was all these and, above all, a horror of joining this mass of dormant humanity, led into their passivity by her own husband. She pictured him as a Pied Piper and they as rats or children – it didn't really seem to matter which. He could surrender without a qualm because he was sure of keeping going, sure of arrival and, if not sure of what they would meet there, sure of his capacity to deal with it. But flying through space like this, with the tattered fragments of her normal daily life torn from her by the furious gale of changing time and place, she felt herself without any of the magic protection that being Mrs William Eliot of 102 Lord North Street gave to her, naked to meet the mysterious demands that would be made upon her by this destination that was coming so rapidly towards her through the darkness. She needed all her powers to retain her identity for herself, let alone to preserve or to create a personality to meet a changed, unfamiliar outside world. I'm like the creatures in Looking Glass land, she thought. I have to run twice as fast even to stay where I am.

At first, as the struggle for and against sleep tore her apart, she welcomed the ridiculous clock changes which brought morning closer and with it the banishment of the breathing zombie orchestra around her. But as the hours passed, she began to feel a strange calm unity with this sleeping world, and then she resented the stupid racing forward of the clock hands. At first her personality had been threatened and now that, in the stillness, she felt some hope of finding it, 'they' were trying to shorten the already brief time left to her. It was not indeed unity, she realized, that she was finding among the universal sleep – even Miss Vines and Mr Colman had now lapsed into puppy-like whimpering dreams, appropriate to their youth – it was sovereignty. She was Alexander Selkirk. Even dear Bill, mouth half open, was a brute in this context, and the white-haired smiling-eyed American lady opposite certainly a dishevelled old fowl in her hunched up sleep. But if like Alexander Selkirk, far better really than he, for she was feeling at least no need of 'alarms' and *could* rule in this solitary place. Let this monstrous forward putting of the hands of the clock only be prevented, and at last, here high up above she did not really know what – Turkey or perhaps Syria by now? – above this anonymous land, among these surrendered people, she would perhaps have the chance to come to terms with the 'In Between', to accept a void and still to remain herself unsurrendered. She felt, as it seemed for the first time in her life, a mysterious mingled calm and elation. But behind the mystery came one of those commonplace convictions of serial repetition, a sense that the experience was not new, had indeed happened to her again and again, though the particular visitations eluded her memory. She tried to thrust the conviction from her, knowing that, in searching her memory, she would dissipate her new found peace.

It was too late; the act of memory woke other activities more destructive still. Her sense of the ridiculous came into play – her vision seemed to her now no more than a childish confusion between 'clock time' and 'real time'. But if this confusion was there she knew it was not integral to what she had experienced. Drowsily puzzling over her muddled thoughts, she fell into an unquiet sleep.

She awoke to a hand shaking her arm and a soft voice lapping over the edges of a fast vanishing, troubled dream. 'Don't miss the dawn, dear.'

It was the old American lady, all freshened with eau de Cologne, her smiling blue eyes full of the hope and beauty that dawns notoriously offered. 'The dawn over the desert,' she was explaining. 'I don't know how many times I've seen it, but it always remains a miracle.'

Meg succeeded in parrying this overture to contact at a deeper level by a smile sufficiently sweet to be appropriate, yet sufficiently vague to suggest isolation. She saw that Bill had left his seat and wondered if perhaps he had already been driven to seek refuge in the lavatory by the same 'spiritual' onslaught. Now that she was awake he would, of course, deflect it all on to her. For her own escape she determined on a deep concentration upon the world outside. The sunrise she found altogether too 'striking' to provide any but secondhand images, but she stared at it as though literally entranced. The thought of Bill's embarrassment, caught alone and fresh from sleep by sunny smiles and eau de Cologne and beautiful morning thoughts, made it difficult for her not to break her trance with giggles, until she suddenly realized that in all his life apart from her – his professional days, the years before they had met – he must often have encountered the embarrassing or the absurd, yet she had no idea of how he would react if she were not there. She felt suddenly so cut off from him that when he returned, red, smooth, and smelling of after shave lotion, she immediately took his hand and pressed it. And when he frowned slightly but comically towards the American lady and lifted one eyebrow to express the horror of what he had gone through, it was only by herself going off to wash that she prevented herself from kissing him on the spot and so even further embarrassing him.

It was not until she returned to her seat that the desert seized her. Looking back later in the full grip of its blank sadness, she could hardly believe that a false introduction – the interposition of an unwanted personality could have prevented her in that first sight from being possessed by it. It was true that the beauty of its subtle range of colours – the endless varieties of brown and grey and white – had been lost to her in the conventional and expectedly 'startling dawn', but even so its frightening sadness must have been there. Or perhaps not; the possession was a gradual one; it was only as it went on hour after hour of rock and of meaningless plateaux and of shelves marked by equally meaningless windblown tracks, of great white lakes that deceptively promised water but were only saltpans, that she found herself lost in it, completely and absolutely bereft of all that made sense of her life, forsaken, and ready for annihilation. She had tried every offer of escape. She talked to Bill about Paris – how incredible that Madame Royaut's mother at their usual little hotel should actually be a hundred years old; how good all the same *Carmen* could be when as at the Opéra no attempt was made to tone down the vulgarity; how incredible that he should have remembered exactly the bookshop in the Rue Saint-Jacques after all these years. She felt only as though she must be appearing to mock his little surprise visit to Paris by the in-attention of her words. She attended to the American lady: how her name was Fairclough; her late husband a hardware millionaire; her widowed years devoted to travel; her favourite corner of favourite England Broadway, Worcestershire, in springtime, so unlike their own noisy Broadway – she was more of a stranger in New York than in London, Rome, or Tokio; her hometown, in fact, Denver; her married daughter devoted to the violin, making that instrument in-deed add to God's harmony; her own life wholly changed by Chris-tian Science, particularly by the banishing of a foolish, old, false claim of bronchial asthma.

But Mrs Fairclough's story evoked neither sympathy nor amuse-ment from Meg. She was only a distracting insect buzzing in her ear far away in the confines of the desert. Yet Mrs Fairclough was hardly a test of the force of humanity's pull against the spell of dead nature. Meg recalled with self-mockery how much their circle exclaimed about her passionate curiosity in people and how much she liked the reputation.

She tried the 'passionate curiosity' out on Miss Vines bringing iced orange juice, tea, fried eggs, and marmalade. Twenty-six, she decided, sexually attractive, but a disappointed mouth – could it be a long, dragging affair with a married man, or an innate frigidity that kept men short of proposing marriage? But she felt suddenly dissatisfied with all this feminine instinct for understanding; it was nothing but women's magazine advice-to-readers stuff. She tried again with Miss Vines, more sociologically: suburban – Bromley perhaps, or Epsom, or no, maybe nearer London Airport – Windsor. Certainly, to use a phrase and, in describing people, a phrase was everything – 'she had become as neat and cellophane-covered as the forks and knives she dispensed to the passengers'. But the phrase didn't work – she didn't care a damn about Miss Vines, who was less than a handful of sand from the desert. And as to the fat, smooth businessman and his young wife, pale skinned and gently attentive, whether they were Siamese, Burmese, Chinese, or any other 'ese' she neither knew nor cared. Her eye had to follow these strange grey-brown patterns to the end of their desolation, to where she herself was utterly lost.

In desperation she turned to her last hope of escape. She opened *The Mill on the Floss* and began to read of Maggie Tulliver's visit to Aunt Pullet. The humours of the book she knew by heart, so that they could do no more than revive laughter that echoed back to her childhood. There was no sound there sufficient to break a desert silence; she had not expected it. But Maggie herself, Maggie (Meg), the girl with spirit enough to follow her thoughts and dreams out of the narrow defeated home she had been born in; surely Maggie's tragedy would work its old spell upon her. She turned the pages rapidly, reading the familiar scenes more quickly to force them into life. It was no good; farmhouses, lawyers' parlours, fields, woods, and fatal river – Warwickshire seemed lost forever.

She sat now listlessly, only her eyes fixed feverishly on the wonderful monotony below them – so much more fearful and more beautiful than Chirico and his kind, by imposing on it their stupid child's nightmares of broken columns, severed arms and piano shapes, had ever warned her.

Bill laid down *The Portrait of a Lady*.

'Yes,' he said, 'it's all very well done. But I don't know that I shall read any more. These high-spirited, upstanding girls like Isobel Archer, out to conquer the world with their youth and gusto, they don't appeal to me. Perhaps I'm too old for them.'

At any other time Meg would have been overwhelmed or driven to fight back. Isobel Archer, and Maggie Tulliver face down on the table, and, in the rack above, among the coats and suitcases, Emma and Lily Dale – all these girls were her, only that, born in a later century, she had avoided their defeats; but their high spirits *and* their high hopes were hers exactly. Now Bill's dismissal of Isobel seemed only to underline the desert that cut her off from him, and, if from him, from all humanity. She turned a very wan smile upon him. His anxious solicitude was immediate and almost paternal.

'Meg,' he said, 'this travelling's worn you out.' He called to the steward for two brandies. 'You haven't slept, my dear, that's the trouble. But we'll be in Singapore not long after midnight.'

She drank the brandy slowly and then forced herself to try to bridge the gap. 'How long does it go on for?' she asked.

'The desert? Oh, pretty well till we get to Karachi, I think. Why? Does it get you down?'

She laughed hysterically. 'Yes,' she replied. 'Just that. I'm down there *and* it's got me.'

For a moment she feared that he would laugh, but he said, very seriously, 'I see. Of course, I'm familiar with it already from the boat but ... Do you feel lost in the immensity?' He could not keep a certain puzzled irony out of his voice as he spoke the cliché.

'No, Bill,' she cried. 'Please be fair. It isn't just adolescent egotism. I've come to terms years ago with the vast spaces of the sky and all that. At least as far as I'm able, which isn't probably much. But this is different. I literally have been down there for what seems hours now. I'm terrified of it but I can't take my eyes off it.'

He said again, 'You're overtired.'

And she answered quite angrily, 'I've been that before now, as you know. Even made myself ill with it. And don't tell me it's agorophobia because I've known that too and it isn't.'

'Well, hardly in an aeroplane,' he said and smiled, but she looked at him and his tone altered. 'Listen,' he said, 'these things change or can do so. Even something as apparently primeval as that desert. In fifty, a hundred years new technical processes may have altered the whole of that.'

'Then I should have come hereafter,' she said.

He took her hand and began to talk to her about the desert lands. She could hardly believe that he could know so much – geographical, geological, metereological facts. Relentlessly, and, as she knew, in purposely boring detail, he ground the whole desert down into facts and figures as dry and dead as itself.

'How do you know all this?' she said after some time. 'I believe you're making a lot of it up.' From her voice he could tell that she was eased and he allowed himself to say, 'Well, does it matter if some of it is a little improvised?' and to his relief, she laughed contentedly.

'I've never had anything like this happen to me before,' she said. 'I feel in a way ashamed.'

'Oh, I don't see why you should be, darling. As I said you're very overtired' – he met her objection to this in advance – 'and it may well be more than that. A really strange experience. After all, things happen to one for the first time when one isn't necessarily very young.'

She laughed again. 'I don't think we need dwell on that aspect of it,' she said.

'We needn't dwell on any aspect of it,' he answered, and, agreeing, she went off to wash. When she returned she found that she could slip with ease into poor Mr Tulliver's financial disaster.

She was only brought back many pages later when she heard Mrs Fairclough's voice addressing Bill in a half-whisper. 'Perfect love,' she was saying, 'casteth out fear.' Meg peered round her book to see an old, freckled hand heavy with rings pressing Bill's arm; she could only glimpse too that he was returning the old woman's deep, sincere look.

She knew now how he behaved in such tight corners: sincere embarrassment, polite but insincere 'sincerity'. Almost her own level, though the sincere embarrassment put him a little above her and this was exactly as she would wish it. Under the table she put her hand on his knee and his hand came down and pressed hers. She tried to return to Mr Tulliver, but Bill, caught in the path of Mrs Fairclough's eccentricity, made her tremble with suppressed giggles. At last, bent over her book, she was forced into open laughter until the tears ran down her cheeks. Mrs Fairclough, who clearly revered laughter as God's image, although herself more given to sweet smiling, said, 'That must be quite a wonderful book, dear, to bring such happiness,' and she peered at the title. Luckily she did not distinguish George Eliot from Artemus Ward or Jo Miller. Meg feared Bill's renewed embarrassment, but instead he pressed her hand more tightly and she could feel his body shaking slightly with laughter that he was just, but only just, able to suppress. Miss Vine's voice, however, came to relieve them with safety belts, and cigarettes to be extinguished, and a stay of an hour at Karachi airport 'during which luncheon ...'.

With less than two hours to go before their destination, they dined in the airport restaurant at Srem Panh. By good luck it transpired that Srem Panh itself was Mrs Fairclough's destination, so there had been no need to atone for their giggles by asking her to dine with them. In this last lap of their journey Meg had lost all her fatigue and depression, she felt now that she would welcome many more days of suspended, immune existence. Bill, on the other hand, seemed irritable at this further delay; perhaps the cramp imposed upon his body in the aeroplane was beginning to exhaust him, perhaps he was tired of the diet of deadened foods in hygienic coverings; certainly the meals at airports had proved regularly so bad as to suggest that they were sampling the various national cuisines only at the station buffet level.

Meg guessed that he had come, too, to hate being shepherded by efficient young women, for he ostentatiously ignored the smiling, moon-faced Badai girl's attempts to place them at the same table as some other Europeans. She walked away with a self-conscious, jaunty swagger. As they sat down at a table for two in the corner, he said, 'I hope all these Asian girls aren't going to look like cinema usherettes.'

Meg looked around her and thought everything more anonymous and beautiful than she had dared to hope for. There was nothing, absolutely nothing in this large glass-fronted room that could touch her. The posters on the walls told of places she knew nothing of; the signs over the doors (if one ignored the English translations, and she felt that she could) were in letters she had never seen before; the chatter, that fought against the aeroplane roar without, seemed to be in a multitude of languages no one had ever told her of; the people (save for a few Mrs Fairkloughs, whom in her present mood she could forget) seemed to be so many beautiful dolls, pretty girls with meaningless smiles, handsome amber men whose enormous eyes said no more to her than would the eyes of cats. Here and there was an absurdity – a young woman (Chinese? perhaps not) in what seemed to be an incongruous and cheap violet ball dress and high-heeled emerald green shoes; a fat, dark brown man with a red fez; a long, thin man (Badai probably, from his amber likeness to the waiters) surrounded importantly by young amber secretaries; some sadder, more European-seeming young amber men guzzling a dish she could not identify, no doubt to assuage their grief – she could look at all these as she would at anteaters or the manatee in the zoo, exotics to whose meaning she possessed no clue.

Great waxen red and pink lilies with huge yellow stamens decorated the room – if she had once known their name at some florist's she had now comfortably forgotten it; even the insects whose crushed bodies formed patterns upon the glass window were creatures she could never identify. Only the large pool of red and blue water lilies outside the restaurant could conceivably be said to be familiar, and then only because in the arc lights they looked like part of an improbable travel film. The country, Badai, the town, Srem Panh, were only names to her; she would never visit there; nothing that happened there could ever concern her. In Singapore, no doubt, and more still in Australia and America there would be impingements; but at this moment she had found a vacuum of peace in place and time.

Not so Bill, who wiped his face, took off his seersucker coat, and then, seeing the great sweat patches on his shirt, put it on again. She could not understand how the mood of happiness they had found on the aeroplane could have left him so easily. The humidity, of course, was beyond even what she had expected, but even so it was cut by the strange, Edwardian-looking electric fans, and outside there were cool pools of rainwater on the terrace and huge dark clouds on the horizon to promise more rain. She set herself, like a child with a tired grown-up, to ask him questions about Badai; but she determined to let the answers drift away in the heat, leaving her calm island untouched.

'The airports,' she said, 'are so deceptive. Like London Airport. So uniform. One has no idea of what lies beyond,' she corrected herself, 'or hardly any,' for really to pretend that this enchanting place bore any likeness to London Airport was too absurd. But he clearly did not find it so. 'Beastly places,' he said, 'and filthy food,' as he allowed the jellied cold soup to liquify in his spoon. 'Not that we're missing anything in not seeing Srem Panh, I imagine, apart from the company of that Middle West lady Messiah. It's almost entirely a modern town. The pride of the Badais since they found their wonderful, new freedom from the Dutch. Some modern blocks, I expect, and a grand hotel. Even the older Dutch quarter is largely *art nouveau.* After all it's a small country; prosperous enough under Dutch rule but never the big affair that French Indo-China was for the French, or Burma or Malaya for us. I believe that there's some wonderful mountain and jungle scenery up country but the people have always been a subject race – when it wasn't the Dutch it was Burmese or Siamese rule. Now, of course, they're an advanced democratic nation, and we have to join in the charade in case they turn to the Communists; but Communism's bound to come sooner or later. I wouldn't invest a penny in anything in south-east Asia ...'

Dutch, democratic independent nation, Communist, Meg let them all flow over her; they had nothing to do with this peaceful backwater into which she had now glided, among the lilies. She felt that she had only to let her hand fall to her side to feel the cool, hardly moving water around her, as she had done so often in punts with David at Oxford. And in any case even had she attended, these questions were outside her range, outside anyone's range, except the experts who ran the world, and they, when you met them, hardly knew what they were doing. But Bill, who became impatient at the least amateur politics from anyone else, was happy now, explaining realistically just where they should cut their losses to Communism and where to hold on. His voice, indeed, sounded full and contented enough for her to venture a quiet, a slow puncture.

'Are you improvising the jungle as well as the desert?' she asked.

To her relief, he laughed. 'No,' he said, 'or hardly.' He began to praise the fruit salad. 'You'll get a lot of this papaya,' he said. 'Do you like it?'

'It's delicious,' she told him, 'all the food's delicious.'

Everything now *was* delicious. She could feel that he was sharing her view of it all, if only at second-hand, in pleasure at her happiness. She was cautious enough, however, to refuse coffee; if that were as poor as she feared it might be there would be no holding him to the idyllic illusion. They walked together to the long glass front of the room and stood watching a Constellation leave on its flight to Colombo. She realized how fully anonymity would be kind to them in the days ahead, once the tedious chores of Singapore were over; kind especially perhaps in relaxing him; for she felt his arm around her waist, even pressing her to him. They stood so for some minutes and she stroked the hand that was placed on her hip. With the Constellation gone, the airfield stretched flat and yellow before them far over to the scrubby bush circling its edges, black outlines only in the moonlight. It might have been Putney Heath or Wimbledon Common, although it was difficult to imagine the circumstances which would have taken them to those places and certainly, had they gone there, his arm would not, as now, have been round her waist. That above all was the sign of how wonderfully it was Srem Panh airfield. They stood there together for five minutes or more, saying nothing; then 'Kew Gardens,' she announced, 'and Versailles.'

'I know,' he said, 'I was thinking that. Red and blue water lilies. We chose conventional places for our courting.'

She took up the slight irony he gave to the last word. '*You* may have thought you were courting, Bill,' she said. 'I was under the impression that we were "walking out together". Besides they were far too crowded to be conventional.' She added with mock wistfulness, 'You'd never put your arm around me at Kew Gardens now.'

But he accepted it on the serious level. 'Wouldn't I?' he said. 'Perhaps not. Things have to change you know.' He turned her round and led her to a nearby table littered with crumbled bread and half empty wine glasses.

'This isn't a very nice table to sit at, Bill,' she commented, but he answered only, 'We've stood for long enough.'

Smiling, the amber waiter proffered a menu. Bill gestured him away. Meg thought, he doesn't realize what overtones of colonialism his manner may have for these people. She said, 'We only want to sit here, thank you.'

But if the waiter understood English, it was certainly not hers. Having retired at Bill's gesture, he now advanced again at her words. She was driven into smiles and signs to express a satisfied appetite. Bill said, 'What on earth's all this pantomime for?'

Annoyed, she said, 'I don't like sitting with all this mess about me.'

At the next table the tall distinguished Badai stopped for a moment in his discussion of the portfolio of papers on his table and spoke to one of his secretaries, who in turn addressed the waiter. In a moment Meg's wishes were met and their table had been cleared. At the cost, however, of the waiter's composure. He leaned against the wall, whispering and giggling in a high falsetto with the two boys who assisted him. Meg smiled and bowed to the official party in recognition of their assistance. This for some reason only seemed to increase the whispering and giggling of the waiter. Bill frowned at them but his expressions did not command as they did in England. The distinguished official turned slightly in his chair and the waiters were silent.

'I wonder what he is,' Meg said. 'I should think a member of the government, shouldn't you? Perhaps the Minister for Culture.'

'Is there one?' Bill asked, looking at her indulgently.

'Oh, I should think so. There always is in foreign countries. He looks cultivated and sensitive. He wouldn't be the Minister for Transport or Agriculture or anything routine like that. He's probably rather lost among his colleagues. That's why he looks a little sad and lonely.'

'And his secretaries?' Bill asked. 'Let's hear about their private lives.'

'Well, the little one with the long flat head like an Egyptian mummified cat is eaten up with jealousy of the Minister. He's probably got a wife who nags him for not rising higher. And the young one with the fat smiling face like a bursting apricot is the Minister's favourite. He's a yes-man, but not without his own ideas. He's got a young wife or perhaps ... do they have more than one wife? I suppose being Moslems, they do.'

'If they were Moslems they might,' Bill said. 'But Badai happens to be a Buddhist country. You're like Sherlock Holmes put down among the Hottentots. As a matter of fact, all this woman's intuition is just a lot of Sherlock Holmesing. You go by the standard thing that you know. "He wore flannels where a suit was called for, my dear Watson. He spoke like a repertory actor. And he drank a third pint of beer when he didn't want it. Obviously a modern parson of a rather old-fashioned kind. The thing's elementary." All that Holmesing won't do here away from the familiar U and non-U of the Home Counties. You have to fall back on describing them as being like cats or apricots.'

A sharpness in his tone perplexed her, she said as lightly as she could, 'Bill, I believe you're indulging in what Viola Pirie calls "only half-teasing". I don't know why my descriptions should annoy you so, after all their faces *are* like that. Cats or apricots. Anyway *you're* always summing up witnesses. How do *you* do it?'

'Not in that sort of way at all,' he said. 'I've no idea what that man's job is. But he's got authority. You can tell that by the tone of his voice even in this jangling language. And by the set of his head. He's arrogant, I should think, by the way his eyes are half closed when people talk to him and by the curl of his mouth. And quite right too. Why shouldn't he be? He's earned the right to it, I expect. And look now, how he's closed that brief case and brought the discussion to an end right in the middle of the fat fellow's argument. It's obvious he doesn't care a damn. He's made up his mind and he'll stand by his own risks. Excellent man.'

'I don't find any of that the faintest bit convincing,' Meg said, laughing. 'You've just substituted John Buchan for Sherlock Holmes.'

But Bill had no concern for criticism. 'If I thought that man was typical of them,' he said, 'I shouldn't believe that the outlook for Asia was at all gloomy. But the trouble is men of his calibre are probably only a handful. It's the material they've got to work on that's so hopeless. That sort of thing for example.' He indicated the table of sad young men in continental style suits, lace edged handkerchiefs and fountain pens prominent in their breast pockets. The food they had guzzled seemed literally to have assuaged their sorrow, for they were talking now in earnest, high, edgy voices. 'Student politics,' Bill said, 'at the age of thirty or so. And one of the customs men off duty with them too. That's a bad sign when your N.C.O.s are mixed up in that sort of thing.'

'N.C.O.s! Really, darling!' she cried. 'What is this Colonel Blimp act? In the first place you've no right to say they're talking politics. They're probably talking about sex. And anyway why do you say they're thirty? They look about eighteen.'

'That's the trouble. Most Asiatics look eighteen when they're forty. Half-fledged with half-baked ideas! And always getting rattled about something. Look at the state of excitement they're in.'

She protested fiercely now, even though she mixed her protest with laughter.

'No, Bill, really. You sound like Tom Pirie's idea of the older generation.'

He looked a little sheepish. 'Well,' he said, 'it's very hot for talking. The sweat's pouring down me. I don't know how you keep so cool. Anyhow I'm afraid I *am* a bit out of sympathy with youth. Perhaps I wouldn't have been if we'd had ...' he stopped and added quickly, 'well, anyhow, for better or for worse I am. As I say, I can't stick the half-fledged and the half-baked; and I hate people who get rattled. In court. Anywhere. It brings all the bully out in me.' He paused as though surprised at hearing his own words, then he said, 'No, put my money on the old boy in authority. He's probably a High Court Judge.'

She had been given time to recover now. When his unfinished sentence hit her, she had been on the point of stroking his hand or bursting into tears – some sort of underlining at any rate that would have made it impossible to turn back. Now it had been half said and the moment of saying, thank God, had been the best that there could be, for she would have all these months of intimacy ahead quietly and gradually to lay bare his wound and heal it in so far as it ever could be healed.

'I see,' she laughed, 'a judge. Much more important than a Minister of Culture.' All the same she had to get away for a moment on her own. 'They'll be calling our flight soon,' she said, 'I'll just make use of the lavatory. I do like their signs. Whatever it says looks much prettier than "Ladies".'

'It'll be very unhygienic,' he said. 'You'd much better wait.'

'No,' she said firmly. 'The one on the plane's like the Black Hole of Calcutta.'

Almost immediately their flight number was called. 'Will passengers in transit proceed *first* to the barrier please. Passengers in transit *first*, please.' That was their call. Meg hastened to move before Bill could call her back. He was inclined to fuss unnecessarily about aeroplane and train times.

As she left Bill, she noticed that the eminent personage, followed only by the fat young secretary, had moved straight towards the restaurant exit without regard for any precedence of passengers in transit. And Bill had stood aside for him. His admiration for the man would almost certainly have been increased by this disregard for official instructions. Such complete certainty somehow always increased Bill's admiration for people out of all proportion.

As she reached the entrance to the 'Ladies', Bill's voice sounded, calling her back. She turned for a second and signalled that there was no need to fuss. The party of earnest young men, she noticed, had broken up. The shirt-sleeved customs official had run up to the eminent personage's secretary and engaged him in some lengthy explanation. They were gesticulating wildly. The eminent personage stood alone at the door, his back turned to all the fuss. Bill, nearby, looked ominously impatient. She opened the door of the 'Ladies' violently to show that she was hurrying.

The place was as dirty as Bill had predicted. The humidity, heavy enough outside, seemed to seep from the pores of the cracked white-washed walls as in some underground grotto. Up above where the ceiling cast shadows, lizards, inert and intent, lay flattened against the moist wall surface. Nevertheless, oppressive, almost disgusting though the narrow, high ceilinged washroom was to her, its privacy and its gloom had given her the moments she needed to retire into herself, to accept the full impact of Bill's preoccupation. Their childlessness had hung ominously over them for so many years, then struck in full guilt at her, and finally through his patient gentleness receded, so that for many years now she had accepted it as much or as little as she did the disparity in their ages. He could not help growing old ahead of her; she could not help being barren. If they did not accept these things they would destroy themselves. And now in the undercurrents of the last few days, in the lightening of the daily routine or in the factitious sense of a new life that their long holiday suggested, Bill had unmistakably shown that his acceptance was hardly, painfully made. Her short moment of retiral had strengthened Meg to face his sorrow, to wonder how much and again how little she could do in these heaven-sent months of intimacy to ease it. It was not, she decided, only as wife that she must give herself up entirely to his renewal, but as daughter.

The single tap of the water basin had a loose washer. As she turned it on there was a grumbling and groaning that startled her out of her reverie. And then almost immediately came the high, clipped Badai voice in its American-English accent calling the final notice of their flight. Startled into eager haste, she turned to the handbag she had placed on a wooden ledge to find her Cologne-soaked tissue pads. In too eager haste, for the bag fell from the ledge, scattering its contents in all the dark squalid corners beneath the basin. She could not see and, to the touch of her finger ends, numbed by the intense humidity, she might have been scrabbling among spiders instead of handkerchief and tissues. Everything seemed soft to her deadened senses. She felt hysteria mounting, then happily her lipstick holder gleamed in the darkness. Methodically she found each object, washed or dusted it, and replaced it in her bag. Then quickly but deliberately she cleaned her face with the tissue pads, peered into the dirty looking-glass, re-did her mouth. Even a lizard suddenly darting across the wall in pursuit of a fly could not disturb her now. She was freshened, ready to see things in perspective, yet not evading her sense that a crisis in their lives had come upon her unawares and that she must deal with it. She was not as Bill had put it 'rattled'.

Above the loud noise of aeroplane propellers, she thought for a moment that she could hear him calling to her and noted how frayed his nerves must be that his impatience could so outweigh his sense of decorum. She heard cries and shouts and hoped that Singapore would not be too noisy. She prepared her phrase to meet Bill's impatience – 'Well, I'm late, darling, but not too late. So I don't intend to apologize.' She swung open the door and walked almost into the arms of Miss Vines.

The stewardess pushed her back through the door into the ill-lit cellarlike room. Even in the gloom her eyes looked out from her rather stupid, regulation-made-up face with a parodied solemnity that hardly concealed her feverish excitement.

'Mrs Eliot,' she said, 'I don't think you should go back into the restaurant yet. There's something I have to tell you.'

Meg's first thought was that she was confronted by a lunatic; she had felt in the plane that the girl was neurotic and unsatisfied; horrors lay so very little below the awful dead monotony of the suburban mind. Then she knew.

'It's Bill,' she cried, 'he's ill.'

Miss Vines tried hard to reach some communication of individual compassion, but it was so difficult – there were so many passengers in her life. She put her hand on Meg's arm, but it was shaken off.

'Don't be absurd, you silly girl,' Meg said, 'I must go out to him.'

When Miss Vines did speak, she sounded as though she were delivering the keyline in a play. 'He's very ill, I'm afraid. He's been shot.'

The strangeness hardly reached Meg at that moment, she thought only, she's using the conventional words to tell me that he's dead. She followed Miss Vines out into the restaurant with a slow, numbed walk. The chattering, excited crowd divided at Miss Vines' words to let them pass through. She saw in a blur out of the corner of her eye the pale student being dragged away by two uniformed men. He was without his glasses, blood was pouring from where his nose was smashed flatter than ever against his amber cheeks.

Meg had a sudden vision of the whole scene as part of some film – this must be how it was on the sets. For a moment she felt a violent anger against them all for making a cardboard scene out of Bill's life and her own. But then the unimportance of anything overcame her so completely; she thought, now I'm supposed for some reason to act with dignity, since there's no point in any action any more.

A second later she saw Bill's face, chalk white, and saw his blue lips moving. She turned on Miss Vines almost as though she would strike her.

'You told me he was dead,' she cried. Those precious seconds when Bill needed her, wasted by this wicked girl's stupidity! She knelt on the tiled floor by Bill's head.

'Darling,' she said, 'can you see me? It'll be all right. It'll be all right.' And as though to echo her, Bill's voice came very slowly and in a whisper she could hardly hear.

'We'll keep going,' he said. But his eyes seemed quite dull and staring.

Her body trembled in a convulsive effort to restrain any tears or cry. A woman's voice behind her said, '*Ah! la pauvre dame!*' And then a tall man was bending over Bill, cutting away his shirt and trousers from his stomach. Holding Bill's hand, stroking his arm, Meg looked up. 'Are you the doctor?' she asked. 'Why don't these fools get a doctor?'

'*Je suis médecin, Madame,*' the tall man said. He had a purple birthmark on his neck. '*Calmez-vous. Votre mari ne souffre pas beaucoup. Il a subi un très grave choc.*'

Were they all mad suddenly that they had begun to talk to her in French?

'*Je vais lui faire une piqûre de morphine,*' the tall man said and, rolling up Bill's sleeve, he plunged the needle into the crook of his arm. Bill's face, so flabby now in its paper whiteness, twitched for a second. The tall man stood up. '*Il ne faut donc pas faire trop grande attention à ce qu'il dira,*' he said.

Meg strove to give meaning to his words. Perhaps he was telling her that Bill would be out of his mind. Well, if so, she would make a life for him somehow, anything so long as he still had a life to make. Always these foreground actors playing some absurd role, and out of the line of Meg's vision this crowd of absurd extras dressed as Chinese, Badai, Americans, Indians, and God knows what. She would not allow them to obtrude upon the reality of herself and Bill.

'The ambulance is on its way, Mrs Eliot,' Miss Vines said timidly. 'I have to go now.' And to echo her words came again the ridiculous clipped American Badai voice.

'Passengers for B.O.A.C. Flight Number five-nine-three please.'

Meg did not look at her. Let them do their role of 'The play must go on'; she was intent on Bill, stroking his hand, mopping the sweat from his forehead with a Cologne pad.

'This is Mr Dykes,' Miss Vines said, 'our Srem Panh representative. He'll look after you, Mrs Eliot.'

What a disgustingly inept time for introductions and strange surnames! Nevertheless Meg made herself smile vaguely in the direction of a silly little reddish moustache and a common accent that said, 'Your husband acted like a hero, Mrs Eliot. The Minister doesn't want to intrude but he's asked me ...'

'Please,' Meg said, 'I don't want to hear all this now. I want to be with my husband.'

'Oh, of course. I quite understand'; the common voice was faintly patronizing. 'We've telephoned to the British Consul.' He said it with pride. These irrelevant emotions in the voices that came to her made her feel, as the words in French had done, that she and Bill were lost among a crowd of lunatics. She dreaded so that this sense of being at the mercy of people with no hold on reality might penetrate poor Bill's clouding consciousness. She held his hand more tightly.

'I'm looking after you, darling,' she said. 'It's Meg. I'm looking after you, Bill.'

His words were blurred now; she could only just distinguish them – 'Can't afford to go out now,' he seemed to be saying. The tall man for some extraordinary reason insisted on shaking hands with her.

'*Je regrette mais il faut que je continue mon voyage, Madame,*' he said. '*Mais vous pouvez me croire, les médecins indigènes sont excellents. Ils feront de leur mieux.*' And a little sallow woman, apparently his wife, for he murmured, '*Madame, ma femme,*' said, '*Soyez tranquille, chère Madame, le bon Dieu vous gardera.*' It was ludicrous.

In the ambulance, seated on a small pull-down seat by the side of Bill's stretcher, she felt thankful for the strange, amber, cat-faced men in white. Where Europeans might have attempted some conventional expression of speech and feature, they gave her decent silence and only the occasional gaze of their large solemn eyes. The anonymous heaven had turned to hell, but even so the anonymity offered its solace.

Bill's breathing had become strained and, although he gave no consciousness of pain, it rose now and then to a kind of involuntary groan, most dreadful to her because it seemed to be taking his humanity from him. He muttered occasionally, but though she strained to hear him she could catch no stray word, no more than a faint sighing. Before they reached the hospital he had slipped from druggedness into death. Meg sensed it only from a slight relaxation of the two attendants, but she had been deceived before, deceived out of precious moments when he needed her; death should not find her again so easy, so shamefully easy a believer.

They came to a halt; the attendants opened the door and a small soft hand took her arm and helped her down. A tiny little Badai nurse craned to hold a huge umbrella over Meg's head towering above her. The rain thundered and splashed around their ankles as they ran into the doorway. Through the now thin, dreary moonlight Meg could discern long glass-fronted balconies above them. She imagined hundreds of faces – brown, yellow, white – pressed to watch their entry. We're giving an all-night show at any rate, she thought bitterly. She saw herself and Bill praising this wonderful modern hospital of which the Badais were no doubt so bloody proud.

They were taking the stretcher in at another door. She turned and ran towards it. 'Where are they taking him?' she cried. With the little nurse in pursuit, crying, 'All right, all right,' she ran, stumbled, fell into a pool of rainwater, bruising her knee, cutting her hand.

A man came and lifted her up. 'Come along this way, Mrs Eliot.' The voice was refined, Edinburgh. 'The doctors are with your husband now. There, there,' he said like any old Scots nanny. 'Come and sit down a moment.'

He was a black-haired, flat-chested man with a little moustache and timid green-flecked brown eyes; beneath his transparent macintosh she could see a white dinner jacket.

'I'm Marriot,' he said. 'British consul. They're a wonderful crowd of doctors here, I can tell you.' He took her into a small waiting room with palm trees in pots.

'Dear me, that's a nasty little cut on your hand.' He called to the nurse in Badai. In a moment everything was washings, dressings, an injection. 'You have to be very careful of cuts here, you know. We're not in England now.'

He was so calm and soothing and nannylike that she wanted to hit him; but she simply stared into space and said nothing. And now to add to the nightmare absurdity a little red-haired, coppery-faced, lioness-like woman, with plastic macintosh covering a long white nylon evening dress, came up and touched Mr Marriot on the arm.

'Ah,' he said, 'the doctor'll be here in a moment with the report.'

For a second Meg looked at him defiantly. She must make up to Bill for her faithlessness, for walking behind Miss Vines slowly, for leaving him alone in those precious moments of consciousness, for accepting his death so easily. Now they would have to tear acceptance out of her. And then suddenly she slumped, exhausted, on the wooden bench. This, she thought, is the first moment of losing Bill, losing the only presence of him that I can understand, oh, pray God that there will come some other presence of him to be with me in these dreadful, dead years ahead.

'There's no need for the doctor to come,' she said dully, 'I know that my husband is dead.'

'Ah, you've known it all along.' Mr Marriot's genteel voice was full of sad kindness; and Mrs Marriot put her hand on Meg's arm and stroked it. But Meg could feel their burden lighten, as though she had owned up to stealing the chocolates and they would no longer have the sad, painful, tiring task of keeping the whole school in.

At their urging she went into the long, high mortuary room in which Bill's body lay, his eyes closed now, on a hospital bed. Memory and love and a terrible pity fought together in her exhausted mind, and an aching love emerged as master; but even so she kept tight a small part of herself, frozen and separate, for she knew that, if she were ever to find him as he would be with her for the future, she must not hold on to him as he had been. Only she wanted to announce to him that everything that in any way had to do with him – even this corpse so soon to be given over to strangers and then to decay – was the object of her utter love and reverence. She bent down and kissed his lips.

It was so difficult not to hate the Marriots and their kindness as part of the whole obscene and sudden horror that had come out of nowhere and engulfed her.

'The great thing now is rest,' Mr Marriot said, as he started up the car. 'Doctor Maung has given us these tablets. They'll help you to sleep, Mrs Eliot. You'll stay with us just as long as you feel the need. If there's anyone at home you want me to cable to, please tell me. Mind you, they'll see it all in the newspapers tomorrow.'

She looked at him through her exhaustion as though he had emerged from the shadows to show her the face of a lunatic.

'Ah, yes, I'm afraid so,' he said hurriedly. 'But nobody'll worry you about it. I'll see to that.'

Her attempt at a smile embarrassed him even further.

'You've come at a terrible season,' he said. 'The monsoon you know. Hence our appearance. I always think these plastic macintoshes make people look like strips of celluloid.'

'I'm afraid,' Meg said, 'that everything appears to be made of celluloid at the moment.'

It was a simple and exact statement – the nearest thing she could find to break her silence in the politeness due to him. He took it as a request to meet at a deeper level.

'Ah,' he said, 'like a film. Yes, I'm afraid it must all seem very unreal. Or rather not afraid, for the shadow-show we all play in is a poor one at best. And if grief brings us glimpses beyond it, well ...'

At the back of the car Mrs Marriot stirred. 'Everybody's bound to seem absolutely unreal,' she said, 'unreal and bloody.' Her voice faintly stirred surprise in Meg – it was not Scotch but a husky strangulated, upperclass contralto. 'The only thing *we* can do,' Mrs Marriot went on, 'is to keep the *other* unreal, bloody people away from you. And one good thing is that after this is over, you'll never see us again. You needn't hate or like us, you needn't remember us or even think about us again. We're just here to keep stupid annoyances away and make things a bit easier.'

Meg strove to acknowledge this kind realism; but how could she, for the reality was simply that she couldn't feel them as individuals at all, only as part of the dead weight that had suddenly fallen upon her; their voices were no more than misconceived sound effects that like the thrashing rain added to the unreality of this improvised melodrama. By some fantastic error they had shot into the audience and killed Bill; now they were asking her ...

But her unhappiness broke through the comfort of such metaphors, she could think of nothing but Bill lying dead in that room. A horrible fantasy that he was only drugged, that at this very moment these wicked cat-faced people were using his body to increase their command of Western skills, seized her so strongly that she put her hand to the door. She mastered her hysteria, turned with a desperate smile to Mrs Marriot in the back of the car, and surprised her greedily munching a bar of chocolate.

'Any shock always makes me ravenous,' Mrs Marriot's boyish grin was the best she could do in apology.

Meg let out a hysterical giggle and then felt suddenly released from them – despite all their kindness, they were indifferent, as remote from her as she from them; the isolation she needed was not really threatened.

A more unexpected threat awaited her when they reached the Marriots' long, low white house. Reporters were already on the spot.

'Mrs Eliot has nothing to say to you fellows,' Mr Marriot told them and added something in Badai. Meg wondered vaguely if his Scots accent still came through, and if he had found the equivalent of 'fellows' in this strange, singing language. 'Helen'll take you up to your room,' he told her. 'I'll have these chaps in for a whisky. If you can't satisfy their curiosity it's always as well to quench their thirst.' He winked at Meg.

'We should like to have a photograph of Mrs Eliot, please,' one of the little men asked, smiling at her. Mistily she returned the smile and apparently roused Mr Marriot's fears.

'Now don't let yourself get involved, Mrs Eliot,' he said. 'You chaps'll have no photograph tonight. But you can all have a wee drop of Scotch to get your insides as wet as your outsides.' His Scots act was clearly familiar and popular, for there was a wave of giggling and immediate acquiescence in his plan.

Going up the broad wooden staircase from the large, circular hallway to the bedrooms, Meg, deadened though all her senses were, was struck by the beauty of the house.

'You have a very lovely house,' she said.

'You *have* to have something in this place,' Helen Marriot told her.

83

'Don't let Jimmie's talking get on your nerves. Tell me if it's too much and I'll keep him quiet. But he'll be a power of strength with newspapers and officials and all that sort of thing.'

'He's a very kind man.'

Helen Marriot turned on the landing and faced her.

'Oh! He's a pet,' she said. 'But there's no need to let him worry you.' Perhaps it was Meg's blank look that made her add, 'Or maybe I'll be the one to get on your nerves. I do on a lot of people's.'

Along the pale lemon wood of the corridor walls hung reproductions of Dufy. Helen Marriot's white crinoline dress and vivid red hair seemed to repeat their decorative, rather chichi effect of splashes of bright colour. Meg longed for the darkness to descend and blot out all this irrelevance.

In the large bedroom the lemon-coloured wood was varied with panels of some lighter, almost white wood. The familiarity of receiving a guest seemed to banish the occasion from Helen Marriot's mind. She flitted about the room, indicating cupboards, a shelf of bedside books, an ivory box of cigarettes; she went into the attached bathroom and turned on taps to demonstrate showers, showed bath salts and fan apparatus. Meg followed her round automatically, saying every now and again, 'Thank you.' She had found it now as the word that would suffice to hold the world at bay in the coming weeks. Helen suddenly went to the door and clapped her hands. Even at that moment the improbability of people really summoning their servants in this way made Meg want to laugh. A moment later a pretty, high-cheekboned Badai girl appeared with Meg's suitcases and – Meg suddenly saw – Bill's. Immediately she felt a desperate need to get Bill's things away from the cat-faced creature. The very existence of these Badais who had killed Bill seemed revolting to her; she must get the girl out of the room lest she should open the cases and touch any of Bill's clothes.

She tried to find some way of effecting this tactfully but she was too tired to invent.

'I don't want her to touch the clothes, please.'

She had said it and was horrified. So, clearly, was Mrs Marriot, though she tried to mask her embarrassment and disgust. She spoke very gently to the girl, who bowed, smiled and left.

'They're very wonderful people, the Badais, Mrs Eliot. A race of natural aristocrats we think.' Meg's tragedy clearly could not excuse her from all censure. 'You must remember,' Helen Marriot went on, 'that for Aung Ma you're surrounded by a halo of heroism. She'll do anything for you. She worships old Prek Namh.'

Meg sat down on the large bed with its scarlet cotton cover. Helen, getting no reply, said, 'Prek Namh the minister.' And then almost irritably, 'You mustn't believe all these stories about the Badais being Communist. Your husband's already a national hero to most of them, the man who gave his life for the minister.'

Meg thought, they'll try to make me accept this monstrous wickedness whatever it is. What have all their hero-worship and their filthy politics to do with us? They've killed Bill and they can't get out of it. And I wasn't there. I went away. She tried desperately to remember why she had gone to the lavatory, but every incident of the night seemed lost in a haze of memories of all her married years. She knew only that for whatever reason she had left him then, she had done so deliberately. 'I wasn't with him when they shot at him,' she said dully, 'I'd gone to the lavatory. I left him alone.' She ended on a cry of despair.

Helen Marriot came over and sat on the bed beside Meg. She took Meg's hands and held them tightly. 'Oh, my poor dear,' she said, 'my poor dear.' Then slowly and deliberately as though she were repeating a spell to exorcise witches she said, 'Prek Namh is the Minister for Education. Probably the most brilliant man they've got. Jimmie thinks so and, although he seems a frightful ass in many ways, Jimmie knows Badai affairs better than anyone, far better than our people at the Embassy. Prek was here from the capital to open the new college. We saw him only this morning. This student or so-called student had some kind of a grudge or so he says. But Jimmie says it's political. So you see, my dear, that your husband's bravery ...'

Meg had removed her hands from Helen's clasp and she now got up. 'I don't want to hear about it all now please. Later, of course, I will. But now I must be alone to think about Bill.'

Helen Marriot gazed in surprise for a moment, then she said, 'Of course. What bloody awful bad luck life can serve up.' But Meg had had enough of her intimacy, she began ostentatiously to unpack. 'Look,' Helen Marriot said, taking a packet from her white evening bag, 'these are the sleeping pills Doctor Maung said you were to take. And there's iced water in this Thermos by the bed.'

Meg looked at the pills. 'I never take those scarlet ones,' she said, 'they're called seconal and they simply send me off to sleep and I'm awake two hours later. I've got my own anyway.'

Helen Marriot stopped by the door. 'Mrs Eliot,' she said, 'please take these. We are responsible to Doctor Maung. And I think you should try to help us a little.'

Meg realized that this was her tone for combating hysteria. Perhaps I am hysterical, she thought; probably. She said, 'Of course, if you think I should.'

To her surprise, Helen Marriot waited. 'I should like to see you take them,' she announced. 'Two, Doctor Maung said.' Meg swallowed the pills as quickly as she could; anything to get the woman out of the room. 'Good night,' Helen Marriot said. 'No one will disturb you tomorrow until you call.'

Stretching out her arms to relieve her exhaustion in the double bed, Meg found only space, void. Her loss hit her suddenly with no soft padding of strange circumstances or of the need to cope. It was the first direct blow. Bill was lost to her; and she was lost to loneliness, back where she had started, lying alone in some country hotel room – at Crowborough was it? where her mother had failed to sell handmade children's toys – with David away at Oxford. At least she had then been wanted, however much she had fought to keep her mother's inarticulate emotions away from her. She drew in her arms, curled up her legs, lay cat-like, in revulsion even at the memory. Sick at her own egotism, she tried to concentrate on Bill, to suffuse herself with remembrance and love of him. Striving to efface herself, she fell into a heavy sleep.

Everywhere a great rocky plateau stretched – grey, pinkish brown, lightening to a lemon yellow, paling to a deathly chalk white. She walked, almost floated over the sand and rocks, terrified yet exulting. Only her mother's voice nagged the solitude. 'To be deserted that's the shameful thing. I'd be far better dead.' The little mouth, lipstick caked in the ridges of the lips, was trembling, and her eyes were imploring and ashamed to implore. She must turn her back on it. Bill would take her away from it. He was there with her. She could not see him, but he was behind her, his arm round her shoulders stroking her breast, the fingers of his other hand tickling her palm. Palm trees all around and the sand stretching down to the blue sea. 'It's the ancients' purple,' he said. And she knew somehow that he was telling her that they were to be at their happiest, to be at Cagnes on holiday. 'I can go a long way.' He meant that he could walk upon the water. And she knew that it was true if they were together. 'With me you can go anywhere,' she told him. The sun was so warm and they were so happy and sure. No woman need be a desert it seemed. Only the sun and the sea.

She woke so safe and warm, that the blackness of the room seemed fantasy. She waited a second for the heavy clouds to pass over. The rain sounded violent and heavy and very near – these Mediterranean storms. And then she buried her face in the pillow, in terror and despair, biting the linen to hold back her screaming. For hour-long minutes she pressed and stretched herself against the mattress, but its softness gave no firm response to assuage her longing. All his devotion, all his love were gone with his body; and hers was useless, could never now offer itself to efface the tired, lonely look from his eyes, the overstrained, resigned note in his voice. Her knee ached; she pressed it against the wooden edge of the bed, trying to gain absolution through pain. Paradoxically the sharp soreness gradually dominated over grief. At the last her own petty physical wound brought her back from her hysterical grief for him.

She turned on her back, switched on the bedside lamp, determined to honour him with her whole being – reason as well as emotion. Shadowy trees were outlined through the large window whose mosquito netting made a blurred pattern unfamiliar to her. Even the single sheet was intolerable in this soaking heat. She turned on the electric fan which seemed to add only a breezeless noise to the air that came from the ventilating screen.

She thought, if Bill gave everything to me, what was my life for? It had no meaning except in him. They had set out together to climb somewhere; but she had been only a rope, not a guide, for she had never known their destination or asked it, only judged its approach by his look of certainty, reading his face for portents of success or failure. There was not a single way that she could live for him now; nor die for him. She had never believed that there was anything more than this life for anyone; nor had Bill. Whatever happened she must live as he would have judged fitting. She tried to imagine how he would have met the sudden loss of her presence. At any rate he would have gone on – not because of other people's judgement, but because there was a pattern that must be kept to. But the pattern for him had the meaning of his work. Her life would be as inert as the large green creature that sat in prayer – mantis, it must be – up by the ceiling above the wardrobe; or the grey lizards in that washroom. Inert, dead lives, only moving when some fly was foolish enough to come near them. Praying mantis. Preying mantis. But she had no prayers – Bill had been all her prayers; and all her prey. The word came to her so easily, was there before she could suppress it. Once again she let the pain from her knee fill her consciousness to drown all thinking.

How could she tell what he would expect of her now? Only that she must wait, hold herself in readiness to live or to end her life, but not to let him down by listening to easeful thoughts of suicide or by catching at stray hopes and turning them into spiritual certainties. She knew at least that he would loathe all such soft ways. All she could do was to fight to keep a sense of his presence alive about her. For herself. To guide her. But where? In the Utrillo reproduction facing the bed, the sun beat upon white walls, and an empty, still street led nowhere. There was nothing for it but to seek oblivion until she had the mind and strength to see how he would have wanted her to live. She got out of the bed. The pain from her knee shot up her thigh. It was swollen and flabby. She took Dr Loundes' pills and sought some respite of her life sentence in sleep.

Through the drug haze that hung around her half woken consciousness there pierced a bright light, spreading out, forcing her awake to face the sun blazing into the bedroom. Resistant, she let her eyelids droop against its compelling power again and again; each time that her eyes closed she saw Bill's face, his look, steady, protective, trusting, admiring. She lay back on the pillows. If she could always feel him about her as she did now, she would have the strength to live on. Suicide seemed suddenly an absurdity because he would have been so ashamed of exposing the depths of their love to a world they had always excluded. No fear now either that she would seek to find him in sweet, cheating beliefs of after life, in all the pitiful round of some widow's churchgoing or medium-frequenting. But she could only keep him with her if she preserved herself as he had loved her, fought the weak fears that for who knew how long would seek to dissolve her personality. She would have his protection as long as she remained what he had respected and loved. And, after all, she had won his respect, even if there had been so much in which she had failed, even if it had been in fact a cheat ...

Action alone could fight the inrush of this destructive guilt. She said aloud, 'I must settle things here and go back.' Her voice far away, small, surprised her. First, there must be no more of these drugs to weaken her control. Sweat poured down her cheeks. The heat was overpowering. Practical, simple actions would make up her healing routine. For example, she must shut out this vile sun, symbol of this vile tropical country.

She got out of bed. Her knee ached terribly. Her leg would not carry her – her leg or this wretched drug. She supported herself with difficulty by holding on first to the bedside table, then to a chair, then to the dressing table. I shall find myself a useful and decent life to fill out the empty years – no, not empty, for he would be with her. But no drugs, for they made useful life impossible, made the floor rise up at her. Holding on to the window ledge, she looked out at a hazy kaleidoscope of colour – purple, green, and something white moving in the distance. She concentrated all her powers on what she saw, away from thought, away from the pain in her knee. Trees – palm trees – and a great mass of purple flowers – B. they were called B. The name seemed suddenly vital to her. B. G. Begum, Buganda, Bagheer. Exotic words all, but not the word she sought. Tears came to her eyes. The word was not in her power, and if not the word, how life? And then, as suddenly, nothing mattered but the moving white object – creature; yes, it was a creature far away at the end of the garden. A white monkey with a dark face. G. B., B. G. A gibbon that swung from one silvery arm to the other along a wire, a rope across the garden. Swing, swing, stop. Swing, swing, stop. And now back again. Swing. And now round and round, white, all arms, white arms and purple. Round and round. White, purple, and green. It was the sun. She groped to find the shutter. But rays of pain scorched from her knee: out, over, through her. The floor came up instead and hit her.

Meg, leaning back on the pillows, gave Helen Marriot the smile which she had adopted to deal with all these tiresome people. They intended kindness and were no doubt doing their best under difficult circumstances, but their absurd behaviour earlier that day, fussing because she'd taken too many sleeping pills by mistake, had shown her that she must get away. As soon as her knee had recovered enough to allow her to be properly mobile, as soon too as she was rested a little, she would assert her authority; meanwhile she could only humour them with a smile.

'I thought the little doctor was very good,' she said. 'I don't think he quite understood all I said, but I suppose they often speak English better than they understand it. When does he think I can leave?'

Helen Marriot sat down on a cane chaise-longue with jade green shantung cushions.

'I'm glad you were happy with Dr Maung,' she said, 'because your nurse will be a Badai too, you know.'

The disregard of her question decided Meg that her smile was insufficient. 'Oh, I don't think a nurse is necessary,' she said. 'I can move about the room for myself already if I hold on to things. But you don't want me here any longer than is necessary and I don't want to stay. When does the doctor think I can leave?'

'It's not a question of your knee. After what's happened we cannot take the responsibility of leaving you alone. You must see that, Mrs Eliot.'

Meg contracted her muscles in an effort to control her anger. She must give no sign that could allow them to continue this intolerable treatment of her as though she were a child. She felt bruised from her fall, and exhausted; the last traces of the drug too threatened her with sleep. She managed somehow a voice that gave some indication of her real personality – a voice at once determined, yet casual and easy. 'I see very well, Mrs Marriot, that you've none of you believed a word I said. I'll repeat. I had no intention whatsoever of trying to take my life. I wanted to sleep and I took too many pills. However, there's no point in going on about it. You don't know me and you can't be expected to understand. The whole situation's a false one for all of us, and that's why it must be brought to an end as soon as possible. If you must bring a nurse then you must, though I really can't see why that girl, Aung Ma or whatever she's called, can't do anything that's needed ...'

'Aung Ma is a respected person in this house,' Helen cried. 'I don't intend to have her treated as you treated her last night.'

Meg stared in amazement. 'I do think, considering everything, that I might be spared hysteria,' she said. She frowned. 'Treated her in what way anyway?' she asked.

'The Badais are not fools,' Mrs Marriot said. 'And if they're hypersensitive, it's because they've known what some Europeans can be like. Only a minority, of course. The Dutch, on the whole, were splendid. But in any case that's all over. There's no room for colour prejudice now. With Communism at the door we can't afford the least sign of it.'

Meg lit a cigarette before she spoke. She noticed with annoyance that her hands trembled. 'Mrs Marriot, please try to understand. I have no colour prejudice of any kind. If I said the wrong thing last night I was hardly in the state to know what I was saying. I remember nothing. But if you want me to be in love with these people, I can't. I don't want anything to do with them that I can avoid. Them or their country. I just want to get away from the place where this ghastly thing has happened.'

Helen Marriot got up and, with her back to Meg, straightened the pink and scarlet gerbera in the bowl on the dressing table. Without turning round, she said, 'I'm terribly sorry, Mrs Eliot. I've behaved abominably. I've shown less than no understanding. But this ... this business needs such careful handling. The least thing might be interpreted in the wrong way and then Jimmie will get the blame.' She paused and when Meg made no comment, she added, 'It wouldn't be the first time, but it might be the last.'

'Look, Mrs Marriot,' Meg said, 'I'm sure we're both perfectly nice people. At least let's hope so. Circumstances are against our showing it to each other. But it doesn't matter. As you said yourself in your very understanding words to me last night in the car, "You needn't remember or even think of us again." And that goes for you too. I see from what you say that life here isn't easy for you. Ordinarily I should ask you more about that,' she smiled, 'I'm thought to be a very sympathetic person. But at the moment I simply haven't room for anyone else's troubles. But I don't want to be a cause of worry to anyone. The sooner I can go the better. It would be such a help if you would stop treating me like a child or a lunatic. If you would answer my question, when does the doctor say I can leave?'

'He spoke of a week.' Helen Marriot made it sound like a year; and it echoed so in Meg's mind.

'A week!' she exclaimed; then she thought, why does it seem like eternity when I have all my life to be alone and only a week to be here with Bill; but she quickly corrected the thought – Bill was with her wherever she went.

Helen Marriot went to the window and looked out. 'I can't get them to use the sprinklers with any common sense,' she said and went straight on, 'If you had someone to accompany you, you might be able to travel sooner.'

'Maybe. But as there is no one we must only hope that the doctor is over cautious.'

Helen did not turn round. 'Yes,' she said, 'although ...'

But Meg's voice sharp, shrilly angry interrupted her. 'Mrs Marriot, you've sent for my brother. It's utterly indefensible. You both of you know exactly what I said about his cable. It's unnecessary and unfair on him. He's a very busy man and he can't afford it. Well,' she paused, 'we'll just have to send another cable cancelling whatever silly thing you've said.'

Helen Marriot turned round. She summoned all the anger that guilt had brought to her. 'Now, look here ...' she began.

But Meg would hear nothing. 'There's no more to be said about it,' she cried. 'You've certainly succeeded in bringing my position home to me as early as you could. And I suppose I should thank you for it. I used to tell Bill that he was arrogant sometimes. Now that he's not here to cope for me, I understand only too well. ... But I don't propose to treat you to my feelings. One thing is clear: there are a number of things I must get straight with you. Will you please ask your husband to come up here?' And when Helen Marriot stood for a moment in hesitation, she added, 'You've said that he may be blamed if things are misinterpreted. I must tell you that *my* blame has to be considered and if you insist on disregarding me I shall see when I get back to England that it counts.'

Both women were sweating now with the intense heat and with anger. Meg thought, at any rate she looks a little less cool now in her green cotton dress; a commonplace woman with commonplace taste – red hair and green dresses. She thought, too, I've gone beyond the point of no return with her, and I'm very glad.

'Please hand me that writing paper and my fountain pen before you go,' she said.

The Marriots were with her again before she had finished writing the cable to David. 'Quite able to return alone. Hope to be back within week.' She paused. 'Will cable you time arrival plane for you to meet. Love Meg,' she finished. 'You see,' she said, 'what your interference has landed me in. I have to make sure now of not hurting my brother's feelings.'

She dispatched Mrs Marriot with the cable. 'Please don't bring that nurse up here until I've finished talking to your husband,' she said. She felt a little alarmed at the unwonted dictatorial note in her voice.

Mr Marriot was clearly more than a little alarmed. She tried to soften her tone.

'Do sit down, Mr Marriot,' she said, 'so that we can talk comfortably. I'm quite myself again.' What did it mean? She could never be what she had been and had no idea what she would be. 'And there are a number of things I must ask you. Things you've had to take responsibility about that really should have been mine. For instance, Bill's funeral.'

'Well, Mrs Eliot,' he began, 'we're not in England, you know, and ...'

'And so the funeral has to be immediate. Mr Marriot, I'm not an unreasonable woman. I think you had no right to send for my brother against my expressed wishes and I said so. However, that's all settled now. But in arranging Bill's funeral I'm sure you were trying to save me distress. I'm grateful to you.' All that remained of Bill traded to repair the breaches in a goodwill for which she did not care twopence. But, of course, that was not all, or indeed, anything that remained of Bill. She said rather primly. 'My husband never made anything of funerals. Nor do I. When is it to be?'

Relieved, Jim Marriot became almost garrulous. 'Well, the arrangements are made for tomorrow morning,' he said. 'I couldn't find any record that your husband was a Roman Catholic, so the service is to be held at St Saviour's, the Anglican church here. And the burial'll be at the Protestant cemetery attached to the Dutch Calvinist church. I shall attend, of course, and the Government's sending a representative. The Minister of Education would like to have attended himself, I think, but we're anxious to avoid demonstrations of any kind. I hope I've persuaded the newspapers to keep their reporters away. So that if Doctor Maung could see his way to allowing you ...' His voice drifted away in face of Meg's inattention.

'Mr Marriot,' she said, 'I stopped your wife last night when you started to tell me how Bill died. I expect you thought that rather strange.' He mumbled dissent which she smiled away. 'Possibly that's what started you off thinking that I wasn't responsible for my actions. You'll have to forgive me if I don't go into the reasons.'

He bowed his head reverently before the privacy of her grief. Noticing a large bald patch on the crown of his head, she felt embarrassed at the obeisance. She thought, my God, can I only stand up for myself by bullying. The old cracked barking of dowagers, impertinence disguised as the wit of old age, lorgnette snubs gave their horrid warning. Immediately she began to give him her reasons. 'You see it's Bill living that I have to hold on to if I'm to keep sane. He was a man of such energy and gentleness and goodness to me. Whatever happened at the end is only a tiny speck of his life.' She stopped, disgusted at her incoherence, horrified that once again she was trading Bill for adjustment to this meaningless environment. 'I ought to have been there,' she said. Trading herself, she became calmer. 'Anyway, please tell me now exactly what happened.'

Jimmie told the story with painfully slow deliberation. Meg tried to control her impatience by considering the importance that he clearly placed now on satisfying her. There was something unsatisfactory about the Marriots' position and probably the handling of this sudden emergency was vital to his career. Listening to the Edinburgh accent, more genteel than ever in slow, hesitating speech, she found the delivery an almost unbearable additional agony. Again and again he reminded her, 'Of course I'm telling all this at secondhand'; again and again he qualified, 'We may get rather a different picture from some other eye-witness who's not yet come forward'; again and again he said as though in consolation, 'but I think we can say that the total picture is a very consistent one.' Even so, from his hesitating, dead narration and her blurred, buried memory of the airport scene, the grotesque, wicked fact of Bill's death was forced into a shape which the authorities recognized as a regrettable incident, some vile meaningless people as disaster avoided, others equally vile and meaningless as righteous assassination freakishly prevented, the newspapers as a front page story, and, Mr Marriot asserted it again and again, all but the fanatics ('probably Communist paid but that's being played down') as Bill's incredible, remarkable heroism.

'I don't know how much consolation it is to you, Mrs Eliot, but your husband showed a very high courage indeed'; and 'One thing stands out. Mr Eliot acted quickly, heroically, and without thought for himself.' The phrase stood before her – idiotic, brutal, impenetrable. All the other blurred figures had leapt into life at the command of words even as dead as these Mr Marriot employed. The thin distinguished Badai's courtesy to passing foreigners veiled Prek Namh, Minister of Education – 'one of the cleverest men in this country, Mrs Eliot, and perhaps the *only* man of real integrity in the Government, though you mustn't quote me as saying just that.' But what did his integrity concern Bill or herself? In any case, a target for a bullet that didn't reach him. Probably a brutal, tyrannical man, a hypocritical Claudio. She had to beat back a hysterical fury as she thought of him living and Bill dead. And out of a pack of earnest, chattering bespectacled students there emerged Bill's murderer.

'There seems to have been some grievance about a University grant. University education has assumed absurd proportions in the minds of many young Badais today, Mrs Eliot. But as I said before there's probably something political behind it. They'll no doubt find out all they want to know. It's a very efficient intelligence system, though I doubt if it'll come out at the trial. You'd best forget anything I've said about that side of it.'

A lost scholarship, a hysterical student, for these Bill had died. She felt only an utter and hopeless depression when she thought of the man who had killed him, but for the man who was saved she felt an utter loathing. It was as though the argument that she and Bill had indulged to pass the time had been carried on into a melodramatic play that was yet no play: Bill to be shot by the young man he had censured, to die for the man he had approved. The actors – Prek Namh, the student, the customs man accomplice, the hired crowd of catfaces and extravagantly exotic supers, the idiot chorus provided by Miss Vines' jolly gentility, the small part players – a travelling French doctor ('a brilliant man apparently, Mrs Eliot' – all the doctors who had let Bill die were brilliant it seemed) these were real enough; but Bill's 'heroism' remained so incredible and so cruel that she had to twist the sheets in her fingers to prevent herself from crying out against it. How could he have lost his life – their life of happiness together – for all this remote, Oppenheim unreality? Even to consider it seemed to threaten an earthquake that would bring the whole structure of their past toppling down around her; and their past was all she had to live for. What these unseeing fools called heroism must have been some ghastly accident.

'Thank you, Mr Marriot,' she said. 'You've made it all as clear as you can. But as you say you weren't there.' She had a peculiar bitterness towards those who shared in the guilt of absence from the scene. 'I imagine,' she went on, 'that, as in most foreign countries, the law here demands written depositions from witnesses before the trial starts. I should like to see copies of those, please, before I leave.' When he hesitated, she added, 'Being the wife of a barrister of international reputation, I couldn't help picking up *some* legal information, you know.'

The humorous tone which she gave to her last remark, far from lessening Jimmie Marriot's anxiety, seemed only to increase his sense that he had failed.

'I must tell you, Mrs Eliot,' he said, 'that my instructions are to keep British commitment in the affair down to the minimum.' When she shook her head, he added, 'I'll do what I can. I don't know how far the police authorities will let such documents out of their hands.'

Meg laughed. 'I only *want* them as far as here,' she said. 'I'm sure they'll agree to that if you ask them.' He looked so sad that she added, 'I'm very glad that you will be at Bill's funeral. Neither he nor I are believers, but the last thing we should want is anything ostentatiously unconventional. Perhaps before I leave we could discuss the stone for his grave. Something as simple as possible.' She decided on heartlessness as the best deception to ward off their pity.

If he seemed a little surprised at her tone, he was clearly relieved at the information it conveyed. 'In that case,' he said, 'you'll not be wanting Mr Tomlin to call on you.'

'Mr Tomlin?' There seemed no end to these invading oddities.

'The rector of St Saviour's.'

'Heavens no!' Meg cried. 'How very kind of him though. Do please thank him from me.' She heard with satisfaction the routine social note in her voice.

A moment later Helen Marriot reappeared. 'I've cancelled the nurse,' she said in the voice of a gruff, sulky schoolboy. 'I hope that'll satisfy you.'

Meg, discerning the guilt buried in the gaucherie, had a panic vision of continual involvement. Nevertheless, she decided, amity, as long as I can keep it reasonably at bay, will allow me to stay in peace with Bill better than the frets and jars of hostility.

'You've both been immensely kind to me,' she said.

'We haven't. We've been absolutely bloody.' Helen had returned to her manner of last night.

'Well,' said Meg. 'Whatever. The least I can do is not to be a nuisance. Be honest with me. What is it you're frightened I might do?'

The question alone seemed enough to alarm Mr Marriot. He looked at his wife as though her face might tell him what labyrinths lay concealed in Meg's words. Then, unprovided with an answer, he said, 'We're just concerned to help you all we can, Mrs Eliot, that's all.'

But Helen Marriot gave an answer. 'Quite honestly,' she said, 'Jimmie simply can't afford to bungle this affair. And by bungling I mean letting the authorities have the slightest excuse for saying he has.' She came behind her husband and put her hand on his shoulder. 'Left to himself, of course, he'd do the job perfectly as he always would. But he won't be, and we need all the help we can get. The British *must* not be involved an inch further than we can avoid. You don't know the politics of it all, Mrs Eliot, but our great aim is not to be identified with any of the parties too much. Though we're a hundred per cent anti-communist. The less that gets into the papers, either here or in England, the better. The first sensation's over and we've got through pretty well but ...'

'In other words,' Meg said, 'you don't want me to shoot my big mouth off. Please don't worry. I promise not to. If I could bring Bill back ...'

She could not understand what had made her use the absurd and unsuitable Americanism, but it was a happy choice. Relieved by her promise, Jimmie Marriot seemed in a transport of delight about the phrase.

'Did you hear that, Helen?' he asked. '"Shoot my big mouth off." Well, I knew Americanization had gone pretty far at home but I had no idea it had caught up with people like you, Mrs Eliot.' He laughed so much that at last the two women were laughing also at his absurdity.

Jimmie Marriot's pleasure at her Americanism heralded the whole tenor of Meg's conversation with them in her days there – days that stretched from Dr Maung's original week to nearer a fortnight. The Marriots seemed drawn by love-fear to England which they had not visited for so long, to which they yet might be returned empty any day. Americanization, rock 'n'roll, Teddy boys, angry young men, new towns, housing estates, television, these formed the substance of all their talk and questions of home. Meg tried to answer as well as she could, but really she wanted to tell them that her life was not lived in the pages of the popular newspapers. Bill and she had been most actively engaged in living, yet nothing of what the Marriots so fearfully sought to find had touched them even tangentially. Once when they had been talking about football pools and their effect on the nation, she felt suddenly as though the world at home was as remote and dangerous as this unknown Asian world that had struck out at her so cruelly.

In the main, however, she was left alone. She lay, giving herself up to happy memories. She had to fill her head with echoes of Bill's voice so that she could endure the years to come; and, above all, with Bill's voice confident, happy, and triumphant to drown the plaintive note of Bill's voice lost, empty, careless of life. But the plaintive note grew louder.

At first she found some relief by fussing each visitor to the room – Aung Ma who brought fresh limes and ice; Helen Marriot who brought Chinese dishes of prawns and bamboo shoots and sharks' fins that, far from tempting, revolted her; Jimmie Marriot bearing, with ostentatious confidence in her goodwill, copies of the depositions – with constant demands that the venetian blinds be more securely closed to shut out every ray of the powerful sun. The heat was unbearable, she said. But the sun's rays were not the voice that ripped her conscience.

Then it became the room itself which refused her tranquillity. The lemon-coloured wood, the jade green cushions; the scarlet bedcover; all these changed from a pleasant scheme doing credit to Helen Marriot's taste; she could not endure such artiness, could not get well amid a pathetic pretension symbolized by the Utrillo reproduction. There were no reproductions in Lord North Street. Saying it to herself, she realized that she had lost her sense of humour but could find no energy to revive it.

Dr Maung was persuaded to let her be helped downstairs each day, and she lay on the veranda in a bamboo chaise-longue with daffodil yellow cushions. There she lost herself, for long moments, even letting Bill's memory slip away, in a mass of strange sounds and colours – the glaring crimson of the bougainvillea, the softer, complex blues and browns and greens of the orchids, the neat and highly gaudy beds of gerbera and portulaca, the whirring of the fans, the fainter sound of the water sprinkler. Then she would be wakened from this half-sleep by chance movements – a spray of water shooting suddenly higher into the air; the gibbon increasing the pace of his monotonous swinging; and she would turn a concentrated attention upon the deposition.

It was only after she had read all these that the amity established with the Marriots was, if not broken, at any rate badly cracked. She found in them no word to support her hysterically held belief that Bill had died by chance. He had moved to protect, all of them said it; some even declared that he had 'flung himself'. Out of her reading, however, came an appeal that broke through her egotism, that restored in some part her normal concern with others.

'Mr Marriot,' she said, as he came out, smiling, to his daily moment of full bonhomie – the shaking of the evening cocktails. 'Mr Marriot, when is the trial of these young men?'

'It began yesterday,' he said, as his face clouded at this banishment of the routine evening talk of scholarship-filled Oxford and Cambridge, or England without domestic servants.

'I should have been told,' she said.

'Now, there's no need to worry yourself about it. I sent your deposition in and the authorities expressed the greatest appreciation of your cooperation.'

She felt the coming battle and said irritably, 'I hope the authorities aren't as foolish as you report them. There was no cooperation. I had nothing to say.'

Mr Marriot's face showed glum and sulky. He gave her the mixed gin and passion-fruit juice in silence.

'I hope they *aren't* as foolish,' Meg repeated, 'for the sake of these young men on trial. What's going to happen to them?' Jimmie Marriot assumed an expression of careful deliberation as though his visitor were asking him some nice point of Badai custom.

'Well,' he said, 'capital punishment is not so generally favoured here as it is in Western Europe. On first consideration I should say that the influence of Buddhism had a good deal to do with that, but you'd need a legal expert to trace all the factors ...'

'Mr Marriot,' she interrupted, speaking each word clearly with an accompanying nod of her head as though she were addressing a provoking child, 'I'm not asking you that. I'm asking you what will happen to the young man who shot Bill.'

Helen Marriot came out on to the veranda at that moment. Perhaps because she had not followed the conversation from the first, she did not divine Meg's feelings as her husband had done. 'I think there's no doubt that he'll be hanged, Mrs Eliot,' she said in assurance.

Meg stared at her. Everything about her was so small and trim – her little thin face with its turned up nose and small white teeth that showed a fraction above her protruding lower lip; her tiny well manicured hands, her neat little feet. And so clean and bright in her peacock green silk cocktail dress. It made her words seem doubly obscene. You beastly, arty, little hop o' my thumb, Meg thought.

'Do you suppose I'm clamouring for a man to die?' she asked, but she strove to be honest even in her distaste. 'Oh, of course, one side of me wants it. No, not even one side, just a primitive instinct to hurt and torture the person who took Bill from me. But what should I be like if I let that sort of thing take hold of me? Far from bringing Bill back I should lose him for ever.' She paused to control her anger, then more slowly she said, 'I can't remember the time when I wasn't against capital punishment. This is the test of my sincerity.'

Helen Marriot said, 'I see. Well, we don't think like that.' Then she asked, 'And your husband, what were his views?'

'My husband and I didn't think the same on every subject,' Meg answered. 'Ours wasn't that stultifying sort of love.' She turned to Mr Marriot, 'I want to make a plea for clemency,' she said. 'Surely coming from the widow and from a foreigner it would have a telling effect?'

Helen Marriot put her glass down on the long, low table impatiently. 'Coming from a woman, and a widow at that, it would have no effect whatsoever,' she said. 'Coming from an Englishwoman it might have quite ghastly consequences.' The note of rising anger in his wife's voice brought Jimmie Marriot to life.

'I understand what you feel, Mrs Eliot,' he said. 'Helen said "we" but it isn't strictly true. I have very pacific feelings too. I hate all cruelty and however you look at it there are some very distasteful emotions involved in hanging a man. But in this case, it's no good. Whatever we feel they'll hang the fellow. Not because he killed your husband, Mrs Eliot, but because he tried to kill Prek Namh. And because they think he's connected with the Communists.'

'All the more reason then why I should protest. I must ask you to forward my pleas to the right quarters.' She was beginning to weep now.

'I'm sorry, Mrs Eliot, I can't undertake to do that. We must not be concerned any further in this business.'

Helen Marriot came over and sat on a cushion beside the chaise-longue. 'You gave your promise, you know,' she said. 'You can't go back on it.'

'I don't know,' Meg said, 'I'll have to think it over. Women aren't quite helpless, you know.' As soon as she had said it she was furious with herself.

Helen Marriot patted Meg's hand. 'Poor Mrs Eliot,' she said; and Jimmie Marriot said, 'Yes, that's right, think it over. But it's true enough that you can't help the fellow, if they've made up their minds.'

'Which they have,' Helen said, 'and it would be very embarrassing.'

Aung Ma was bowing to announce dinner. With stick in one hand and the other holding Jimmie Marriot's arm for balance, Meg went in to a dinner of stringy chicken, okra, and potatoes, which she did not want.

The next morning as Meg was seated again on the veranda beneath a striped umbrella canopy, watching a large yellow and black bird flying in and out of a bottle-shaped nest, a Badai came up the drive pedalling a bicycle rickshaw in which sat Mrs Fairclough. She paid off the man with many smiles and advanced towards Meg – a harmony of blues. Her dress was bright cornflower blue linen, her large panama hat was draped with forget-me-not ribbon, she wore a turquoise necklace and turquoise ear-rings, her blue eyes smiled, brave but sad. It's hardly worth her while blueing her hair, Meg thought, if she's going to provide it with such competition.

'Why do you come up the drive in blue
Fat white woman whom nobody knew?'

she murmured. But it wasn't really fair because Mrs Fairclough wasn't fat and, after all, *she* knew her, although only slightly. She began to smile and then, remembering Bill's embarrassment and his subsequent happy suppressed giggles, she felt very pleased to see the old lady, if also horribly tempted to laugh in her face.

'I'm so very glad, dear,' Mrs Fairclough announced, 'that you've found the peace of this lovely garden.'

Meg thanked her for being so glad, asked her to sit down and offered her refreshment. To her surprise Mrs Fairclough specified the refreshment she required. 'A pot of coffee, dear. I always think it's so much better when it's stood in a pot. And a glass of iced water. You can't live long in Italy without knowing that coffee gets lonely without iced water.' She added that she was not particular about the food. 'Biscuits, sandwiches, or whatever they've got.' Meg reflected that rich old ladies who lived in hotels probably got used to commanding in this way; it was only fortunate that the Marriots were out. With Aung Ma she now had such a complicated relationship of mutual smiles to efface the past that she was quite reconciled to clapping her hands and giving orders.

Until the refreshment was served, Mrs Fairclough confined herself to talk of the garden's beauty interspersed with little jokes like the one about the coffee and the iced water, and with examples of the quaint, human goodness of simple people – peasants or natives – in the many countries she had visited.

'If only,' she said, 'the wise of the world could learn from that,' and 'Only a little coloured boy no more than knee high but what a mighty truth he proclaimed, bless him, without knowing it.'

Meg was reminded of a childhood book, *Peeps at Many Lands*. When Aung Ma had served a lavish display of home-made cakes, fruit, and sandwiches, Mrs Fairclough set to with relish and she threw aside pleasantries for a more serious tone, though still smiling forth a radiant harmony. She put her hand on Meg's bandaged knee, and when Meg grimaced in anticipation of pain, she gave her a full, personal, and intimate smile.

'I am with you always even unto the end,' she said. 'Truth denies sickness, sin, and death. They are not lost, they are only gone before. Hold on to that thought, dear; we are children of God, children of light and the light knows no darkness.'

Meg could not think how to answer but there was no need, for Mrs Fairclough kept right on talking, though often, with all her eating and drinking, it was not entirely easy to hear what she said. 'Truth is real and eternal,' she told Meg, 'matter is unreal and temporal.'

Meg speculated how far the old woman was consciously aware of the discrepancy between her doctrine and her greed, but she could find no answer. The truth was that far from resenting the intrusive visit, she found pleasure in the presence of someone who was so pleased with life; particularly someone whose happiness was enough tarnished with self-satisfaction to allow of ridicule with a clear conscience.

'I have been thinking of you so much, my dear,' Mrs Fairclough said, 'and I've been working for you. Once when I woke in the night I declared the truth about this whole business. Error can seem so real in those hours of darkness. It came to me then that I should find you in peace and sunlight. The peace that passeth all understanding.' She smiled and smiled. '"Still, still with thee when purple morning breaketh, when the tired waketh and the shadows flee." That's from one of our hymns, dear.' Then suddenly the glitter went out of her large blue eyes, and the faintly lipsticked mouth ceased straining with little powder-caked lines and wrinkles. She looked quite serious.

'It seemed to me,' she said, 'that you would like a visit from someone who had seen you with him. Someone who could tell you that even in that little time she had seen with what a deep love he cherished you. He saw you afraid, and his love was enough to banish that fear. Love like that can't die just because he has put off this life, and put on the life immortal. You know all this, of course, but I thought that as there was no one else here who had seen you together, you would like to hear it from me. Was I right?'

Meg felt that, even if she could not accept all that Mrs Fairclough had said, she could honestly say, 'Yes. Thank you very much. You have helped me a lot.'

Whether it was that she had now said all that she had come to say, or whether that she had eaten everything Aung Ma had brought to them, except for a large mango that would have shamed even someone less dainty and fragrant than this baby blue, shellpink old lady, Mrs Fairclough now sat in rather embarrassed silence.

'I'm afraid,' Meg said, 'that I wasn't very friendly on the aeroplane.'

Mrs Fairclough's blue ribboned picture hat shook a little involuntarily.

'Oh, I didn't feel that at all. An old woman travelling on her own is glad to feel such great love as you and your husband gave to one another. You seemed so rich in love, my dear, that you couldn't help spilling it over on to others.' The sweet smile she had resumed seemed, in her nervousness, embarrassingly insincere.

When she got up to leave, her legs below her short skirt were so matchstick-thin that Meg was overwhelmed with pity. She felt that she must show her some affection.

'Could I tell you something in confidence, Mrs Fairclough?' and when the old woman had sat down again, she told her of her wish to help the young men on trial. 'They say it's no use,' she said, 'and I feel so powerless.'

'Blessed are the merciful,' Mrs Fairclough announced, 'for they shall obtain mercy. All things are possible if we believe. Mrs Eddy tells us in *Science and Health* ...'

But Meg could not let it all run away like that. She wanted to prove the old lady as fine as she now believed her to be.

'Would you help me?' she asked. 'It wouldn't be fair to go over the Marriots' heads to the Embassy or the Minister or the police. But this is the man who is defending them.' She had copied the name from the reports. 'Would you try to find him and tell him that I would like to see him? Perhaps *he* could make use of my support.'

Mrs Fairclough seemed a little bewildered, but she assured Meg that she would arrange it. She, too, had something to give Meg before she left. It was a reprint of one of Mrs Eddy's hymns in red and black lettering on a card with scalloped edges.

> 'Mourner! He calls you, "Come to My bosom.
> Love wipes the tears all away".'

Meg read. When Mrs Fairclough had gone, Meg was alarmed to find tears coming to her eyes. She felt less embarrassed when they merged into hysterical laughter.

The pleasure of Mrs Fairclough's visit kept Meg elated for some time afterwards. To have talked to someone who had spoken to Bill, however absurd the encounter, released her from isolated fear. To have talked to someone from outside, to have enjoyed a ridiculous person, did more; it made her feel that she was not entirely cut off from the woman she *had* been, the woman who liked people and laughed at them. Looking back, she felt that she had hardly been herself, had hardly been on top of the world, fulfilled and mocking, since before that wretched send-off party that had so strangely presaged the miseries to come. And then too Mrs Fairclough would set in motion her plea for these wretched men, would allow her conscience to work as it always had done, commanding right where it saw that right should be done.

All the same her conscience told her that the appeal to the defence lawyer differed in no way from any other appeal as far as the Marriots were concerned. She had simply wriggled out of her impossible promise to them. She found it necessary to tell them what she had done.

To her surprise, they took it very calmly.

Helen Marriot said, 'I'm afraid you're very naïve, you know. What makes you think a stranger like that will take all that trouble? And even if she did, I don't think their lawyer would do more than thank her profusely and forget about it. The pleas of widows are hardly likely to help his case here. If, that is, he's putting up a serious case at all in view of the government's attitude.'

Jimmie Marriot toned it down a little. 'Helen's got a powerful imagination,' he said. 'We don't *know* what'll happen. All the same the views of strangers and especially of women don't carry a lot of weight. But you've done as your conscience bade you, Mrs Eliot. Please don't think I've any hard feelings.'

Meg found it difficult to speak to them for the next few days. No word came from Mrs Fairclough or from the lawyer, and at the beginning of the second week there Aung Ma told her with a gentle smile, 'These bad men are hanged.' She had become devoted to Meg and tried hard to master new English words in order to speak to her.

At first Meg was so utterly disgusted with herself for not having battled more fiercely to save them that she felt a physical disgust with her own body. It seemed monstrous to be living when she had run away from Bill and he had died; when she had run away from her conscience and these men had hanged. Yet by the evening a strange lassitude had come over her. Always in her life she had got what she wanted, trying only to see that what she wanted did not defy her conscience. Fighting against her mother's feeble plaintive will, and later backed by Bill's strength and affection, she had gained her points in life. She had kept her will within bounds, never listening to the courtiers' voices of hysteria that had bade her defy the great ocean of things beyond her control. Even when war, that ocean that had engulfed so many citadels, threatened their happy life, Bill, with foresight, had propelled her into Red Cross work; and, though he had been absent on military service for some months, it had not been long before he was back with her, working in the legal branch of Admiralty in Whitehall. They had both been immensely useful at their jobs so that conscience and will had kept in pace.

As she thought of the war, the memory of their only casualty made her shudder for a moment, as though her mother's shadow had cast a chill misery over her. Poor, pluckily battling, bewildered Mother, washed up with a dozen or so other lost impoverished old ladies and buried with them beneath the rubble of a private hotel in Bath. A Baedeker raid, and poor Mother had found so little time or place in life for works of art. Meg forced the image of her mother out of her mind – it had troubled her peace increasingly in this last year, when mysteriously, despite all their secure happiness, the roaring of the ocean without had sounded again and again in her ears and not even Bill's presence had been able to still it. And now, Bill had gone and she would have to face it alone. She would have to circumscribe her will most deviously if she were not to meet defeat. Yet if defeat was so easy to take as her failure over these men ... She pulled herself up in disgust – an acceptance of the hanging of two wretched youths was a pretty sort of triumph over her will. But disgust could not keep back the tranquillity that took possession. The last act of the airport tragedy was over. Perhaps, she thought, vengeance was what she had really wanted despite her life-long principles. She was too drowsy and peaceful to pursue the thought.

As her last days in Badai came upon her she felt an increasing distaste for leaving. The Marriots too seemed easier, less intrusive since the hanging was over and done. They left her largely alone. She sat at her bedroom window idly watching the tropical rain beating down in great pools on the gravel drive. Or, when the sun shone fiercely, in the shade of the veranda, pretending to read the air mail letters of condolence, but the very names of the senders reminded her that a whole world of doing and coping awaited her, and she left them unread. She wanted to bring neither Maggie Tulliver's Warwickshire nor Emma's Surrey to life. She was able now to walk with a stick, and early, before breakfast she went round the garden, finding an immediacy of pleasure that she could hardly recall in her past life. She had often 'admired' flowers, but it was a perfunctory action compared to the detailed intensity with which she looked at the orchids Helen Marriot had grown over old tree stumps. 'I only wish you could see the cassias and the jacarandas in flower, Mrs Eliot,' Jimmie Marriot said, and she longed to say, 'I'll stay just for that.' When she praised the frangipanis, Helen Marriot laughed.

'My dear, they're a disgusting, withered sight now. I ought to have the dead blooms cut off but I never remember. They were rather heaven though a week or two before you came.'

If she stayed a year she would see them in full flower, and really there was nothing to prevent her being here where Bill was. Nothing except the conviction that to escape so would make nonsense of her existence. She had made one escape from her mother's world into the life that she, or she with Bill, had planned; to turn back on it now would be to deny herself and Bill. Even David had seen this, for he had written:

'I have taken you at your word and left you to make your own way home. We may be in need of each other more in the coming years, so that it seems to me essential that I should not begin badly by interfering where you tell me you don't need me. But don't, Meg, delay your return, if you take my advice. Sorting out is bound to be painful and the sooner it is over the better.'

So back to the problems she must go. Even Mrs Copeman had seen this, kindly offering to leave Lord North Street as soon as they found somewhere else. And indeed, she would want the house, for whatever provision Bill had made, she was bound to need some new

resource – perhaps to let off the top floor as a flat, although she revolted at the thought. She could only then relax in this new tranquillity, the wonderful lethargy induced by the overpowering heat, wet
or shine, and husband her energies for the horrible lonely return.

Helen Marriot wanted to take her on drives round Srem Panh,
'though God knows there's little enough to see. One temple that's
rather heavenly,' but she preferred to remain in the Consulate, for she
feared that any excursion might reawaken the first day's horror of
Badai. She read willingly enough, however, in an absurd little guide
book – 'Srem Panh has no past to boast of. It is not one of those towns
the mere approach to which recalls their ancient glories and grandeurs.
Our step does not slacken into reverent pace, nor is our fancy fevered
with the glorious pageants of the past, nor are we fired with poetic
fervours beyond bearing.' A dull, ugly little town really; a week ago
she would have found extra horror that Bill had died there; but now
its blank past seemed only to increase its anonymity for her, for Bill.
He would lie there in a place that had no claim on history, no claim
on them either of past or of future.

The Marriots perhaps ventured a small claim on her, but it was not
serious. One afternoon Helen Marriot, lying sewing in another chaise-
longue, had filled in some of the gaps in the story of her marriage. But
it was all so much what their emotional undertones had already told
Meg – Helen's grander social background, her marriage on a rebound
from a broken up first marriage, her admiration for Jimmie's goodness and knowledge, her protectiveness of his insufficiencies in his
career – that it was a twice told tale.

'I've had to push poor Jimmie,' Helen said, 'so that I sometimes
feel I must appear as a ghastly shrew to other people. But he understands; and we'd neither of us wish for a moment different from what
it has been.'

And Meg said, 'Bill did any pushing that was wanted. But he knew
I was there if he needed me. And heavens, yes, every minute was
what it should have been.'

She could see that Helen's avowal scratched no deeper below the
surface than her own; nor did either of them intend more. It was
simply a conventional outline for a woman's heart to heart, serving as
an apology for past dislike, a signal that all claims their consciences
might make of unseemly treatment could now be cancelled.

At the last even the sight of the airport – Meg's last dread in Badai –
was managed without too great a shock of memories by the Marriots'

careful timing – avoiding the restaurant and arriving by special permission only a minute or two before the plane left. The presence of one or two photographers so long after the newspaper fuss had died down – or so Jimmie Marriot had told her, for she would read none of it herself – reminded Meg of how much peace and decency she owed to his watchdog guardianship in the first days after Bill's death.

'You've been so much kinder to me than I've realized,' she said, 'so much kinder than I've deserved.'

Jimmie Marriot said, 'It's been a privilege to help you. I only wish you had known us at a happier time.'

And Helen cried, 'Don't worry, she will. We shall descend on you, Mrs Eliot, when they ship us back to England.'

'I shall expect you to keep to that,' Meg said. But of course she didn't and they wouldn't. She could wave to them as the aeroplane began to taxi along to the runway, and smile with real friendliness, because they were no longer in her life. It was an unknown England that now filled her with terror. As the plane took off from the ground, she had to grip the arm-rests in order not to scream out, 'I can't leave him behind. I can't. I don't know what to do without him.'

BOOK TWO

JOBS FOR JOB

DAVID PARKER, making as little noise as his very thorough morning ritual of washing and gargling allowed, heard a faint creaking and rustling in the corridor outside his room. Else, it appeared, had also decided that she must be up first on this 'important day'. If his own stirrings had the same power to penetrate the consciousness as hers, they must, in their anxiety to disturb no one, have successfully woken Gordon from his fitful sleep. David had felt sure that not even Else would stake a claim on half past five, still dark and cold for early October. Now he pictured her, looking more than ever flat and emaciated in her tightly girdled grey woollen dressing gown (school-boy style), with her pepper and salt bun straggling a little – for even Else's neatness would be daunted by this early hour. Her lips would be bluish and her well-shaped nose red; she would probably be carry-ing her old sand-coloured Jaeger slippers until she had arrived down-stairs, for Gordon had once said that they flapped.

Years of self-discipline had made anger a rare temptation for David, so that even irritation with another human being's actions was a cause of concern to his conscience. Yet irritation he did feel at her forestall-ing of his well-laid plans to get away from the house that morning without the distracting jars of human contacts. He had no right to be irritated, he told himself, every duty not to be so. Else denied herself all comforts, poor thing, as it was, except lying in bed until Mrs Boni-face had made breakfast. To give up that small luxury was surely no pleasure to her; only her kindness could have led her to it. She was no doubt already cutting him sandwiches for his journey. Her love for him and for Gordon was the one strong emotion in a self-effacement that, however admirable, came perilously near to negation: he should be glad to receive it, even when as now it irked him, if it gave warmth to her bleak life.

Nevertheless another thought pressed hard upon him: she, he, all of them perhaps – for he anticipated others upon the scene in the next hour – had determined to be up the first simply out of the superstitious feeling that by so doing they would have mastery of the day, power over its fateful happenings. It was, of course, pure superstition. Of the two plays that were being enacted that day, the one depended not on them, not even upon the doctors, but upon certain mysterious organic changes in Gordon's body; while the other, the horribly irrelevant second feature, which would keep him from Gordon's side where he longed to be, depended upon the extraordinary chaos of a dead man's finances and the reactions of Meg, almost after all these years a stranger, to her changed fortune.

He had written to her that they might need each other in the years to come, because when he wrote the letter of condolence he was so deeply oppressed by the realization that Gordon too might have followed Bill into oblivion before many months were gone. Now he wished that he had not written it. He hoped that she would have no need of him. He was determined that if he lost Gordon, he would need neither her nor anyone else. All the same superstition persisted: himself, Else, in some degree many others who worked and lived at Andredaswood, all indeed who had come under Gordon's extraordinary influence, seemed at times of crisis to vie for mastery and power. Some years ago he would have speculated whether this meant that in their search for peace of spirit, their fight for disciplined living, they had suppressed too deeply some inherent need; but now he was strong enough to dismiss such ideas. Gordon laughingly would ascribe them to the Devil; Else would seek to repair some gap in her unity with the world of creatures; himself, more agnostic, accepted the impulsive cynical thought as a destructive element inherent in the human psyche, a quirk to be ignored in the struggle for integration. He smiled at the inadequacy of the terms; he had known too long the limits of his metaphysics to allow speculation to encumber the immediate and supreme demand of moral activity.

Suddenly the morning bird chorus started up from the nearby copse. He looked at his watch – ten minutes to six. He pictured Else, pouring the boiled coffee into the Thermos, listening intently, drawing a strength purged of any sentimental sweetness from this creature signal of a new day begun. There had been a time when he had envied her the certainty of her symbols, however inadequate her pantheism; but now he was secure enough in his own path merely to note other roads with sympathy and to maintain his own way.

He hesitated for a moment whether he should put on a suit out of deference to Meg's conventionality – for as likely as not the shock of her experience would only have accentuated her narrow sophisticated way of life, as snails draw into their shells when touched. His physical distaste for the constriction of ties, the weight of coats, was too strong. He put on his usual corduroy trousers, open necked khaki shirt, and old wine-coloured pullover, ran a comb through his thick, prematurely grey hair, wiry as steel wool, and was ready for the world, even for Else Bode's stolen march.

Through the kitchen window the sun was rising over the distant South Downs, gold and pink, lurid yet soft and hazy, in a combination peculiarly repulsive to his taste.

'I can't say I care for dawns,' he said. Else Bode looked first to the window, then at him, and smiled. The light gave a sweet, rose pink glow to her thin, white face. David looked away.

'Oh!' she said, as dismissing a child's nonsense, 'you remember bad art too well, David. We have to look at things as they are, not trailing memories that spoil our vision.'

Her English was fluent, but her accent markedly German and in some way governessy. She smiled with approval as she noted his clothes. She thinks I've dressed to put Meg in her place, David thought. He wished he had worn the suit. And yet it was natural that Else, who knew his sister only casually as a superficial smart woman, should resent the intrusion of Meg's tragedy into the anxiety of Gordon's illness. After all I resent it myself, he thought. He would have made no comment, but Else carried her approach further by a small squeeze of his arm. It drove him to protest, though he tried to soften any priggishness in his rebuke with a teasing smile.

'Yes, Else,' he said, 'I didn't dress up for the occasion. But don't let's make too much of it. However I approach it, today will be difficult. The manner of approach won't make *that* much difference.'

'No. It must be a bad time, of course. But it's good that you are going to be yourself. It will be easier for Mrs Eliot to be herself too. Maybe then you can reach her in order to help her.'

Her clear, sapphire blue eyes looked sweet and sad, her long mouth in smiling drew the wrinkled, white papery skin tight across her cheekbones. Mater dolorosa, David thought, fourteenth-century, in wood; then he remembered the challenge to charity that times of stress offered. He had, after all, settled long ago for the lump of sugary hardness in Else's wholesome cake. The impingement of personalities could of all things diminish that surplus of inner strength he would need today if he was to fortify Meg, to give her the conviction of his being all hers in her distress, when in fact he would be more than ever all Gordon's.

'Mayonnaise, Else?' he said, looking at the sandwich filling. 'You're indulging yourself again by spoiling me.' He had intended at all cost to eat breakfast at leisure in some roadside hotel.

'I would have given you breakfast before you left,' she said, 'but the leaves in Ashdown are already turning. Eat your breakfast quietly in the forest. The autumn trees will give meaning to your sadness. I used to go sometimes in the autumn, you know, David, to spend a holiday with my grandmother by the Bodensee. I was always complaining that the lake looked so sad. And I was sad too. Do you know what is the awful, meaningless sadness of seventeen years old? My grandmother was an Anthroposophist. There is much so stupid in the Steiner teaching, but also so much good. She used to say to me "Mingle your sorrow with the sadness of the season." She was right. Our sorrow is good when the season is in tune with it. I have not forgotten the lesson.'

'I have no time to enjoy the sorrows of autumn today,' he answered; and then because he always feared to treat Else with insufficient seriousness, he added, 'No, no, your grandmother was quite right. As a general proposition, I agree: the mood may be mellowed by its setting. But today I need the sharp edge of distress to keep me on the alert, not a sweet, sad soporific.'

'All the same your sister will have to find some road from despair to acceptance.'

David's bony, equine face, almost tapir-like with its long nose, wrinkled into innumerable lines as he frowned, partly from annoyance at Else's interference, partly in conjecturing Meg's state of mind.

'Perhaps she has done so already,' he said brusquely, 'I'm not speculating until I've seen her. She has great resources of courage.'

'Oh, yes. I think so, David. To say that she did not need you. That was very brave. Poor woman! She must have wanted all her resources with this terrible publicity,' Else said primly.

David gave her a sharp glance. She had stressed her horror at the news aspect of Bill's death so often that he had begun to wonder what needs had been suppressed by her passion for an anonymous private life. She should have been an actress. And why not? He rebuked himself. Not everyone felt the same distaste for histrionics as himself. And if it were true, her exclusion from the part she should have played in life was only an additional cause for compassion and admiration.

'Don't let's distress ourselves too much about the publicity,' he said. 'From what she wrote in her letter the consul seems to have protected Meg very well. And we coped, which is all we can ask. After all the newspaper reporters have to live.'

'Do you think so? I remember the German newspaper men in thirty-three, you know. No, I don't find it easy to kill ... what do you call those enemies of yours? Wireworm and leather jackets. But newspaper men, that's different.' Then, worried lest her exaggeration should be taken as a serious exception to her pacifism, she said, 'Except those good men who write the holy words for my bible up in Manchester.' She had learned to mock herself with painful discipline in her years of refuge in England. She did so somewhat crudely. But now she could laugh to take the conversation away from Meg; and David with the identical aim joined in the laughter. Immediately, however, she put her finger to her lips. 'Sssh,' she said. They were both still, remembering Gordon asleep upstairs. He had slept in the last months so little and so lightly.

'What time are you due at the hospital?' David asked. In his state of tension over Gordon's illness he constantly forgot these details as soon as he was told them.

'A quarter to midday.' Else's voice sounded patient. 'Doctor Blackett says that we may expect the results of the X-ray in two days. I think that is quite good.'

David recalled with irritation that it was he who had given her this information. He limited his annoyance to saying, 'It isn't an X-ray, you know.' He did not say what it was. He had tried in the last weeks of anxiety about Gordon to confine his conversations with Else to practical details. If, in the worst event, she and he had to find a basis for living together without Gordon, any intimacy brought about by their present stress might only be a hindrance to a tolerable, mutually independent relationship. His fears that she did not feel the same need for caution seemed realized, for she turned towards him and said:

'David, I am sure that Gordon has already won his battle. And we are still full of fears. Our fears cannot help him. Shall we talk a little about it while he is not here?'

David saw no hope of evasion; even to give his reasons for avoiding intimacy would lead them straight into the heart of it.

'Else,' he said, 'don't you think that we would be wise ...'

She looked so defiant at his warning tone. 'There is no wisdom more important than love,' she said.

He resigned himself at least to meeting her demands upon his sympathy, although, to his distaste, he knew that out of prudence he would not be wholly frank with her.

'You will be hurt, David. You must be, by something I shall say. But perhaps with all that is hurting you now, it will not be much to add. Yours is a more cruel part than Gordon's because you have not his faith. This makes your duty to give him strength, yes, even out of your weakness, a very hard one.'

Her honesty was clearly to be complete; David hoped that he could bear it.

'I believe that I can help you almost not at all,' she said, 'but if I can, you must tell me. Will you please tell me now if there are things ...'

But that, of course, was exactly what David knew he must not do. Any things he told her now would be distorted. He admired her, was grateful to her, very fond of her after ten or so years; but at the moment he resented her; and she, if her love for Gordon was as deep as it seemed, was deceiving herself if she did not resent him too.

'There really isn't time now,' he said. But she would have none of such feebleness.

'No, David,' she said, 'there is tension between us and that makes it harder for him. No matter what it costs us, we must discuss it.'

But time was in fact on his side. Voices came from the lobby by the back door.

'Aren't they lovely? Not that I'd *pick* dahlias. I don't think they're a house flower really. I prefer the delicate shades like the Michaelmas,' Mrs Boniface was saying. David thought, she'll be as much refined cockney at fifty-five as she is now at thirty; Sussex will never change *her*.

'Climbers'' voice came in a hoarse whisper, like an actress playing a schoolboy over the radio. As though she had a set of plums in her mouth instead of a cluster of projecting teeth. 'I thought a bit of a riot of colour in the house would cheer him up when he gets back from this ghastly hospital trip. And I shan't have a moment to cut flowers today, Mrs B. Tim Rattray's jolly good, but he doesn't know the ropes, so everything will fall on me.'

'I came over early just to give Mr Parker a bite of something before he goes off to meet that poor Mrs Eliot.'

It embarrassed David to hear all this devotion, which he and Gordon had somehow gathered to themselves, declared aloud. Perhaps Else noticed this for she smiled.

'Why are we women such fools?' she asked.

And David said, 'I don't know. Why do men put up with it?' It had come to him that if Gordon died, he would only feel free outside in the Nursery. In the house he would be delivered up to this monstrous regiment. He was disgusted with himself for the egotism of his thoughts.

'Climbers' Lake's face peered around the kitchen door. In her surprise at seeing them, she looked more than usually crazy. Her thick black hair was tied in a piece of old purple silk, her array of protruding teeth seemed unconnected with her wide grin, her nose was as red as her withered apple cheeks. Below her whiskered chin she held an enormous bunch of cactus dahlias as though her head had come to rest in a colony of starfish.

'Good Lord,' she said. 'Everybody's up with the blinking lark.' She might have been commenting on a 'lark' in the dormitory.

'Now, Climbers, don't drop any earwigs from those dahlias,' Else said. She treated Miss Lake kindly, but as though she were in fact as mentally deficient as her features suggested.

And now Mrs Boniface had joined them, her contribution to the harrowing times a chin up, 'cigarette and cuppa' jollity. 'Well,' she said, 'I shan't let Arthur know about this. He's grumbled enough already. Me getting him and the kids up before it was light. But when I told him I'd got to give Mr Parker a bite of breakfast before he went off to meet Mrs Eliot, he piped down all right. He'd do anything for Mrs Eliot since he's seen her picture in the papers. You tell her from me, Mr Parker, that she's breaking up my home.'

'I think,' Else said, 'that Mrs Eliot will not want to be reminded of the newspapers.'

'Now don't you come the duchess over us, Miss Bode,' Mrs Boniface laughed, 'just because we like to read the *Daily Mirror* doesn't mean we're morbid.'

And Else softened. 'No, dear Mrs B, you are very good to everyone.' David remembered when Else had been mistrustful of the Bonifaces. 'Peasants' came into the many categories of those whom Hitler Germany had shown to be 'not good people'. But, thanks to his own and Gordon's persuasions, Bode and Boniface now met in friendship.

'What about you, Miss Bode,' Mrs Boniface cried, 'getting up to cut sandwiches like that when you love your lie in so! And mayonnaise too. Aren't you a lucky boy, Mr Parker, with all the girls running after you? You ought to give him your flowers, Miss Lake.'

David was unsure what 'gawped' meant, but that was undoubtedly what Climbers did as she thrust her huge bunch of dahlias into his arms.

'Oh, you look like the blushing bride, David,' she cried, 'I wish I had my camera.' And now it was loud laughter, cigarettes, and cups of tea; and all hands on deck to get Gordon's breakfast ready, although God knew, he could eat little enough. Oh, they were a happy household, thanks to Gordon and himself, where German crank, cracked English gentlewoman, and cockney good sport could lie down together lion-lamb fashion – loving lambs with lion hearts. So David worked off his spleen. He was not prepared to consider any of his feelings deeply at the moment; too many of them were worthless chunks of buried waste thrown up by the times' upheaval; they would sink again when it was ended. Nevertheless he must get away from these women; he would give his last instructions to Tim, say good-bye to Gordon, and be off.

But as soon as he moved to the door, Climbers followed him. 'I wanted to have a word with you, David,' she said.

'I'm going to the office,' he answered. 'You'd better come with me and tell me what it is, while we're walking. I mustn't be late.'

'The office!' Mrs Boniface cried. 'You're going to get the slipper, Miss Lake.'

Else spoke kindly but firmly. 'Don't keep David too long, Climbers,' she said.

He walked rapidly down the passage from the kitchen to the hall, leaving the dahlias on the long, low glass table in front of the hall fire; Else could cope with the earwigs. Climbers thumped along briskly at his side in her Wellingtons. Her words came in a breathless torrent.

'I don't want to open old wounds, David, you know that. And I feel awful speaking about it at a time like this. In any case you and Gordon know best. And as soon as he's found his feet, I'm sure Tim Rattray will be absolutely super. But he isn't altogether easy to work with. Of course, I know he's frightfully good and he's got all the new methods. I'm going to learn a terrific lot from him myself, I can see that already. Only yesterday he showed me a grafting that was quite new to me. But it isn't the same as knowing the place, is it? And then some of the girls feel ...'

But they were outside now. It was exactly the kind of day that David loved most – bright sunshine, a cold keen east wind and puffy white clouds driving fast across a pale blue sky. It was the weather that had urged him forth as a boy to take long, solitary walks over the Downs, leaving behind his mother's mute demand for pity and Meg's claims for his support in refusing it. Now he felt free to forget all pities for the moment – even the minor pity for poor Climbers's adjustment to her new subordination.

He allowed only wisps of her breathy monologue to drift through his consciousness – 'that silly girl Annie crying – larking with them one minute, shouting at them the next – upset Tom terribly over that staking business – fuchsia gracilis not fuchsia magellanica – I'm sure Colonel Ashley will be frightfully upset.'

Such a day made him feel so spontaneously free and happy that he could forget everything but the scene before him, each detail of which seemed a matter for pride. How right he had been in refusing the claims of business to bring the nursery up to the front of the house. He had insisted on the small formal garden to replace the Victorian lawn. And so it stood, with its greystone parapets, low box hedges, tall yews, and baroque figures bought in Franconian junk-shops, on their first holiday the nursery's success had allowed them, five years ago. And the house itself; about this he and Gordon had fought so many battles with friends and advisers. What did they want with a place so large? They were going into business, not setting up as country gentlemen. But it was the elegance of the house that had made the first years' slavery tolerable, that had given enough room for privacy and communal living, for the quartet and for writing their book. One had every right to a setting, if that setting made a good life more attainable, if it was tempered by sensible self-denial.

They turned off to the side, behind the yew hedge, into the nursery. The display beds, now massed with dahlias and Michaelmas daisies, came into view. Behind these stretched the long herbaceous borders beneath the walls of the former kitchen garden; and, to the side, the glasshouses where the bedding out annuals were beginning life for next spring's sale. The 'regular trade', they called this side of the nursery. It was only by his own insistence that it was there, with its regular profits, for Gordon, with eye trained for the contemporary market, had wanted to specialize only in shrubs. In the end they had compromised and served both sides of the chalk line. Azaleas and rhododendrons for the richer soil of the expense-account, weekend gentry who were their neighbours in the Forest to the north; delphiniums, dahlias, the most ordinary regular annuals for the 'new poor' ladies below the chalk line to the south, from cottage gardens in the Downs to sad, windswept gardens without hope in the seaside refuges of the retired. And shrub roses for the more sophisticated – the rich 'resting' stage stars, the lady novelists, and the local friends of Glyndebourne. It was a triumph of practicality over self-indulgence, David reflected. And his self mockery did not lessen his approval of the reflection.

Gordon and he would dearly have loved to have cultivated exotics. With their successful establishment, they had indeed permitted themselves two stove-houses last year, but they were even so to be devoted to the Christmas market for poinsettias. Financial bohemianism or, for that matter, anarchic generosity were not part of the unorthodox quietism they had tried to build up. Financial competence, even success, so long as it did not merge into greed, were external marks of a sane, ordered inner life. For David, despite his agnosticism, Quaker thrift as well as many other Quaker practices seemed a model. While to Gordon, 'render unto Caesar' meant exactly a prudent consideration of material resources. It was this attitude that made Bill's and Meg's fecklessness so abhorrent to David – worldly values were bad enough, but worldly values built on financial sand seemed to him the final folly.

He looked over to the far corner of the nursery where in the clear light he could still only dimly see the high rhododendron bushes, with their second flowering hardly distinguishable as blobs of pink, red, and white. They had been discussing of late the acquisition of land far over on the other side of the main road. Seven assistants, nobly led by old Climbers, had swelled now to thirty-six, directed, when he and Gordon were not there, by a fully trained specialist, Tim Rattray, B.A. of Reading University Horticultural School. Log Cabin to White House, he thought with amusement. Well, why not? As Gordon had said rather tartly to Else, when she complained periodically that Martha was driving out Mary, 'Conceit of failure, my dear Else, is one of the Devil's simplest snares for the godly. What on earth do you suppose God gave us a mind and a pair of hands for if he didn't want us to use them competently?' And man without God must strive no less to keep the rules, David thought. But suddenly he remembered that in a year Gordon might *not* be there, and the little puffy clouds grew monstrous and sadly grey and the sunlight went off the nursery.

'After all,' Climbers was saying, 'we have built up a sort of tradition here which newcomers can't just ignore. I mean Andredaswood is more than just a nursery garden run for a profit. It's a kind of way of living, isn't it, David?'

David felt the full force of parody of his own sentiments. The nursery is exactly what it is, he thought, a well run commercial garden, supplying its customers with value for their money, paying its workers good wages. If there are any 'ways of living' they're in the house; and, even there, the virtue, such as it is, is an indwelling thing, a self-mastery, hardly to be communicated, certainly never consciously or else it would vanish.

'Climbers,' he said, 'you have your own special value to us. But we asked you to accept Tim's authority when we engaged him. I know it's not easy for you but you must do it.'

'Oh, I know, David,' she said. 'It's only that I care so much about the place and, after all, Rattray can't know our customers as I do. He's *got* to learn.'

'Exactly,' David said. 'Just as you had to. Remember "what about a nice climber, a real hardy climber?"' He saw, as she smiled back at him, that she was weeping. He felt disgust at his sentimental humorous appeal to the inept phrase she had used so continually to customers in the first days – the phrase which had given her her nickname.

'You've just got to accept it,' he said. 'We've given you sole charge of the display gardens and of personal interviews with customers because, as you say, by experience you know their needs. But Tim Rattray's orders go for everything else when Gordon and I are not here. That must be understood.'

She stood blushing and blubbering like an ugly schoolboy. 'I think it's jolly unfair,' she said and stumped away.

He felt disgusted with himself for reducing a good, simple woman of fifty-five to such ridiculous pathos. Nevertheless, Tim Rattray was young, skilled, competent, and not ridiculous. From the large hut which served as an office he could hear Tim crooning – 'I'm a little babe that's just lost in the wood. Won't you be good and watch, watch over me?' He remembered Gordon saying, 'No, even if poor old Climbers weren't so goofy, we would have to have a man to work with. Especially for you, David, if I go sudden like.' And now Gordon might go, though perhaps not sudden like.

As he was about to enter the office, Climbers came running back. Panting, she said, 'I've been absolutely beastly and selfish, David, when you've got all these troubles. Of course, it doesn't matter. You're not to think about it again. And you're *not* on any account to worry Gordon with it. He'd get in a frightful stew.' Embarrassed, she stumped off. He reflected wryly that Gordon had in fact a far greater acceptance of human sorrow than he had.

Tim Rattray, seated on a high stool and crouched over the desk top, checking yesterday's mail orders seemed to fill the small office. The span of his bent shoulders was vast, his buttocks humped out over the edge of the stool.

'How many of those revolting songs *do* you know?' David asked.

Tim turned and slid to the ground. Standing, he was as tall as he was beefy; blond and fresh-faced, with piggy features and an amiable, squashy smile. 'The handsome porker' Gordon had called him after their first interview.

'Haven't you got any soul? No love of good music? All Baching and Blowing. You're like Eileen. Before we know where we are the poor bloody infant's going to be ashamed of his poppa's pop numbers if momma has her way. Anyhow be your age, David. That number just about started life when you were bursting into flower. Man, don't you have any twoway memories?'

It continued to surprise David, even after the four months that Tim had been with them, still to find that so much jolly facetiousness did not irritate him. But so it was. He felt always refreshed by Tim's presence; and this although he had decided that Tim's loud voice and even louder laugh betrayed a lack of adjustment somewhere which touched his own paternal feelings. It had taken him some time to find a note that could respond, ever reassure, without breaking through to an intimacy that might demand too much of both of them. He had learned from wartime experience that neurotic extroverts needed careful handling. He had settled for his own facetious note in response – everyman's caricature of the whimsical old scholar. By exaggerating the difference in their ages it gave an easy farcical note to their relationship.

'There was a time when I was young, Tim,' he said, 'and I should impress upon you that when I say young I mean very young, when I used to delight in a popular tune about bananas or rather the lack of bananas. But I'm glad to say that my sister very wisely and properly put an end to that. She pointed out to me that all popular dance music was monotonous in rhythm, utterly uninteresting in melody, and entirely revolting in the sentiments that it sought to express. Her words impressed me deeply, and, although I was only six at the time, I took a solemn oath never to allow any of what you call "numbers" to penetrate my consciousness again. Given the conditions of the world it's been a hard battle but I've won it.'

Tim gave a roar of laughter, then grimacing with pain, put his hand to his forehead.

'Christ!' he said. 'Sorry. But I was out with the outfit last night. We collected quite a few odd beers.'

David's smile was washy and perfunctory. He had shared Gordon's amusement at first over Tim's Five White Aces, so incongruous with the reputation of their own quartet; but the dance band seemed an increasing bore to him now.

Whether Tim sensed this or whether he had suddenly identified the sister David had mentioned with Meg Eliot, widow of the newspapers' five-day hero, he looked self-consciously grave.

'Mrs Eliot arrives today, doesn't she?' he said. 'Eileen asked me to say that if there's anything she could do – you know, a woman's hand.'

David could not easily envisage Eileen Rattray's up-to-date housing estate mothercraft being particularly serviceable to Meg. 'Please thank her,' he said, 'I've no idea what the next step's going to be. My brother-in-law's left his affairs in appalling confusion. My sister's going to be very badly off.'

Tim looked shocked. 'Well, I hope there'll be a thumping great compensation from someone or other,' he said. 'A brilliant man like that. You probably don't realize the feeling there's been among ordinary people in pubs and places. Even down here. After all Englishmen don't become heroes every day these days ...' His voice trailed away in embarrassment. He looked a very pink pig. 'Anyhow if she decides to come to Andredaswood I hope you'll let her know that everybody will respect her need for privacy.' He seemed to be offering himself as a watchdog.

It was quite another aspect that dominated David's mind; and he felt that it should be impressed upon the young man.

'That must depend, Tim, on the result of Gordon's examination at the hospital. He goes over to Brighton today, you know. In any case I doubt if he'll be well enough to have strangers about.'

Tim looked perplexed, but the hearty note returned to his voice.

'Oh, don't let the doctors get you down. They're always pessimistic. Most of them get a rake-off from the undertakers.' He laughed loudly.

David stared for a moment at a corner of the room where two tulip bulbs decaying into powdery dust were enmeshed in a dirt-hung spider's web. 'I think this room ought to be cleared out,' he said. 'I may have to stop in London with my sister for a little, I can't say. If so, I don't want Gordon to be worried with business. Try to trouble him as little as you can. But tactfully, won't you?'

Any impatience or distaste that Tim's obtuseness over personal matters, his insufficient appreciation of Gordon, had aroused in David was soon banished when they discussed the practical affairs of the nursery. He was so knowledgeable, so competent, and, though fully aware of it, so modest. Gordon had been mistrustful of the value of a horticultural diploma, he tended to despise all formal education; but some buried loyalty in David to the academic life he had renounced was appeased by the obvious advantages Tim's training had brought to the place, even in the few months he had been with them.

Yet it was more than a good, up-to-date training, David reflected; Tim, for all his hearty naïve exterior, had a high I.Q. and his intelligence was applied to the job to the full. For Gordon and himself, running the nursery had been the sealing of a bond of their life together; making a success of it was the disciplining of their dilettante interests, an external pattern for their inner lives without which they might have succumbed to a corrosive, anarchic existence. Yet it was always and however pleasantly a discipline, a renunciation of over indulgence in music or in books, or even, as Gordon admitted for himself, of an exaggerated selfish engrossment in the life of the spirit. Theirs was the achievement; but, David reluctantly admitted to himself, Tim's was the efficiency. He was amused and a little irritated at his reluctance.

Only perhaps in relation to the rest of the staff was Tim's easy naïveté at a disadvantage; he was hardly to be blamed, for the choice of Climbers and, indeed, of one or two of the others was hardly orthodox. As Tim said, 'The trouble is, David, that I feel you and Gordon are on a kind of personal footing with them which is bound to make me resented.'

'It's a matter of time ...' David began, but Tim, having reached the subject informally, at an unexpected moment, felt freer than he had ever done when they had met to 'discuss the staff'.

'I'm not so sure, you know,' he said. 'With old Bob and Collihole probably. But with someone like Climbers, I don't know. You see she's the sort of person I've never had to deal with. I don't know what you call them – distressed gentlewomen or whatever it is. They aren't in my line. She's bound to resent me.'

'Whatever Climbers' feelings,' David said, 'they won't have anything to do with any stereotype of her being a gentlewoman. She has the great virtue of having entirely personal emotions.'

But Tim did not take it. 'Well, I think she feels pretty personally about me,' he said. 'And she gets so worked up about some of the others. Annie, for example, is the sort of wench I can deal with any time. She's not a bad girl but she's a bit of a lazy bitch and you have to tell her so sometimes. But Climbers rushes in as though I was acting like the king of Soho or some other brute like that. Honestly I think she's a bit psycho at times.'

'She's a very hard worker and a very good gardener,' David said, trying by the note of fair pleading in his voice to avoid a priggish rebuke.

'Oh, yes. That's perfectly true. I wouldn't have believed it when I came. But all the same, David, I think you and Gordon should have had the courage to get rid of her.'

David tried to consider the suggestion dispassionately.

'When she's a good worker, wouldn't that be a bit unjust?' It sounded so housemasterish that he saw at once he must stick to the whole truth. 'Besides,' he said, 'she's not young and she's poor.'

'All right then,' Tim said. 'Let her be in charge, at any rate, nominally. I could make it work.'

'No,' David cried, 'you have the qualifications, you must have the job. Look, Tim, you won't get anywhere by veering from side to side. People have to accept unpleasant things, and they will if the things are just. But you have to approach them equably, from a distance and with love.' He measured the words slowly, but, on seeing Tim's face at the sound of the last word, he laughed. 'Oh, I don't think she expects that sort of love from you,' he said.

Tim, too, roared with laughter. 'Well, it's just as well,' he said, 'because then I *should* resign.' They parted on a note of easy facetiousness.

David, as always, knocked on Gordon's door before going in. They had decided from the moment of taking Andredaswood that there would be no ease of living there unless each surrounded their close friendship with a total and conventional regard for the other's privacy. The deep voice that told David to come in contrasted oddly with the tiny body sitting up in the large crimson canopied bed, even more perhaps with the little, drawn face, greyish yellow against the piled up white pillows. He seemed, now more than ever, all bony Roman nose and large brown eyes; but the eyes, like the thick copper-tinted brown hair, lacked lustre. David found that Gordon's changed appearance distressed him every day afresh, not only for the threat it carried but more still just from hatred of the physical change itself. The surface of his conscience made him ashamed of this purely physical reaction, but his deeper feelings told him he should be proud to feel it.

Gordon was tickling the stomach of a small tortoise-shell cat rolled over in play, its back legs kicking against the hardly-touched breakfast tray.

'She's an abominably randy cat,' he said.

It had taken David years to habituate himself to Gordon's animal loving, and more years still to accept his easy delight in his pets' sexual powers. He felt glad to tease him by saying, 'What's abominable about it?' The first remark of the day, so difficult for him now, had been made.

'Nothing except that we should never have let poor Oliver be cut. It's still one of the worst sins on my conscience. Now this poor thing's got to go out for her fun.' Oliver, the fat neuter ginger cat sat on the windowsill, snoring faintly. 'I don't suppose,' Gordon said, 'that he even has a wet dream now.'

Apart from the cats, there was a clove pug asleep in a royal blue velvet lined basket, a borzoi stretched on the hearthrug, and a pink and grey Australian cockatoo climbing with beak and claws over the roof of its ornate Victorian cage. David's sense of hygiene had not found it easy to accept this menagerie that slept in Gordon's room. But Gordon had insisted. 'I won't allow them to go into *your* room,' he said and he had trained them to keep out of it. 'Though why you should worry I don't know,' he had declared. 'My animals don't smell.' He was quite right, they didn't. The room was entirely clean, which again was surprising considering that it was filled like a junk shop with a jumble of pleasing, valuable antique furniture and hideous, worthless bric-à-brac. This incoherent taste, too, had for long worried David, but Gordon was equally firm. 'I like tatt,' he had said.

'I slept well,' Gordon announced with a slightly mocking smile. David had agreed not to discuss his health, but he, in return, had promised always to declare if the auguries were good. David felt it a mark of their friendship's achievement that when Gordon said they were so, he could be sure there was no deception intended to allay his fears.

'Oughtn't you to be gone already?' Gordon went on.

'There've been a lot of delays,' David said. 'Else got up to make me a picnic breakfast. The leaves have turned in Ashdown Forest.'

'Oh, hell. That's what comes of confusing God with his creatures. Well, she won't get far with her conversions if she tries to make them at breakfast time. Leaves turned indeed!'

'I don't mind as much as that, you know,' David said. 'Then there was Climbers fussing.'

'About what?' Gordon asked with a mock imperiousness.

'Oh! Things.'

'Fussing about her seniority. Poor old war horse! I'll have a good get together with her this evening. "Sing away my little tart, if it's going to ease your heart",' Gordon had six or seven quotations, of which this line of Blok's was one, that he used often and only with the vaguest relevance. 'Does Climbers ever sing, do you think? Oh, yes, she does. She came with me once to Christmas mass and bawled to the faithful to assemble round her. Perhaps that was why I never urged her to come again.' He grimaced with self-disgust. 'I suppose it's because I'm a whole-hogger. I can understand *your* position. Although of course it's only real shilly shallying disguised as intellect, no doubt. But this sort of once a year at Christmas business, it's like Else and God in the trees, it seems to me such nonsense. But, of course, it's spiritual pride on my part. I should have watered Climbers' mustard seed. How difficult biblical similes are, it makes Climbers' faith a sort of mustard and cress grown on flannel. However, one always pays. Now I have to sit by and see an old woman I respect and like hurt like a child.'

'Would she be any less hurt if she were a regular church-going Anglican?' David asked. Strangely to him, he only felt eased from his anxiety about Gordon when, as now, he was entirely involved with him, giving questions and answers in a pattern fixed over years.

'Yes,' said Gordon with certainty, 'she would. You mould all unbelievers, or half believers for that matter, in your own high fashion. Oh, I grant the height of it, David. For heaven's sake, I couldn't clothe *myself* in a self-made iron corset. As you do. But it's personal.'

'And faith?' David asked, 'is that uniform?'

'No. But it's one and indivisible. And that's good enough.'

'I see you all,' David cried, 'floating on a cloud at one high level.'

He saw quite clearly the degree to which the image touched upon all that he feared, but in Gordon's presence he could accept the temptation.

'No. There *are* bumps. But at its lowest we're sustained and that does help.' Gordon seemed happily intent on the argument, until David was about to answer, when he turned his head away and began to play with the cat. 'Oh Lord!' he said, 'I've had more than enough of this nice green stuff.' And he laughed.

David, recognizing the Grimm quotation as a half sign, laughed too.

'There are some things about Meg,' Gordon said, 'that I must say before you go.'

'I know them. First I must urge her to accept any money from you that she may need. Second I must urge her to come down here if she wishes.'

'Oh yes, you know them, dear David, but do you feel them? The money wouldn't amount to more than a temporary help but that may be everything at the moment. You seem so set on seeing her as too independent to take it. It's a sort of family snobbery, David. All right, the Parkers are very independent. But now may not be the moment to show it. And as to her coming down here. She may hate the idea of it, hate the place and us even, after she's got over the shock; but at the moment she surely needs a gesture of love.' He looked at David, his face screwed up into a puzzled frown.

David waited for him to go on. The whole breathing space of happiness had vanished in these last moments. All his anxiety and his anger had returned; and, above all, the awful knowledge that he couldn't communicate with Gordon at a time when he so longed to be close to him.

If Gordon had meant to pursue the subject, he changed his tack. Lying back on the pillows, his voice croaking a little with exhaustion, he said, 'I've thought about them both a lot the last day or two. I don't know that under any circumstances I could be a close friend of Meg's. I won't say her ambitions are too conventional but they're not my conventions. But I've always liked her. She's got such energy to skim over things.'

'She's not an entirely stupid woman,' David said ironically. He hated to hear what he felt to be patronage coming from Gordon. 'She knew a lot of unhappiness when she was young.'

Gordon laughed. 'Misery doesn't always make for good sense even in your sad pagan world. But, seriously, you're quite right, of course. I've no doubt she's known the abysses beneath the surface even as she skimmed. But if she couldn't ... Well, sometimes it's wise to go on skimming for a long time in life until you know how to dive. And I admire those who skim gracefully. Of course, she's fallen with a bump now. But heavens, we all need charity.' He paused for a moment. 'Perhaps,' he said, 'it's because, as you know, I always found Bill so attractive. Always? We met about three times and could hardly find a shaky plank over the enormous gulf. He was tedious, of course, but he seemed so reliable and sad. If I were her ... to have him throw away his life ...'

'I don't really think you can say that in saving someone's life one *throws* one's own away. I admit that the choice seems a bit random. This Badai minister what's-his-name. But then Bill's whole life seems to have been a bit random.' David frowned it all away.

'Oh, of course, it's a heroic deed. And one must admire it. But for Meg, it seems to me, there must be an awful sense of not having counted enough or, rather, not having made life count enough for him, that it could all happen so suddenly and apparently senselessly. Oh! I don't know. But if I were you, I shouldn't say anything about the heroism.'

'I shan't,' David said. He realized that he had hardly thought out what he would say. 'You seem to think ...'

'I know,' Gordon said, 'that you'll be good and kind as always. David, you must go now.'

'Yes,' said David, 'I'll phone tonight about ...'

'About everything. Yes,' Gordon declared. He turned again to fondle the cat. But as David was opening the door, he said suddenly, 'I can't leave it like this, David. It's silly. Look, I want to help you. And it will help you in the end if you do all you can to help Meg. Listen. I've considered every possibility. I'm a lover of life in my own way so it hasn't been easy. But with prayer and thought I'm not only reconciled to dying now, but I'm truly happy for it to come if it shall come. That doesn't mean that I regret my life – far from it; or that I'm any the less fond of you. Please think about that and about why you should be happy to hear it. I think it could help you.'

Meg Eliot, shivering slightly from many concurrent causes, looked from Donald's window on to the sharply sunlit Bloomsbury street. Passing taxi, hospital nurses brightly chattering as they went on duty, dim greenglassed window front that gave a glimpse of a poky cobbler's shop, eighteenth-century doorway, all swam in front of her. Pressing her hand on the windowsill, she steadied herself. Beneath the rush of a hundred jostling thoughts and emotions sounded a continuo – I can't bear this cold, I must get some suitable clothes out of store.

Without turning round, she said, 'Before we discuss the practical implications of what you've told me, David, before we start saying what I can do and what I can't do, I want you to understand that the blame, the whole blame for this lies on me.'

David, his thoughts upon some specialist, some surgeon perhaps, God knew, anyway someone unknown and loathsome who within a few hours would be pronouncing upon the examination, knowing abominably, before Gordon knew, Gordon's fate, forced himself to attend to what his sister said. Sister – loving, loved, claiming, fighting against the claims of poor, inadequate-to-claim Mother, fighting perhaps unknowingly – and if unknown to her, how could *he* tell? – fighting for Father, vanished and so without defending voice – sister, if only momentarily and in fragments, stood before him. And married sister, in her own world husband-centred? self-centred? he could not judge – finding no contact with him in his world, self-effaced? Gordon-centred? self-centred? – he would not judge – married sister also stood before him, but now only momentarily and in fragments too, obliterated almost by a student's shot. And, hey presto, now, summoned to life by the same shot, this widow, her loss marked only by drawn, tired lines at the corners of her large, lively eyes and of her small, too small, birdlike mouth – but seeing her so seldom, how could he tell if these were lines of loss or marriage lines? – but loss certainly shown in her too bright, too constant, capable, determined talk.

Well, if the chatter meant fright, as well it could, he must do all to support her in meeting that fright, or rather in concealing it until she was free to meet it in the long fight – months? years? – ahead of her. He could at least check the flow that she might later regret.

He said, 'Dear Meg, all that you were for Bill and he for you is yours and his. And damn anybody else.'

Meg, hearing his voice, thought, he has his own life; if we had time we could be again perhaps as we were, but we have no time and if I ask anything now I shall get charity. There must be no more delaying false comforts; I must keep the distance.

She said, 'Yes, I know I'm talking too much, David. But I'm bound to at the moment. In any case I always have done. You've forgotten in your quiet world what a chatter I keep up. Besides,' she said, 'I say this to Donald. He's known all along that I was to blame. I realize that now. What I don't understand, Donald, is why you didn't tell me?'

She looked at him sitting there in his elegant, rather fussy, Victoriana strewed, bachelor flat of his. He was still a fat, doctored cat, but he was not purring. He had an instinctive tact, she thought, which David, because of the family tie between us, and because of his tortured rectitude, can't manage.

'Don't you think,' Donald asked, 'that you're seeing the picture too plainly now. Looking back at it, I mean, what? Bill gambled the money away because he was overworked. He drank, smoked, and so on only moderately, and he needed some other kicks to relieve the strain. After all, he knew that he could always earn as much as he wanted and more. And of course, he was going ahead. Probably would have become a judge, what? Accidents happen. Yes, but we don't live by them. We'd be fools if we did. Don't think I'm saying you shouldn't think of blame. At times like this we're bound to think of everything. But you blame yourself because you think someone might blame *him*. If they do, they're fools. He couldn't know he was going to die. In any case they don't. They think him a hero for as long as they think at all.'

'Hero!' she said angrily.

'No.' Donald's loud voice had for a moment a note of annoyance. 'Don't object to that. He did a brave thing. We'd all much rather he hadn't. But don't refuse him the praise he deserves.'

To David's surprise, Meg, who at the airport had at first refused to see Donald, went over and sat on the sofa beside him.

'Donald,' she said, 'I believe that you see it all exactly as I see it. I have got somehow to live with that picture. If I can talk to you about it, it will help me. I don't suppose that we shall see each other again. No, I'm being dramatic – let's say, not often. We have nothing in common except that you were really fond of Bill. I know that is a lot, but it's a memory now. *You* have no need to live on memories. I don't intend to. But if I'm to live with this picture, I must estimate its truth, get it into focus. You can help me to do that. Please, if only because Bill would have wanted you to help me, let me say what I believe was true. David must make what he can of it.'

Donald said nothing and she took his silence for assent.

'I drove Bill and I fed on him at the same time. Yes, I know,' she said as she saw Donald frown, 'that's an exaggerated statement. Bill loved me and he could count on my love and in a way on my support. And there are a hundred other things which only I can know and which, thank God! count on the credit side for me. But broadly it's true. I married Bill because I loved him, but also because he could offer me a way of living that, for a thousand reasons David knows, I wanted, well, I suppose one could say wanted obsessively. I thought Bill wanted the same life, and so up to a point he did. I respected and admired him, thought him brilliant. And he was. And, of course, he was ten years older than me. It was easy, all right, natural if you like, for me to repose on that and I did. I felt that if I gave him my love and trust he could do all that he wanted in life.'

'I don't see that you could have done much more, what?'

'You know, Donald, that I could and that I didn't. I was for ever priding myself on trusting, on not interfering, but it was just an excuse to accept what I wanted. You told me on that last evening, at that awful party, that Bill's life had gone dead when he gave up criminal law. All right, you didn't tell me, you tried to tell me and I wouldn't listen. I see now that when the decision was made, he tried to tell me the same thing himself. When I asked him, "Is it what you want?" he said, "I think it's the right decision if we're to live as we want to." And I happily accepted "we", because it was what I wanted. I didn't count the price Bill paid. And then there were all sorts of people to tell me how wonderful it was for Bill to give up those sordid criminal cases, how much more "our sort of world" his new life would be. Our sort of world! The sort of dead crowd that you saw at that wretched party, Donald. Bill was bored and stifled in it.'

Donald had to boom in excess to silence her excited flow.

'Oh come,' he said, 'you're forgetting the reality of what you felt then in your determination to paint this picture. Your friends weren't all fools or knaves or walking corpses.'

'No,' she admitted. 'You're quite right. We had a lot of pleasure. Many of the people we knew were happy, good, intelligent people. But what they wanted wasn't what Bill wanted. Nor even what I wanted. I only kept going because of my outside interests.'

'Well?' Donald cried, 'Lady Pirie's been telling me a good deal of what you do for Aid to the Elderly. That's useful, what?'

David, searching his heart, found something that he and Gordon had always commended. 'You've taught yourself to really know something about ceramics,' he said.

'Do you think I'm happy to have sold Bill for a Nymphenburg harlequin or a Meissen magpie,' she said, 'or for the comfort of old Mrs Bloggs for that matter? Besides, most of that I could have done without making a mess of Bill's life. When I think of the way that I patted myself on the back for not fussing Bill about his gambling; and all the time I knew that something was wrong, that he was getting obsessed by it, absurdly elated or depressed by this or that horse winning or losing, getting feverish about the stop press of the evening paper or the Stock Exchange page of *The Times*. I told myself that it was all on a par with his evening bridge, though I knew it wasn't. Happily married people need to live separate lives!'

David said firmly, 'My dear Meg, everybody, happy or not, married or not, who is worth anything, has to cultivate his own garden.'

Donald, looking dismayed at the intervention, said, 'I still think that Bill gambled because he worked too hard. And again I say, he couldn't, you know, have told that he wouldn't live.'

Meg looked at them in turn with a certain contempt. 'His own garden! David,' she cried, 'it must have been a bleak, windswept sort of garden that forced him into this. Overworked, Donald! Overworked at what he didn't care to do in order to maintain things as I wanted them. And,' she added, 'as to his not knowing that he was going to die, there's an irony to that. I told you that night of the party that he'd just seen Doctor Loundes and learned that his blood pressure was normal. He'd thought he'd got thrombosis, Donald.'

'So he might have had; pressure of work and boredom combined. But it can also be imagination. Bad nerves, what? His nerves were in a shocking state; anyone with less self control would have shown it.'

'He thought that he might be dangerously ill, Donald. And as you say he might have been. I thought, like you, that he was simply neurotic about his health; that last day in London, something – going abroad perhaps – made him go to Bobby Loundes in desperation. And he was all right. That was the first evening for months when I didn't see him rush to the racing results. I believe he'd have given up gambling altogether if he'd lived....'

'Resolved to give it up, what?' Donald interrupted.

Meg knew that out of concern for her he was deliberately trying to lower the intensity of her emotions; but she still resented the remark and ignored it. 'Out of a sense that he had time to put things straight. And between us we would have done so. But in those months before, when he thought he was dying, he was concerned with only one thing, to recoup what he'd lost. He didn't think he had time to do it by work. He wouldn't even see the doctor for fear he had too little time to do it at all. That's why he speculated so crazily then, and gambled to forget the failure of his speculations. He was desperate to pay off the mortgage. Oh! now I know how much he must have hated the house, not only because he felt guilty knowing that it wasn't really ours, but because the whole way of living it implied was the root of the trouble. All he was thinking about was not leaving me in the lurch. Me! the person who had started him on the whole thing because of the demands I made on him. He never thought of himself. So don't blame him.' She paused and then turned to Donald; fiercely she asked, 'Well, am I right?'

But again it was David who answered. He was himself surprised at the statement that so imperatively presented itself to him.

'Meg,' he said, 'Bill loved you very much and so he thought only of you. But it isn't what happened in the last months that worries you, is it? He wasn't himself then. He thought he was dying. It's before that time that you believe things had already gone wrong. May it not have been a more simple thing that lay behind it, simply that Bill wanted children?'

Meg, surprised too, registered in passing her brother's apparently compulsive need to raise the subject.

'Oh! that,' she said. 'Yes, that he felt terribly. And there I was blind again. When I learnt that I couldn't have a child, he was wonderful to me. And when I got over it – early Vincennes cups and old Mrs Bloggs, you know – I took it for granted that we both had. But he *hadn't*. I learnt that only when we went on this trip.' Suddenly she began to cry desperately. 'I was going to do all I could,' she said, 'to help him to accept it.' Her words were hardly intelligible from the convulsions of her sobbing.

'Look,' Donald said, 'this isn't helping *you*, you know, is it, what?' David said nothing.

After two or three minutes Meg recovered herself.

'How funny men are,' she said, 'I'm not more unhappy because I cry. That's how I feel all the time, only I try not to show it. You understand that, don't you, David? But I suppose it's more embarrassing for you when it appears on the surface, Donald.' She paused and turned to her brother. 'But you're wrong about my not having a child being the cause. It's kind of you to try to take the blame from me,

David; if it was that, certainly I wouldn't feel guilty. Sad, yes, but not guilty. I can't blame myself for what I couldn't help. No, it's what I've told Donald that I have to live with. And I still ask you, Donald, is it the true picture? Am I right?'

Donald got up. 'I'd like notice of that question,' he said. 'I asked my woman to put up a few sandwiches for us and a glass of sherry. I'll just see what's been done about that. And then I'll try to answer you.'

Donald out of the room, David said, 'He's like an undergraduate pretending to be a don.' When even to this Meg answered, 'He's a very good man, I believe. I've behaved very badly to him,' David saw that there was no way of stemming her mood and he remained silent.

Donald, returning with a tray, announced, 'Cold chicken. Rather dull, I'm afraid, what? But the Fino Delicado has its virtues. It's better than the Amontillado they're sending over now.' He handed sandwiches and glasses of sherry slowly and deliberately.

Sitting down, he said, 'You rather reduce Bill to a cypher, don't you? He had guts, you know, and ability. You say life had gone sour on him. I can't presume to judge that.' Meg raised her hand in protest. 'All right,' he said, 'something went wrong. Agreed. Though the how much and the what are more than I shall care to say. We judge actions in court, you know, but few of us, I think, care to judge people. I certainly don't. But if we were to make that judgement, quite a lot of people would say it was his own fault.'

David sat thinking that Meg found herself closer to Donald than to himself. He was shocked that his only reaction was 'Well, that lets me out!' They must, he thought, have been horribly friendless for Bill to dig up as executors only a man whom Meg disliked and a brother-in-law for whom he had no regard. The man certainly had all Bill's pomposity; perhaps Meg would find the way to his heart. If she had ever found it to Bill's ...

To his surprise, she said, 'You disappoint me, Donald – for a friend of Bill's. He was never pompous and especially he was never evasive. I don't care what "quite a lot of people" would say. I want your opinion.'

Watching his sallow face grow a little pink, she thought perhaps I can only get through him by making him angry. I'm sure that Bill must have burst that swollen balloon sometimes.

He was making a visible effort to accept her words without anger. He said, 'I was trying perhaps to say that Bill, like most of us, was as he was. A platitude, if you like. But not quite. If there was an empti-ness, if the gambling filled it, perhaps it went deeper than anything to do with the life you led, to his giving up criminal pleading, or perhaps it was too deep to be changed. Even someone as close as you were to him could only palliate. If I didn't say it, you see, it's because it's rather impertinent. What?'

As he spoke, she wondered why she was so bothered to secure his acquiescence in her view. To get close to one of the few people Bill liked? But what she had of Bill was complete, her own, and needed no outside support. More probably it was a desperate search for some coherent line of thought. She would, no doubt, make many such cul-de-sac, meaningless pursuits in her present distress. And leave them off as suddenly.

She said rather flatly, 'I don't really believe in determinism of that sort. But even if it's true, I didn't palliate enough.'

Donald was clearly somewhat cast down by her casual reception of his views. He spoke to her now in a more direct tone, which she took to be his search for a greater intimacy. She listened attentively out of politeness only, for she had seen clearly now that her approach to him had been no more than an attempt to make up for the failed contact of the past – an attempt that had no meaning now that Bill was dead. It's only one of the many things, she thought, that can never now be repaired.

'All I can tell you, Meg,' he said, 'is what I know about. And that is that you were sun and moon to Bill. Everything he talked about in some way referred to you. A man doesn't do that unless his wife's given him a great deal in life, what?'

Meg thought, that's nonsense, Bill would never have forced me upon those who didn't like me. What sort of a bore is he trying to make Bill out to have been?

She said, 'Yes, of course. As I said there are a hundred things that Bill and I had together which only I can know of, and they must be my consolation. Thank you, Donald.'

She left what she hoped was a decent pause and then said, 'Poor Donald! And poor David! This *is* being executors to the widow with a vengeance, isn't it? But I promise you I'm not so entirely impractical. I've understood most, I think, of what you've told me of the financial situation. Let's see if I've got it straight. Bill has left debts of four thou-sand five hundred pounds. You agree that by selling the house now we could pay off the mortgage and Bill's debts and leave me with about fifteen hundred pounds. It seems an incredible gain on what we paid in nineteen forty-one, but that after all is what I've read about rising property values. I've tended to think such things had nothing to do with *my* life, like a lot of other things – Far East politics, for example. But for once reality's working in my favour. You ask me how much of the furniture I can claim as my own; and I think you suggest that I should claim as much as I can. Bill's generosity being what it was, I can, in fact, claim quite a lot of it. And, of course, the porcelain. I believe I might add another four to five thousand, possibly a little more, to the fifteen hundred that will remain to me. The additional bookmaker's debts of Bill's I shan't attempt to meet, since you tell me I needn't. It seems in a way rather dishonest but they've had quite enough out of him. And anyway I've no intention of being a martyr. My needs are infinitely greater than theirs. It looks as though I shall have more than what Mother would have called enough to meet sudden doctors' bills. Which reminds me that I shall have to leave Doctor Loundes and get a sensible National Health doctor. Bill agreed with National Health in principle, and I was a great defender of it when any of our more extreme Tory friends attacked it. We compromised by going to Bobby Loundes, who charges rather a lot but is competent as well as being a friend. Well, that's one of the sort of things that will have to go. Not that it matters because I'm never really ill ...'

She spoke not so much with bitterness, David thought, but as though tired with everything about her old life. It could after all be the preliminary to some real change in her, but the tired note made him doubt whether she had the will power. Disgusted at his own priggishness, he said aloud, 'My dear Meg, anyone who's been through what you have is bound to be exhausted.'

The irrelevant interruption surprised Meg. Suddenly very youthful and laughing, she said, 'Thank you, David dear. You're so thoughtful.'

Nevertheless he found it more and more difficult to listen to her. The only contribution that he could make was to press again Gordon's offer of a loan and try genuinely to make her accept it. But to wait with this on his mind only made him dwell on what was happening to Gordon at that moment and this, since it could help no one, he knew it to be his duty to eschew. It seemed to him that times like these – Meg's first months of widowhood, and for that matter the days waiting for the doctor's report on Gordon – times usually denominated 'critical', should, in any sensible approach to life, be treated as entirely dormant intervals. Every gesture, every speech was simply a formal measure improvised to fill in time, while the emotions and thoughts rose, sank, and reshaped themselves to fit the new mould that the future offered; a little ballet between the acts not intended for serious attention but simply to cover the noise of scene shifting. That, in fact, society demanded a continuity of real decisions and of meaningful statements at such times seemed to him so contrary to psychological truth that he could give no convinced attention.

Meg's voice sounded in his ears – the words, merely what she said because she had to say something, the emotions behind the words – hardness? fear? bravery? What was the sense of estimating them, since it would be some months before Meg emerged as a reshaped person?

His attention wandered over Donald's room. The nondescript, heavy, comfortable chairs and hideous frill-shaded standard lamp bore the mark of some dowdily furnished service flat – and indeed, it seemed that a man and wife did in fact 'do' for the bachelor tenants. In absurd contrast were the Victorian 'finds' – a large papier-mâché model of what looked like St Pancras station, the elaborate wool and beadwork cushions and footstool, wax fruit, a Byronic mandolin with incongruous tartan ribbons. The pictures too bore witness to the man's heavy assertion of a taste out of touch with his times – for he felt sure that Donald Templeton's Victoriana were intended as a defiant rather than an amusing gesture: a smooth Etty-like nude, a Martinesque apocalyptic scene with lowering storm clouds and fabulous rainbow, something pre-Raphaelite and medieval, called no doubt 'The Tryst', announced the eclectic range of his defiance. But here once again the mood was broken by a large pastel of a woman, snake-necked, vacant-mouthed, large-eyed, the hair making a shell-shape on the forehead in the style of 1915: Templeton's mother, no doubt, by Lavery? The picture went so well with the service flat furniture and, of course, ultimately with Donald. He was surely, David thought, that rare 'period' thing – a bachelor in full right, no homosexual, but the full Edwardian or Great War genuine article; up those stairs should have come frou-frouing skirts or elegant hobbles and panniers to little supper parties with rose coloured lamps and Russian cigarettes. Was all the man's mannered, Edwardian utterance and clothing then only an attempt to fit himself to the period of his sexual tastes, or ...

David determinedly checked the train of thought. He was here to help Meg, and he had long ago decided that these aimless speculations upon other people's lives were a dissipation of spirit, if they were not indeed worse, an idle intrusion into human privacy, only a degree better than idle gossip. Donald was less than Hecuba to him, but, unlike that queen, he was a private person with rights to privacy. If, David told himself, he were properly occupied at Andredaswood, cultivating his own garden, there would be no occasion for these time-wasting thoughts; however, he had now another, if less congenial duty. He concentrated on his sister's words.

'I know what you're both thinking,' Meg said, 'that there's no reason to sell the house. You will lend me the money to meet Bill's debts and to pay the mortgage interest each year. I'm sorry that I can't accept the offer. I really mean "sorry" because whenever I've offered anything to anybody I've been hurt when it wasn't accepted. It seems like refusing friendship.'

She thought, I really *am* talking too much. I shouldn't have said that, because, of course, it is exactly true. I can find no reason for friendship with Donald or indeed with David acting for Gordon.

'I feel very much against the idea of debt at all at the moment. I know you'll say that's an unreasonable, emotional reaction which may be purely temporary. All my emotions probably are at the moment. But they're the only ones I've got and I'm not clever enough to see beyond them to more durable feelings. And if you mean the debts to be the sort that are really gifts, I couldn't ever accept those. David could explain that to you, Donald. It's to do with our mother, although goodness knows I don't think I'm like her in most ways. But she had what she called a "horror of debt" and a worse "horror of charity". My father was what's called a ne'er-do-well.'

'Meg,' David said, 'for all that, you know, Mother would have been willing to borrow money on a sensible basis to secure a home for herself, especially one she loved.'

Meg said, 'Maybe. The truth is, David, I admit, that one side of me still says keep the house at any cost. But I *know* it's the wrong thing. I couldn't afford to live in it except by taking lodgers, and truly I doubt if that's practical. It's a small house. There'd be no privacy either for myself or for them. But in any case, the other side of me, and I'm sure the right one, is glad that I can't go on living there. I've lived in the Ark, David, snugly and smugly and not knowing it. Well, now I do know, I'm not going to sit there waiting for the rainbow. I must take a plunge and it won't do me any harm if it's off the deep end. You remember how Mother used to say that to me if I was in a temper. "Don't go off the deep end, dear." I'm not in a temper now but I *am* going off the deep end.'

'I think, if you feel like that,' David said, 'that you're quite right, Meg, not to want to live there.'

'It's a point certainly,' Donald said. 'With lodgers and so on. It wouldn't really be her own house, what?'

'Well,' David said. 'Yes. But much more than that. Meg's looking for peace of mind. Not the peace of dead memories. That's no peace at all.'

'I'm looking for life,' Meg cried, 'life to fill the desert inside me.' She caught a look of embarrassed distress on Donald's face. She said to David, mimicking her mother's voice, 'Your father was always such an actor.' And to her pleasure, he replied in the same voice, 'I often wonder whether his life wouldn't have been different if he'd gone on the stage....'

To Donald's evident surprise, they both burst into laughter. It was the only moment of contact they had made that day.

Hastening to free Donald from embarrassment, Meg said in an easy, conversational voice. 'Yes, David, what were you going to suggest?'

And David, anxious for the same end, said a little solemnly, 'I would like you to consider, Meg, accepting a larger loan from Gordon to pay off the whole mortgage. If Templeton likes to contribute, I think you should accept his offer too. Then you could still sell the house and have a sizeable capital to play with.'

'Play with?' Meg said, laughing. 'You don't mean that, David, but in fact what you do mean comes to much the same thing. Playing at flower shops or interior decorating or perhaps at a house agency with awful witty advertisements. No, thank you. Especially not with a debt to repay from the start. I know you wouldn't recommend a life just because it meant "being a lady", but that's what it would be, David, or else selling my life away in order to be my own boss. I can see it's worked all right for you with the nursery, but, for one thing Gordon has a lot of capital, and for another I shouldn't like that life. Nobody would recommend it if I was a girl in my 'teens, however much of a lady I was, well, I don't see why I should take it because I'm forty-three. It seems to me as cut off from the modern world as my own life has been. I must know what's going on, David, so that I won't be hit hard again by something I don't understand.'

Donald Templeton made a gobbling sound, and she continued,

'Yes, I know I couldn't expect to know the ins and outs of Asian politics, Donald. But there is a connexion between that and my sheltered ignorance all the same, I'm sure. Not a logical one, but logic isn't all there is. In any case what time would I have for learning anything about the world with plucky responsibilities and debts to pay off around my neck? I might do better than Mother but ...'

David felt suddenly a wave of remembered anger. 'I really think, Meg,' he said, 'that you needn't ...'

'I'm sorry,' she said, 'I don't want to tread on family corns, my dear, but the situation makes such a depressing parallel. Let me say once and for all. I want to be an employed person in a largely employed world. With the disadvantages and the benefits. But just to show that I'm not being a romantic martyr, I'll tell you, that when I've decided what I'm going to do, I shall use the respite of the little money in hand to get proper qualifications for a decently paid, reliable job. I've preached qualifications to others, I don't intend to be idiot enough myself not to get them.'

David fancied that Donald must also be drawing a breath of relief at her evident determination. They had done what they could. Donald, indeed, was looking at his watch – a heavy, old-fashioned gold hunter on a waistcoat chain.

'In ten minutes,' he said, 'I intend to call a cab and trundle you both off to Wheeler's for a bite of luncheon.'

'Good heavens,' Meg cried, 'I shan't want anything for hours after all those sandwiches.'

'Nonsense, chicken sandwiches are all right with the preprandial sherry, but they're not a meal. What? Now before we go, I want to point out to you, Meg, that you either missed completely, or purposely ignored, my principal suggestion to you earlier this morning. If you don't want to live in the house, let it. You can borrow to pay Bill's debts. Your brother and I between us won't notice that. The rent from the house'll pay the annual interest on the mortgage and leave a small income over. Something to add to the earnings of your qualified job.'

David looked to see if Donald Templeton's sharp tone of voice had annoyed Meg, but she was smiling.

'I'm glad something's roused you, Donald,' she said, 'even my proposed wretched little qualifications.'

'Roused?' he queried. 'No. I don't understand your passion to be involved with the modern world, but if you want qualifications, get them. You won't have any trouble I'm sure. Most of these modern degrees and certificates only demand a smattering of this and that. You could do it on your head. You're interested in social work, why not do one of these social science courses? You'll get every Shibboleth of the modern world there – economics, social administration, whatever that may mean, psychology. I believe they throw in the common law of England to make weight. But, for the Lord's sake, have a bit of money to fall back on.' Meg was about to reply, but he said, 'No, don't answer yet. I'm going to telephone Wheeler's for a table. Tell me what you think when I come back.' He stumped out of the room.

David said, 'I won't say anything, Meg. If you want, we can talk tonight. But I'm always available and, if a moment comes when you need someone, call on me. Myself I think it may be a little time before you can make any decision.'

She said nothing, only shook her head in dissent. She caught his eye for an instant. This is the second moment of contact, she thought, a recognition that there is no lasting contact between us, that the present, for both of us, can find no good in the past. But he began again, in a voice overloud, like a speaker who tries to efface an ill-received opening.

'You know you are welcome to come down to us now or at any time. Gordon specially asked me to say that to you. You'll find him a bit of an invalid, but of course you wouldn't say anything.'

She said, 'It's very sweet of you. And of Gordon. But really, no, David. I find it freezing enough in London. But the South Downs!' She shuddered.

After a pause he said, 'I wouldn't take too much notice of Templeton's show of temper. I live so out of the world, I'd forgotten what personal pity people feel it necessary to assume. I think the angry clubman is only part of the general pose he's expected by now to put on.'

She said, 'I very much hope not, David. His being angry is the only time that I've felt him to be really human.'

He thought, I simply don't understand her. And why should I? One can only understand the people one is with every day. And then it's mostly illusion, even with Gordon. One loves or likes or neither, but it only carries one a certain way; the rest is invention, invented intrusion.

He said, 'He was a great friend of Bill's.' She answered, 'Yes. Or rather Bill had no great friends. He was too self-sufficient. Or else too shy.'

'He's a very kind man,' David said, 'and sensible in his own way. He wouldn't be difficult to make friends with.'

'I imagine that's how Bill saw it,' she said, then a moment later, she turned to him, 'Or do you mean me, David? Do you think friends are what I am needing? Or that I should choose them because they're kind and can give sensible advice?' She was less scornful than genuinely puzzled. To David's relief Donald returned at that moment, allowing no time for him to answer or for her to reply.

'I apologize for this lengthy wait,' Donald said, 'but I had some difficulty in securing a cab. However, one is now on its way here. Well,' he continued, 'now tell me what you have to say to my suggestion.'

Meg said, 'It's a very good one, Donald. To refuse it would be quite illogical. But I'm going to do so. I shan't be able to afford to be illogical in the future. So this is my last fling. You see, I want to be finished with the whole thing – house, mortgage, all. I won't say it's what Bill would do ...'

'Good Heavens! No, why should he?' Donald barked.

'I'm not going to say that he *would* do it. I think that's the sort of shabby pretence people often make about the dead. But I'm quite certain that *I* should and I'm going to. I'm afraid,' she added rather lamely, 'that you disapprove very much, Donald.'

'Disapprove? It's not for me to approve or disapprove. Bill appointed me executor, what? And I want to help his widow if I can.' He paused; then, 'All right, if it'll make you take a more sensible line,' he said, 'I'll tell you that I think it's a piece of emotional indulgence.'

He's not a very sensible man, David thought, he's admirable but silly, or perhaps that's what we mean when we say 'sensible' in that rather loose, looking-down-our-noses sort of way. Meg said nothing, and Donald, retreating perhaps from this silent announcement of her indifference to his views asked abruptly, 'What about the sitting tenants anyway? They may rather get in the way of your scheme.'

'Poor Mr and Mrs Copeman! You will keep on calling them sitting tenants as though they were partridges. Perhaps you think I'm too sporting to shoot a sitting bird; if so, you're wrong I'm afraid. Mrs Copeman offered to leave so that I can live there. She said that Bill's death had affected them both very much. I can only suppose she meant the circumstances. Anyway I shan't hesitate to accept and then sell.'

David said, 'Wouldn't it be better to tell her what you're going to do?'

'It might be more honest, but it wouldn't be better. She might change her mind.'

David said, 'Ah!' Donald said, 'I see.' He went into the hall and came back holding her coat for her to put on. 'This is a bit thin for a cold October, what?'

'It is indeed,' Meg said, 'I intend to get my fur coats out of store as soon as I can. I'm not going to sell *them*, they're much too useful.' She laughed, but they neither of them responded. She shrugged her shoulders in despair. David saw the slight gesture. Her hardness is hysterical he thought. She needs some gesture of affection to steady her. He found such physical contacts difficult, but he took her hand and pressed it. Oh, dear! she thought, if only he would laugh a little to ease the atmosphere. Donald came back with a light grey overcoat, black hat, umbrella and washleather gloves.

'Well,' he said, 'I think we'd better talk about other things now, if we want to digest our oysters, what?'

As they were getting into the taxi-cab, however, he said suddenly, 'Have you got something to go on with?'

'To go on with?' she asked, then, seeing his embarrassed look, she understood. 'Oh, yes, thank you, Donald,' she said, 'I've got about three hundred pounds in my own account at the bank. We never had a joint account. I was much too frightened of Bill knowing how extravagant I was.' It was a slightly arch piece of conversation-making that she had often fallen back upon in Bill's lifetime on sticky social occasions; only when she had said it, did she realize how bitter it must now sound. She could not look at Donald during the whole taxi-drive for fear of his interpretation. It's one more reason for not seeing him, she thought, I'm bound to put my foot in it. She wondered why she didn't consider David's reaction. After all he seemed to have become severely censorious in his nursery garden of Eden. They must *live* on the fruit of the knowledge of good and evil down there, she thought, by the way he sits in silent judgement about everything. But his judgements did not touch her. The wires of communication with Donald were so tangled, that there was nothing to do but to cut them; those with David, however, had simply rusted away.

In the weeks that followed Meg found that most of her communication lines were dead. The three-day gale of newspaper notoriety had shaken some of the posts and toppled others over. The happily married young middle-aged couples who were the friends or acquaintances she had shared with Bill, did not get into the newspapers, except, of course, where the husbands' speeches appeared in reports of important legal cases or of the annual general meetings of companies. If they had any ambition towards publicity it was strictly confined to the Honours list. Bill had died as a kind of hero in an accident. No one, of course, could help accidents, but they were hardly to be sought after. As to heroism, that was surely more a wartime action – the unemphatic bravery of 'mentioned in despatches' shared with other friends. Heroism like Bill's, no doubt, seemed to them somehow unconnected with their lives, more like saving someone from drowning – a splendid action rightly rewarded with the George Medal, but faintly connected with Boy Scouts, certainly not with one's friends.

They were genuinely sympathetic to Meg, but it was an embarrassed sympathy. As she might have expected, the news 'had got about'; nor, despite all her caution, were these friends unaware of the financial distress Bill had left her in. He had borrowed at times, it seemed, from some of the men; and, although he had always repaid, they were not themselves borrowers and had noted his actions with doubts. Doubts that were now triumphantly justified.

Kind invitations came to her by every post. She dined in Belgravia and Chelsea, Knightsbridge and Kensington, Hampstead, and even Highgate. One or two wives, on behalf of their husbands, found an intimate occasion to press various offers of help upon her, one or two husbands, with less sympathetic wives, offered manly counsel that served as an excuse for proffering loans without embarrassing her. There was kindness and sympathy behind it all, but there was also embarrassment and a kind of setting her apart which she found impossible to accept. Was it her mother's pride, or touchiness, or simply self-punishment in her present mood of guilt? Probably a bit of all three, but the fact was also that she *was* set apart. These people were happy, married, rich, and established, she was none of these things. Apart, she decided, it should be. After a fortnight she began to refuse the invitations; gradually and, she hoped, with tact, she severed the remaining lines.

Only the three lame ducks remained. At first, for all her closer friendship with them, she had been very unwilling to see them. Even though she knew that her picture of her past behaviour to them was coloured by exaggerated self-criticism, that she had probably in fact never allowed her impatience or her ridicule to be apparent to them, had indeed never found difficulty in concealing any such emotions because of her very real affection for them, she nevertheless felt sure that they must have sensed some patronage. She could not blame them if they mixed their sympathy now with the same leaven, but she had no wish to offer herself to it. More particularly, though she tried to make less of it, she remembered Bill's uneasy tolerance of them. She could not bear any implied blame of him, yet she could not be surprised if they mixed it with the sympathy they offered; nor could she be surprised if they suggested a criticism of his spoiling adoration of her, for they must know that this was the origin of his mistrust of them – a fear that they might tire or bore her.

The lame ducks, however, broke down all the defences she put up against them; they were not only consistently kind and sympathetic, they proved to be so exactly the same as they had always been.

Lady Pirie had sent a closely written airmail letter to Srem Panh containing nothing but her memories of what Bill had done and said. ... If the wisdoms and witticisms recorded there so exactly recalled to Meg rather Bill's manner of dealing with 'dear old fogies' than any utterances she herself could have wished to remember, the true admiration Lady Pirie showed in recollecting them and the natural tact she evidenced in her one reference to the shooting – 'a thing so apparently cruel and meaningless, Meg dear, that without faith I do not know how you will be able to accept it; only that knowing you and your courage I know that you *will* find the way' – were sufficient and more to make up for any naïvetés. She had added to this letter a postscript saying that if Meg needed a man to come out to Srem Panh to deal with officials 'and that sort of thing' she suggested Mr Templeton. She had seen him more than once since that party and he seemed so clever. Tom, of course, would gladly come out there if Meg wanted him, and would be a tower of strength – as he always was in a crisis – but officials might be more impressed by an older man. The absurdity of Viola Pirie's loyalty to her son and her manner of noting yet modifying the world's estimate of him had been one of the happy signs by which, in the strange isolation of the Marriots' house, Meg had felt that, among so much in England to which she dreaded returning, there were humours and affections she would be glad to know again.

Meg, avoiding Kensington hotels as emblems of the plucky reduced gentility she feared, had temporarily chosen a small hotel near

Victoria Station, where the genteel was seasoned with the disreputable and both were sufficiently transitory to create a rather colourless, seedy atmosphere. Here on the first morning Viola Pirie, informed no doubt by Donald Templeton, telephoned to her with a simple welcome home. Only when a week had passed did she press an invitation upon her. 'I know how busy you must be, Meg,' she said, 'and the last thing you'll want is to feel tied up with invitations. But if you suddenly know you must see someone, my dear, or the hotel menu doesn't attract you, just put your bonnet on and come round. There's always something fairly substantial here to eat, because there's a man in the house. Anyway,' she said, 'I can never eat hotel food without stomach rumbles afterwards. And then all the people in those lounges look at me.'

She made no complaint when Meg did not follow up the invitation, but merely wrote her a note saying, 'The committee need your services as soon as you can spare the time. Talk about the blind leading the blind, it's old crocks helping old crocks now. And they're so slow about it. Cackle, cackle, cackle. Darlington and I just pray for your return to speed things up again. Anyway, it's time you were in harness. Mrs Masters kicked up an awful fuss about Miss Rogers taking that course. She's not a bad old stick but she does like things her own way. I think she felt that Miss Rogers wouldn't be her protégée any longer if she had any qualifications. She started a moan, as Tom says, when we said the Committee ought to pay for the girl's course. However, Darlington and I had been doing a bit of lobbying and old Purdyke stuck by us nobly, so we pushed it through. The course is doing Miss Rogers a power of good. She obviously feels she's there in her own right and she doesn't sulk so much. So you see how much we depend on you.'

It was a letter that helped Meg a stage further in adapting herself to her new life. Whatever she decided to do, she would not be available for afternoon committees. She knew, indeed, with a certain measure of self-ridicule, that no job would satisfy her that allowed it. Independence of that kind was too strongly associated with the life she had left behind her. No more 'open prisons'! The reality in front was vague in its outline, but she knew that it must begin with the circumscribed hours ordinarily demanded of the wage earner. Less welcome was the realization that she doubted her ability to control the committee once they knew her to be no longer a goddess descended from the heights of chic worldliness, but only poor Mrs Eliot, can we give you a lift? To resign from the committee was obviously a step towards the new life, not as immediate or pressing as selling her porcelain, but, she had to admit, a good deal less unpleasant. First, however, she must write to Viola to tell her what she was going to do. It meant speaking openly of what she felt sure Viola already knew – her changed financial position, but at least she could do it on her own terms, saying simply that she and Bill had lived beyond their income, that she would be a good deal poorer and, in fact, have to earn her living. 'I'm grateful to you,' she wrote, 'more than you can realize for roping me in on the committee. As a result of my work there at least I shall have no illusions that I'm anything but rich compared to many people, and I can also thank God that I'm young enough to be able to fend for myself.'

Once again Lady Pirie's reply pleased Meg. 'I had heard something about your money bothers,' she wrote, 'but I knew you would know just what you wanted to do with your life without a lot of interference. I remember when Herbert died far too many people were busy telling me what I should do. Of course I had the widow's pension from the Colonial Office and just as well too, because I'd never have been any good at a job. But Tom was still at school and they would keep on interfering. Tom and I knew just what we wanted without outside advice. It would be different if I could offer you the sort of advice that a man could. But there, I hear you have your brother to help you. Of course, I'm very sad about the committee and so will Mr Darlington be, but you know best. I wonder if you've thought of taking up social work professionally, you'd be so good. And it's something you would find interesting even if things took a better turn later. But you're sure to have thought of everything and worked it all out for yourself. I *am* going to fuss you about one thing though, and, if you don't like it, just forget that I wrote it. A hotel's no life for you and the food won't be anything like sufficient if you're working all day. Why don't you come and P.G. with me? I've got the spare room which will make an excellent bed-sitting room. I kept it for Tom to invite friends to stay but I don't think young people do that sort of thing nowadays. I'm being quite selfish really because I'd decided for some time that I must let it. It's wrong to keep a room empty with so many people needing somewhere to live. And I could do with the money. But to be honest, Meg, the real thing is that Tom and I are too much alone together. He oughtn't to be with an old woman all the time. And you and he get on so well together. Forgive me for being so selfish and if the idea's quite impossible don't feel you have to refer to it again.'

The idea was, of course, quite impossible, but, nevertheless, deserving of a full and grateful reply which Meg hoped that she provided. For the time being, she wrote, she wanted to be quite on her own. No doubt that mood would only last a short while and then one of the first people she would want to see would be Viola; and Tom, too, of course, if he felt like it. She didn't see herself living with anyone else, but if ever she felt differently, Viola was the only person she could imagine being indulgent enough of her general untidiness to make such a thing possible. As to social work, she was glad Viola suggested it, because as a matter of fact it was one of the things she had in mind. If she should decide on it, she would expect Viola to write her an absolutely first rate reference and she hoped that Viola realized that she had committed herself to it.

After she had written the letter, she saw that, however it might appear from her words, she did in fact intend to see Viola Pirie; that it was a link unbroken.

And so also it happened with Poll and with Jill. Poll's first reaction had rather depressed Meg. The letter of condolence she sent to Srem Panh had been so very stilted and conventional that except for a certain illiteracy of phrasing it seemed to have nothing of Poll in it. However, a few days before she returned to England another air mail letter arrived of a far more characteristic kind and she realized that she should have known that, at times of birth, marriage, or death, Poll would revert to the conventions of her upbringing.

In her second letter Poll said, 'I do think Bill being killed like that is the most awful balls up and makes me more mad than ever that people talk about God being good and all that. Of course, in my church they wouldn't do that. To give them their due they don't pretend in that kind of way. In fact sorrow and sin are their standbys. They'd probably say it was a special dispensation to bring you into a state of grace. But although that's more sensible really, I still think it's jolly nasty and it's one of the reasons why I lapsed really. Apart of course from wanting to be divorced. But anyhow I expect you have all your own ideas about that. As far as I remember you and Bill were rather proud of being nothing, which seems funny to me too in a way. What *has* made me absolutely mad has been the papers. About how Bill gave his life for this unpronounceable man. I shouldn't think it was true, would you? And if it was, I think the unpronounceable man ought to be shot for letting it happen. Bill was one of the most attractive men I ever knew. I told you not to go to those awful foreign places. And anyway why are you staying out there now? I should think you would have had enough of those beastly yellow people by now. And the consul must be quite ghastly. Don't let him bully you or anything, will you? They're quite unimportant people. Even now, I mean, when quite a lot of kinds of people are more important than they used to be. I hope you're not *brooding*, Meg, are you? My Mum brooded after Father's death, although we all told her not to and how she ought to be glad, nicely, of course. But she went on brooding and really she did get to be like an old hen and of no interest to anybody, like hens. And before he died she'd been rather a nice, interesting sort of person, at any rate much better than him. Of course, I can see that when you've lost a top attractive kind of husband like Bill you would want to brood. I never did but then the only one I had that *died* was Robson and although he was really the best, he wasn't exactly up to *brooding* standard. But you *mustn't*. Because although I keep on saying how attractive Bill was, so are you, and you know I don't go much for having women about. But like Americans say "you're a truly lovely person", only not of course all the awful things they mean. And seeing you turn into a hen would be very sad. Except that with your loud voice and looks it would be more like a peahen which would be better but not much. Anyhow there's an awful song that they sing on Saturday nights in a pub I go to at World's End. Only I don't go any more because I can't bear the kind of pubs where they sing. I couldn't really write it just like that, could I? but as the name of an awful song I can. Come home soon.'

A few days after Meg had been at the hotel she returned to find a present of two dozen large yellow Korean chrysanthemums and a bottle of champagne. With them was a note from Poll.

'I don't know why you're staying at a hotel for tarts,' it said, 'I had a terrible time finding where you were. I'm not surprised you've concealed it. I had to ring up that sex repressed beard, Lady Thing's son. I should think your staying at that hotel would give *him* ideas. He tells me you're going to be rather poor. Poor you! Actually you won't find it so bad as you think. I don't. I shall write to those beasts of trustees and tell them I must have the money to pay you back what I owe you. It might break that bloody trust. The champagne isn't very good but nice to have, I thought. P.S. Don't talk to any of the tarts. I've done so once or twice in pubs and they're *always* insolent.'

A few days later a letter came to say that the trustees had been un-able to make Poll a special payment to repay her debts to Meg; 'so I shan't be able to pay you. I've written the beasts a stinking letter, but I shouldn't think it would help, should you? What I did think was that you oughtn't to stay in that hotel brooding. I've made inquiries about it and it isn't only a place where tarts go, but also respectable people like clergymen and "mademoiselles" from grand girls' schools on their way to and from Paris. Only neither know that the others go there. I can't think why, can you? I always know tarts and clergymen, and mademoiselles too for that matter only I don't see *them* very often. Why don't you come and stay here? You could have the room for nothing, only I'd probably borrow from you at the end of the quarter. I shouldn't think it would work out for long, should you? But it would be rather heaven while it lasted which is more than one can say for most things. And you'd be doing me a good turn which I know you like to do, because, as it is, such a lot of drunks ask to be put up for the night and if *you* were there there wouldn't be room. Anyway you wouldn't be able to brood because there are always people here – not by any means all drunk and lots of them rather nice. Do do it.'

To this letter Meg replied that she thought it wouldn't work out for long enough to be any good, because she was so set in her rather overtidy ways. At the moment, she said, she wasn't brooding but job-hunting all day which made her very sleepy and boring in the even-ing; and as she loathed being sleepy and boring in company she wasn't seeing anyone. As soon as she was settled, however, the first person she intended to see was Poll. And, she thought to herself, I really be-lieve that she is.

Jill Stokes's letter of condolence had not been at all disappointing, for Meg could not remember a time in their long friendship when Jill had allowed her emotions such rein. Thinking of the embarrassment that Jill would normally have shown even on hearing one quarter of the things she had written in her letter, Meg was, however, surprised and a bit embarrassed herself until she remembered that she had never before received more than a short note of thanks or acceptance from her. Distance, it seemed, gave her courage.

'People have been saying to me,' Jill wrote, 'who have read the papers and knew that I knew you, "how dreadful for her to be so alone out there." I haven't felt that and I have a feeling that you won't have felt it either. You *are* alone now and you're much too intelligent – and you were much too happy with Bill – to want to have people pretending that you're anything else. It is the most awful thing that can happen or that ever will happen. Don't for a minute let people try to tell you that it isn't. When Andrew was killed some good kind people did try to make me feel that it wasn't. I knew they were wrong, but the unhappiness was so great that I selfishly tried in some way to belittle it, to see it as they said "philosophically". Those are the only moments of which I am ashamed, they were the only moments when I betrayed the greatest happiness, the real fulfilment of my life. And I truly believe that if one goes on thinking in that way – Time is the great Healer and all the stupid *and* wicked things people say – then one can be left with nothing. And deserve it. Only, of course, as I write it I know that what I found in Andrew was too great ever to have allowed me to lose it by such selfish "false comfort". And I'm sure, Meg, that you will find the same. Of course the agonies are less often with one as time goes by. People say that they're a form of selfishness anyway. But selfish or not they still come back and they're still as intense. And I'm quite sure of this, that only by knowing them, by feeling them fully – I don't mean awful outward expressions of grief, they seem to be a sort of show people put on who can't feel enough – can we keep something with us. At any rate I've never tried – except for that short while I'm ashamed of – to pretend that I'd lost less than everything; and as a result I have regained so much – Andrew is with me always now and in a far more real way than in the first years after his death.'

In the strange, isolated misery of the Consulate, Meg had found this letter, alone of all those she had received, acceptable to her, if only because it alone gave the same weight to her loss as she did, really sympathized where the others only strove to do so. That it was only a complete identity of situation, she realized even then, for she doubted if Jill's experience of widowhood was likely to be any fair guide to her own. Yet this, too, was exactly in keeping with what she had always felt about their friendship – that, with no agreement of outlook or interests, an intimacy existed between them below the level of their differences. It might be merely the length of their association; but whatever it was, it allowed them a mutual insight that persisted through all incompatibility.

That Jill, at any rate, knew *her*, another passage in the letter seemed to confirm. Jill had written, 'I admired Bill immensely, Meg, and it didn't alter *that* a scrap that I knew he didn't really like me. How could he have done? He hardly knew me before Andrew was killed so that he only knew me when I lived in the past, and he was active in the present. But he was one of the few people whom I wished that I had known before I became a bore. With most people I simply don't care. Fond as I am of you *and* knowing you much better than him, I have always thought you were very lucky. Perhaps too lucky. Although he seemed to go his own way so completely I used to feel that his life had been given to you. You're a very infectious person, you know, Meg; you're so sure of what you want that it's not easy to resist you. But don't blame yourself; if it hadn't been that, it would have been something else. You'd be surprised how much I blame myself for shutting Andrew off from Evelyn when she was little. But saying these things doesn't help. One just has to find one's own level ...'

Whether it was that Jill felt embarrassed at her unusual openness, when Meg returned to England she sent a short, more characteristic note to the hotel. 'Just to welcome you home. But, I suppose, only in transit. I imagine you'll be off somewhere warm so long as the house is still let. I shan't intrude myself on you because I know you'll have so much to do and so many people to see. I'm surprised at the hotel you've chosen. So close to the station and in the days when I knew of such things, not at all your class of place. But for all I know, nowadays the Ritz may be a dosshouse. I can't help envying you the West Indies or whatever it's going to be. They say we shall have a very bad winter and the price of electricity seems to go up every year. I hope rest and sun will make the world seem a little brighter for you. Jill.'

About a week later, however, Meg returned to the hotel to find an envelope containing a Yale key and a covering letter. 'My dear Meg, I felt so ashamed of my last grouchy note, written when rheumatism's first twinge was gnawing at me and when the first mention of Christmas cards this year made me think how much I hate working in the stationery department. And now I hear from nosey gossips that you have been left badly off. You know how I bore everybody about being poor, so that *I* can't pretend that there's anything to like about the condition; but you'll do better than me at it I dare say. As with everything else today people seem to think that one's financial affairs are a common concern. I think such nosiness is quite detestable and I'm not going to add to it. This note is merely to say that, of course, I'm always glad to see you if you feel the need to unburden, although I warn you – as if warning were needed – that I'm not a very gay companion. But still we have a lot of the past in common which can be a help. I shall not be a bit surprised if you want to be left alone, but I *did* think that sitting in that wretched hotel might really be too unpleasant, and as my flat is so near I enclose a key. If you want to be on your own in the day just go there whenever you like and make a cup of tea or what you will. It's hardly palatial but the sitting room gets the morning sun when there is any. Just to show I'm not altruistic, I would say that if you could look in on a Tuesday morning when my woman comes, it would be very kind. It's so impossible to check if she does anywhere near a full two hours since I'm always out at work. Her name's Mrs Beazley.'

To this Meg also replied that she was not seeing anyone at the moment but that when she did Jill would be among the first; nor would her job hunting allow her much time to sit in the flat, nevertheless she would keep the key just in case; and certainly she would try to look in on one Tuesday morning.

So there they were, she thought, her three best friends; or, at any rate, those who looked like being her three only friends. She remembered what she had asked David – are my friends to be chosen for being kind and sensible? Well, the three lame ducks were kind, and their kindness seemed less intrusive than that of other friends. Sensible? It was such a loose word. She supposed that, in fact, they were not very sensible, or, at any rate, less intelligent, less cultivated than a great number of others she knew. There was about all three of them that mixture of sentimentalism and selfishness – if one counted poor Viola's devotion to Tom as a kind of selfishness – which on general principle she had always disliked. But there it was – no general principle could apply. All her other friends belonged to the circumstances she had left behind; Viola, Poll, and Jill beckoned her to the circumstances to which she was now called. What, however, endeared them to her was the tact of their beckoning. They made no urgent canvass of her to join their particular sort of distress; they did not even so much as remark on her demotion to their gentlewomanly ranks. She could find no trace of covert satisfaction and, if any trace of patronage, certainly a great deal less than she merited. She realized that in her present mood of self-recrimination she was in danger of extending the poor estimation she had of herself to others; and she was grateful to all three of them for demonstrating to her the falseness of such a view. They had simply shown her that they were fond of her for herself; and this, without changing at all from the very ordinary women they had always been. Their demonstration of unaltered affection tempered her self-dislike with a sense of having not failed with *them* at any rate so completely as she had supposed; it warmed her enough to admit to herself how nearly she had frozen; and it gave her the knowledge that she need not be entirely alone, without in any way obstructing the solitary path she had decided to take. She would not see them now, but she would see them in the future; and she was glad of it.

Certainly she found need of remembering it during those weeks in the hotel. Although she had found so little in common with David, although so little had remained to either of them of what they shared in the past that she felt some embarrassment in his presence, there had been in compensation, even in the few hours they were together, moments of some sort of empathy, some kind of vanishing of time's changes, that had given her a physical relief from the strain and anxiety and misery that she felt. The assuagement had been enough to make her hope for David's presence again in the future – if, she thought, they could have sat together silently in a cinema, it would have calmed her. But two days after his visit to London he telephoned to her to say that Gordon was to have an operation. Three days later he telephoned again to say that the operation had been successful, but there was apparent even to Meg, so certain that she was no longer attuned to his overtones, a note in his voice that suggested a formula prepared for the general public. For a moment she felt hurt at being treated as an outsider, but when she reflected how little she had tried to extend her understanding to her brother's life, she felt that she could only atone for it now by making easy his desire to remain a stranger. Andredaswood was hardly yet a place for visitors, he said, but would she like him to come up to London? She answered that she was too busy by day and too tired in the evenings, and he accepted *her* formula with evident relief. His telephone calls, his suggestions of a visit, her refusal, and his relief at it became now only a twice weekly ritual, sufficient to satisfy convention. It left her, however, without one of the solaces, always it was true only potentially effective, on which she had depended. In the blur of misery through which she still saw life, she had to meet chagrins and shocks entirely alone.

They were numerous. Some came unexpectedly, suddenly and un- invited. Others, although she felt them as acutely, she knew that she had half expected all along. Yet others, too, proved more vexatious because she had preferred to forget their existence. And all these day- time mundane troubles had to be met with an energy depleted by her fight against the melancholy of the evening, the fears and despairs of the night, which in their turn gained upon her more easily because of the days' exhaustions.

To begin with she was forced to realize that the shreds of the old life would not slough off the more quickly simply because she was resolved, and truly resolved, to begin the new life with intelligent realism. The delays of lawyers and probate authorities were not charmed away by her admirable courage. She saw clearly that one of the results of being 'sheltered' as she had been by Bill was to lead her to suppose that she had only her own moral struggle to fight, that if she could satisfy herself all else would come to her. Her failure, her abject failure, to present a petition on behalf of Bill's assassin had been a lesson in limitation; but as with all the lessons of Badai, it had told her only that there was a wide world outside her realm which knew her not. To learn the same lesson in England was more distressing. She could not get the estate 'cleared' the quicker by any discipline of self, nor sell the house, nor even secure accommodation to Mrs Copeman's taste which would give her an empty house to sell. She could only dispose of the china and that not as quickly as she could be rid of the circle of friends who had made up the Lord North Street social life.

It was in the course of disposing of the porcelain indeed, that she met an unexpected setback, the more wounding because she had made no advance to 'deserve' it.

Miss Gorres had proved kind, kinder than Meg had any right to expect, or indeed, than duty to Mr Sczekely should have allowed.

'Yes,' she said, 'we could, of course, find a customer for your collection. Very easily.' She paused and, offering Meg a cigarette, she went on, 'But you realize, I am sure, that your collection is not quite of the kind that will be valued *as* a collection.' She looked at Meg for a moment as though she were an object. 'Mrs Eliot, let us have a glass of sherry,' she said.

I'm being shown, Meg thought, that I'm valued even though I am no longer a potential customer. She dwelt on the thought as Miss Gorres dived about in the cupboard, because in the look she had been given there was a strange and less welcome suggestion that she was an all too familiar object of pity.

'Yes,' Miss Gorres said, when their sherries were poured out. 'Your collection is a very – I think I shall say – pleasing one. There is no object there that personally I do not like. I envy you your collection, Mrs Eliot. But it is composed of objects of very different values. Some will fetch a good price from any serious collector. Others are charming but they are your own choice. It may be difficult perhaps to find the other person who will regard them so highly. In a big collection, of course, this is usually so too, but there the number of pieces that are – shall I say? – of idiosyncratic taste will be balanced by the number of very valuable pieces. That is in a big collection. Of course, I know that you will say the collector's taste is of the essence of the collection. True, of course, historically and, perhaps, with one or two very outstanding living collectors.' She paused and raised her glass in what Meg imagined was her idea of a 'gallant' toast. 'Mrs Eliot, if I advise you something, will you be very discreet?'

Meg, annoyed by all this mystification, said rather briskly, 'I can't say until I've heard it, Miss Gorres.'

Miss Gorres smiled approvingly. 'You are quite right, of course. A confidence is a matter of trust on both sides. Well, I trust you. Take your collection to one of the big sale rooms. There each object will have more chance of getting its true price. All the dealers will be bidding; and don't believe all these stories about dealers' rings. I will help you. But you see that I am being very naughty.' She gave a look of coy *gaminerie* that Meg would never have supposed likely. 'Mr Sczekely would not be pleased.'

There was something in the way it was done that had not pleased Meg either; but she reflected that no kindnesses came unmixed and this was, she felt sure, a true kindness. She accepted Miss Gorres' offer.

'You won't regret it,' Miss Gorres said. 'You know, Mrs Eliot, I see so many mistakes made, but, of course, it is not my job to prevent people making them. You are exceptional. It has all reminded me so much of what I experienced twenty years ago now. I came very early to England, almost immediately after Hitler rose to power. I was already an assistant in the Stadtsgalerie at Bremen and so I had not much trouble in getting work here. But then in the following year or so came many of my friends; some of them who had been more – I shall say – gods than friends – private collectors, benefactors of the Gallery and so on. A few of them managed to bring their collections with them – the lucky ones who came out early. Among them also there were people who had delightful small collections like yours and they could not believe that they were not going to make fortunes by selling their collections as collections. It was natural really. But I am afraid they had not your good sense, Mrs Eliot, they would not listen to advice. Oh, it was extraordinary really. Many of them, formerly rich people, thought they could at once become experts – private dealers or curators at the Victoria and Albert Museum. They had no idea of the limitations of their knowledge, that they must know so much besides ceramics or tapestries or ivories or whatever they had collected, and so much more about even those things than they did. And, of course, above all they could never see that to buy for one's own pleasure is not always the same as to buy and sell for others.' She smiled. 'I don't think you will have much difficulty in *your* troubles, Mrs Eliot, if you are always so ready to take good advice as you are this afternoon. I propose your health. Good luck!' She drained the last of her sherry.

Meg seized on the gesture of dismissal as though it were a last minute reprieve. She almost bounded from her chair. But Miss Gorres had not quite finished. 'I am so glad that we have met not entirely so officially this afternoon. I feel that my indiscretion was not only helpful to you but to me. Perhaps we can now meet again as friends. I have myself one or two pieces that I think you will like. This is my telephone number. Please come and have a glass of sherry one evening. Either Finchley Road or Belsize Park stations are in easy walking distance of my flat.'

Meg walked along Bond Street feeling as though she had been caught in some ridiculous attitude in public – that her skirt had come down or that she had fallen through a chair. She did not believe that Miss Gorres had intended to put her in her place – she wished in a way that she could so believe – but she had clearly only been reminiscing. Nevertheless it now seemed, although she had never thought of it before, that one of the ideas she had most cherished was that of working with some dealer, collector, or department of ceramics; and also it seemed quite clear that this idea, held in reserve, had been a ludicrous one. She felt unfairly exposed as a pretentious and ignorant fool.

It was only in the bus that another aspect of Miss Gorres came home to Meg. I suppose it was an invitation to see her etchings, she suddenly thought. She wondered how she had been so naïve as not to have 'placed' the situation before now. Other women had made advances to her and she had always seen them coming a mile off – seen them with a mixture of amusement and perplexed desire not to hurt. It had never occurred to her to suspect such emotions in Miss Gorres because, of course, as she now saw all too clearly, she had always 'placed' her below any real personal contact. Her management of 'difficult' Miss

Gorres had been, for herself, that mixture of affability and patronage which she had always hated when her mother had preached it – 'one has the duty to be unfailingly pleasant to people who serve one, Meg,' and again, 'everybody is a human being'. But of course being human didn't mean that they were qualified to associate their personal lives with one's own. It seemed that she had been all too successful in making Miss Gorres feel that she was a human being. She wondered if perhaps she had thrown sex appeal about equally liberally elsewhere in her desire to please. What annoyed her most, however, was her own serious, guilt-struck reaction to the incident. Shall I never react again to anything simply by laughing? she thought.

This crushing rejection of aspirations she had never even declared to herself decided Meg that she must at once set about exploring the field of social work which had been in the front not only of her own but of others' minds in considering her future employment. She could think of no better, more experienced or more honest adviser here than Mr Darlington. Accordingly she rang him up and asked him to tea at the hotel.

A disgusting tea it was too that they had, as they sat in the huge dusty cretonne covered armchairs in a corner of the dark little lounge. Meg had chosen it in preference to a tea room because although derelict and depressing, it was also quiet. That afternoon, as it happened, there was a party of bright, hearty South African schoolmistresses which seemed somehow to have become divided into two so that they shouted to each other across the room. Meg and Mr Darlington were forced to perch on the painfully hard edges of their deep chairs in order to hear one another.

Mr Darlington, no doubt in order to show Meg that his admiration of her was unaffected by her change in fortunes, seemed to find it necessary to praise everything – he preferred tea on the strong side and bread and butter thickly cut; he was delighted to see apricot jam. Meg, finding it unbearable, eventually asked him if he also liked madeira cake that was as dry as the desert sand it resembled. She said it in the tone of the jokes they had formerly shared, but Mr Darlington, for whatever reason, refused to meet her.

'I'm not very particular about food,' he said rather primly, and then added as though this might have been misunderstood, 'My wife, luckily for us, is my idea of the perfect cook. Nothing exotic, you know. But always reliable.'

It was a smug little statement, but not, Meg realized, as smug as it suddenly seemed to her, for as he said it she had immediately thought, I don't want to know anything about his wife, I don't really even want to know anything more about him, I simply want his advice on this one thing. I'm being unfair to him, she decided, I'm expecting him to meet me for the first time outside the Association's offices and for the first time in my changed position in life. It's no easy assignment with these ghastly colonial women whining so loudly through their teeth. She decided to ask about Aid to the Elderly affairs. This proved altogether better; at any rate, to start with. Mr Darlington twinkled and even giggled in the way that Meg had always found so promising in her past dealings with him. He told a dryly amusing story about a set-to between Mrs Masters and Annie Pratt – one of the toughest of the old women – in which Mrs Masters had been worsted. 'She said,' Mr Darlington ended, 'that she would not have believed anyone could have spoken in such a way who'd been in service in a good part of Eastbourne. She was quite relieved when I pointed out that she'd mixed the files and our Annie had worked all her life in a Bermondsey tannery.'

The atmosphere seemed so 'right'; Mr Darlington so level-headed and lively that Meg felt convinced she would get sound and encouraging advice from him. She was about to plunge, when the harmony seemed disturbed once more in a more subtle way. Meg had asked whether Mr Purdyke had finally succeeded in getting satisfaction from the hospital where it was clear enough that one of their protégés – an old ex-sea captain – had been disgracefully neglected. 'I'm sure,' she said, 'that you were quite right in urging that since Mr P. knew the head house surgeon a private complaint would be far more effective than a formal protest from the committee.'

'Yes,' Mr Darlington replied. 'It would have been. *If* he'd done anything about it. But, of course, they're members of the same club. It wouldn't have done at all to worry a fellow-member with some wretched old pensioner's grievance. Most out of place.'

Meg looked at him in surprise. 'Oh, I think you're wrong. I don't know about men's clubs, of course. But I don't think they're like that at all. I'm sure Bill, my husband, wouldn't have hesitated to raise a point of that sort with anyone he knew at his club.'

'I expect your husband had more guts than Purdyke.'

'Poor old Mr Purdyke. He's a cautious old man but once he's said he'd do a thing, I should have thought ...'

'Well, he hasn't done this,' Mr Darlington broke in savagely. Meg thought, I hadn't realized that he took these things quite so seriously; or, perhaps, she reflected, I no longer feel so strongly about the Association.

She was about to lead the conversation on to her own needs, but Mr Darlington spoke now with real anger. 'Poor old Mr Purdyke,' he copied her, 'I'm sorry, Mrs Eliot, but it's depressing to see how you all gang up together. It's exactly what the members of the committee said when I talked to them about it. Even Lady Pirie. I certainly didn't think you would. But after all, you've no interest in the matter now. I must say I'd love to get it across to the *rest* of them that about the only useful function they can perform is to pull strings to get things done. After all they're "influential people". That's why they were elected, presumably.'

Meg reflected that despite all the criticism of the committee's work that she had shared with Mr Darlington, she had not seen this as its sole function. 'I see,' she said, 'you don't rate the work we do very highly.'

He looked for a moment embarrassed. 'I rate the work *you* did *very* highly,' he said. 'You kept the rest of them from interfering and messing things up.'

Meg laughed. 'Rather a negative function,' she said.

'I can't imagine a more useful one. They can only be kept down by snobbery. Good heavens!' he cried, 'you don't want a lot of voluntary, untrained idiots mixing themselves up with the actual work, however good their intentions.'

Meg was about to say sharply, 'Well, you've quite lost your shyness, haven't you,' but she stopped herself in time. 'I've often been surprised that you took a job with a voluntary body, Mr Darlington,' she said. 'I'm pretty sure I should feel happier with a Home Office or local government appointment.'

He looked at her with amusement. 'You sound like my father,' he said. 'I can't see what on earth difference it makes whether a thing's a private charity or not. Except that for some large-scale things it works better under the government. But as to who you're working for – I suppose Home Office inspectors and so on are better, they're trained; but it's like Trade Union officials, they become remote from the real work. As to local councils, why should they be better than a voluntary committee? In any case so long as we have *voluntary* charities they'd better have properly trained employees.'

Meg said, 'Although I worked for the Aid to the Elderly, I must say I've always thought it should be a government service or at least run by the local councils.'

He said indifferently, 'You may be right. I'm not political.'

The moment to raise her own affairs seemed to have come, not because the conversation had been naturally led to it but because without some fresh topic it threatened to cease altogether.

'And what did you feel about our telephone conversation?' she asked. 'Do you think *I* would make a competent trained social worker?'

There was a tension in the second's pause that followed which made Meg ask quickly, 'Do you think I'd ever get through the training course?'

The flicker of relief in Mr Darlington's eye showed her that she had been tactful – if tact were relevant.

'Oh certainly. My only fear is that you'd find it too elementary. But if you've never dabbled in the social sciences, I think you'd find it interesting. It sets one to reading more. I enjoyed it enormously, but then I'd never taken a proper university degree.'

'Nor have I,' Meg said.

He seemed somehow surprised and a little disappointed. 'Oh, in that case I think you'd enjoy it considerably and, of course, you'd pass with ease.'

'Good. And after? What about a job?'

'Oh, no difficulty there. They're crying out for people in all branches – work for the aged, hospital almoner, probation officer, problem families, factory welfare work. I should think you could take your choice.' He concluded with a finality that suggested the end of the topic; but Meg wanted to know more. 'Do you think I'd be *good* at it?' she asked.

'I should think so. How can I judge a thing like that?'

She was now far from content. 'Mr Darlington,' she said. 'This is very important to me, you know. It's the whole of my future life. Please be honest with me. You've got some reservation, haven't you?'

He asked her permission to smoke his pipe. She found all the preliminary packing and lighting quite intolerable. He's all right, she thought, but I couldn't stand him about me for long. At last, 'Quite frankly, I am a bit doubtful, Mrs Eliot,' he said. 'How would you fancy, for example, being in my place or perhaps, more to the point, Miss Rank's *vis-à-vis* the committee?'

'I thought you believed that I managed the committee very well.'

'Now, Mrs Eliot, *you're* not answering *my* question quite honestly this time, are you?'

'I suppose all employers can be difficult,' she said, 'but I'm not the sort of person to put on airs, you know. I don't want to be a "lady" graciously taking on a job. Is that what you're frightened of?'

He seemed surprised. 'Oh! Class,' he said, 'I don't think that's very important. We have people of all classes who are social workers. I doubt if such a thing's noticed much in England now if you haven't got the money to back it up. No, I was thinking of personality. I think, you see, that you expect results, and quick ones. And, of course, you've always been in the position to get them.' He blushed. 'I'm being very rude,' he said. 'I'd better stop.'

'That's all right,' Meg conceded. 'Please go on.'

'Well, in our work, you often don't get results at all, or the wrong ones, and certainly they don't come quickly. You've probably got too much imagination, too quick a mind. You'd get impatient and lose interest. I'm thinking, you see,' he went on, 'not only of committees and colleagues but of the people you'd have to deal with in your case work. Old people, factory workers, delinquents, whatever it was. I think they'd interest you enormously. You'd get on with a lot of them well, understand them and like them better than most of your colleagues. And those you didn't like I'm sure you'd take even more trouble with. But that isn't really the point. It's impossible to talk about it except in platitudes. You see what you'd be there for is to help them to help themselves. And I don't believe you'd do it. You'd carry them along with you, charm all their troubles away, make them feel they were interesting and that they were liked, but when the time came for them to stand on their own feet they'd be just where they started or almost so. And then you'd be annoyed.'

'I see,' Meg said. She hoped that she did not show her annoyance now. 'Charm's my trouble, in fact.' His own charm, she thought, was rapidly vanishing; he seemed like a schoolboy trying not to sneak on the others.

Now he squared his shoulders and clearly took the offensive. 'You remember how dull much of the work of the committee is?' he asked. She could hardly, recalling her all too apparent boredom on certain afternoons, deny it. She said nothing. 'Well,' he went on, 'the committee get the pick of things. Three-quarters of *our* work is simple, dead routine.'

'I've got a sense of humour, you know,' she said. 'You'll admit that. Surely it helps. You must know, for you've got such a good one yourself.'

'I hope,' he said, 'I've been able to live up to you there. It's interesting to have such different personalities on the committee, but it's not always easy to adapt oneself to everybody.'

For a moment she could say nothing. It was not only her 'special' relationship with Mr Darlington that seemed to have been hit for six, it was the whole sacred nature of 'humour' – the purest, most truthful of all human characteristics, her touchstone of whether a relationship was real. She said, not caring about the obvious irony in her voice, 'Oh, I think you're very adaptable.'

But if he knew her intention, he ignored it. 'Well, that's what I mean. You have to be in social work. Adaptable to weeks of dreary routine and ready to adapt yourself to the sudden flap, or the odd unexpected interesting situation that suddenly comes up.' He smiled at her and she felt that he was asking to be forgiven for disappointing her hopes. He looked at his watch. 'I must fly,' he said, 'or I'll have to adapt myself to some very black looks from my wife.'

After all, she thought, it would have been so easy for him to say what she wanted to hear; only real kindness could have made him go through such an ordeal of shyness. 'Thank you very much,' she said. 'You've been very honest with me. You're probably right in what you say. I'll have to think it over.'

Nevertheless as she watched his neat, stocky figure disappear through the hotel swing doors, she reflected that people's honesty looked like being a most inconvenient part of her new life.

Try as she would, Meg could not get past Mr Darlington's advice. It had been so definite, so without any personal motive. She tried to believe that he was actuated by spite, that she was his whipping boy for the sins of the committee; but it was just not so, and to start believing such things for convenience, she realized, opened a dangerous floodgate for a lonely, bewildered middle-aged woman. She could believe, indeed she must, that he had no such particular liking for her as she had supposed; but in that case his view was only the more disinterested – a mixture of general benevolence, bent ever so slightly towards her because of their particular association, and of concern for the good of his profession. A prig, then, she might call him, and an insincere man in his professional relations; to do so would not decrease his competence at his job which was the test of the value of his advice.

Nor were priggishness and insincerity charges she felt happy to throw around lest they rebounded and hit her. He was colder, more calculating than she had supposed, but that hardly impaired his judgement. And in any case he only calculated with the committee not with the old people. Her own position had changed and no doubt from that changed position she would now see different facets of the world she knew. Only the three old faithfuls seemed no different, but it was hardly fair to Mr Darlington to expect him to preserve faith with her as they had. She must, she decided, adopt a rule – she would see the friends of her married life no more, but remember it as a charming one; she would forget Miss Gorres' disturbing 'pass' and remember her as that friendly, helpful little German woman at Sczekely's; Mr Darlington should remain the surprisingly lively, humorous, intelligent secretary she had got on so well with. If there was patronage in it, that was better than rancour.

Nevertheless to take Mr Darlington's advice meant the suppression of her own esteem of herself, her own will. This might be excellent as a general discipline, wise on this occasion, but she feared for her future if she was not to be her own guide. And, more important, she realized that she had pinned too much on the idea of social work; she found no other idea to fall back on.

Her little bedroom at the hotel was ugly – the more hideous for having been recently redecorated with a standard 'contemporary' wallpaper. All over the walls floated gay little blue and pink café tables, around them a few Vermouth and Pernod bottles and the word 'Montmartre' in pretty childish script. The design was no doubt carefully chosen to enchant cross-Channel travellers; it had no message for Meg. In the first weeks she had sought every excuse to be away from the room; but now suddenly the wallpaper, the pink, bevel-edged, modernistic mirror, and the furniture of shaded pink and silver began to give her a sense of anonymity. They were so remote from anything she knew or cared for that she felt free, safe, and hidden. She was free to fight her way back through the tangled, wounding branches of guilt and self-recrimination to the inner recesses of the past where she and Bill were still in unity. She was safe from the present desert of the London streets where, no longer Mrs Eliot of Lord North Street pausing in her busy purpose to enjoy the human variety around her, she felt herself only unknown; a creature without place or purpose; ageing female of the past, everything to be despised. Above all she was still hidden from the future that sought to prise her out of the last fragments of her protective shell and expose her for whatever absurd and ill adapted creature she was henceforth to be labelled.

'I suppose the fascination of gardening lies a lot in the way one can plan for the future. Especially in such an insecure world. I open my morning paper and read of some fresh new horror the scientists have devised and then I plan some change in the garden that won't be fully realized for at least five or six years. It's illogical, of course, but it's some comfort. Don't you think so, Mr Parker?'

David, as always, smiled a sort of agreement. It was an observation that in some form or other seemed to come from so many of their customers after a certain period of trading. David, it suggested, had been discerned to have a mind that could appreciate the deeper aspects of his trade; with such a man business relationships must henceforth bear some of the ornaments of friendship. Since Gordon's return from hospital, however, David had found that the remark inevitably heralded an inquiry about the invalid's health. Little Mrs Glaisher, one of the many customers now coming from Crawley New Town, was no exception.

'Is Mr Paget still going on all right?' she asked.

David wondered if she would realize the tactless juxtaposition of subjects and blush, but she did not; none of them did. It was true that external appearances were saved by the fiction they had generally reported of Gordon's 'successful' operation; yet he knew that such a fiction could not have long been truly preserved in a country district; he was sure that most of their neighbours and customers must now have heard that Gordon was dying. The fiction of longevity inspired by gardening was always coupled with the fiction of Gordon's health; he knew that no unkind motive inspired these friendly people, yet the compulsion seemed constant. The embarrassment that the dying caused to the living was clearly not only general but less deeply suppressed than he had supposed. However he was able still to answer, 'The winter's not easy for him, of course.' And then Mrs Glaisher, like all the others, was able to cluck sympathetically. She was less easy in her transition remark than some others, it was true.

'The hopes we all place in the spring!' she said.

David wondered how anyone could get out of a remark like that, but here she was passing on to the best means of preserving her dahlia tubers and the fungicide she had used to keep her tulip bulbs from mildew, had she chosen the right one? Spring raised such practical problems.

Nevertheless, he reflected, sitting alone in the little office when she had gone, the idiotic sentimentality about 'gardening and the future' was right in its general line. Over the years he had built up a life encompassed by simple immediate duties and recreations – an ordered present; but an ordered present demanded at least the fiction of an immediate future with simple duties and recreations to be planned. Only such a life, he had come to believe, could allow one to cross the shapeless tract of human existence with grace and with gentleness; if the path was a meaningless progress to the grave, then the more necessary to take each step as a deliberate progress to the next; he could see no other way of preserving the fiction of civilization, and nothing to recommend the indulgence of exposing it. Now in this cruel November, prelude to Gordon's last few wintry months of life, careful ordering of the future had become more than ever his aim. The present was only a matter of giving the very little to Gordon of all that he would have wished to give, and more still of keeping from Gordon all the things that he and others, in indulgence of their affection, might have imposed. It was as an aid to this discipline of emotions, his own and others', that planning and attention to the coming year's duties and routines proved so valuable. If it meant an outrage of his own feelings in dwelling on the time when Gordon would be dead, that must be nothing if in result it assisted Gordon to be free of vexation. Pain, the great enormity, only the doctors could in some measure ease, but added vexation it was *his* task to remove.

The one compensation in this crisis of his life was that his way of living proved of value. He had thought once that it was one which, by small example and through long stretches of time, might yet 'save humanity' from the grosser absurdities of self destruction; this was a dream he had now rejected. History, after all, offered so many examples of 'the proper course', and so few conversions. Perhaps the hope itself had been only one more of the self assertions, ideals, ambitions, and pious interferences which were the weapons by which man was destroying himself. But in the last year or so, he had wondered if, even in his own life, he had applied the rule too rigidly to himself, had dogmatized a means of salvation when all he had found was personal safety. After all, he had no doubt that in the howling wilderness sweet voices sounded, and that their sound was the only thing worth hearing. Selfishness, self assertion, ideals, dreams and so on lay behind *those* voices. Up to now he had answered this contradiction simply by measuring the magnitude of the voice; Beethoven, Shakespeare, Flaubert, Mozart – what the local W.E.A. man called 'the big chaps', in their wide variety of 'big chapness' – were the only ones that could defy the discipline of living. The rest of us had the more to make up in self-denial to earn the bounty of those above the rules. But doubts he had had of it all lately, even for the few small self-assertions he had refused himself. Now those doubts were gone. The climax of life – and for him Gordon's dying was the climax – seemed undeniably to prove him right. He could meet it, he believed, decently for himself and, within the great limitations of human aid, decently for others.

He had been lucky perhaps that his love, and the object of his love, had declared, so openly and once for all, that loneliness was the condition of man, a loneliness to be endured and fulfilled in the constant disguise of human contact. It was so simple a truth, but so many lives – Meg's for instance – seemed shaped to hide it. If the whole discipline of his days, then, was designed to accept this reality, he could at least congratulate himself on his luck rather than on his superior wisdom and so preserve his self-effacement. He smiled with anticipatory pleasure when he thought of the amusement he would give to Gordon in telling him the smug conclusion of all this self-inquiry.

This at least was also a consolation of their way of living. His thoughts could still be communicated to Gordon even though they involved his reactions to Gordon's death. Gordon could speak of his own death, and did so bravely, casually, and no more than was practically required. Gordon could and did urge certain courses of action upon them all – David would be foolish if he did not do this, if David were wise he would see to it that Else did that – after he had died. Gordon had certainly no wish to suggest that future should not still follow present in its daily, monthly, and annual trivialities. In the past he had participated, led, in the 'business of daily life', now he hardly did so any more; soon pain and then death would withdraw him altogether. But it was nevertheless the triumph of their life together that they could still communicate, from their distant stations of belief and ordered despair, without a single lapse of the truth they both so respected. Indeed they were closer if anything than at any time before. They had each, always, held the other's personality as so separate a thing, so inviolable, so supremely more than any communication could hope even to glimpse – he in his conviction of man's utter loneliness, Gordon in his conviction of man's relation to God. Now, when they were in fact to go their own ways, the separation perhaps seemed less important, the communication more valid. And their love, as he had always told himself it would be, was the less impaired by death because, as a Christian, Gordon could permit it only so limited an expression. And accepting this, he himself had changed his way of life to fit Gordon's.

There had, of course, been failures and disappointments in their meeting of this climax; but, distrusting perfection, he felt that it should be so. With his own strong sense of insufficiency, it was difficult for him to judge how often he had unconsciously failed Gordon. Too often, certainly, for once would be too often; but also, no doubt, very often. Yet it was his nature to exaggerate his own failings, and to do so at this time would perhaps make him over self-conscious, upset the rhythm of communication that at present so happily flowed between them. Yet, too, it was easy to face one's failings, and, in accepting, leave them free to grow. What was certain was that on a few but important occasions he had thought Gordon to have fallen below what he had hoped for. Each time he had been disgusted with himself for making such a judgement of a man already in pain and looking beyond it to inevitable agonies and death. But at last it had seemed to him that to deny the judgements would be to lower his regard for his friend.

He had wished then, more than at any time he could remember, that he were able to say, I observe, I don't judge. But this sentimentalism, that passed as a wide and deep love of humanity, as the gentle wisdom taught by the years, was surely the negation of real respect for men. It would never do, least of all where respect and love were involved. Where you respected and loved, you esteemed, you judged. If these self-styled adult 'observers' simply meant that judgement should not impair one's love, they spoke in platitudes; if the love was deep enough, no judgement would impair it. But if they really meant 'observe' of someone that one loved, then they could not mean real love – you don't love microbes. Or perhaps their love meant no more than Pavlov's love for his dogs. Better really that they should limit it to that; that word 'observe' had a sinister ring for any greater love. In any case, he had long felt that the patronage, the godlikeness implied in this sort of compassion from above was far more displeasing than the action of judging. So he had judged Gordon on these few occasions and found him wanting, even as a dying man – not by a standard that anyone else would have passed, but by Gordon's own magnificent standards. And he had loved him, of course, no less; nor (stupid modern sentimentality) the more. He had railed against the disgusting physical nature of man that should impose such tests upon Gordon's fineness; had railed as everyone presumably did when those they loved died (his mother was the only other and he hoped that she had known no time to show courage or panic before the V2 from no-where annihilated her) and he had seen the folly of railing. More use-fully he had used these judgements to step warily himself, so that cir-cumstances should defeat Gordon as seldom as possible.

The first occasion had been so simple, or was it? – in one sense, failure itself? in another, no failure at all, certainly not one that he could judge. *He* had received the surgeon's verdict soon after the operation. Shortly after he and Else had got back from Brighton that evening, Terence Loder, their doctor, had come round to Andredas-wood.

'It's too far gone,' Loder had told him, 'the liver's affected as well as the gut. You'll say, I'm sure, that the photos ought to have shown this without subjecting him to the strain of this operation. They don't always, I'm afraid. But the verdict's very final now . . .' It was clear that he had a competent line of patter to carry his audience through the immediate shock.

When, apparently, Loder had judged him to be 'composed', he had said, 'It's a wretched business. He's a fine man. We'll spare him all the pain we can, I promise you.'

He had answered, as he realized, angrily, 'I hope that you can spare him *most* of it.'

Terence Loder hadn't answered, but after a pause, he had said, 'One thing I should like to know, Parker. Does he have any idea?'

'He has thought for a long time that he may die, if that's what you mean.'

'I see. He's a deeply religious man, isn't he? That often helps them. All the same I think we should stick to my usual rule in these things. Let time break it to the patient. We have only to say that we can't tell at this stage. It's kinder, you know. The knowledge of certain death is a terrible thing to live with. One wants to spare anyone from it as long as possible. If he's as aware as you say, he'll probably guess what the non-committal verdict means.'

Looking back, he realized that this illogical statement of Terence Loder's had come nearer to making him lose his temper than anything that had happened in that ghastly week. He had managed, however, to

168

say icily, 'Does a non-committal verdict, in fact, never mean that you don't know?'

And Terence Loder, surprised as well as ruffled, had said, 'No. Of course not. I was just considering every eventuality ...' The voice had trailed away.

David had said then very formally, 'It would be quite out of the question, doctor, to keep the truth from Gordon. Apart from other considerations, he is as you say a deeply religious man.'

'He's not a Roman Catholic, is he?'

He had found considerable assuagement of his unfair anger in explaining to Terence Loder the nature of the Christian preparation for death, a need not confined to Roman Catholics.

Terence Loder had attempted some self-defence. 'I think it's exceptional with Church of England people, but still what you say alters the case. Do you wish me to tell him? I'm used to it after all. Or would you prefer to do it yourself?' David had said that he *would* prefer to do it. They had agreed to a non-committal statement until Gordon was back at Andredaswood and recovered from the immediate effects of the operation.

He remembered the evening he had chosen for the telling as clearly as he could the details of so many nightmares. But had he chosen it any more than those?

Gordon could eat little and his skin was already stretched on his bones in the way that had now given to his eyes the timid-seeming stare of a lemur. He had taken egg-white whipped with brandy and much powdered with caster sugar, which pleased his sweet taste. The first hard frost had come and they sat in the drawing room before a blazing, pine-scented log fire. They had played the records of *Salome* and Gordon had more than usually delighted in the irony of the music transcending an absurd 'decadent' theme. He had made his usual comment on the pleasure of not seeing Welitsch in the flesh. Little owls screeched and barn owls hooted. They had agreed how pleasant it was that Else had gone to a meeting in Haywards Heath on Nuclear Disarmament. She invariably shuddered at the owl's ill omen; whereas they had long ago agreed that the sound of owls on a cold night reminded them, with delicious, selfish pleasure, that some Wordsworthian figure – solitary traveller, leech gatherer, or idiot boy – was miserably lost abroad, while they sat in comfort at home.

Then Gordon, feeling perhaps that comfort was for him an illusory sensation, or perhaps feeling comfortable enough to consider a future

– it was just this vital matter of Gordon's mood that he could never now know – spoke suddenly of their next book. 'We ought to get on with "Africa", you know. The gardeners of England can't remain suspended among the flora of the New World and of the Antipodes for ever. Besides if we ever get to Asia we might have enough money to see some of the damned things in their lovely natural settings.'

They always spoke of their very successful series of books in this slightly forced facetious vein; it had never quite ceased to worry them both a little that their joint hobby should have proved lucrative, and, indeed, esteemed – *Garden Flowers from the New World* had been given leading reviews by the senior critics of the two major Sunday newspapers. There were many phrases from these reviews that they used as happy catch-phrases in their daily life – 'how pleasant for a change to find wide reading so little paraded' (That's you, David); 'Flower plates have become all too depressingly familiar on the walls of our country hotels. How clever, then, to have found more than fifty that are at once unfamiliar, exact, and decorative' (That's you, Gordon); but their favourite was 'Alas, I cannot follow the authors in their enthusiasm for the showy cineraria.' As Gordon often said, 'All together not too bad for a book put together on an entirely haphazard arrangement of continents by authors who have never visited them and who owe their material to a lot of ill-written naturalists' and travellers' tales.'

In fact, of course, they had both done a great deal of hard work on them, and, no doubt, Gordon was right when he had said, 'This, David, is the price you pay to your conscience for not going on with that vital work about Richardson's influence on all those French bores.' The decision to work on 'Australia', the first of the flower books, had been the final curtain to his academic career.

But, faced on that evening with the direct question, he had hesitated, and Gordon had suddenly said, 'Or shan't I be alive to see the end of "Africa"?'

The casual tone, at the time, had genuinely seemed to him to come from a man, sure in faith, who had accepted imminent death. He had answered directly.

That Gordon, for perhaps two minutes, had not been able to control a physical shaking, that his body had refused to help him in disguising his panic terror had been only a sadness for him to see; few men, hearing their death warrant, were not afraid in that moment, and, besides, what was this 'absolute faith' he was expecting of

Gordon? Was his own doubt so 'absolute'? These were childish terms.

When the shaking was under control, Gordon had burst out angrily. 'Why the hell did Loder leave this to *you* to tell me?' He had defined the remark quickly, it was true. 'Loder had no right to leave such an unpleasant job to you.' Nevertheless he had known that Gordon was conscious of having shown terror and that he would rather have shown it before anyone else. Respect of privacy had been the keynote of their relationship, but he had never supposed that, for Gordon, this had involved no call upon ultimate compassion. He had tried always to understand and sympathize with Gordon's religious beliefs; could it be that Gordon yet thought he would pounce upon a moment's failure in faith with triumphant glee or mockery? Or was it that Gordon supposed his respect to be so shakily founded as to be lessened by that second of doubt and fear? Whatever the cause it could never now be discussed or explored. The most he could hope to do was to bury it in silence. Nevertheless there was a rent in the close-knit fabric of their understanding.

The incident of the animals was discussed, but discussion had only made him realize that, however unjustly, he had been disappointed in Gordon. David liked the animals so little, had so accustomed himself to ignoring them, that it was only on his second visit to Gordon's room that day that he had noticed their absence. The dogs and cats might unusually have been out on the prowl, but Rosie, the cockatoo, never left the room except in the hottest days of summer. 'Where's Rosie?' he had asked.

'Bobbie Telfer's taken her with the others,' Gordon had answered in an over-casual voice.

He had not understood. 'Is there some animal pest about?'

'No. And I doubt if there was that parrots and cats would be threatened by the same one. You do say the most stupid things whenever you speak about animals, David. You're always the same when you're not interested in something. You simply speak before you've thought.' He had sensed the tension in Gordon's voice and had not answered. But Gordon could not leave it alone. 'I hope you're not going to fuss about the animals,' he had said.

'Good heavens! I only wondered what had happened to them.'

'I've got Bobbie to gas them.'

'Gas Oliver!' If he had a liking for any of them it had been for the old cat.

'Oh, for God's sake, David, don't be sentimental. I made pets of them all and they became attached to me. We have a duty to be humane to the brute creation. They've become habituated to my treatment, they'd be miserable with any other regime.'

'But they enjoy life so.'

'Enjoy life! Really, David. Their appetites were satisfied and their habits were not disturbed. But they don't have souls.' He had paused and then said, 'Or do you think I should have left them to you as a sacred trust?'

'No. I suppose not. But Climbers adored Rosie, she'd have done anything for her.'

'Anything except feed her sensibly. The bird would have suffered from constant bellyache. And Else would have taken the dogs for a ten-mile walk one week and forgotten to let them out of the house the next. No, my pets die with me.'

There was some arrogance in Gordon's tone that had provoked David perhaps, for he had said, 'Well, it's just as well you haven't got a troop of slaves.'

And Gordon had said scornfully, 'It takes a humanist to lower men to the brute level out of sentimentality about animals.'

And so it had been on the Thursday evening of the First Bartók Quartet. There had been a lot of discussion about doing the work at all. Mary Gardner, with her jolly, loud business background, was in most local social affairs inclined to say 'the more the merrier'; she was fully aware that she owed her own general acceptance to a breaking down of barriers. But where music was concerned she made a defiant insistence on standards. 'I'm sorry,' she said, 'but I don't think Miss Bode's good enough. We've made a concession, *I* think, in doing Mozart and Haydn in practice with her. But while we're looking round for a new permanent second fiddle she'll do. This is quite different. It's silly attempting the Bartok with her. She just isn't good enough.'

Utterly uncultivated in any other way, Mrs Gardner had put all her values into music. She knew that she was a very good amateur cellist.

Reggie Green, on the other hand, the 'cultured Group Captain' as Gordon called him, was nothing if not all round – local brains trusts, art exhibitions, play readings, all were grist to his mill – but he was *not* so very good a viola player and he knew that. Snobbish and exclusive in local social affairs, he thought Mrs Gardner made too much of herself.

'Oh, come,' he said, 'nothing venture, you know. It's not as if we were professional.'

And himself, who usually was dead against the amateur emphasis – what Gordon and he called, 'making music can be so jolly' – nevertheless came down on the Group Captain's side. 'I really think we ought to give it a trial, Mary,' he had said.

He knew how much Else set store by being involved, and how badly she needed some indirect sympathy – she would find any overt demonstration impossible to take – during these days of Gordon's illness; how much Gordon would be helped by a less strained Else. It was two against one; and as first violinist and organizer his view carried great weight. Mary Gardner had given way. And really, now that they had practised a good deal, if Else was not adequate, she was less inadequate than might have been expected. The Group Captain was enthusiastic.

'Bravo, Miss Bode,' he said, 'I really think we make a pretty good showing, don't you? And by the way, what a splendid work it is.'

On that Thursday there had been their first limited audience of friends and neighbours. He had been particularly pleased to see that Eileen Rattray, who at first had come solely as a protest against the jazz activities that took Tim so often from home, was now not only a regular attendant, but had struck up a friendship with Climbers. Poor Climbers who gawped at the music she comprehended not at all, but who would have hated to be left out! If Eileen Rattray got on well with Climbers that might help the Tim–Climbers situation to improve. Without Gordon, he really would not be able to cope with a quarrelling staff. And there in the centre of the audience, like some Banquo's ghost, sat Gordon, the stick on which he now relied for supporting his enfeebled body laid on the floor by his side.

The first movement went remarkably well. Even Mary Gardner gave Else a smile at the end of it. Only when Gordon with great difficulty raised himself to his feet, and Climbers, with gasps and growls that expressed her overgrown child's alarm, handed him his stick and with Eileen Rattray's aid helped him from the room, did he realize that all could not necessarily be accounted well because Else had got through her part without disaster. Gordon had turned his face to them for a moment, tears were streaming down his cheeks and his body was trembling like a mouse caught in a corner. It was with the greatest difficulty that Else was persuaded to carry on to the end of the quartet; but she had only been upstairs a few moments before she returned again, her long grey cheeks unwontedly red, her eyes refusing to face the company. She drew David aside.

'Oh, it is terrible, David. It is dreadful to see him so weak like a baby. I wish I had never agreed to play.'

It was Eileen Rattray who brought the evening to a close. She came down to the drawing room and told them to go. With her genteel discreet make-up, soft wavy black hair and rather silly, round brown eyes, she seemed appropriately the nurse-in-charge. 'I honestly think we'd better all push off, David,' she said. 'Gordon just isn't up to visitors, you know.'

Had it been only that Gordon, so austere and undemonstrative in his love of music, had been reduced to maudlin tears by a very inadequate performance of a work he knew well, it would have been easy, though sad, to accept it as one of the indignities of a mind and body weakened by pain and stress; but it was what had happened the next day that had been so difficult to think of as coming from the Gordon he knew, yet also impossible not to see as springing from some habitually encouraged wilfulness. Gordon at that time – only a week or so ago – did not leave his bed until after luncheon; now he scarcely left it at all.

At eleven o'clock Mrs Boniface had brought a note from him. 'My dear David,' it read, 'I'm afraid there can be no more music *of any kind* until after I am dead. I cannot risk a repetition of the shaming exhibition I gave last night. Also I cannot tolerate the idea of music going on without my being there. I'm sorry but there it is.'

His own first thought had been: rather than that this sort of thing should happen again, let him die soon. He particularly felt the selfishness of destroying Else's morale. And, although he had rebuked himself again and again for the selfishness and cruelty of such a thought, he knew that his reaction had been a healthy one. In the play of Gordon's death, by which the whole repertoire of their life together was then being judged, the only uncertain actor was the dying man. Every further day of playing the ungrateful role might prove too much for his endurance, might lead to increasingly selfish hugging of the last pathetic rays of limelight.

The spluttering of the flame in the oil stove suddenly grew louder, breaking into David's reverie. The office was in any case fiendishly draughty. It was all very well to refuse oneself remembrance of the past years as too sweetly false; indulgence of the vinegary bitterness that the last few weeks had left was even more senseless and perverse.

There had been failures, but on the whole Gordon was dying true to his life; and they, his disciples, the household of Andredaswood, had not entirely failed to support him as he would surely want.

Attention to the future was the only sane course. He must see Climbers about the Christmas orders for cinerarias and poinsettias; he must go over the proof of the spring catalogue with Tim; and – surely this was a triumph? – he could now see them together without undertones of hostility. Then he must pass an hour with Else, letting her talk – of her first sight of Rosa Luxemburg in Berlin, of her visit to the Bruderhof settlement near Lindau ('such good, good people, though quite childlike'), of her work with the Basque refugees at the Cadbury settlement in Birmingham, of Gordon's mother and Gordon, and of Gordon again; talk was her only relief. And then, when Father Hill had left the sick-room at six precisely, his weekly visit of comfort concluded, David must read aloud to Gordon from *Prancing Nigger* or *Valmouth*, for only Firbank was tolerated now. A fixed routine, in fact, of people and places; only so could he hold himself apart, and, his soul not invaded, have the energy to endure to Gordon's end and beyond.

Meg, as November fogs thickened, looked out of her bedroom window and, craning as she would, could not discern the outlines of the Cathedral. Only an occasional drunken Irish voice or the high giggle of some Teddy girl reminded her that, incongruously, her long nights of memory floated, in all their varied scenes of her life with Bill, above the squalors of Vauxhall Bridge Road darkness. Nightmares beset her drugged sleep, waking her suddenly at two or three in the morning, lost in the desert, or taking off in an aeroplane with a burst of gunfire or a cry (some motor car or drunk, no doubt), Bill drowning in the sea below, Bill buried in the sand, Bill falling from the window of the plane. She woke to the reality of her dark, stuffy safety and would lie an hour or two with soothing memories of all their shared happiness; only, as the morning noise grew, to be jolted back into remembrance of her failure to help him. Or, on other nights sleep would wrap her round in a heavy sweetness, dreams ill-defined but reassuring, vague presences at her side in shadowy scenes that soothed her fears. From these, too, she would wake, but now gradually, slowly, to a final terror that he was *not* with her. She would lie for hours forcing back panic and hysteria until the night porter collecting shoes along the corridor told her that morning's safety had come. She argued with Bill now, and with herself, even in the day hours when she pottered in her room. Only when the chambermaid, an old 'character' with a Lancashire accent, came at eleven or so, saying, 'I'll have to make the bed now,' did she make her way to the lounge with *The Woman in White* as a barrier against intrusive conversation.

One morning the old woman remarked, 'First sign, you know,' and when Meg looked blank, she repeated in a tone half jocular, half maternal, 'Talking to yourself. I've never heard anyone like it. They say it's the first sign, you know.'

Meg, with effort making any communication, said, 'I must look out, mustn't I?'

The old woman answered solemnly, 'It's the money worries that are the killers,' so that Meg was left wondering whether she had been doing sums aloud.

It was the head waiter, however, who unwittingly brought Meg's retreat to an end. One morning at breakfast a new young waitress put rolls on Meg's table. The head waiter came up and said fussily, 'No, no, Mrs Eliot always has toast.' He stood for a moment over Meg. 'We're getting to know your ways, Madam,' he said. 'You can't think what a relief it is to have a regular in a hotel like this. I've been used to country hotels and it's terrible to see the faces change every morning like they do here.'

And then after breakfast that very morning the anaemic-looking cashier, who had seemed as genteelly hostile as she was sickly ladylike, said, stamping the week's receipt, 'Well, that's four weeks, isn't it? Our oldest inhabitant, I think.'

Meg answered the dismal smile as brightly as she could. 'Is there a bonus for long residence?' she asked, and they both laughed.

When Meg came up to her room she saw it suddenly as a squalid, hideous prison. She heard suddenly her mother's voice. 'Well, Margaret dear, I only hope *you're* never up against it. We'd all like to sit day-dreaming with our noses in a book, you know, but some of us have to think where the next meal is coming from.' It was then that she had begun the secretarial course which her marriage had interrupted.

And now she realized that under all the half sleep of the last weeks she had been forming the resolution to take up such a course again. There were ladylike secretaries, she knew, but she need not be one; nor would she be stamped as the bright, embittered career woman; that was the peril of the unmarried woman, not the widow. The demand for private secretaries was considerable; the pay good; the work, if she chose the right job, would bring her into contact with some part of the world outside that, until she had met it, would continue its desert threat; and she could change her milieu as she wanted. 'I'll nibble up this damned world bit by bit. Nothing can really hit me so hard again as I was hit at Srem Panh; but at least if I *haven't* been punished enough yet, I can try not to be caught in ignorance again. I'll go out to meet it.'

Then she laughed at herself; Alexander conquering the world, or even Oliver Cromwell leaving his farm to set England's wrongs to right, was hardly the correct mood for becoming that two-a-penny thing, a competent secretary. All the same, she knew that this, for the moment at any rate, was what she wanted – to be subordinate, but independent, to be 'in the know', to work with a man, having his confidence and identifying herself with his work.

She was surprised to find how much the idea of working with a man mattered to her. 'She became the boss's boss,' she thought. And, why she did not understand, she felt suddenly freed from care of seeing herself as a ridiculous figure. Only, of course, to become qualified at her age would not be easy. She had acquired before her marriage only a measure of proficiency in shorthand. The course, she decided, must be intensive, whole hogging – she would plunge wholly into the cut-off routine of study, drive memories and guilt away by the sheer weight of memorizing – and emerge, she could not tell what, but not, at any rate, the same.

Finding the right secretarial college did not prove easy. The one she had attended twenty years before turned out to be all too much a general finishing school – talks on modern affairs, little scrap ends of a nice girls' finishing off about pictures and books and the changing world around us. She had not remembered how incomplete her emancipation from her mother's vision of her future had then been. Wherever else, she had no place among the almost right type of girls for whom 'abroad' was out for cash reasons, and whose homes could not contain too many women doing nothing – girls about to do a job in London for a year or so until ... She checked herself; she had not known such rich suburbia still existed, why therefore should she suddenly wax angry about it? She would have to meet many young girls now. She must not allow middle-aged rancour to canalize her unhappiness. The semi-finishing schools were not for her, that was all. Nor, with the desire for self-torment vanishing in her new mood of determination, had she any intention of joining the stifling smells and the mass-personality of the large scale typing schools, to giggle and squeal her way to the slaughter market. At last, however, she found the place she wanted – Garsington Secretarial College.

The principal, Miss Corrigan, small, white-faced, with bright red hair, reminded Meg of Ellen Wilkinson, who had been one of her heroines in her youth. Miss Corrigan was not at all fiery, however; indeed her deliberate rather cold manner seemed to have chilled her physically. Although her small office, partitioned off from the great drawing room first floor of the large Victorian house in Gloucester Road, was almost furnace hot with two electric fires full on, Miss Corrigan wore two woollen jackets, one pink, one blue, and another of mauve was draped over her shoulders. This regard for comfort at the expense of appearance predisposed Meg in her favour. Miss Corrigan's practical, direct manner completed the effect.

'You won't find the shorthand easy at your age, Mrs Eliot. I had much better say that now. And the course is a six months intensive one. It means really hard work. But I can say that, unless you prove to be one of the rare persons who just can't learn, which is very unlikely, you'll be fitted to take a really good post at the end.' There were courses in commercial French and German, but as Meg had a good working knowledge of those languages, she would advise Meg to pick them up if and when she needed them. 'You'll need all your energies to memorize the shorthand,' she said.

Her interest in Meg's story was certainly no more than politeness required. 'Yes I read about it in the papers,' she said. 'I suppose you're recovered from the shock. I ask because if your health isn't up to it I shouldn't recommend you to waste your money on the fees.'

As to Meg's decision not to follow her mother's course of running her own business, she merely gave a little laugh and said, 'Well, times have changed haven't they?'

Nervousness, perhaps, made Meg elaborate her explanation. 'I think some of my friends will be surprised that at my age I don't want to be my own boss. Or, at any rate, go for one of the "refeened" sort of jobs which so many distressed gentlewomen do.'

Miss Corrigan paid no regard to her ironic tone. 'Will they?' she said. 'Other people's suggestions are never much help.' When Meg emphasized her straitened means, she said, 'We have a canteen which provides a cheap snack lunch. *And* saves time. You'll find most of the girls very young,' she said. 'They're a mixed lot in background, but young people today are very sensible. There are one or two older women. Anyhow, I don't suppose it matters. You won't be coming here to make friends.'

And so it started, a life of dictation and the first steps in shorthand, of various model typewriters, of duplicating and book-keeping in the great drawing rooms and the bedrooms that overlooked a garden at the back and the little maids' bedrooms that overlooked almost nothing. Only the embossed dadoes and the gold and white porcelain bell handles remained functionless to speak of the past Victorian glory. For the rest the rooms with their desks and collapsible chairs were coldly functional, the walls distempered ice blue, the paint white; but every room, unlike Miss Corrigan's office, had central heating and the lighting was good. Meg ate bridge rolls with cheese or sardines and drank a bowl of tomato soup at lunch time, and made conversation about the morning classes with Miss Corrigan's 'mixed' girls. She found them uninteresting but easy; when she chose to read a book with her snack no one seemed to be offended. All her energies and thoughts, as Miss Corrigan had predicted, were taken up with her work.

The only feature of working at the Garsington which irked Meg was that convenience seemed to demand her living in Kensington – the very centre, she felt, of the genteel penury she was trying to avoid. Determination to leave the hotel, to seek anonymity in a bed-sitting room, had been the starting point of her new mood of determination, but she had hoped to find a characterless district of London, or at least one that had no associations for her. However, she discovered that her picture of Kensington was as out of date as Miss Corrigan's laconic manner had shown her protest against 'ladies' jobs' to be. It was true that many of the old poor genteel hotel residents were still to be seen in the streets, and even some of the older stratum of rich house-owners, but the whole pattern of the Kensington she detested was now overlaid by such an influx of clerical workers and students and foreigners of every kind that she soon saw that her mother's world had vanished for ever.

She took a good sized bed-sitting room in a hideous terra-cotta coloured pseudo-Dutch house in a garden square near Gloucester Road station. The furnishing once again was 'contemporary', but characterless and 'restrained' in taste; it was a room that at least she would never notice. The two gas rings she resolved never to use for more than breakfast's tea and boiled egg. She realized with amusement that her picture of a straitened life was extremely vague, but that certain timeworn clichés, such as that 'you cannot decently sleep and live in a room which smells of cooking', coincided with her own feelings. These, at any rate, would serve as a guide at first. She found a nearby Italian restaurant, of the old-fashioned kind with paper carnations in vases on the tables, at which she ate each evening rather tough but well cooked escalopes, or fritto misto, and drank very good coffee. The prices of everything – and especially of the bed-sitting room – were a great perplexity to her. At times they seemed monstrously high and at others absurdly modest. With the limits of her small capital still uncertain, she had no guide to what she could afford save the vague knowledge that her old standards could be no guide.

She had hardly ever, at any rate in her adult life, known a routine of combined difficulty and tedium such as her new life gave her. At first the very novelty held some fascination, but, after a week, she found in herself a power of application to the daily task that she had not expected. It was not only pride that kept her determined, but an appetite for order so that she now made tables of her days at the beginning of each week and gained an absurd satisfaction from ticking off each lesson in her shorthand book, seeing new groups of sound symbols absorbed from the mysterious mass in front of her, noting the increase in her typing speed. She disciplined all her days to one end; she forswore all reading or cinema going as an unnecessary additional strain on her already fully taxed eyesight; she refused herself an immediate return from the Garsington to her room, when the day ended at four, for fear of having no recreation; she gave herself instead a short repose over tea in some café and then a walk in the park; on Sundays she made herself sleep on until eleven or so in the morning. By natural inclination she liked books and cinemas, disliked walking and lying in bed, but this subordination of all activities to an end eliminated choice and, in so doing, distracted her mind from her indifference to everything.

In a week or so, too, she found that the regime she had imposed by decision was the one that in any case her body demanded; with the day's work and the evening's preparation she was too tired for books or cinemas, longed for half an hour's fresh air and luxuriated in her Sunday laze. The nightmares became less frequent; her memory was too active upon syllabic symbols to allow for review of the past; the enlarged vision of the moral pattern of her life, that had obsessed her since Bill's death, faded each day; the gnawing guilt found some satisfaction in the performances of tedious work or was forgotten in concern over an ill-remembered lesson. She no longer felt that, in order to regain unity with Bill, she had to use all her energy to suspend Time's passage; now it seemed that, if she could subdue herself to a hard discipline, each day that passed would bring nearer that state of ordered quietude in which alone she could hope to purge her memories of waste and decay, and recall the essential past in which she had been at one with him. If at the moment all was confusion within, then only an ordered outer life could give hope for clarity; meanwhile she must stun her imagination and emotions with fatigue.

Christmas she dreaded, both for the strain it would put upon her acceptance of loneliness and for the well-meant demands that it would bring from her friends. The large circle of acquaintances she had shared with Bill, however, were clearly content to accept her rebuffs. Their Christmas cards, sent no doubt to show they had not forgotten her, seemed, when she remembered the parties and presents exchanged in earlier years, only to suggest that they soon would. Andredaswood presented more of a problem. Gordon, in a shaky hand that she found almost undecipherable, had written to ask her to stay; but by the same post came a letter from David, telling her of Gordon's condition and asking her to find an excuse not to accept. To Gordon she wrote that she was already promised to an old friend, but her letter to David, inept as she felt it, only made her feel that grief, far from enlarging, had narrowed her power of sympathy.

Jill wrote to say that her son-in-law had magnanimously allowed Evelyn to invite her down there for Christmas. 'As it means being with the baby for a bit I'm swallowing my pride and accepting. If I were on any footing but sufferance with Leonard I should suggest your coming down with me, but as it is, I must be thankful to be invited at all. Anyhow, Christmas isn't really for the old, so you're well out of the fuss of it. Apart from going to church *I* should certainly disregard it if I wasn't a grandmother.'

Poll somehow got hold of the name of the secretarial college and, much to Meg's embarrassment, held her in lengthy conversation over Miss Corrigan's telephone.

'What are you doing for ghastly Christmas?' she asked. 'Do you go to that brother? Or is there a breach? I've never known.'

'No, there's no breach, Poll. But his friend's ill.'

'Oh! poor him! All the same he must be very sensitive. I shouldn't put off Christmas just because a friend was ill. Or perhaps it's just an excuse. Anyway I don't suppose you're mad with anger. What will you do?'

'Oh, stay in bed probably.'

'Lucky you! *I* was going to do that and ask some nice people for a lot of gin in the evening. I mean you and some other ones. But now my Aunt Mary – the one who's not so bad but rather too keen on opera – has asked me there. It's miles away in Lincolnshire. Only the house is warm because she's frightfully rich. She said to bring a friend and I thought of asking you but I should think you'd much rather go to bed.'

'If it isn't rude, I think I won't say yes.'

'Rude? Well, I suppose it would be if I told Aunt Mary you'd rather go to bed than stay with her, but as she's never met you I shan't say anything about you. Anyway *I'm* only going because she's got lots of lovely "mon" and might leave it to me. She hasn't got anyone else except a sort of young man that lives there that she thinks might become a singer. But I shouldn't think that would last, should you? But she wouldn't leave any to *you*, so there's no reason why *you* should go there. I suppose I couldn't take a man and say I thought she meant that by "a friend"?'

Meg could hear Miss Corrigan, tired no doubt of her rather icily courteous withdrawal, fidgeting in the passage outside. 'I really can't say, Poll. I don't know your aunt.'

'Oh, she isn't all that different from other aunts. All the same I expect it had better be a woman. Who do you think I should ask?'

'I really don't know. Miss Corrigan's waiting outside ...'

'Who's *that*?'

'She's the principal of the college.'

'I don't think I could ask *her*. Even if I wanted to. I mean Aunt Mary *did* say a friend. Why? Hasn't she got anywhere to go?'

'No. I'm speaking in her office and she's waiting outside until I've finished.'

'Whatever for? We're not talking about *her*. Or at least we weren't until you started.'

'I really must ring off, Poll.'

'Oh, all right. Is that a good place? It doesn't sound it. Anyhow, sleep well. And get a lot of food in. If one sleeps all day one often wakes up ravenous.'

It seemed, then, that Meg might spend the Christmas holiday entirely alone. She planned to pass the three days involved between sleep, work, exercise, and the indulgence of reading the new Hartley novel – he and Forster alone of modern novelists aroused the same craving that she felt for the English novelists of the past. She saw the days as an exercise in relaxing, if only a fraction, the discipline she now found so necessary, in preparation for the years to come when some relaxation would be inevitable. Even so there lurked a panic behind her resolution. She had not, since beginning the course, had so much time to fill with no outside aid. Above all the prospect of providing food seemed entirely repugnant. She bought fruit and a bottle of Beaujolais, a camembert, a French loaf, and some *pâté*. The smell of the camembert in the room disgusted her and she threw it away. The loaf she could only imagine as it would be on the third day – stale. The wine she suspected would prove as nasty as it was cheap. The *pâté*, so reminiscent of the Dordogne on the Soho counter, looked only greasy in her room. The fruit alone seemed edible.

The day before Christmas Eve Lady Pirie rang up and said in her gruffest voice that she supposed Meg was going to her brother's; no? then Tom would come round the next evening and fetch her in that terrible old car of his. There was no need to pack an evening dress since they would be very quiet over the holiday.

When Meg demurred, she said, 'You don't suppose you're going to stay in that room by yourself, do you? You can cut your old friends off as much as you like at ordinary times, but Christmas is Christmas. And those are orders.' Meg accepted them.

As Viola Pirie had said, they 'were very quiet'. Meg wondered in how many English homes Christmas festivity had now shrunk to this skeleton caricature of its old fat family self. Not that she had ever known the days of game pies and brandy snap and the old bachelor family solicitor pulling crackers with the spinster aunt, of which her mother had always spoken so nostalgically when serving the only turkey she could find small enough for their oven at the sad little Christmas dinners of David's and her own childhood. Such Edwardian and Victorian lavishness, however, had always been part of her myth of happy childhood to set against their own 'learning to be pleased with quite simple little presents'.

Now, at Lady Pirie's, the faded little festivity suited her well. The 'spare' room turned out to be comfortable and without the slightly stuffy 'snugness' that somehow hung round the rest of the flat. More light came into it than into the other rooms; it was not encumbered with photographs, and with the offerings of primitive utensils and basketware and weapons made to Sir Herbert by grateful islanders, as was the drawing room. It was, as Viola Pirie had claimed, a bed-sitting room, with a pretty walnut bureau, two harmless neutral covered armchairs, and few ornaments. Two Lowestoft plates adorned the chimney piece. Meg supposed that they were the pieces Viola Pirie had so often said would particularly interest her. No doubt she had kindly put them there for Meg's benefit. Meg normally scorned Lowestoft, but she realized that she was pleased to see any tolerable pieces of porcelain again. She was able to work or read in such a room; and no one seemed to mind her being on her own.

When they sat together Viola rambled on about this or that – the Island days, the governesses she had known, the wrongness of the Church in refusing to remarry the innocent divorced, Aid to the Elderly, Tom's childhood, the wickedness of a woman she had once known who had refused her husband his conjugal rights, the girl at Barker's provision counter who managed so splendidly despite the loss of her leg in the bombing, and Sir Herbert's lovable if difficult fads about home-made jam. It was, Meg thought, as soothing as a purring cat or a kettle singing on the hob.

On Christmas morning Viola went to church. Tom looked more deathly than ever in a yellow dressing gown. However, he was in high spirits. He had met a man the evening before who might be very useful to him.

'I was saying,' he told Meg, 'that most of us were pretty sick of all this stuff about the Angry Young Men. I mean most of my genera-tion. As a matter of fact as I was telling him you don't have to have been to a grammar school or whatever to have ideas. A lot of the people who went to public schools have got quite a few ideas about how things ought to be. And this fellow turned out to be a free-lance writer who's published a good deal of stuff all over the place. He said I ought to make some articles out of it. He's pretty certain he could get them placed, so long as we can find a gimmick and a good title. He suggested "The Real Young Men", but I don't think that's got what I want. I thought something more like "We *don't* make news".' He looked a little sad when the title came home to him in all its flat-ness; nor was he elated by Meg's asking after the play.

'I've put it in cold storage,' he said. 'I don't think there'd have been much difficulty in getting a management to take it. Technically it has what it takes. But that was part of the trouble. It was in danger of being slick. I was probably covering up for a certain immaturity.' He seemed to recover his spirits as he analysed its defects. 'There's nothing against an immature work in itself, of course. As long as it's faced. That's why I've started this novel. It's frankly autobiographical as one's first work's bound to be. I've been running away from that, of course. But if I don't get a lot of personal stuff off my chest I shall never get started. Anyway some of the best novels are autobiographical. The only snag is libel.' He looked very shrewd. 'But I shall show it to a lawyer, of course. Templeton or one of these fellows.'

Meg was surprised to hear that Tom, too, was now familiar with Donald. He read the first chapter. It began, 'At that time I still believed in the One and Only Girl. Irene changed all that for me. She'd been around a good deal more than most of our set realized. She only wanted one thing, but she wanted it pretty badly. When she dropped me I was hurt pretty hard. She was a bitch, I suppose. But I'm grateful to her. She taught me a lesson I needed to learn. After that it was hello and good-bye.'

When he had read for a while, Meg suggested that she should read the rest at her leisure.

'Did you ever know anyone called Irene?' she asked.

'Oh, the names had to be changed, of course,' he said rather grandly. 'It's frightfully good of you to take an interest.'

She had really enjoyed herself for a few minutes giggling at him, but now, a little conscience-stricken, she said, 'I wish I could be of any use.'

'Oh, you are,' he said. 'It makes a lot of difference having you around. I wish you'd come here more often. Mother gets on my tits a bit when we're on our own.'

His manner was a little patronizing, Meg thought, and the smile he gave, instead of appearing gallant as she supposed he intended, was a most unpleasant leer. She couldn't remember his having used words like 'tits' to her before either. I suppose it's what people call 'deteriorating' – too much Irene, she thought and giggled to herself. She felt unusually relaxed.

Indeed the days passed pleasantly enough. Lady Pirie and her son bickered now and again, especially on Boxing Day and the Sunday that followed. The excess of rich food and the more than usual drink produced the usual indigestion; and the rainy weather prevented any exercise to counteract it. Tom was untidy and clumsy; he left litter of newspapers everywhere and knocked over full ashtrays. He had promised to mend a cupboard catch and to take a parcel to an old nurse on

Boxing Day. He did neither. 'I have my methods,' he said, 'I'll get round to it.' 'Not to worry,' he always said.

Viola most of the time was gruffly amiable with him, but her excessive devotion sometimes allowed the gruffness to emerge too tenderly. Sometimes on the other hand the gruffness hardly disguised an angry bark. She had the habit of what Tom called 'picking on' things that he said. 'Not to worry' clearly worried her a good deal. 'Not to worry!' she would exclaim. 'Why don't you say "don't worry" like anyone else?'

At last Meg said, 'I think it's the new catchphrase, Viola.'

After that Lady Pirie always gave a little laugh when she heard it. 'Oh, so that's the new phrase,' she said, and a little twitch of annoyance jerked her cheek.

At times Meg noticed each of them watching the other to see if their snapping had thrust home. Once Tom burst out, 'Oh, for Christ's sake, shut up, Mummy.' On the whole though the bickering was intermittent and on a very simmering level.

Meg was surprised to find how little their love–hate tussles disturbed her. She had rested so long from human contacts that she felt quite withdrawn. When both Viola and Tom said that her presence had eased the atmosphere she felt pleased.

On Boxing night seven or eight people came in for drinks after dinner. Meg heard without interest that morning that there was to be a party, but as the day went on she felt unaccountably depressed and even, by the afternoon, tense with anxiety. She told herself that the dull pain in her stomach was Boxing Day indigestion, but she knew it was alarm. It was only when Viola tactlessly said, 'I'm afraid it won't be up to the standard of your parties' and then blushed, that Meg remembered that this would be her first after-dinner party since the last night at Lord North Street. She realized suddenly that she had firmly linked her anxieties that evening with Bill's death; and with this realization came the knowledge that somewhere beneath the rational chain of events leading up to Srem Panh lay a whole irrational history whose hold upon her was no less powerful. Who could say which was valid? The thought occurred to her that at any rate the irrational could not make the awful demands upon her conscience that she had suffered in these last weeks. She knew that some censor should act to repress such a frivolity; but it didn't. In a quite foolish, giggling mood she heard the first guests arrive.

It was just as well, for the party threatened to be a sad, tepid little affair. Most of the guests were friends of Viola's, people whom she had known in the colonial days; people of Sir Herbert's age, retired now and doing odd jobs to make ends meet. They knew that the world was not interested in what they *had* done, and *they* were not much interested in what they were doing now. Much of the conversation was about the old days in the Islands. A retired admiral talked to Meg a little about the coaching work he now did at a well-known crammers'; Viola brought up a rather silly widow of a planter who was considered to be rather dashing because she did film-extra work and modelling; a fat man talked to her about hypnotism as a cure for smoking. It was a measure of their dimness that they all considered Viola with her downright manner a 'tremendous character'. Almost everyone was twenty years older than Meg and forty years older than Tom. One old woman had brought her granddaughters. The elder of these, a rather pretty blonde of about twenty with a hard, aggressive manner, engaged Tom in argument. 'I think that's a pretty poisonous point of view,' she said loudly, and again later, 'Well, it's lucky some of us have a slightly less feeble attitude to things.'

It was obvious, however, rather to Meg's surprise, that the girl was very attracted by Tom. She kept edging towards him as she was talking and her hard laugh had a sexy, edgy note. Her sister, a tall, rather fat girl with dark hair, whose cheeks burned more crimson as the evening went on, only giggled. Once she turned to Meg and said with pride, 'They're at it again. Vanessa's on the warpath this evening.' Meg hoped for a moment that the remark had a double meaning; but it wasn't so. Tom was clearly very pleased with himself.

The only event that disturbed Meg's apathy was the sudden arrival of Donald Templeton. He recalled too closely the Lord North Street party. She also thought it embarrassing that since nobody else was in evening dress he should have chosen to come in a dinner jacket with a crimson, embroidered silk waistcoat. His ebullient manner seemed far less tinged with nervousness than at any time she had known him. She could hear his laugh braying out heartily over the little room and always a second later the laughter of the person he was talking to. He laughs at his own jokes, she thought, I've noticed that before but, of course, that's one of the things I don't care for; all the same the others were following up with genuine laughter. Indeed he was clearly a great success. He seemed to be giving them a sort of cultural travel guide.

'Stay at the small hotel on the hill,' he was drawling, 'and ask for the *truite gelée*. Don't let them persuade you into having any of their vintage wines. What? The local red is a very good simple table wine. The church is passable Romanesque, but nothing more. You'll have seen quite enough Romanesque by then anyway. But take a look at the crypt. Don't be put off by the old chap that shows you round. And don't listen to a word he says either. You *read* French, I suppose. Well, for once there's a good local guide. There's a small *librairie* where you can buy it. Just opposite the Café de l'Univers, as I remember. Most of the cafés there stake this universal claim, what? The point of the crypt is the Carolingian stone carvings. They're not beautiful, of course, but you won't see anything else like them, what?' He seemed almost to be shouting in anger now against some imagined opposition. 'And go out to Rémy les Asiles,' he cried. 'It's five miles of very bad road but there's a fourteenth-century Tree of Jesse – a very well preserved bit of painting – that's not to be sneered at. You're going in July? Well, get them to give you a thing they make with fresh raspberries and a very decent local sweet white wine to go with it. Don't fuss with the crayfish, you'll get them better and cheaper farther south. What?'

Amid this dogmatic, assertive speech, unfamiliar to Meg, the interrogatives seemed more affectedly irrelevant than ever. And what a wine and food carry on! she thought. She realized suddenly that the party had formed into two groups – one around Donald and a smaller one around Tom. She was left alone. For a moment she was annoyed. Then her old social sense returned to her. This shut-off, quizzing attitude was too like some embittered old maid compensating with 'Jane Austen sense of humour'. In any case, why should she sneer at Donald? She liked European travel, food, wine, buildings as much as another. To call the voicing of that taste 'wine and food snobbery' was simply to fear committal. And as to his patronizing the company, there was no evidence that they felt it to be condescension. It was only a measure, really, of her own estimation of them; Donald was less intolerant, that was all. She was about to make herself join his circle, when Viola Pirie touched Donald's arm and indicated her isolation with a glance. She had paid the price then, Donald was to be 'nice' to her.

And in truth she had to admit that he did all he could to be nice. He sat with her on the sofa and told her of Bill's conduct of many of his cases. His admiration for Bill was complete and sincere. As the stories progressed Meg listened fascinatedly; to hear anything of Bill that she did not know was to increase the living part of her, to add, if only secondhand, to the stock of memories which she was building up as a counterweight to the dead routine life that was to be hers in the future. But as Donald ended one of the stories, she suddenly felt a distaste for hearing any more. She did not want to know things about Bill from other people, things in which she had not participated, especially not from Donald. She sought some means of bringing the conversation to an end; but she felt that she could not do so without a gesture of friendliness in response to his, something that did not commit her to seeing him again soon or often.

She said, 'One thing I didn't mention, Donald, about my affairs, if you'll forgive my bringing them up. Mr Marriot, the consul at Srem Panh, started to talk to me about compensation from the Badai government. I shut him up. At the time I couldn't bear to hear about it. As though there could be any compensation for what had happened! I still feel that, but I do realize that I oughtn't to refuse any money I can get. I don't think I could bear to handle the thing myself. Do you think you could do it for me? I expect the Foreign Office have gone ahead even though I said not to do so. I *don't* want it if there's to be any publicity or fuss. But I know you'll handle it tactfully.'

He seemed a little surprised, she thought, although he promised to do all he could. The subject of the compensation had occurred to her quite without premeditation; it seemed a polite means of disengagement. If, as she now saw, it marked him off as a business adviser rather than a friend, she could only welcome the chance result.

She got up and began to circulate among Viola's friends. She found that the deadness she had sensed at the beginning of the party had gone – thanks perhaps to Donald – but, benefiting by it, she was soon amusing and entertaining them at the top of her form; a good deal less noisily, she could not help reflecting, than Donald. After the guests had left Viola Pirie said, 'You're wonderful with people, Meg. Thank you. I thought it was going to be very sticky.'

Meg wondered at her own motives. Had it merely been pique at finding herself for a moment a wallflower? Had she wanted to put Donald's nose out of joint? Or was the desire to be 'good socially' – the desire that she had placed at the head of that list of follies with which she had spoiled Bill's happiness – so naturally strong in her? The lightheaded frivolity which she had felt during the evening was not routed by these questions, she could not answer them and she didn't care. Instead she found herself giggling at something Tom said.

'That Cynthia Robertson's a bit nympho,' he announced in worldly tones. Meg had to go out of the room, it struck her as so funny that he should want to lessen the value of his conquest by attributing it to nymphomania. She could hear Viola saying, 'Now, Tom, you really shouldn't. You've shocked Meg'; and she could only laugh the more.

The next day Viola said, 'You've got a wonderful friend in Donald Templeton, Meg.'

Even this did not really annoy her. She said only, 'He was Bill's friend.'

On the Sunday evening she returned to her room. The visit had not proved as irksome as she had feared; although when Viola said, 'I shall have to let that room soon, Meg. Why don't you come here as my lodger? You can see now how independent you would be,' she thought, 'Not for more than three days, thank you.' She looked at the dead anonymity of her own bed-sitting room with considerable relief.

About a week later Meg caught a very bad cold. She hardly knew how to get through the afternoon classes. This was a time in any case when, after absorbing the first shorthand lessons very rapidly, she seemed suddenly to have fallen behind the younger students. She longed for a memory that was not so over-stuffed with the irrelevant minutiae of forty-three years. Miss Dacres, the shorthand teacher, drew her aside in the passage and told her not to worry. 'There always comes a period of mental blockage,' she said, 'after the first week or two. If you've started to learn when you're older, I mean.' The intention was kindly but Meg was only the more depressed. She had obviously shown her anxiety which she had no wish to do; and to be comforted by 'teacher' – especially when 'teacher' was ten years younger than herself – annoyed her.

She gave up in the middle of a shivery walk by the Serpentine that evening; it was dark, with a cold east wind too harsh to permit even a gentle melancholy. How anyone could be invited to easeful death by that black, freezing water is beyond me, she thought; at any rate, I'm no suicide.

The melancholy chill of her room gave quite other thoughts. She made herself a cup of tea but it seemed thick and bitter in her mouth. She took three Disprins and went to bed. The blankets were inadequate, the water bottle burned her feet and then, as she lay awake so long, turned toad cold to her feet. 'Cold as paddocks' – she repeated the phrase, which had always before had an archaic charm but it failed to exorcise her thoughts. Lonely old women in their hundreds went through her mind – old women smiling inanely from frightened, timid eyes; old women leering crazily from clownish painted faces; old women smiling and nodding, with cracked shoes and skirts done up with safety pins; square faced, bobbed haired old fighters for women's rights reduced to depressive silence; and bird eyed, gaunt old socialite women (Meg Eliots these) chattering their manic nonsense.

The disgust that this fever of self pity aroused in her gave no assuagement, for the circle revolved endlessly in her mind. She tried to think of all the useful, cheerful, self-dependent old women who had conquered poverty and loneliness, but they could find no place in the crushing ranks of the defeated old women that crowded into her memory. She tried to efface the particular in the general and a voice, clear, detached, a little pompous – the voice of the BBC Question Master – gave the answer. 'The panel have been set the following problem. You are in charge of a lifeboat. A liner is sinking. There are only two more places that can be offered. You must make the agonizing choice of saving these two from among a number. The possible candidates are a young girl engaged to be married, her fiancé a brilliant young atomic scientist, a famous ballerina, a mother and her fourteen-year-old son, an elderly woman once famous as a beauty and a society hostess, a surgeon, a stevedore ... Well,' the voice continued almost cheerfully, 'I think the panel have little difficulty in their first elimination. The elderly woman after all has had her life, she has no one who depends on her, she is not frankly going to be of much use to the world ...' Commissars scratched out the names of old women from the lists of those worthy of bread tickets, even humanitarians averted their eyes from old Jewesses packed into cattle trucks, steeling themselves to think rather of the children and of the active.

Meg fought the hysteria desperately. I am forty-three, I am strong, I am not stupid or cowardly, I have humour and experience on my side, a new life can begin for me. Barren, spoilt, ignorant of the world around you – a world that has no place or use for you. It is my intention (and I'm fully aware that the whole of this dialogue is absurd and humourless) but it is my intention to learn about this world (if the whole business about my not knowing it isn't itself a hysterical mystique born of a chance tragic happening) to learn about it and make myself useful. But, as her will seemed to be conquering her hysteria, the dialogue changed. You pity yourself because you think you have a *right* to a better life; it's worse for you because you weren't expecting it, it's unfair because you didn't know it was coming; all the old women who haunt you have been comfortable, rich, beautiful, spoilt, that's all you pity in them. The voice seemed to jeer, to mimic her mother's voice – I don't care what you say, it's worse for women who had been brought up as ladies. She answered, declaring all her hatred of her mother's view, protesting all she had done for the old working women in Aid to the Elderly. I'm lucky, she said, I know it – at least I've had something, they've always been poor. But the voice said, You *do* think it's worse, it *is* worse, isn't it? It's degrading. It's a hateful world that has no place for you.

On the superficial level of her mind she tried to ignore the whole, sordid hysteric struggle, told herself that it was the fever, lay on this side and on that, turned the pillow over, tucked up her legs, stretched them; and at last fell into a sleep where the dialogue assumed more active nightmare forms.

She woke in the night once, crying; and then in the morning, with the fever gone, but sneezing and streaming from the eyes. The anonymity of her room now told against her. The house was one of five converted into bed-sitters – there was no resident proprietress, even the housekeeper lived two houses away. The maid did not appear until eleven; she was Latvian and not very bright, but she promised to phone to Miss Corrigan and to make some few purchases for Meg. Instead of the sponge cakes and grapes that Meg had asked for she brought macaroons and some very shiny, red, soft Australian apples; she had understood 'eggs', but what she might have said to Miss Corrigan Meg dreaded to think. She made some tea for Meg, and then, suddenly darting across to the bed where Meg was eyeing the macaroons doubtfully, she thrust one of them into the cup of tea and held it out. 'This is good,' she said. The episode restored Meg's spirits a little, but she spent a miserable day between the bed and the electric fire that roasted her feet and left her body a target for the numerous draughts.

The next day she went to the Garsington and braved the doubtful looks of the others at her anti-social sneezing and coughing. That evening she rang up Viola Pirie and asked if she could rent the bed-sitting room. Whether it was her weaker, hysteric side that had broken down at the first real discomfort or whether it was her stronger, rational side that had recognized the end of one phase and the need to embark on another, she really could not tell. She had reached the limit of self-examination where the answers seemed to be no more than arbitrary choice. She only knew that she feared to be alone any longer.

The first weeks at Viola Pirie's passed easily, soothingly. The pattern of Viola Pirie's life unfolded before her but it impinged on her own very little. Viola's days were spent, it seemed, in a continuous, exhausting round of benevolent activity. There was no end to the charities, private or public, in which she was involved. She was also an ardent Conservative party worker and concerned in some parish activity for St Mary Abbots' which Meg never really comprehended. None of her daily work, however, was allowed to delay by a minute her return home to prepare and cook dinner for Tom and Meg. When Meg asked to help with the washing-up, she demurred. 'You must stay and talk to Tom,' she said, but Tom was busy with his novel, so in the end she agreed.

In the first three weeks Tom returned rather late. He was now in partnership it seemed, with a friend who was opening a combined paint and carpentry shop to assist the 'do it yourself' householder.

'The point,' Tom explained, 'about all this do it yourself stuff is that nobody has the faintest idea how to go about it. And we shall advise as well as sell the materials.'

Meg's friends had not included a lot of people who 'did it themselves', even so she had an idea that this sort of shop was not entirely new. However, Tom spoke of it as a money spinning novel scheme; Viola was delighted; who was she to question it? After a week or so the partnership seemed to peter out and Tom found that the novel required all his time.

'I'm not,' he said, 'giving the thing a chance to live. Once I've got this thing off my chest, I shall look out for a *real* job. Anything I do while my mind's on the book I do half cock and I'm not prepared to work like that. Of course it may be a best seller,' he added, 'although one can't count on it, because the first book's always a gamble.'

Meg suggested that the gamble was rather a wild one. Viola looked worried. But Tom told them of a friend of his, with capital behind him, who was setting up in publishing simply to give new writers a market. 'And he's not the sort of man to throw money away. He may tell us that he's doing it for art but if he publishes anything it'll have every chance of being a money spinner. As good a chance as any first book can, which is all I ask.' His mother's anxiety seemed to vanish at this news. Meg thought it best to say nothing more at the time, but later she voiced her doubts to Viola when they were alone.

'Oh, I don't think we can say too much about it,' Viola said. 'These young men have their own ways of doing things, haven't they?'

Tom, it seemed to Meg, had his own way of doing nothing. She had not minded his giving no hand to the washing-up when he was working in the day, but now it annoyed her. Once again she decided not to provoke a direct battle, but one evening after dinner as they were arguing about emigration – when Tom felt depressed, Meg noticed, he always spoke of emigrating, 'all the cream of my generation have had it here' – she told him that he must follow her into the kitchen if he wanted to talk to her. Viola looked bewildered at Tom's appearance there, but Meg handed him a plate.

'You can dry that while you're talking,' she said.

Soon he was happily stacking plates and glasses, explaining all the while that it was exactly this sort of thing that made life impossible for people who wanted to get anywhere. The next night Viola Pirie said, 'You two stop here and talk, Tom isn't to wash up.'

Meg protested, 'Dear God, Viola,' she said, 'he's got a pair of hands.'

But the expression that Viola so liked to hear from Meg caused no amusement this time.

'I'm sorry, Meg,' she said, 'I don't like to see men doing women's work.' She was both determined and angry.

The same pattern of relationship emerged when Meg suggested cooking some of the meals. At first she thought that Viola's refusal stemmed from pride in her own good but plain cooking; but when one evening, in her enforced absence at a Mothers' Union outing to a musical comedy – 'there's no way of getting out of it without offence' – Meg cooked a risotto and Tom enjoyed it, everything was changed. Viola would have handed over the cooking entirely, if Meg had not been firm. From then on they cooked on alternate nights. Viola's devotion to Tom seemed curiously without jealousy. She did not mind his preferences for Meg's dishes – a preference simply due to boredom with his mother's repertoire – indeed she went into pantomimes of delight at everything Meg served, partly to encourage her to do more, partly out of pure pleasure at Tom's satisfaction.

This spoiling of her son, Meg soon saw, was only an exaggeration of Viola's general high regard for men. Despite the genuine humility that made her take on everyone's cares without regard for herself, she was, as Meg knew from Aid to the Elderly, very decided in her views and often quite ruthless in getting her own way. The women she worked with she regarded as fools and did not hesitate to tell them so. Some few were excepted because they were younger and had a full life. 'It was so splendid of them to take on committee work.' Meg, with her Lord North Street life, had been one of these. It was not a matter of snobbery, however, for there was for example young Mrs Martin. 'She looks after a husband and four children, Meg, *and* runs a sweet shop. I wasn't going to have all the old tabbies bossing her around just because she isn't what they call "our class". I think somebody like that is absolutely splendid. I *always* vote with her at meetings.' To a few women, then, she gave way. To only a very few men she did not – men like Mr Purdyke, who acquiesced too much and so earned the title 'an old woman', or subordinates like Mr Darlington who could only be 'given their heads' to a limited extent; but from Sir Oliver Lacey, the chairman of the Child Care Committee, or from Colonel Randolph, the Youth Club governor, or, for that matter, from Mr Marcus, the tailor who was on the Prisoners' Aid Committee, she accepted anything they chose to tell her. 'Men know what they're talking about, you see,' she taid. It was, Meg felt, a sad mischance that Viola should have a son who so evidently contradicted this rule.

The tension between mother and son was too endemic ever to break out fiercely, though the restraining influence of Meg's presence upon their bickering grew less as time passed, especially upon Tom's. Yet, for Meg, life in the little flat remained quiet and restful: they made no demands upon her support except in assuring her that her presence was helpful, they never intruded upon her privacy, and if Tom did not make any practical additions to his mother's care for their visitor's comfort he eased her sense of loneliness by his evident admiration for her.

She was still putting most of her life into her work and had caught up again in her classes as Miss Dacres had predicted, but she found that, freed from the depression of the bed-sitting room life, she could read or go out on a few evenings in the week without falling behind in the lessons. She started on a re-reading of Proust; she saw Poll a few times and found the fun she got out of her company worth the squalor of her King's Road flat and the hangover she inevitably suffered the next day; she dined a few times with Jill and appreciated Viola's virtues the more.

They were both, she found, a little jealous of her living at the Piries'. Poll said, 'I shouldn't think it would last, should you?' Jill asked every detail of the Pirie budgeting. 'Lady Pirie can't really live on her pension,' she said with a little laugh at Meg's ignorance of the current cost of living. 'People seldom tell one all their means. Of course, she's doing quite well out of you. But you're probably wise to put comfort before economy while you're still doing this course.'

Life, on the whole, would have been quite tolerable if she had not ached so much for Bill's presence. All her distress and guilt about their life together had now fallen away, to be replaced by a simple, but almost continual physical aching to hear his voice or to feel his arms round her again. She thought of Jill's declaration that Andrew was always with her; she could only believe now that such feelings were deceptions, or that those who claimed them asked less than she did. Bill was somewhere in her mind always; and memories of all kinds, happy, sad, and sad-happy, were often so intense that in them she lived with him again. But he was not *with* her, she knew now that he never again would be and no memories could compensate for that. She wondered at times if she could have reconciled herself more easily if the tearing apart had not been so sudden. She no longer believed that such time would have allowed her to atone for anything; but at least she might have grown used to the idea of losing him. David's letters, that came now each week instead of telephone calls, showed such resignation to the loss of his friend; and although she could not find it possible to compare his attachment to Gordon to her own love for Bill, she knew that he was deeply attached and she had to envy and admire his powers of resignation.

Then suddenly there came a letter from David that blew her out of her self-centred bolt-hole. His resignation had broken down before Gordon's suffering. It was an incoherent letter of anger that zigzagged across the writing paper like random flashes of lightning. He accused his own carefully built up detachment of being only a self-induced blindness to the Evil that governed the Universe. He railed against the childish conceit that had let him suppose his own will and reason to be meaningful in the logic of nightmare. 'God forgive me for prating about humanism, pretending that pain and evil could be reduced to a pigmy human stature.' He equally fiercely attacked the monstrous Christianity that forbade Gordon the right to suicide, and the wicked idea of a good God and His gift of an Immortal Soul that added the humiliation of patience to Gordon's suffering. 'When I was in the Friends' Ambulance Unit in Libya I was praised, heaven help me, for my detachment in face of the worst cases, before hopeless, screaming, dying men. A stoic dignity! What right has anyone to dignity in such circumstances! It's disgusting even to consider such a triviality.'

A letter followed almost immediately asking her not to read 'the stupid letter I sent this morning. I have no excuse to offer but the strain of seeing someone I love dearly in agony and of having nothing to give him but the decency of silence.'

She was shocked by the unexpected hysteria of the first letter; and then moved to tears. The fact that its cry had gone out to her only as a name to write to, without any real personal contact, made her ashamed of how little she had let herself become for him. All she could do, she thought, was to try to satisfy the piteous demand for love that underlay this letter. She wrote without reference to what he had said, recalling incidents of their past together, of all that she had received from him when she was a girl, evoking as far as she was able the atmosphere of their childhood. I have never said all this before, she thought, because I've feared to be insincere. It seemed to her now that this sincerity she made so much of in herself and in others – David, Jill, Viola, Poll – was a gagging of their love. Do I *mean* it? Do they need it was a better question. At least let me seek for the words, she decided, and with them I may discover my emotions.

In this mood she sought a more positive relationship with the Piries. The result with Viola was oddly unexpected; she interpreted Meg's greater interest in the affairs of the household, her questions about Sir Herbert and the Island social life, her concern for Tom's future, simply as a sign that the first shock of Bill's death was over, that Meg was ready for a return to life. Little dinner parties were arranged, Sunday luncheons and Saturday tea parties were held. It was a mark of Viola's unselfishness that her sole reaction to Meg's concern for her was a demonstration of her own concern for Meg, or was it possibly too a mark of her reticence? Meg could not tell. She only knew that this rather futile social round was not what she had sought.

It would not have been irksome, however, if Viola had not decided to kill two birds with one stone and succour Donald Templeton's loneliness at the same time as Meg's. This was too much. Meg had carefully conducted all her own financial business – getting Mrs Copeman to leave, selling the house, selling the porcelain – expressly to avoid being beholden to Donald as executor; and, she thought, she had done the job pretty well. Donald, however, whether from professional pique or from masculine vanity, professed the view that she had been cheated, and Viola accepted his opinion obediently. They clucked away together about the profits she had missed. When he was not clucking, Donald made constant efforts to entertain her, urged on, Meg imagined, by Viola.

She was prepared to believe now that her distaste for him was due to jealousy of his friendship with Bill, that it had always been so. She could not *feel* any jealousy, could not remember ever having done so, but she snatched at any motive to explain her wish not to be with him that was deep seated enough not to be easily eradicated. If she declared her feeling to be simply dislike, as she half suspected it was, she would feel the need to conquer it. If it were a complicated jealousy, she could believe *that* too late to cure. She had, after all, involved herself further than she felt true to her feelings by asking him to deal with the compensation. To go further still in order not to hurt his or Viola's feelings would only involve her eventually in more ruthless behaviour. The compensation, he reported he was keeping an eye on, but it seemed luckily that there was little he could do; the Foreign Office had it in hand and they, in turn, waited on a Badai government anxious not to aggravate a current wave of anti-Western sentiment. The menacing world, here at least, had saved her from having to be too grateful to Donald; she would be wrong to put herself in a similar position again.

She managed at first to be pleasant and yet to avoid him at Viola's little surprise parties, but it grew increasingly more difficult to do so. In his turn he seemed to be surprised at the stream of invitations he was receiving and he gobbled his 'Whats?' like a harassed turkey being driven to Christmas slaughter. His respect for Lady Pirie, however, was as great as hers for him and he obeyed her summonses. At last Meg decided to help both herself and him by picking on arguments with him, each time, that were near enough to a quarrel to bring home their relationship even to Viola's myopia.

Viola's only reaction was to treat them as a sort of Beatrice and Benedick. Such rose-coloured obstinacy opened Meg's eyes: she should have guessed that, with her gruffness and her sentimental heart, her friend was likely to be a Mrs Jennings, a matchmaker. Now she managed to be out whenever she knew that Donald was coming.

This was the easier because she had decided that if she could help to free the Pirie impasse at all it would be through Tom rather than through his mother. She had few illusions about him, less now that she had lived in their flat. In the past she had thought him a not very bright young man trying to think for himself in reaction against a

Philistine background. Twenty-four, she had thought, was late to be so conventional a 'rebel' son, but he would come through the phase and settle down as a rather uninspiring, well-meaning young business man with the saving, if commonplace, grace of having once tried to be different. Now she saw that his opinions were secondhand, picked up from the last 'interesting man' or 'rather unusual fellow' that he'd met at some pub or club or coffee bar; and these unusual and interesting people themselves seemed seldom to pronounce more profoundly than the popular papers reporting the views of the younger generation. His natural intelligence was probably low enough, but it was further befogged and retarded by his emotional immaturity. He was spoilt, selfish – and yet engaging, not by any design, but by nature.

Remembering her lesson with Mr Darlington, she hesitated to attribute his charm to his sense of humour – in any case he only possessed more humour than one would have expected from him, which did not mean a great deal. She felt sure that she liked him not *only* because he admired her – his admiration, though soothing at first, was becoming progressively more annoying. Other people liked him too, although they clearly thought him absurd; it was probably because he was so friendly and, for all his conceit, trusting. She saw little hope of his ever becoming anything positively good; but great danger – especially when, with Viola's death, all his props had gone – of his becoming something positively bad – a dreary, fifth rate, 'minor public school type' crook. If on no other ground – and she had her affection and gratitude to Viola to consider – she ought to do everything she could to help any human being in such a predicament. If she could take over some of his mother's propping she could perhaps ease him along a little to find some perch, however insecure and at however low a level; and she was, at any rate, an attachment – a mother substitute, if she had to use such terms – without strong emotional strings.

Well aware of the comic aspect of the psycho-analytic role she was assuming, she felt safe to pursue it so long as she kept the absurdity well in mind, referring to her friendship always to herself as 'the transference'. The disgust at her own self-absorption, which David's letter had aroused in her, welcomed any opportunity for an active helpful relationship that demanded some unselfishness.

She went to the movies with him, to pubs, to his chosen coffee bar and to a terrible little club near South Kensington Station. She met his friends; they were, as he said, 'a pretty fair mixture of types'. She met duffle coats, jeans, a few absurd Robin Hood caps and very hunting jackets, and some dark suits so slept in and foodstained that they attracted her notice more than the various uniforms with which youth now advertised itself. Tom called them his friends, and indeed they were always very friendly to him; even those whom she judged to be reasonably intelligent, and therefore presumably either amused or bored by him, seemed pleased to see him; nevertheless he was always quick to tell her of each individual or group that he 'didn't see much of them now. They're rather superficial.' He was continually moving her on. 'I was getting pretty bored with that lot,' he would say as they emerged into the street. She was also introduced to numerous girls – coffee bar black jeans, saloon bar plaid jeans, art student black or grey tweedy skirts, and a few grubby smart dresses.

Tom's manner with them was diffident and leering. Again he rushed her away from them. 'God!' he would say. 'It's not their function to *talk*.' She supposed that he wished to imply that he slept with all of them, but she decided that his sexual experience was probably small, possibly non-existent.

She couldn't say that she liked or disliked his 'friends', for she seldom learned more than that they were on the fringe of various occupations – or more truly, though of course that was not necessarily their fault, unemployed. Their jobs ranged in scale of security from publishing and copy-writing, through all the creative arts (writing, painting, dancing, acting) to selling everything secondhand. In fact most of them only nominally followed their profession but were actually working as temporary clerks or temporary shop assistants or temporary post office sorters. Some were students. Others managed not to do anything at all. All of them, male and female, were younger than Tom, but few probably were so naïve. For the rest she knew nothing of them, for apart from a few of the bowler-hatted young men, and the tweed-skirted, bright-scarfed art student girls with 'nice' homes, none of them spoke to her further than absolute politeness demanded, and many not as much as that. This age segregation was something so unlike the behaviour of her own generation in their early twenties that she took some time to grasp it. When she did at last see that their ignoring of her was not due to shyness, she tried to feel an intruder.

After all, she told herself, her own generation's determination to ignore age barriers was the first blow in a battle to end the long tyranny of respect for elders. That battle was now over and youth could afford to look down on middle age. In the end, however, she decided that it was a retrograde step. Her generation had treated people as individuals, not bothering about age; these young people were returning to a seclusion as narrow as the 'secret lives' of youth in Victorian times.

She could have forgiven them if they had at least tried her out and found her failing; but they hadn't even wanted to know what sort of a person she was. She had done nothing outrageous to offend them, she had not, for example, pretended to hold the views of youth, the cardinal sin of the middle aged in her youth – she had just been herself. But they didn't care about human beings; they only wanted badges, and they weren't interested because she didn't wear their badge. It was clearly a mark of Tom's naïveté that he had taken her into the forbidden zone, but it suggested – for good or for bad, and, after seeing them, she was prepared to say 'for good' – that he did not belong there. That, no doubt, was part of his trouble. He could hardly be blamed for not wanting to live in his mother's moribund world. She remembered his censures on her own social set at the Lord North Street party. They were censures, however parrot-like in his mouth, which she now believed to have much justification. If perhaps she could find some group into which he *could* fit ... but she was hardly in her present life a useful guide.

Then one evening Poll telephoned. 'What kind of people say "guess what"?' she asked.

'I don't know. Americans perhaps.'

'Oh,' Poll paused doubtfully, then she said, 'Well *I* am saying it this evening. I've been saying it to masses of people. I tried to say it to you, only your telephone was engaged. I suppose it was that Lady Pirie using it.' There was a long pause, then Poll said rather crossly, 'Well. Go on.'

Meg said, 'I'm very pleased to hear your voice.'

'That isn't guessing.'

'I didn't know there was anything to guess.'

'That's what "guess what" means.'

'Oh, I didn't realize you were saying it to me. I don't know. You've been burgled.'

'That's a silly guess. I shouldn't be phoning lots of people, I should only be phoning the police. Anyway I don't think you say "burgled" now. That's a long time ago. Cat burglars! It's "broken into" now.'

'Well, I'm glad you haven't been broken into.'

'Are you? I'm not sure. It sounds rather nice. Anyway I'll tell, because I've heard all the boring guesses people give now. I've broken the trust.'

'Oh, Poll, how wonderful! How did you manage it?'

'Well, I didn't really *do* anything. But it seems the trust was only to go on until Teddy's youngest boy was twenty-one. And he is. But as I never see them and didn't know whether he was alive or dead, it was such a surprise that it's quite as good as if I had broken it. But the main thing was I thought I must have a party, because now that I can touch the capital I'm bound to be absolutely penniless in next to no time. At least I should think so, shouldn't you, knowing me?'

'Well, I do think it's very important, Poll, that you should have a clearer idea of what you're spending. It's so difficult if one's been used to a regular allowance, as I know myself.'

There was a long pause and then Poll said, 'Well, the party's any time from ten on.'

'When?'

'Ten.'

'No. I mean what day?'

'Now, of course.' Poll sounded quite angry and rang off.

Meg was furious to think that her moralizing might have spoilt Poll's pleasure. She had not expected any invitations for late parties; normally she would have refused them, even Poll's. They didn't fit in with her picture of her present life of hard work and regular hours. Not to go now, however, was impossible; it would only seem a continuance of her wretched priggishness over Poll's expenditure. She had not been to one of Poll's parties for years, hardly since her marriage. She knew that Poll had kept up with some of their old Art School, United Front friends of the pre-war days; she had heard that Poll's parties were 'more wild than ever' or 'much less wild' or 'not wild at all', just as she had been told that Poll was now 'a complete drunk' or 'drinking much less' or 'hardly drinking at all'. The few six o'clock parties to which she and Bill had been invited were perfectly ordinary cocktail parties, rather nice ones, with plenty of drink, Poll being very amusing, and one or two 'lion' guests – painters or writers – whom she had been interested to meet and liked sometimes more, sometimes less than she had expected. She took it that the late parties were different, largely because she and Bill had never been invited to them. Whatever they were, she thought, there was a good chance that Tom might meet people there who would satisfy his notions of Bohemia, while yet being a little less washed up and half-baked than the usual crowd he mixed with. In any case he and Poll had got on very well at the Lord North Street party.

He gave a strange little giggle when she asked him to accompany her. At one time she had taken these private laughs and smiles of his as evidence of some personal vision of life, a promise that he might in time emerge as an interesting individual who had been hidden away under a protracted adolescence; now she thought that it was just zany laughter expressing only the emptiness within.

'Sounds like we're going to get us a good party,' he said. He affected on occasion a rather feeble American accent and never appeared more feeble than when he did so. Looking at him as he drove the old car, she thought how unlikely it was that any of Poll's friends would rush to cultivate his acquaintance. She realized that she had only asked him to come with her because she was shy of going there alone. Shyness was an emotion new to her; I haven't really taken the best precaution against embarrassment, she thought, by bringing a bearded zany as an escort.

In fact Poll's little mid-nineteenth-century artisan's house was packed so tightly with people that there was really no question of being shy about anything or anybody. Meg saw nobody that she knew, but there was at any rate no danger of her appearing isolated because she was too securely wedged. It was one of those parties, she decided, where one could keep fighting one's way around the little house, listening to various conversations and always seeming to be about to join somebody else. Most of the young people – and there were a good number of them – looked like Tom's 'friends'; in fact many of them were, and Tom was soon introducing her to a small group.

One of the two young men smiled at her; the other scowled, and the girl said, 'Do you live near Guildford?'

Meg said, 'No. I don't, actually.'

The girl said, 'Oh, I thought I'd seen you there.'

Meg was pleased that someone had taken notice of her existence. She thought that perhaps a scatty sort of conversation would give an Ionesco note that they would like. She said quite untruthfully:

'I had an aunt who lived there, but she left because of the badgers.'

The scowling young man roared with laughter, but unfortunately not at Meg's crazy wit. He said, 'Ha! ha! An aunt!' He made it clear that the comic thing was to hear someone speak of an aunt.

They now ignored her. 'John says that she threw a lot of money down the loo and went on crying,' the girl said.

Tom asked, 'Is John still working on that play about the nuns?'

The scowling man said, 'Yes. But that hadn't anything to do with it.' For some reason they all laughed, but not, Meg thought, at Tom.

'They got this grandmother up to London,' the girl said. 'It was exactly what you'd expect that Mrs Freeman to do. I can't think why Ann always went on about her so. She's an awful creature. She's just the kind of person to send for the grandmother.'

'She's the one who's always in a dressing gown, isn't she? I thought she was just the landlady.' The smiling young man spoke. He was fair and anaemic.

'That's what I mean,' the girl said. 'Ann makes up stories about people being different. Just because they did the pools together! Well anyhow the grandmother's put her in this place.'

'But isn't she very rich?' the pale young man asked.

'It wouldn't make any difference,' the scowling young man said, 'she'd be only the more keen to get her own back on Ann.'

Tom asked, 'Can we write to her?'

'You *could*,' the girl answered, 'but I don't think it would be much use. Most of the time they're giving her fits.'

'It could be quite interesting if she wrote it all down as soon as the fits were over,' the scowling young man told them, 'there's a moment just as consciousness returns when formal patterns emerge without any associative values.'

Tom looked impressed. 'I don't suppose Ann'll create much from it,' he said.

'Well *I* shouldn't,' said the girl, 'if they'd been giving *me* fits. Anyway they wouldn't let her have anything sharp like a pencil.'

The pale young man said, 'I don't think any of us are very interested in all that abnormal vision stuff, Ralph.' He smiled at Meg again.

Now she thought was her chance. It was only a question of hitting the right note in order to get on with them. She knew that two strong vodkas were working within her – it was now or never. Frivolous but basically serious was surely the key.

'I must say I agree,' she said. 'All this Huxley mescalin stuff seems to me a terrible bore. Three quarters of what they say they see, one could guess at in advance.' She was pleased to join in opposing the scowling man. Gathering confidence, she said, 'The terrible thing about all breakdowns, and madness for that matter, is how frightfully comic it is to the outsider.' Their faces appeared very blank. She decided on another tack. 'All the same I hope they don't give your friend E.C.T. If it's a very expensive place they probably won't. But at the hospitals they do. They have to, really, because of the great number of cases.'

The pale young man asked, 'Can I get you another drink?'

Meg was brought up with a jolt. 'Oh, thank you,' she said, giving him her glass, but she felt an urge to carry on. 'While there are so few trained psycho-analysts,' she said, 'and analysis takes so much time and money, they're bound to use short cuts. But nevertheless E.C.T. is a disgusting business and it isn't anything but a short term measure. It simply gets people back to work.'

'I say, Simon hasn't brought that drink for your friend,' the scowling man said, 'you go and get her one, Tom. There's masses of drink,' he explained to Meg.

She thought that she had been talking too much, but, as nobody said anything, she went on. 'That's why they use E.C.T. in Soviet Russia. Wherever things are on a large scale.' She heard her voice fading out and decided that she must pep up her remarks. 'All the same I *do* think, however necessary it is, it's up to everybody to emphasize that it's only a *pis aller*.' She realized that by her vigorous tone she was appearing as an obsessed victim of shock treatment. Her audience seemed most embarrassed. 'Not that I've ever had it myself,' she said, giggling to lighten the atmosphere. Nobody giggled back.

The girl said very sternly, 'Well, I don't suppose they give it unless they have to.'

The scowling young man said, 'Neurosis is the least interesting form of evasion.'

Suddenly Meg saw the whole situation as very funny. 'What's the *most* interesting?' she asked.

The young man didn't reply, but the girl laughed and said, 'Good.' She gave Meg a friendly smile.

'Well I *have* enjoyed this talk,' Meg said. This time the young man smiled. 'And now I'll go and have another one somewhere else,' she added. The young man said, 'Good,' but his tone was not rude.

He added, 'Tom and Simon have no manners,' and again he smiled at her.

Meg fought her way to one of the tables of drink, feeling that she had been at the same time excluded and accepted. She thought all the people looked a bit scruffy and fifth rate but very nice. Poll came over to her and said, 'I shouldn't think you'd like this party very much. But let me tell you here and now that I love *every*body here.' She was glassy eyed and redder in the face than even her Dutch Doll rouge allowed for. She seemed still to be angry about the telephone conversation. She looked at Meg's black cocktail dress. 'Well, anyway, you've come dressed for slumming,' she said.

Poll was wearing the only evening dress in sight – a low-waisted beige-pink muslin dress, short and backless. Meg's mood of elation was not pierced by this rudeness. Poll was too old and plump for this return to the twenties, she thought. She said, 'Poll, the drink's lovely. It's all lovely.'

She found herself shouting it at Poll's receding back and a skeleton thin, knocked about looking, middle-aged woman with dirty black hair, absurd false eyelashes and little broken veins in her cheeks turned upon her in surprise.

'You must be one of the happy ones of life,' she said. 'I wish I was.' Then she told Meg at great length about her lover. 'He has two locks on the flat,' she said, 'mortice and Yale. And he gives me no keys. So I can't get in. I never know when he's going to get back – sometimes three, sometimes four. I used to just stand about in the passage, but then the porter got rude. I told Charles, "You're lucky that I've not been run in. *That* would look good for your precious reputation." But he never listens. So now I just go to parties and stay on and on.'

Meg said, 'He sounds like a sadist.'

'Oh yes, and a bore to boot.'

Meg had assumed an expression of sympathy, although she could not help feeling that the whole party had been staged especially for her as a comic show; at the 'to boot' however, she suppressed a hoot of laughter and spluttered her drink on the woman's dress. It seemed to make no difference.

'He wouldn't treat me like it if we were married,' the woman went on. 'And I've given him a child. Surely that's an act of trust. The poor little thing's locked up all the time. His wife's a Roman Catholic so there's no chance of divorce. And I say that's the one little bit of luck I *have* had. Think if I was tied to him for life!'

It all seemed so sad and illogical that Meg could think of nothing to say. Luckily Poll came up and said to the woman, 'Are you talking to Meg Eliot? She's one of my oldest friends and an absolute darling.' To Meg she said, 'You must forgive me, darling, I was at the rude stage. I *knew* it all right though. Doctors and people say you don't know the stage you're in, but *I* always do.' Then she took the woman away.

Meg wandered from room to room having dotty conversations with various people. She thought they were all rather ghastly – most of them seemed to be pub or club pickups of Poll's, or people these pickups had brought along with them – and when she thought of Poll and the amusing, intelligent world she had once lived in she felt rather sad. But most of the time she also thought that the people were rather enchanting as well as ghastly – at any rate for the purpose of a party – because she felt so elated and everything made her laugh so much. She knew that she was a little drunk but after a while everybody else seemed more drunk than she was. Only one conversation threatened to upset the evening. A fat, pink-haired woman, who appeared to be the manageress of Poll's local launderette, recognized her as Bill's widow.

'I don't think I shall ever get over that,' she said. 'The day I read about it. I felt proud for England when I read what he'd done. Of course, you know the circumstances as well as I do, dear; better probably. I only saw what was in the papers. But one thing I am sure of, and you can say what you like, if that had happened when we were young there'd have been a war about it.'

Meg tried hard to answer her frivolously, especially as a lot of people had gathered round them. 'Well, I'm very glad there wasn't.'

'I don't know. Might be the best thing there could be. Bring the world to its senses. But you won't get it with this lot. Anybody could invade England tomorrow and all they'd do is talk. Her husband was a hero,' she told a bald-headed, red-faced, oldish man who looked like a farmer.

To Meg's surprise he spoke in a very cissy, common voice. 'Oh, really,' he said. 'What did he do?'

The woman was indignant. 'Gone today, forgotten tomorrow. That's the world for you. If you don't remember William Eliot, thousands do. Greater love hath no man,' she said.

Meg felt so angry with her that she wanted to hit her. I mustn't do that, she thought, she's not wicked, only stupid and a bit drunk. She tried to reassure herself of this as she would have comforted a child.

'You've been through a terrible ordeal, Mrs Eliot,' the woman said. 'A lonely vigil, the newspapers said.'

Meg knew that she must stop the woman or she *would* hit her. She said, 'Please don't talk about it. I'm afraid that I shall cry.'

She had never in fact felt further from tears except those of rage.

'It wouldn't do you any harm to *have* a good cry,' the woman told her. 'I should find a room upstairs all by yourself. You don't want all this shouting and noise after what you've been through. And have a good cry.' She seemed to realize that this was hardly practical advice in view of the crowd, for she said almost fiercely. 'No. Better still, go straight home. That's right, you go straight home and cry your fill.'

Meg was surprised to find how little the incident had affected her; as soon as the woman had moved off she felt quite as elated as before. She continued to have a series of ridiculous conversations. An Indian student told her that in Calcutta the liberals were crowded twenty into a room.

'How monstrous,' she said, 'I'd no idea the Nehru regime was so tyrannical.'

It was only after the Indian had got quite angry with her that she realized that he had said 'labourers'. She refused to recede from the position.

'Economic tyranny's even worse than political,' she announced.

'I am afraid,' he said with alarming coyness, 'that you are a parlour pink. That is your privilege as a beautiful lady.'

A beery, tweedy man who said he was a newspaper cameraman, pointed out Poll to her. 'That's our hostess,' he said. 'You wouldn't think to see her pissed like she is that she's in Debrett.'

'She isn't,' Meg said, 'her father made buttons. Very successfully,' she added. She didn't want to let Poll down.

'Who told you that stuff?' he asked contemptuously. 'Everybody knows old Pollyollyoodle. You can see her any night between Oakley Street and World's End doing her round of the pubs. She's a duke's daughter. She may be *détraquée*, as they say, but she's strictly U. And she'll let you know it if she's in the mood. Pissed or not, she'll stand no nonsense.'

Some hours later, as it seemed, Meg found herself with Poll and Tom. Poll put her arms round them both.

'I like the beard,' she said. 'But I'm not sure that he likes me.'

Tom in answer embraced her very tightly and gave her a smacking kiss on the lips. Then he kissed Meg. She thought, dear God, Poll's was on the lips but he's trying to stick his tongue into my mouth. Only two people besides Bill had kissed her like that since her mar-

208

riage. She determined to consider none of the implications of this; she only hoped that her distaste for the kiss was not solely caused by the prickly beard. When Poll said, 'Mmm,' in a rather thoughtful drawl, Meg for a moment feared that she was going to be angry, but it was all right. 'I *should* have liked just the beard and me, but I shouldn't think he would have liked it, should you?' Poll said, then squeezing both of their waists she added, 'I'll just say I think you're *both* adorable people.' This vaguely benevolent sentiment sounded more like some silly American woman's than Poll's. They stood there rather foolishly. Meg thought, Poll'll have time to get angry if her attention isn't distracted. As though sent by Providence, a huge gorilla shaped man with long arms and mutton chop side whiskers pushed his way through the crowds towards them.

'Leonard darling!' Poll cried. She withdrew her arms from Meg and Tom and threw them round the gorilla man's neck.

He said, 'What a bunch of phonies! I adore you, Poll, but when I see the crowd you gather around you I think, you silly old bourgeois cow.'

Poll said, 'Whatever I am, I'm *not* bourgeois. I'd have you know I've ridden to hounds. Again *and* again.' She put a bare shoulder up to her chin and smiled like a silent film star. 'I'm a lady to my finger tips,' she said in a mock refined voice, but Meg thought, she means it, it matters to her.

The red-faced man with the common, cissy voice, said, 'Old-fashioned camp,' by way of sociological comment.

Poll said, 'I may be camp but I'm *not* bourgeois.' She was quite angry.

'You are,' said the gorilla man. 'You're as middle class as they make them.' Before she could reply he began kissing her violently.

Meg wondered whether this was what they meant by Poll's 'wild' parties, or was this one 'not so wild'? I suppose, she thought, people would say how good it was for me to have such a new experience; but it isn't really so different from some parties I went to in the thirties, only the people here, if funnier for an hour or two than more intelligent people, would become an awful bore if one saw them often. She was amused to think that Poll's invitation to her must mark a recognition of her changed status. Is it because I'm poorer? she thought, or because I'm on my own? She wondered too whether it showed an increased affection or less regard. She decided it was time to go home.

As she made her way to the basement where the coats were strewn on an old double divan bed she saw that some couples were getting down to more than embraces. She wondered for a second that the expression 'getting down to' should come into her thoughts, then realized her wish to reduce all this drunken sexual pleasure to the lowest level. She had often challenged Bill for his contempt for what he called 'kids' dirty games'.

'All right,' she had been used to say, 'it's *not* grown up. We aren't asked to the children's parties, so what does it matter? Top people take *The Times*,' she had teased him, 'but we can't all be top. Someone's got to buy *Reveille*.' She had hated to hear him censorious. But now she thought, I liked his success but I didn't want the constrained outlook that went with it. Perhaps if I hadn't driven him so, he would have been more easy going in his attitude to others; perhaps he envied them a life that the blending of all his energies towards success made impossible. She rejected the thought angrily; in whatever else he had been frustrated, his sexual passion, his ease of lovemaking had always woken an answering desire in her.

Suddenly her longing for him was so intense that she felt that her legs would give way on the staircase; sheer misery made the hall and the people crowded there shiver and scatter before her eyes. She held on to the banister. For a moment or so the thought was with her to stay at the party and get drunk – any oblivion from this loneliness. Then, horrified, she realized that, half-formed in her mind, was the image of some man, any man taking her – if she were drunk enough she could forget that it was not Bill. She ran down the stairs now, buffeting her way through the vague figures in front of her.

By the time she had found her coat she had recovered from the fright her thoughts had given her. A young couple were strained tightly against one another behind the half open door. In the corner on the floor, propped against a cupboard door, sat a dark, flushed faced man. With his points of hair, his up-slanted dark eyes and his long curling lips, he must once, Meg thought, have been handsome in a rather showy, Mephistophelean way. Now his eyes were bloodshot and a heavy blue jowl had taken the shape from his face. Leaning against his bent up knees was a thin blonde. She, too, Meg saw, must have been noted for the shapely bone structure of her head – one of the many distinguished Dietrichs of the pre-war days. Now her face seemed merely bone with the skin stretched over it. He had unzipped her dress at the back and was feeling around her breasts. Scrabbling old rat, Meg thought. But the woman seemed hardly to notice his hand. She was staring straight ahead with her deadened blue eyes and her little wrinkle-edged mouth was snapping away in talk.

'If they think I have any intention of putting myself out for anyone,' she was saying, 'they've got another guess coming. I've had my fill of helping others and you may as well know it.'

As she went up the stairs Meg determined to think no more about it all. It's not my world and that's that, she decided, but there's no point in being censorious. Then she asked herself why she was always so anxious these days not to appear priggish. It's as though I were an old virgin afraid of turning sour, she thought. I'm not going to pretend. I *don't* like a lot of public promiscuity; the middle-aged ones at any rate are ugly and squalid. She must have spoken the last thoughts aloud for a little, jolly, grey-haired Lesbian said, 'Well! *Thank* you.' Instead of apologizing or explaining, Meg found herself excusing her argument. 'I dare say it's all right at any age so long as they're really *enjoying* it.' The little Lesbian said in a slightly bitter tone, 'How very big-hearted of you.' Meg, thinking that she must be much drunker than she'd supposed, found herself at last outside in the street.

It was only then that she remembered Tom. The altruistic reasons she had found for getting him to accompany her now seemed more threadbare than ever. She wondered why she had pretended to herself without any evidence that Tom would find a more valuable set of friends by going to Poll's party. I suppose, she thought, I wanted to be of help – for 'be of help' read 'hand out patronage', she amended. 'You've got an awful lot to learn about yourself, my girl,' she said aloud. 'You're so used to knowing the "right person" that you can't believe you haven't always got the answer to everyone's needs.' But still that was that. She could only hope that he had enjoyed himself, was doing so now, would do so, because really after his kiss she couldn't suppose that he was absolutely sex shy, at any rate when he was filled up with drink. She set off to look for a taxi. Even now she found herself deciding that Tom probably never went much further than 'pawing about'. People who boast a lot of their sexual prowess are never ... She asked herself on what experience she based this long-held view – on her own behaviour, on Bill's, on the behaviour of people they knew. People of good taste are silent about their sex life. She saw it high up on a building in Piccadilly Circus flashing in and out in green and orange. What a lot of utterly tasteless prejudices of 'good taste' I've collected over the years, she thought; I *have* got a lot to learn. In any case Tom was no model of good taste. Good luck to him! She was reminded of a rather sinister, fat classical master at David's school. 'I hope he enjoys himself *to the full*,' she said, smacking her lips in imitation of the master's manner. And come to that, she thought, *I* enjoyed myself; if I couldn't take the 'wildness', well that's my affair – in any case it's not surprising if drink makes me a little hysterical at the moment, nothing to worry about. In my own way I enjoyed myself. I shouldn't want that particular way very often, but there are hundreds of other ways. I shall enjoy them all *to the full*, she said, smacking her lips again and giggling. I must be very drunk, she thought. But whatever else, it was a comfort to know that all the 'learning about herself' that lay ahead of her wasn't going to be an entirely miserable experience; a great comfort.

A motor horn sounded loudly; someone was hooting at her. Another of the things she'd been warned about years ago. Really, it seemed that life was almost too like a nice girl's guess.

It was only Tom. 'What the hell are you doing capering off like that without me?' he called. Meg thought, dear God, he's aggressive drunk; he looks so pathetic when he's trying to look tough, that absurd little beard! I must treat it all very seriously. We don't want a scene.

She said, 'I thought you were having fun, Tom, I didn't want ...'

He flung open the car door. 'Get in,' he said, cutting her short. She thought his manners really are appalling.

She said sharply, 'I never asked you to ...'

'Get in,' he shouted.

She thought it best to obey. Seated next to him, she said, 'I hope you didn't hate it all too much. Poll's collected a rather terrible crew round her. But I thought it was quite fun. At least ...'

Tom said, 'Shut up.' She looked at him in amazement; then she realized that the drink had made him not angry but randy. Dear God, she thought, some girl's turned him down and he's too drunk to remember who I am. Automatically her voice took on a maternal note. 'Tom, dear,' she said, 'watch your driving, won't you.' He immediately swerved across the road and, when she gave a scream, swerved again. He righted the car.

'Frightened?' he asked. 'Good, I like that.'

She wondered what fantastic picture of himself he had built up out of what ghastly 'tough' novels. She did not know whether to be more alarmed by the thought that he was completely drunk in charge of the car or by the growing doubt that he was not so drunk as all that. After all, he seemed in complete control of the steering, and, if so, he must be perfectly conscious of all the nonsense he was spouting at her. Spouting, indeed, was the right word, for every time he spoke, he showered her with spittle; but that proved nothing, he always spat when he spoke. She could cope with him, she felt sure, once they were back at the flat; she would have to do it soothingly because she wouldn't wish Viola to be brought on the scene; but then nor would he, unless he was much drunker than she now believed. It was in the car that she felt so powerless; she had a dread of motor smashes that the absence of traffic at that hour hardly reassured. He might try to give her one of those unpleasant bristly kisses, but it would not be difficult to avoid him so long as he continued to drive. If he put his arm round her shoulder, she would let well alone – ignore it and talk.

In fact, he put his hand up her skirt. She grasped his wrist firmly; for a moment she thought he was going to tighten his hold on her thigh, but then his fingers relaxed and he allowed her to remove his hand. She forced herself to keep silent, knowing that anything she said in her surprise and anger would sound, at any rate to her own ears, ridiculous. They drove on for a few minutes in silence. She was shivering with the suppression of her feelings. She found a cigarette. He took his lighter from his waistcoat pocket and flicking it with his left hand, gave her a light.

Then suddenly he braked and stopped the car and, turning towards her, began to pull her to him. His grasp was stronger than she could have expected; she had to exert her full force to push him away.

'Don't be a bloody fool,' he said. 'You know you want it.' His voice had taken on an artificial, virile, insolent note, yet she knew as he said it that he believed it to be true. With his hands on her shoulder blades he began to bend her back on to the seat. With difficulty she took her cigarette from her lips and deliberately brushed its lighted end against his hand.

He let out a sort of puppy's yelp. 'You cow,' he said, but he still held her with the other arm. She edged towards the car door. 'I suppose,' he said, 'I've said the wrong thing. I forget you're still so much the blasted lady. All right. *I* want it. Is *that* better?'

Fumbling for the door handle behind her, she could still register relief that he was in fact very drunk. She pushed his mouth away with her right hand, feeling his saliva on her fingers, and with the left at last twisted the door handle downwards. As the door swung open, he seemed to give up the struggle. He was, she thanked God, not drunk enough to start the car again as she was getting out.

He leaned drunkenly through the open door. 'All right,' he said. Sleep seemed to be overtaking him, for he could hardly get the words out and his eyelids kept closing involuntarily. 'All right. I'm sorry. I've behaved bloody badly. Please get in. If you've got to put me in the dirt with Mother, I shan't blame you.'

She said, 'Tom, you're too drunk to drive, and too drunk to talk to. Let me take the wheel.' For a moment she thought he was about to become angry again, but he fell across on to the passenger's seat. 'It's all yours,' he said. He was asleep in a minute.

Meg did not herself find driving all that easy – houses and lamp-posts seemed so unsteady that night. She crept along slowly and her heart pounded violently when a policeman appeared in one of the deserted Kensington streets. Bill had always driven when they returned from cocktail parties. A man and a woman were quarrelling outside High Street Kensington tube station. Their raised voices woke Tom. He smiled strangely – with self-satisfaction and ironically, she thought. Then he spoke. 'You don't know what you've missed,' he said. 'You're so bloody tightened up. Always have been. Married to an old man. You've never had a proper screwing.' Outside the dismal block of flats she left him sleeping in the car. I hope he gets run in, she thought, a spell of prison would do him no harm. She would *not* touch him now if it were needed to save him from death.

She slept as soon as she was in bed and woke at half past five with choking indigestion. She had gone to bed raging against Tom, she woke still angry with him, but her rage was turned against herself. She looked back on the past weeks with acute embarrassment; she saw herself going about with him from café to pub, acting the gracious, amusing, understanding surrogate mother, but regarded no doubt by his friends as his rather elderly next lay – no wonder that they had been embarrassed by her presence. Who knew what mission tales of releasing her from sex starvation Tom had been preaching while she had been playing the woman of the world aunt? She should have guessed at his feelings weeks ago, when first her reduced status had encouraged him to drop the odd dirty word at her, to give her what she now realized were lecherous looks. Instead with her 'friendly understanding' she had been encouraging the wretched – no, not wretched, *her* folly didn't excuse *him* – the filthy little brute. Bill had always said he was that – 'he'll get himself into trouble some time, expose himself or something'. But as Bill's voice echoed in her ears, she knew that he had been as wrong as she about Tom. Tom was neither a pathetic child nor a delinquent one; or rather he was both, but he was also, she felt sure now, a young man, who for all his inadequacy in other things, got plenty of sex of the kind he wanted. Yet even that she didn't really know; perhaps his outbreak had been the drunken release of years of repression. Whatever it was, she saw clearly now where she stood in his fantasy – the grand lady who'd been knocked off her pedestal, and it would be no comfort if some psycho-analyst were to tell her that she was only standing in for his mother in the great degradation scene.

Almost more revolting to her than the squalid, dirty dreams he'd presumably always had about her was the idea that she had ever encouraged them by appearing so untouchable, like some Victorian *grande dame*. Nevertheless what he had said of Bill was unforgivable; absurd, untrue, cheap, but still unforgivable. If somehow she could have managed the whole affair better, cut him off from the moment he made the first pass in the car, it would never have been said, she need never have heard it; and it was no excuse for her ineptitude to say that she was not used to such scenes; at her age she should have the instinctive power to put an impertinent boy in his place. Now – and the frustration of it increased her fury – she would have to find some way of tolerating his presence for a week or so until she could find a plausible excuse to give to Viola for leaving the flat.

She set off for work angry, tired, and with a headache that racked her with every step she took. In the dictation class, taken by Miss Corrigan herself, she made four stupid mistakes, and, rattled by her sudden failure, asked two questions that suggested ignorance about things she knew perfectly well. Miss Corrigan said with a little laugh, 'Not your bright day, Mrs Eliot.' Some of the girls giggled a bit spitefully; but Meg thought, I can't blame them if they dislike me, I've never really bothered with them; but then, I'm not here for that, I'm here to become an efficient secretary.

At the end of the afternoon's work Meg felt quite unable to face a return to the flat. She had heard Tom's voice, before she left that morning, grumbling at his mother when his breakfast tray was taken in to him, so that there seemed no hope of his having been arrested, or, if that was too monstrous a wish, none that he had been too shame-faced to return home. Even if he were to be out this evening, she had no relish for dining alone with Viola. She almost regretted that some little dinner party – an ex-Colonial servant and his wife, or even Donald – had not been arranged, but Viola had begun to lose heart before Meg's lack of enthusiasm. She rang up and said that she would be out to dinner.

At first she had included Poll in her anger. Now she felt that this was unfair; although she wouldn't care to be involved very often with Poll's set as she now knew it, she had enjoyed herself and it was her own fault that Tom had been there at all. She decided to ring Poll up and thank her. As soon as she was in the telephone box she realized that she wanted to tell Poll about her trouble with Tom.

When Meg declared that she had so much enjoyed the party, Poll said in her flattest, most conventional tones, 'Did you? I'm so glad.' Then she added, 'I think everyone did. It was a very *good* party.'

It was difficult to tell from Poll's voice whether she was in a bad temper; perhaps she was still angry over their previous telephone conversation, or perhaps she was piqued because Tom had only kissed her on the lips. Meg said very enthusiastically, 'Well, I *certainly* thought so.'

Poll didn't reply to this. Despite this lack of encouragement, Meg felt a desperate need to talk about the Tom situation and Poll seemed the only person she could discuss it with. She said, 'I'd like to come over to see you, Poll.'

'Yes, you must. When will you?'

'Now, if I may.'

'Oh!' There was a pause. 'I haven't got another party and there isn't any food,' Poll said dampingly.

'You must come out with me. We can go to some little place in the King's Road.'

'You do make things sound unattractive, Meg. Anyway I'll take *you*. After all I owe you some money and now the trust is broken I expect I'd better pay you. Only such a lot of people are borrowing from *me* now. Perhaps I could pay you back by taking you to lots of "little places".'

'Yes, do,' Meg said impatiently. 'I'll come round straight away.'

Sitting in the bus, Meg thought that she was making a mistake in going to Poll's. She's obviously in a stinking temper, she thought, and even if she isn't, I'm not sure it's a good thing to tell her about Tom. She realized that it was the first time that anything unpleasant had happened to her without Bill being there to comfort her. The odd thought came to her – 'except, of course, his death'. She pushed the thought away angrily. Anyway Tom's behaviour would have been embarrassing to report to Bill, he would have flown into such a rage. Yet however unwise it was to tell Poll, she knew that she would do so; she needed so much to confide in someone. I ought not to be going there, she thought. But it was too late.

Poll opened the door, holding a large glass of tomato juice in her other hand. Meg had somehow expected her to show the effects of the night before – to have pouches under her eyes or to be wearing a dirty housecoat or dressing gown. In fact she was dressed and made up exactly as usual; her face showed no sign of fatigue or hangover. Surprise added to Meg's nervousness. She said, hearing herself sound foolish, 'Tomato juice! What a good idea!'

'I don't think it would be, if it was,' Poll said. 'It's a Bloody Mary.'

Then to her horror, Meg heard herself say, 'The hair of the dog?' She couldn't think how the awful phrase had come into her head. Poll ignored it.

If she showed no effects from the night before, the house looked like Hangover Hall. Empty glasses and full ashtrays were everywhere, even on the stairs. A small space had been cleaned around the sitting room fire like an animal's nest in the undergrowth. They sat down and Meg tried not to think that vodka would further upset her digestion.

Poll said, 'You haven't said anything about the mess the house is in. It isn't always like this, you know. Mrs Taylor couldn't come in today because her mother's ill.'

Disastrously Meg said, 'How like chars.'

'Is it? Well it isn't like Mrs Taylor. Nor like her mother. She's never ill. She's a wonderful old woman. She walks all the way over Albert Bridge to bring me cakes she's made.' Poll made it sound very feudal.

Meg felt too flattened to say anything more. Perhaps Poll noticed it, for she suddenly brightened up and began a long and very lively inquest on the party. Meg could scarcely recognize the people she had met the night before as she heard about them. She had found them funny because they had been incongruously assembled and because, since they were all a bit drunk, their remarks had been absurdly inconsequential. Poll missed none of this absurdity. As they recounted the various conversations, she reiterated an expression that recalled to Meg their old art school days. 'Wasn't she a scream?' she cried. 'Or didn't that make you scream? It did me.' But she attributed other positive virtues to her guests that Meg had not found, and, as the adjectives she used were as vague as they were emphatic, it was difficult to tell exactly what these virtues were; but there was a definite implication of active merits where Meg had found only incidental entertainment.

When Meg told her of the launderette manageress's embarrassing remarks about Bill's death, she said, 'Oh, Alma! She's *too* extraordinary, isn't she? Of course having a face like that helps her to be so amusing.' Of the Indian student she said, 'I can't *think* what goes on in his head, can you? But he does it all to the manner born.' The red-faced, cissy man, it seemed, was called Hilary. 'He's one of the regulars at the Antigua. I *was* angry that he didn't bring his friend. He's marvellous anyway, of course, but he's a hundred per cent funnier when his friend's there.'

Meg didn't like to say that the newspaper photographer had told her that Poll was a duke's daughter, so she merely said, 'He thinks you're very grand.'

Poll looked vague. 'Well, I suppose he'd know,' she said. 'He's tremendously up in things.'

Meg had believed that she could always tell when Poll was speaking ironically, but in all this she sensed a certain serious estimation, or, if not that, at any rate a refusal to accept last night's crowd only as funny people who had been collected together. She wondered if perhaps Poll was very reasonably unwilling to treat them entirely as a joke because of some personal affection for them. She selected at random the lady whose lover locked her out, and said, 'She seemed a very likeable woman.'

She was snubbed for her dishonesty, however, for Poll said, 'I wouldn't know really. I don't care much about "likeable" do you? She and Garry are an awfully *mad* pair. And I don't mind, do you, as long as people are entertaining.'

As to how they had to entertain in order to win Poll's approval, Meg could get no clear answer. There was a clue, perhaps, in her attitude to the gorilla-like man, Leonard.

'*He's* not very funny,' she said, 'coming in and saying my party was full of phonies. I suppose he wants me to have all the bores here.' She named some of the people whom Meg had expected to see there. 'I don't have people here just because they're well known,' Poll said.

'But they're not as well known as all that, Poll, and they *are* old friends of yours.'

Poll looked suddenly very cross. 'Well, I *don't* have them here.

They don't mix well and they fuss about what one's doing. If the people I have here aren't good enough for you and Leonard that's your look out.'

'But I liked them very much.'

Poll's face once more took on a vaguely blissful look.

'Yes, aren't they amusing?' she said, then, as though considering, she announced, 'When one's young, Meg, it's all right to collect people. But now I'm older I like people to collect *me*.' She poured out more drinks. 'Don't let's go to that little place of yours,' she said, 'it's sure to be scampi or snails or something I couldn't eat. I'll make a delicious omelette later. With chives. Don't you love chives?' Meditatively she said, 'I shouldn't like it if Leonard *didn't* come here. He's immensely strong.' Then, 'And *you*,' she said, 'the beard was terribly put out when *you* disappeared like that.'

'I was very put out when he found me,' Meg said. A light tone would allow her to skim over it all quickly if Poll proved unsympathetic. 'He made a pass,' she said.

'Well, I suppose so,' Poll replied. 'I must say I shouldn't have minded.'

'Well, I *did*. I burned him with my cigarette.'

Poll looked surprised. 'I'm rather glad he *didn't* take to me if *that's* what he wants.'

Meg felt in danger of crying. Poll's judgement at that moment seemed of the greatest importance to her. If she thinks I've behaved stupidly I don't know what I shall do, she thought. But Poll's tone changed.

'My dear Meg, surely you haven't let the beard upset you? Anyone can see he's in a bad way about sex. You'd better tell me what happened.'

Meg told the whole story. When she repeated Tom's remark about Bill, Poll said, 'Silly little beast! Anyone could see that you and Bill had a marvellous time in bed. He *must* be in a bad way about you to have said that. Well, you mustn't go on staying there. He obviously thinks of you as the marble statue he'll bring to life with his kisses.' She gave a great raucous laugh.

Meg said, 'That's what's so awful, Poll. I'd no idea that I went about behaving like the untouchable grand lady.'

'Well, you *did* rather, dear. But I can't see why not. You didn't *want* anyone except Bill to touch you. And you could *afford* to be the grand lady.' She got up. 'I think we'd better have something to eat,' she said. As she was heating the omelette pan, she remarked, not look-ing at Meg, 'Well, you haven't to worry about all that now. Being the grand lady, I mean.' She broke the eggs into a basin. 'I must say I don't think you seem to know what you're doing.'

'I managed things very badly last night, I know.'

'Oh, I don't mean *that*. All this typing and shorthand and living at old Lady Thing's.'

'Living at Viola's obviously has been a mistake. But I can't see what you have against the secretarial course. It will get me quite a well-paid job; and if I don't let myself get stuck in a rut, which I don't intend to do, I might get involved with all sorts of things I don't know about. I've lived in such a narrow world, Poll.'

'Lucky you,' Poll said, 'I can't think why anyone should *want* to know about most of the life that goes on in England now. Of course, I do see all those successful middle-class people you had to keep up with because of Bill's work must have been rather ghastly. But you don't *have* to keep up appearances now, Meg. What on earth do you want to go and work in some ghastly little office for?'

'I must have some money, Poll.'

'Well, you won't get any that way. How much money *have* you got?'

'A very few thousand pounds. It isn't quite certain yet ...'

Poll interrupted. 'But, good God,' she said, 'you don't have very expensive tastes. You can almost *live* on that for a while. And then you know lots of people to borrow from. That's what *I've* always done. And as you saw last night I meet masses of interesting people if that's what you want. And you needn't *do* anything. That's the main thing. Doing things is so awful. I have a heavenly time. Even without breaking the trust, I mean. And anyway that won't last long.'

Meg looked at Poll in surprise. It was clear that she meant what she said; she *did* believe that she had a full, interesting life and it was obvious that she really enjoyed it.

'If one can't be *really* rich,' Poll said, 'I don't think it matters how little one has.'

Meg said, 'I don't think I'd be very good at borrowing and so on.'

'You'll learn, dear,' Poll replied with mock sharpness. 'If it's some silly moral scruple, you'd better get rid of it at once, Meg. Nobody cares about *us*, why should we care about *them*?'

Meg said as tentatively as she could, for she didn't wish to puncture Poll's optimism, 'I really don't think I should like your life.'

She was afraid that Poll would be angry. People never liked to have their way of living criticized. But she need not have feared.

'Oh, my dear, you can't know what it's like then. It's absolute bliss. I get up when I want to. And I know where all the people are if I want to find them, and none of the lots of people have anything to do with the other lots unless like last night there's a special party. And sometimes I just go to pubs I don't know where there are blissful strangers.'

She gave Meg a list of all the pubs and clubs she visited and which group frequented which of them. It takes, Meg thought, 'talking on their own subject' to make people into bores.

'And they never come here. And if they do I don't answer the door. And usually I can borrow from them if I'm hard up, or else they can borrow from me, they know when my cheques arrive. Sometimes it's rather hell and we're all broke together, but then we can all grumble together.'

Meg said, 'I don't think they'd like *me* very much.'

'Oh, I should think they would, shouldn't you? After all you say funny things and look quite nice and there's no specially awful thing about you like bad breath or any of those things.' She laughed again loudly. 'Besides,' she said with a look of concentrated thought, 'I should think you'd be wanting sex again some time. And it would be so awful to have one of those office affairs that they have in the women's mags.' Meg made no comment on this; Poll said, 'As a matter of fact you could go on being as grand as you wished. Most of the people that bum around think they're against everything like that, but they're tremendous snobs really. If any of them get tiresome I just tell them what it was like being a deb and about all the balls and things. Of course, they make a great show of laughing at it, but they lap it up really like any *Evening Standard* reader.'

Meg saw that Poll had invented a whole mythology of an aristocratic past. It seemed impossible that she could truly be as euphoric as she seemed. Meg now felt that she must puncture her satisfaction. 'And you don't regret giving up painting?' she asked.

'Oh! I should if I'd been any good. But it's ghastly to do things you aren't any good at, like muddling all the papers up in somebody's office.' She got up and took a brown paper bag from the kitchen dresser; out of it she produced two very shrivelled chicories. She looked at them closely. 'I shouldn't think it would be worth making *that* into a salad, should you?' she said and threw them into the sink.

221

'I don't believe you've come to terms or whatever it's called with your new life at all, Meg,' she said. 'You've got all sorts of ideas about fulfilling yourself and finding a what's its name for yourself. But there just isn't any place for women of our age and upbringing who haven't any money. It's hell if you don't accept it, but once you do it couldn't be more cosy. You just have to settle for being a slut, that's all. And goodness knows nobody can make a better slut than a lady born and bred if she sets her mind to it.'

Meg suddenly felt disappointed and annoyed to hear this missionary note in Poll's voice. She said sharply, 'It sounds wonderful, Poll. But isn't it simply what our grandparents called Bohemia?'

'Did they? I never knew mine. Yes, well I suppose it is. Why? Shouldn't it be?'

The surprise was so evidently genuine that Meg was forced to consider. She realized that this was simply another of her own prejudices. 'Bohemia' like 'wine and food talk' had always been stock jokes to her, and rather stale ones at that; yet she liked a little of the sort of life Poll led, just as she shared moderately in Donald's enthusiasms. It was not an absolute difference only one of degree. Nevertheless there was a depressing emphasis on 'lady' in Poll's gospel that seemed a mad version of her own mother's views ... but there again the criticism was pointless. Poll had created a rather 'ham' part for herself as the grand lady down the drain, but in her own mind it was a star part and most of the time she was clearly entirely happy playing it. Such trouble as she gave to other people was no doubt compensated by the entertainment, conscious and unconscious, that she provided. It wouldn't do for herself, Meg thought, but that was not Poll's fault.

She tried to rest content with this 'live and let live' view, but it was no good. Puritan or not, she was made differently – made to judge; and at this critical juncture she must make judgements or cease to exist. The truth was that Poll could be as happy as she liked, her life was still a sort of animated death. Behind her clown's face nothing except perhaps mistrust and hatred. She had, it was true, accepted them, turned them into a kind of punch-drunk bliss. It didn't make any difference, of course, to her affection for Poll. 'Loving the woman, yet hating her life.' Meg mocked at the conclusion she had reached. It was surely the most priggish of standpoints. Yet priggish or not, she knew that she must hold it. She was not looking for punch-drunk bliss or any other sort of plucky death in life.

She said, 'Thank you, Poll, it all sounds marvellous. I'll think about it.'

She knew that she would not and she guessed – this saddened her – that when Poll saw that her invitation to 'settle for being a slut' had been rejected she would find Meg's company less and less desirable. Wholehoggers were like that. Meg's depression grew on her. She refused an invitation to go to the Antigua Club; and managed to slip into her bedroom at the flat with no more than, 'I must have an early bed, Viola. You'll excuse me, I know,' to Lady Pirie's call from the sitting room to join the company.

It was not long, however, before she realized that her relations with Viola could not remain for ever on this evasive footing. Meg had feared that her inefficient management of Tom on the evening of Poll's party might have seemed inconclusive enough to stimulate him to further 'passes'; or again she was anxious lest her rejection might, by adding to her 'haughtiness', have increased his ardour. They were groundless fears for Tom now treated her civilly but with an off hand, uninterested ease that truly placed her in the aunt-like role she had always supposed herself to occupy. He even seemed willing, though in no way eager, to let her continue to be the friendly, 'good fun' aunt she had sought to be. She tried to think he was embarrassed, but he was simply without interest in her. It made things easier; but she still found herself remembering what he had said even if he did not, and she was still determined to leave as soon as she could do so without hurting Viola's feelings. Indeed she saw that it must be very soon, for, by staying on her own terms, she now risked upsetting Viola anyway.

Viola, it was clear, had welcomed the secretarial course as a useful bridge by which Meg could cross from sudden tragedy to a sensible life more in keeping with the lively, fashionable young woman of harnessed energy that she had always admired. Now that Meg, depressed by the failure of her sally into 'life and people', was more intent than ever on evenings devoted to shorthand, Viola clearly thought that prudent means had become foolish ends.

'Anyone,' she said, 'would think you were studying Chinese, Meg, the amount of time you give to that wretched shorthand.'

'I doubt if Chinese would be more difficult.' Meg gave a laugh which she heard as hollow. Laughing to stave off conflicts of opinion was beginning to prove a tedious and fruitless ruse.

'Nonsense. You're not going to tell me all these typists spend hours studying in the evening like you do. They're far too busy gadding about with their boys. And quite right too.'

Meg thought that she had commented too often already on the difficulties of age and on varying standards of competence, so she only smiled.

'You'll wear your eyes out. I know it doesn't sound kind, Meg, but your age is exactly the time when you have to take particular care of your looks.'

Meg wanted to say 'and my position too, of course', but she merely registered the increased necessity for moving.

A few days later Viola said suddenly at breakfast, 'Meg, it wasn't very kind not to answer Donald Templeton's letter about the compensation.'

A childlike rage seized Meg, so that she had to put down her cup for fear of spilling the tea. Interfering old bitch, she thought. That Tom was at the table did not help; however, he was apparently entirely absorbed in his newspaper. He even interrupted his mother's next remark. 'Here's another brilliant engineer clearing out,' he said. 'He's had as much as he can take. But I don't suppose what the younger generation feels seems important to either of you two.'

As he spoke, Meg had a sudden vision of Sir Herbert, whom she had never known, speaking exactly so – 'I don't suppose, Tom, that what the older generation feels interests you,' he must have said. But Viola was demanding her attention.

'You *must* know, Meg,' she was saying, 'what a jolly busy life a barrister leads and yet you seem to take all Donald does for you for granted.'

Meg could sense that she was deliberately provoking a quarrel. She answered shortly. 'The letter simply said, Viola, that the Foreign Office were still hopeful. There was nothing to answer.' They finished breakfast in silence. But as she was leaving the flat, Viola called after her.

'Oh, Meg, I've asked Colonel Randolph and Donald Templeton to dinner a week today. Do you think you could do something to please me? *Don't* work that evening. Give us the pleasure of your company.'

It was the sweet first scolding of a naughty child; soon, Meg thought, she'll give me 'what for'. She knew that she should ignore it – accept it for this time and make sure she was gone before there was a next. Illogically, however, the fact that she had to protect Viola from hearing of Tom's conduct made Meg the more furious at this rebuke. She walked back into the dining room, put her bag and her books down on the table, and said, 'Viola, this has got to stop. You think you're being kind, I know. But interference of this sort isn't kindness. No matter how many times I am forced to see Donald Templeton I shall not like him any better, in fact I shall probably dislike him more. I know that I ought to try to like him because he was Bill's friend, but I can't. In fact I haven't any doubt that that's why I dislike him. I don't understand why Bill had to choose a pompous bore as a friend, and I don't understand how a pompous bore like that can have known Bill's true needs in life better than I, but he did. To see Donald only makes me remember the side of my marriage which was a failure. As I can't do anything about it now, I don't see any point in upsetting myself. I don't intend to do so. I don't intend to see Donald even to please you.'

Viola's thick neck had flushed as Meg spoke, but she only said, 'Oh, Meg, what stuff and rubbish you clever people think up about yourselves. All this psychology!' She picked up the tray on which she was collecting the breakfast things and walked towards the door. To her own amazement, Meg found herself shaking and shouting after Viola's stocky figure.

'You'd do a great deal better if you thought a little more about your own motives. What on earth sort of mess do you think you've made of Tom?' Viola walked straight on out of the room.

Meg found it difficult to attend to her work that day. To have chosen Viola of all people on whom to release her pent up nervous distress shocked her. It was irrational and cruel; she had always been pleased to think that such cruel feelings as she had were under her conscious control. Viola was being tiresome, but she had always had her silly side. In the past under Meg's influence she had shed her prejudices and shown only her good sense. Meg saw that she no longer had that influence. Viola was only another of the people who, without realizing it, had adjusted their attitudes to Meg's changed position. It would have been more tolerable, if she had to hit out at someone, to have attacked Poll or better still Tom. To have considered their feelings and not Viola's seemed peculiarly cowardly. It would be easy enough to say that stupidity was too heavy a tax on the temper; the fact remained that she had made the decision not to criticize Viola's treatment of Tom, kept to it all the time they had known one another, and now she had broken that resolution in a moment of temper. Everything suggested that she was completely incapable of managing human relationships, unless, as in the past, she could play her part from a position of advantage. All the more reason, she thought, why she should stick to her determination to involve herself with the world around her. Women, after all, were given a likelihood of longer life. She might have thirty years or more ahead of her. She felt increasingly sure that she could only hold on to Bill's memory if she were fully alive. If she hoarded up her thoughts of him now and curled round them defensively, she would wake in the end to find them mouldered away.

Meanwhile she must do penance for her follies longer than she had hoped. Having spoken in anger to Viola, she must stay on at the flat for a while to try to repair her unkindness, must put up with Tom's presence and with the remembrance of what in her incompetence she had allowed him to say.

She returned to the flat that evening resolved to pocket her pride, ask Viola's forgiveness, and accept the dinner with Donald. A telegram awaited her from David announcing Gordon's death. She sent a telegram in return. She wrote a letter saying no more than that she was ready to do anything that could help David – to come down there, to go abroad with him for a while. She tried to get some comfort from the fact that if he accepted, she would have to give up her cherished course at the Garsington in mid-term, and that she truly knew she would accept this sacrifice gladly if it would assist David in his misery. But she knew that he would not accept, and the realization of her genuine if impotent affection for him was little compensation for not being able to act at once as a successful sister would do – to telephone, to be at Andredaswood that night, to take over all the tiresome chores, to speak from an intimacy that would comfort him. It was this that Viola Pirie would expect if she told her and, unable to face further failure in Viola's esteem, she suppressed the news. In her distraction, she also found no power to make the resolved apologies. She did, however, sit with Viola after dinner instead of going to her bedroom. She tried to read of Marcel keeping the Guermantes waiting for their dinner. Somehow it only made her annoyed. No wonder he found society an inadequate end in life, she thought. Then she laughed at the Philistinism of her thoughts. It must be Viola's influence, she decided. All the same Proust could afford to find human relationships insufficient – or at any rate he could make Marcel do so – because he knew that he was to find an answer in his writing. I've got to learn to find some end in life itself.

She put down the book and tried to give herself up to immediate sensation. She needed a rest from thinking. The room was warm, the coal fire – what Viola called her 'one antisocial indulgence' – glowed in fiery caves and mountains. Outside, the February snow had already been trampled into dung-brown sludge: this was comfort as great as anyone could hope for. Gazing into the jutting, craggy landscape of the fire that flickered and glowed each instant, she was carried back to the thousand times she had peopled with her thoughts these burning caves and mountains snow-topped with wood-ash – Alice-like, drying her hair, or like Maggie Tulliver, her book fallen to the floor. The dreams then had seemed to have a magical power to command the future; and so she had commanded it with Bill and Lord North Street. Tears came to her eyes; but it was for her house that she was weeping, not this time for Bill. If only she could have relaxed her will, given up her dreams, followed the advice of others, she could be there at Lord North Street now. With lodgers and a pretence, lonely existence. No, the magic had gone from that as from all her other dreams.

She was roused by Viola's voice. 'Meg,' she said in her kindest, gruffest tones, 'We've got to talk about it, my dear.'

Meg, pulled from far away, said, 'I'm very sorry, Viola. I had no right to speak as I did. I'm rather keyed up these days. I expect it's as you say – I'm overworking.'

'You know best about that. I shouldn't have interfered. That's the trouble, Meg, we're both interfering. I did it for the best. I thought you would be happier here.'

'I *have* been. You can't think what a relief it's been after the wretched bed-sitting room.'

'I'm glad. And I've been happy to have you. But I never believe in shutting my eyes when things go wrong. It doesn't work. I ought to have known it could only be a temporary measure. You can't have two women in one house, any more than you can have two men.'

'That seems an extravagant sort of statement, Viola. Lots of households do.'

'Yes, poor things! Mothers and daughters, or fathers and sons that can't get away from one another. But the natural arrangement is a man and a woman. And children.' She hesitated for a moment. 'Or just a man and a woman is often enough. But two women or two men, they both have the same roles to play. It's bound to lead to

227

tension. As it has done here. It's beginning to get Tom down. I can see it.'

Meg, in her turn, hesitated for a moment, then she said, 'You thought it would be so good for Tom to have me here. Now you don't. Why, Viola?'

Lady Pirie turned in her chair, as though looking round the room for some means of diverting the conversation. Then she burst out.

'Why you wanted to go running around with him at your age, Meg, I can't think. He's only a youngster. I give him a comfortable home and, as for what he does outside, he must find his own feet. That's the only way he can become a man. You think I spoil him, but I don't interfere with his life. A young man, any man must run his own life. I'm sorry, my dear Meg. I imagine he behaved stupidly with you that night you went to that Mrs Poll's or whatever her name is. I don't ask to know about it. I don't want to. But one can sense these things. If it is so, I don't blame Tom, I'm afraid, I blame you. You should never have got yourself into such a position with a boy of his age.'

Meg made no attempt to defend herself. She said, 'I'm afraid I've gone down in your opinion a lot, Viola.'

'My opinion's of no value. I just don't want to see you waste yourself that's all.' She paused for a moment and then said, 'All this careers business, Meg! I'm surprised to find you so old-fashioned.' She cocked her cigarette up towards her nose in a jaunty errand-boy sort of way that showed she was very pleased with this phrase. 'A woman needs a setting and a background that only a husband can provide – especially an attractive, talented sort of woman like you. You know I don't mean that she should sit at home like some Victorian house-wife. When Herbert was alive I entertained for him, and a full time job it would have been in the Islands for most women. It certainly was for old Lady Argles who was there before me. But I still found time for social work. That's what I admired in you. But now you seem set on a career. It's only another name for an old maid's pretence, and widows can become old maids as much as any virgins. Oh! I know I've been a fool. I've pushed Donald Templeton at you far too soon. But he's got so much to offer to a woman like you.'

Meg did not know whether to laugh or to be angry; she contented herself with saying, 'Apart from a thousand other things, Donald doesn't want to marry me as far as I know.'

'I don't suppose he's thought of it yet. But he soon would. Any attractive woman as young as you are who can't make a man fall in love with her isn't up to much. But there it is; you don't like him. And I've been an impertinent old fool. Only for heaven's sake, Meg, don't put marriage out of your mind. And don't leave it too late. And don't be too choosey. You've had everything with Bill. You can't expect that again. A woman isn't complete without a man.'

'You didn't marry again, Viola.'

'My dear, plain of face can't choose. I was lucky to get one husband and such a fine one. In any case, I have Tom to think about. And to be honest, Meg, it's chiefly because of him that I'm forced to say that this arrangement doesn't work. I'm sorry about it, my dear, but there it is. You'll take your time finding somewhere else, of course. And I hope there are no hard feelings.'

There were, but Meg saw no point in voicing them. In Viola's mind Meg should settle for being a woman, just as Poll thought she should settle for being a down the drain lady. She had no wish to follow the advice of either; if the 'bohemianism' Poll suggested was a stale joke to her, Viola's 'calculated marriage' scheme had always ranked among the few things she regarded as immoral – only acceptable even in Jane Austen's novels as a historical phase. Perhaps she was as narrow-minded in this judgement as she had been in dismissing Poll's view of life, yet she was even more certain of her feelings. What Viola urged upon her was exactly that side of marriage which was now the most distressing to her; it was this 'setting' as Viola called it, which she had forced upon Bill to his cost. To seek it again with a man she didn't even love would be as near a calculated wickedness as she could imagine. Nevertheless until she was firmly secure in whatever new life she was to make, neither Viola nor Poll would forgive her for not taking their advice. Apart altogether then from Tom, she must leave the flat. But the prospect of returning each night to a lonely room seemed desperate to her as she lay in bed that night. She hoped that by some freak David would write asking her to go with him for a while abroad, anywhere, so that she would not be alone. Two days later a letter came from David.

'My dear Meg, your letter was good to receive. The only letter that didn't talk of a merciful release in some circumlocution or other, for which I was especially grateful. For the last days Gordon was seldom conscious which was all I could ask for. There is nothing, as you know so well, to say at these times and alas, vastly too many people here saying a great deal. But that like everything else will be over in time.

Gordon has left everything to me. His mother and the others are very good people really, and about this, which I suppose they might well resent, very kind. All the same I wish them all in the Sahara, or anywhere not here. My main task now is to resume the routine of my life as quickly as possible and persuade the others that they will help the most by resuming theirs. Gordon had a great and natural peacefulness and imparted it to others. My spirit is too unquiet to ease others, but that's what I have to do and at least all these years with him have given me powers of reserve and calm that I must be grateful for. Meanwhile I admit that I find all the noise and clamour of the goodness and the kindness of the people around me hard to bear. Good and kind they really are, but like most of us they need to protest so much to persuade themselves that they exist. Gordon's mother has some of his inner strength but like so many Quakers – or so I have found – her quietness speaks in so *personal* a voice. It's kind of you to suggest being with me, but I don't think we can help each other – at any rate, at the moment. As for leaving here even for a short while, pleasant as it might be to get away from everyone here, it would solve nothing. But thank you. Please let me know if I can help *you* in any way. Much love to you and peace of mind. David.'

The February snow had melted away under an unusually hot spell of winter sunshine. David, muffled in an overcoat it is true, had been able to sit out on the terrace by the south wall of the house. He was preparing a bibliography of the books he would need in writing 'Africa'. The small south garden by the terrace had been of Gordon's making – an entirely private garden given up to flowers that they never cultivated for sale. As a result, bulbs and corms abounded. At the moment iris reticulata gleamed purple and gold here and there in the sunshine, and a great mass of mauve iris stylosa still basked in the dusty, rubble-filled soil by the wall. Next there would be knots of crocus, daffodils, and fritillary edging the lawn – in what Gordon had called 'our very pleasing, vulgar little spring show'. Later the beds were massed with tulips and later still with lilies. There were rose beds with hybrid tea and floribunda – for they were no rose specialists – but in Gordon's words 'never a chic shrub rose'. Perennials and annuals were largely banished except for odd species that were not in their sales catalogue. At the far end was a shrubbery unmarred by any azaleas or rhododendrons to recall their trade. At the moment a daphne gleamed with purple flowers.

David had never happily accepted this concession to their private tastes. His own formal garden at the front of the house was, after all, not purely private, it provided an impressive first view for visitors to the nursery. Although he loved the south garden, he had already determined to let it go gradually to waste. To tend and care for it would be to accept Gordon's concessions. They had agreed in Gordon's last weeks that life at Andredaswood must, for the future, be the honest expression only of David's view of life, inevitably different now from Gordon's which had been its source of inspiration. Besides, to tend Gordon's garden would seem a sentimental plan to keep his memory alive, and David believed that memory must persist unaided or die.

Nevertheless David was glad to bask here for an hour or two today. The house was still beset by people. The nursery routine, to which he looked to give his life the shape inside which he could seek his goal of self-effacement, demanded too little of him at the moment. February, in this respect, was an unfortunate month for Gordon to die in. There was comparatively little work to do. The preparing of the composts for the annual boxes hardly demanded even Tim's supervision. There were, it was true, late orders for shrubs and perennials to be dispatched; and with them the usual telephone calls from customers, late in ordering, who yet complained that their deliveries had not been early; there were also inevitably complaints of shrubs arriving in the two frost- and snow-bound weeks that had preceded the sunshine. At first David had insisted on dealing with all these customers personally, but to do so had meant either to offend Climbers, or to receive her understanding 'You do as much of the work as you want, David, if it helps you'. Climbers could easily cope with the customers and she knew that he knew it.

Above all he wanted to be alone, but not inactive. The long weeks of Gordon's dying had given him full, too full, time for thought. He had considered the future, sought to make sense of the hideous present, suffered the involuntary pouring in of the past. Above all he had tried desperately to fuse into an indivisible trinity the three seemingly forever divided persons – David then, David now, David to be without Gordon. 'Africa' now seemed the only escape from the senseless recurring cycle of these thoughts.

Yet 'Africa' occasioned the same inconclusive debate in him as everything else connected with his life. There was no need for the money the series brought in. It had started as a pleasure common to them both, and one that in the early uncertain stage of the nursery brought in extra cash. It had served to hide any incompatibilities of interest that might arise in their life together. It had finally cut him off from the distracting remembrance of his academic past. It had seemed too obviously popular and dilettante a work to make any pretentious claim. It was pleasant to compose, quite pleasant to write, and absurd enough not to matter. Yet what could be the point of his going on with it? If it was a matter of filling in time he would choose to listen to music or to try to evolve some system of meditation that would help to loosen the bonds of personal will. But was he not busy with personal assertion in making all these changes after Gordon's death? He had decided to let the private garden run waste, he had decided to give up the stove house, for the Christmas poinsettia sale could not cover up the fact that they had accepted exotic growing for their own pleasure. He'd decided, he'd decided – and all this in the cause of self-effacement. No, he would work away at 'Africa' as a gesture of in-differentism; letting it go on while the daily Martha tasks were few enough to allow it, throwing it over when they pressed.

A score of problems of conduct, in fact, now faced him to test the practical validity of his ethic; but the truth of what he had come to believe only seemed more striking when he considered the behaviour of the household in the last few days of crisis.

The funeral itself for a start: what absurdities and wastes of emotion that had brought forth! Mrs B. crying hysterically in the car to Brighton, then shocking Else and Gordon's mother by announcing that she would take the opportunity to go to *Mother Goose on Ice* instead of to the funeral ceremony. It was fantastic that intelligent women like Mrs Paget and Else should have let themselves be shocked; but then they had indulged in such an orgy of sentiment over the simple char's grief that her change of plan had to be seen as of equal significance. How incredibly they had lost all sense of proportion was clear when Mrs Paget, a woman who normally tempered life with an easy sense of humour, had said, 'Even if it had been an ordinary, old-fashioned pantomime I could have understood it better' and had not laughed. Nor was Mrs Boniface so simple that her behaviour had not been cal-culated. She had genuinely grieved for Gordon, but she had also felt the need to show everyone that she did so in her own way. 'I'd no idea I'd upset the old things,' she had told him, 'but I'm afraid I can't help it. Mr Paget wouldn't have wanted *me* at the funeral service if I didn't feel I could take it. He liked people to be natural, and he knew what I was like, a proper cockney, up one minute, down the next.'

Not that the more intelligent and sensitive had proved less determined on personal demonstration. Mrs Paget, her bony old horse's face set in obstinate lines that made nonsense of her gentleness, had said in her cracked old woman's voice, 'I shan't come to the Anglican service, David. Gordon always knew that while I respected his faith I did not understand its expression. My presence would be dishonest. I have arranged with the Brighton Friends for a short meeting of remembrance after the burial. I shall be so glad if you will come to it.'

He had no time to say 'yes' before Else, her bloodless cheeks suddenly aflame, had shouted, 'Oh, no, that's too paltry, Ada. To put your own beliefs before Gordon's at this time. You will please excuse me from being at the Meeting House.'

'Of course, Else, you must do as you think right,' Mrs Paget had answered, her gentleness all suppressed aggression now. And there they had sat in the car to Brighton, trembling at each other, refusing to speak, until Mrs Boniface's tears had united them in admiration for the grief of the simple.

Yet that very evening, back at Andredaswood, they had cooed away to one another, talking of their activities in the Nuclear Disarmament Campaign. 'David takes no part in the campaign,' Else had said sadly; and Mrs Paget, 'Oh, David, I hope you've not lost your pacifist convictions.'

'No,' he had told her, 'but I'm afraid I feel more and more that it's myself I have to pacify.'

It had been impossible not to sound priggish without a full explanation which he had not wished to embark upon. But he need not have worried, for both women had felt quite equal to understanding and refuting him before he had spoken. Else had cried, 'Oh, David. If we could make ourselves perfect! I'm afraid, my dear, the hydrogen bomb will have disposed of us all long before that.'

And Mrs Paget had glibly chimed in, 'Surely, David, we can only make ourselves ready, "toward", so that peace can enter into us.'

'But, of course,' Else had cried, 'soon the leaves will be showing and spring will bring a new peace to our minds.'

Mrs Paget had smiled with a little secret amusement. 'Well, yes, spring is *one* of its symbols, Else. But meanwhile, David, there is work to do.'

'Oh, yes, Ada, so much work.' He had left them arguing vigorously about the relative values of large scale meetings and small groups. He had gone to find some ease in a beer at the local with Tim.

All the same he had been disappointed that Gordon's mother had shown so closed a mind.

Breaking in on his thoughts came a thumping sound behind the swing door that opened on to the terrace. He turned to see Mrs Paget herself, pushing open the door with her rubber-ferruled stick. Her tiny, thin body was so bent now with rheumatism that she had to twist her head upwards to speak, and her hands were so gnarled and twisted that she used her stick to push her way through wherever she could. With her bony face, mat of untidy white hair and long, shapeless brown dresses, she wanted only a conical cap to make her the conventional fairy story witch. She manoeuvred herself, with long-acquired turns and twists, into the bamboo chair beside him.

'I shall be leaving before supper, David,' she said.

Had Gordon been there, *he* would have said, 'Supper, mother? When is that?' for she liked to be teased about the homely language she affected. David hesitated to make the remark.

Perhaps she unconsciously missed her son's comment for she seemed put out. Knowing her belief that silence healed, David made no attempt to carry on a conversation. But she was clearly nervous, for she slipped the old-fashioned silk sewing bag down her arm from which it hung by its two bone hoops. Her sewing days were over some time ago, but she was never without the bag, its tasselled end swinging as she walked. It never contained more, as far as David knew, than two packets of Player's Weights. She lit herself a cigarette and then said, 'Would you like me to take Else away with me, David?'

He guessed what she intended, but he preferred to let her say it. He asked, 'Do you think she should have a holiday?'

'No,' she answered and she laughed. 'You know I didn't mean that, David. Don't pretend with me after we've known each other so long. For good. She'd come if I told her to. She's fond of me. And I'm fond of her. She's a good creature for all her fancy talk about Nature. Besides I've known her a long time, ever since she came to us as a refugee. She knew my husband. She was an encumbrance I wished upon Gordon, there's no reason you should take her on. I have the feeling that you and she get upsides of each other at times.'

'No, no,' he said. He had made up his mind that living with Else was to be one of the Martha tasks of his life so long as she wished to stay there. 'We get on very well you know. If it hasn't seemed so, it's just the strain of the moment.'

234

'Ah,' she said doubtfully. 'Well if you ever feel you don't want her, let me know and I'll say that *I* need her. She has to be needed, poor thing. I'm going to leave her some of my money when I die. I asked her to take it now. Go back to Germany if she liked. Anyway learn to be independent. You'll have to be so some day, I told her. But she likes to think she's needed here. She's frightened you'll get your sister down to keep house instead of her. It'd be natural enough if you preferred your kin, David, you know.'

'My sister's got her own life,' David said, and thinking he saw a glint of contempt in her eye, he added, 'She offered to come down as soon as she heard the news.' He was going to stop there, but he reflected that 'the news' could not mean Gordon's death for ever, so he added, 'of Gordon's death. Or to go abroad with me for a holiday. But I said no, of course.'

'Why of course? You're a contrariwise to me, you know. You've no faith, yet you've got enough puritanism to do for the whole Kirk of Scotland. They say "gloomy atheists", don't they? But you're not that. You love the pleasures of life. At least what I call the worthwhile pleasures – music, books, and so on. Yet you're always denying yourself things. You've got enough people to carry on here while you go abroad for a month or two. Why refuse it?'

David smiled. 'It isn't puritanism,' he said, 'I don't believe that the difficulties of life vanish just because one's been on holiday.'

She said, tapping on his knee with the handle of her stick, 'What *are* all these difficulties?'

He raised an eyebrow, and she said immediately, 'Oh! Good heavens! I don't mean your private affairs. I'm that nonesuch, you know, an old woman who isn't inquisitive. I don't care a jot about other people's business.' He reflected that, considering how little she had ever fussed about his friendship with her son, this was probably true. 'But I am interested in people's ideas,' she said. 'What was all this about pacifying yourself the other night? I didn't follow it up when Else was there because I thought we'd had as much argefying as was good for us.'

David hesitated before he spoke. He felt an aversion from expressing his views. Mrs Paget was as good a recipient as any other: she was sympathetic, reasonably intelligent, and he had no particular emotional link with her. His aversion was a general one: he felt desperately the truth and importance of what he had to say and yet feared that, voiced, it would sound puerile utopianism. As he phrased his reply, he could hear Gordon saying, 'I'm not here for a tutorial. Why can't you talk naturally?' but a conventional academic form *seemed* the natural voice to him for the statement of any ideas.

'I think it might be best to begin –' he said. He could see the same glint in Mrs Paget's eye that would have appeared in her son's; but he would make no concession, this was the way in which he found it natural to answer. 'I think it might be best to begin,' he repeated it, aware of the pedantic effect of repetition, 'by saying that if there's one word widely used today which I really abhor for its evasion and its looseness, that word is "humanist". But the word has acquired by constant use a compendium significance combining a number of rather ill-linked views about life which, if only by their rather negative nature, it seems sensible to apply to me. I must accept, I'm afraid, being called a humanist. I say that,' he gestured to the old woman as though she had contradicted him, but she sat attentive, yet looking as though she needed a pad of paper to make notes of points for refutation. She assumes a 'committee look', he thought, as easily as I do a don's. 'I say that,' he went on, 'because the practice of life I've been working out over these last years – the "difficulties" you asked about – is, I suppose, more usually associated with people of religious faith.' His voice rose to an odd falsetto, 'Gordon, as you know, influenced me deeply, as he did everyone whom he met. I suppose I've had to fuse his way of life with my agnosticism. But I remain unconvinced by any transcendental arguments or, even more important, by any transcendental experiences that have been described to me.'

'Gordon, you know, respected your sincerity so much,' Mrs Paget said. David thought impatiently, I'm afraid she's more stupid than I'd thought. He wished that, like Humpty Dumpty, he could say that observations were unnecessary and only likely to put him off. He longed to ease the solemnity of her remark.

'I'm glad to say the tribunal took a similar view,' he said. 'I was one of the few non-religious objectors whose conscience was taken seriously. I suppose I'm rather proud of that. But I've never felt that the pacifist attitude could be confined to physical violence. I think that passivity – I don't say quietism because that has religious connotations – is an entire way of living. It's not quite as platitudinous as all that,' he said, for he could see that she had put down her imaginary pencil. 'I'm not saying that the passive way of living is an absolute good, right at all times of history. I'm afraid the tribunal would not have cared for that, had they known it. Only in ages like the present one, where violence and self-expression and complication of motive have become so great that we need a *détente*. It's the commonplace of the newspapers when they talk of the cold war. But I believe this disengagement should take place inside all of us. We need a simmering down of human personality, of human achievement too if you like, in order that we can start up again. Otherwise all will be lost in the boiling over.'

She said, 'You started talking to me like a schoolteacher, David, but you've turned into a preacher. I'm glad of that.'

He said, '*I'm* not. That's why I was wrong to let you uncork me. It's a way of living, not a declamation. All this talking to you is a perverse indulgence in self-expression.'

She said, 'Many people would say that it's absurdly utopian.'

'Meaning that *you* would like to say so?'

'Meaning that I would *not* like to say so. But perhaps that I think it.'

'It is. But, at the boiling point we've reached, no more so than anything else that's offered. You nuclear disarmament people are always admitting that your scheme runs this or that immediate risk. So do the people who want to hold on to the bomb. Yet neither of them, for all their difficulties, even professes to go very deep. Mine at least is radical. It might take centuries. Extinction may put an end to *all* man's schemes. Certainly violence will supervene many times. Violence masked as greatness. But meanwhile if more and more people simmer down we may eventually reach a safety point. On all accounts,' he laughed, 'during this age, no more greatness.'

'You don't have to worry much about that today,' she said. He saw that his last remark had shocked her.

'Or mediocrity claiming greatness. That makes an even louder noise. We've got enough past greatness to feed on for centuries. I shouldn't even encourage a Beethoven if he lived now.'

'I should think,' she said, 'that most folk would put an end to themselves in such a despairing world. No greatness! No God!'

'No,' he cried, 'that's the whole point, the whole difficulty. We must keep *alive* – but on the simmering level. I offer you a life of Martha daily duties, and of meditation.' He laughed.

She too seemed to feel he had said enough. She said rather solemnly, 'I don't know how I should live without the power of God's peace.' After a moment's silence, she told him, 'You seem to have encouraged Else with her fiddle anyway. I'm glad you've made that exception.'

He smiled. 'That's been one of the difficult decisions,' he said. 'She's not good. I'm afraid that our cellist, who is really good, will leave the quartet if I encourage Else too much. We can get another cellist, but *he's* not good.'

She said, 'Oh, David, you mustn't let Else ruin your quartet. Gordon had such a high admiration for the musical standard here.'

David said, 'I shall let Mary Gardner, the cellist, go and keep Else. Now perhaps you see something of the kind of decision I've been speaking of. We lower our presumptions and our achievements deliberately.'

She said, 'You're a self punisher. That's all it is. Or perhaps you've sacrificed your music to make living with Else easier.' She sounded bitter. He answered, 'No. There's a double motive in most things, of course. But I know why I made this decision.'

She sighed deeply as though the very idea of his existence wearied her. She said, 'I'm glad you have Tim Rattray. Gordon thought he was an excellent man for the nursery. And he was *your* choice, wasn't he? It's so important for you with all this army of women here to have a man to talk to.'

He said, 'Yes. I feel that.' He fell immediately into a depressed silence. Her remark had touched the one difficulty he did not care to consider. Hopeless love had dominated his life for so many years. Only the good fortune of Gordon's rare personality had saved him from being destroyed by his emotions. If he drifted into another hopeless attachment he would deserve destruction.

Mrs Paget must have felt this time that the silence was a healing one for she closed her eyes.

Renewed loneliness cast a sinister bogey shadow before Meg. What she had dreaded on leaving Viola Pirie's was a return to nights of melancholy and of macabre dreams. That way seemed the short road to some sort of breakdown. It was essential, too, that she should be able to work in the evenings, for although she felt satisfied with her progress, the final test was now only two months ahead, and she had a gnawing fear that if she were beset again by neurotic distraction her memory would lose its grip on the complicated network of symbols she had so laboriously assimilated. The Garsington was becoming tedious to her. She had begun to dislike the faces of the young women and of the teachers, to know too well the patterns made by dust or cracks on the classroom walls, to detest the sardine sandwiches and the tomato-filled bridge rolls. It had served its purpose well; Miss Corrigan had spoken the truth when she said that the course was concentrated, hard, and effective. But Meg had chosen to work there as anonymously as possible. She still thought that she had been right to do so; to have made friends with any of the girls or the teachers would have been a distraction the work could not allow to her, and a meaningless distraction since she would never see them again. On the whole everyone was pleasant to her. Nevertheless her own attitude of polite withdrawal had inevitably left her in isolation, and now that she had returned to evening solitude as well, she would have been glad of some greater social warmth during the day. She began to long for her first job, her first real committal to some new personal relationships.

Meanwhile to avoid a recurrence of the nightmare life of the Gloucester Road room or of the Victoria hotel, she decided to spend more money than she could really afford in order to live in a hotel that offered at least comfort. She saw it as a temporary expedient until she was through the last weeks of the course and the early difficulties of her first job.

She chose a large hotel in the borderland between Kensington and Knightsbridge. Her room was small but comfortable in its faded pseudo-Louis Quinze furnishing, unchanged, she imagined, since the nineteen-twenties. The food was quite good. There was a lift, and porter service. The décor in the public rooms was rather more depressing, because newer and pretending to something more chic than the dowdy, once de luxe bedrooms. The lounges and dining room and the hall had all been redecorated after the war in the deadest of gold and white Regency. The management, as though to atone for this glacial, sad decoration, employed an ex-R.A.F. type and his wife to give colour to the rooms with flower arrangements. To Meg's eyes these splashes of bright tulips or cinerarias seemed never to be in place for more than a few hours before the busy couple were replacing them with other tulips or cinerarias of a different bright shade. She wondered if they worked at piece rates. More permanent splashes of colour were provided by the smart hats of the chic old women who lived in the hotel and by tacit agreement always occupied their same chosen chairs. Meg was surprised to find that there were so many rich middle-class old women still in existence. She reflected that, if Bill had died in his sixties and left her rich, she might have been one of them. It was a comforting thought, at least, to know that she had avoided that. Beside the macaw-bright old women the parties of Australians and Americans, who stood disconsolately in macintoshes about the hall waiting for hired cars, seemed very sober. It wasn't, she thought, a place that she could like, but it would do.

Loneliness, nevertheless, caught up with her after the first week, not in its old nightmare, hysteric form, but in a strange restlessness. After dinner she would sit in the faded blue satin chair in her room trying to concentrate on tomorrow's lesson. She would stare at herself in the oval mirror, or wonder why the ovals of satin on the wall had faded to a different shade to that of the chairs. Then she would go down to the bar and drink a whisky and soda she didn't want. She would sit in one of the lounges and turn over the pages of *Country Life* or *The Queen*. She would concentrate on the stories of antique-buying American tourists, or on the old ladies discussing hairdressers or bridge or psychic experiences. Once or twice she even started conversations with other lonely residents, but as soon as she saw that the barriers had been broken down she wanted desperately to go away. She would go into the television room and immediately what she saw and heard from the screen weighed upon her like lead. She would go out to the cinema and become physically uncomfortable, simply from a sense of the futility of cinema-going.

The weekend proved a horror of claustrophobia. Rain made it impossible for her to walk in the streets. At last after luncheon on Sunday she got on a bus and took a ticket to its terminal point at Acton, but as soon as they reached a part of London unfamiliar to her she was reminded that long bus journeys had been her favourite treat at the age of ten. The regression seemed intolerable. She got down and went into a very dirty café, so old-fashioned that it had plates of coconut tarts in the window.

As she drank her cup of tea she knew that she must find the company of someone she knew. She was aware that her feelings about Poll and Viola were exaggerated. Viola might perhaps show some embarrassment if she went there, but it would only be the shame of a kind-hearted woman who felt that she had behaved badly. Poll would probably be pleased to see her. Yet she could not get away from the belief that they had judged her and found her wanting. They had dictated the terms on which she could regain their respect, and she had refused them. They had asked her to conform to their patterns as the price for their intimacy. On any other terms she suspected that intimacy would now be impossible, until at any rate she was established enough to dictate her own. Yet it was a sense of intimacy that she so desperately needed. She could make no new intimacies while she was still on this station platform waiting to change trains. She had not realized how completely identity seemed governed by milieu and, without any identity card to offer, she found no means of approach. She was too old, she thought, and the thought angered her, to manage a stateless existence.

In desperation she went to the nearest telephone box and rang two of their Lord North Street friends. At the first house there was no reply. At the second house the foreign maid said that they were away in Austria, ski-ing; they would be back next week, the weather had proved unfavourable. Meg said, 'Of course, all this rain.' She didn't leave her name. There were so many more she could have tried, but her courage failed her. She was disgusted to discover herself shy from pride.

It was only then that she asked herself why she did not ring Jill, why indeed she had seen her so seldom. She knew at once the answer – that Jill, in her embittered isolation, represented the life she feared to fall into. It was an answer that, in its lack of charity and facile condemnation, at once challenged her. She dialled Jill's number, almost hoping that this was one of the rare Sundays when Jill's son-in-law allowed her to go down there for the day. Jill answered. Yes, she was in. No, she was not going out; she seldom did on very wet Sundays. No, she was doing nothing. Yes, Meg could come round. She had nothing to say, but no doubt after such a long interval Meg had lots to tell. No? Well, in that case, she would advise Meg to bring a book. She had only a little fish in the flat, but if Meg had got used to tins now she was on her own, they could eat their evening meal together. She usually listened to the serial of *The Modern Comedy* on the wireless on Sunday evenings, but if Meg found Galsworthy too middlebrow she was quite happy to miss this evening's episode.

Meg went back to the hotel and got her shorthand notes. When she arrived at Jill's small flat in the mews behind Westminster Cathedral, she found her dripping oil into egg yolks.

'I don't expect you've quite sunk to my level of food yet,' she said, 'so I thought I would make a mayonnaise, if you can bring yourself to eat tinned lobster.'

Meg took a chance and roared with laughter. To her pleased surprise Jill laughed in return.

The evening from start to finish was a great success. They enjoyed their food. Jill made excellent coffee afterwards and even produced a bottle of brandy. 'I expect you think I only have it here in case of illness,' she said, 'but actually I don't. I always buy brandy whenever I can afford it because I like it so much. Sometimes I even have wine.' She giggled with pleasure at her own high spirits in a way that took Meg back many years into the past. They had hardly been listening to *The Modern Comedy* for five minutes before Jill turned it off. 'I can tell you the end if you want to know,' she said. 'It's very surprising. Old Soames gets killed by a picture falling on his head. And his daughter feels awful about it because she'd been so hard.' At that she laughed a great deal more and poured out another glass of brandy for each of them. They laughed so much over stories from their girlhood, and Jill so excelled in her old dead pan manner of telling them, that Meg forgot even to mention her recent difficulties. Jill never asked Meg how she was getting on; she was enjoying herself too much. They might never have been hard-luck widows.

She returned there several times that week. There was never a repetition of the gaiety of that evening: the food was sparse and poor, Jill, if not exactly gloomy, was perseveringly flat. Nevertheless Meg was deeply touched by the effort her friend had made to relax on that first visit; it suggested an affection and a loneliness that answered her own emotional needs. She discovered too that Jill was one of the rare people who could sit in a small room and neither vocally nor silently distract another's concentration. Meg found the task of memorizing easier than she had yet known while Jill sat at the other side of the gas stove reading the newest volume of travel, autobiography, or war memoirs. The department store at which she worked allowed its employees a cut rate subscription to its circulating library.

It was a strange setting, Meg knew, in which to find peace – this small room with its almost improvised furniture – the odd cheap chair or two, the divan intended for Evelyn if ever 'the little beast' should allow her to stay the night, the leather cushions, the now fast fading, carefully nurtured azalea – a Christmas present from Evelyn – and, on the mantelpiece, desk, and table, photographs of Andrew in uniform, of naval groups at Gib and Malta and Alex, pictures of Evelyn in every stage of youth, one photo of the baby. Meg rather maliciously picked on the dark young man who appeared at Evelyn's side in one photograph.

'Is that Leonard?' she asked.

'Yes,' Jill said, 'wearing his usual self-satisfied smirk.'

It was her only reference to her son-in-law. Meg thought that he was very good-looking.

She fished rather warily for Jill's opinion of her decision to take the secretarial course.

'It seems a very good idea,' Jill said. 'After all it's a way of getting a job. You're lucky to have had the money to pay for it.'

One evening Meg told her of the difficulties with Poll. Jill said, 'Weren't they rich trade? That sort of people always have to pretend to more than they've known in life. They don't feel happy unless they're the trout among minnows. She's lucky to have a trust to break. But still it's her life and if she enjoys it ... She must be a fool to suggest your doing nothing all day when you haven't any money.'

About Tom Pirie she was more final. 'What a very unpleasant young man,' she said. 'It does rather serve you right, Meg. I must say I've never believed that "being taken out of oneself" helps in the slightest unless it's with people one cares to be with. I suppose I ought to be glad that Evelyn didn't marry anyone like *that*. The "little beast's" far too keen on his precious career to behave badly in that sort of way. Of course, I never meet the young men of today, but judging from those that come into the shop they all seem to be wasters or what used to be called bounders. So I suppose Evelyn had to marry one or the other.'

Her indignation was reserved for Lady Pirie. 'I don't see how you could *ever* forgive her, Meg. Hasn't she any idea of what your feelings for Bill were? I think if anyone had urged me to marry again so soon after Andrew's death I should have smacked her face. Of course, most of those colonial service people are quite impossible anyway. You should have heard what people in the services had to say about them. I suppose Templeton never realized what she was up to. Otherwise as Bill's friend he must have been furious. Anyway why should she think that after years of being a bachelor he should want to saddle himself with a widow without any money. No offence to you, Meg. But it isn't very likely, is it?'

Meg found no offence to take. There was something comforting about Jill's tactlessly frank and low estimate of her position. She expected nothing and yet also she made no interference. It was the same in all things. Jill had always had good sense, but the acceptance of the natural prejudices and conventions of her family, which was largely an emotional need, had prevented her from ever developing her intelligence. She was brought up a sailor's daughter and had married a sailor. She thought as they did, but she was quite clever enough to know that other people thought differently and, as long as they didn't threaten her family affections, she left them to it. So now she knew that Meg 'always read novels', while she, like Andrew and her father before that, read memoirs and biographies. But she did not, as they would have done, think that hers was the superior act; she knew, in fact, that Meg was more 'highbrow' – 'very nice for her', she would have said, 'but we have our own ways'.

In politics, perhaps, it was a slightly more strained situation: once they had both, from different positions, been 'anti-Munich', now Jill's conservatism under stress of post-war social change had taken on a more diehard hue, but she had always regarded Meg's more liberal views as the luxury of a wealthy woman and she was prepared silently to wait for penury to bring her better sense. In any case they didn't talk a lot and when they did they were held together by a common sense of the ridiculous that ironed out their differences. Jill's laughter had a slightly more bitter note than Meg's, but her comments were accordingly rather more pungent. There was between them a girl-hood tie that had slipped loose as they travelled such different paths in life but that had never been broken by any disagreement about the people they loved; and that, for Jill at any rate, was the only kind of disagreement that counted. She thought it odd, however, that Meg should have lost touch so completely with David, when in their youth they had been so close.

'I used to envy you having a brother,' she said. 'Rex and Jack were all right but they *were* only cousins. I always liked David. And for all his being so clever he seemed so sensible. I was awfully upset when all that pacifist business happened. I felt so sorry for your mother.'

'Yes. So did David. I think that was one of the troubles. He thought that I ought to make it up to Mother for her disappointment over him. He never would admit that nothing I did mattered to her. "Marrying well", as she would have called it, was about the best thing I could do for her. But when I did, it didn't really give her *much* pleasure. Not that David and I quarrelled about it. We've never quarrelled over anything. It's just that he so obviously didn't want to have much to do with us. And I must admit that once I saw that, I didn't try very hard. I had all I needed in Bill.'

Jill said, 'Yes, of course. And, after all, you stuck to him during the war. You were right, of course. But not every sister would have done it.'

'I shouldn't care for the sort of sister who didn't. Not that it made much difference to him. At first perhaps, with all those tribunals. But after he'd met Gordon Paget nobody else counted for him. I never really liked the man. Not just because he was so odd, but I don't care for people who go about influencing. And in the end they had such an extraordinary ménage down there – a lot of cranky women! Funnily enough when Bill and Gordon Paget met they got on like a house on fire. But I think Bill was a bit embarrassed by it. I'm afraid David's going to be very lost now that Gordon's dead.'

Jill said, 'I think all men feel very deeply about their friends. Andrew felt it dreadfully when Neville Easton was killed. It was one of the only things I could do absolutely nothing about. It's something quite apart from their feelings for us, I think. We've just got to accept it.'

Meg said, 'David's never had any feelings for women.'

Jill said, with no difference in her tone, 'Oh! I see. Well, I suppose that's something we have to accept too. The papers are always telling us so nowadays. I can't see it matters very much anyway now that the whole world's gone to pot.'

'I wish I could think that it had made David happier. However, Gordon's left him all his money, so he'll be quite well off.'

'Oh,' Jill said. 'Then that *does* make your chances of seeing much of him pretty impossible. It's the greatest barrier of all when one's poor.'

Meg thought that this, like so many of the beliefs of her friends, was something that she could not judge without more experience. She said only, 'I don't imagine David will live very grandly. He seems anxious to immerse himself even more in that nursery now that he's alone.' She began to study her notes. She did not particularly want to talk about David and in any case the conversation had run to the limit they usually allowed for talk over their after dinner coffee.

Yet Jill left Alan Moorehead's *Gallipoli* lying unopened. After a few minutes' silence she said, 'Isn't it a bit grand of you, Meg, living at the Rodin? What do you pay?' When she was told, she said, 'Good heavens! and you don't even have dinner more than three times a week. That can't go on.'

'It's only temporary,' Meg said, 'I really couldn't face a bed-sitting room or a boarding house until I'm settled.'

'I know. You haven't learnt to be alone yet, have you? It'll come. But meanwhile you certainly mustn't spend all that money. I think, you know, that you'd better come here, at any rate until you've got a job fixed up. The divan's very comfortable. You'll save money. You can pay me for your food. I'm used to being alone but I won't say it isn't pleasant to have you here for a while. It wouldn't do as a permanent arrangement and, of course, if by some extraordinary chance his lordship allows Evelyn to bring the baby here for a night I'll have to turf you out. But it only happens once in a blue moon, so you needn't worry too much about that.'

And so it was arranged. Meg moved in the following week. It proved a regime that allowed her to work without undue depression, without restlessness, and without sudden panics. She managed to improve the food a little and, since March that year was very cold, Jill made no serious attempt to economize with the gas fire. They found, it is true, less to say and there was a monotony of existence which Meg knew would prove intolerable over a long period. On some evenings indeed their remarks were confined to announcing aloud whatever they were doing. 'I'll just put the kettle on for the bottles, Meg,' or 'One more chapter and I shall go to bed,' but, Meg reflected, this was at least better than talking aloud to oneself. The little surplus of affection that Jill had to offer after she had concentrated her love so fiercely upon her daughter and her granddaughter was suddenly unfrozen and flowed over Meg. She was solicitous for her health and her comfort, she showed an interest in her progress at the Garsington, sometimes she was lively and amusing as she had been on that first evening. Meg, on her side, felt wanted, which was all that she could ask.

The weekly letter from Evelyn with its Ipswich postmark was the centre of all Jill's expectancy. Evelyn's life appeared from the excerpts that were read aloud to be even more circumscribed than her mother's. It was clear that, like her mother, she too lived in and for her husband. She was tactful enough to say little about him in the letters, confining her news to the baby. However, there was always some item about Leonard's success. 'Leonard may be going to the Philadelphia branch for a couple of months in the autumn. It would be tricky because he'd be sent there over the heads of a number of senior men. But we're keeping our fingers crossed,' Evelyn wrote. Her mother read out the passage to Meg. 'I shall keep my fingers crossed too if he goes,' she said. 'After all planes can crash and boats can sink.'

Meg could detect no trace of humorous suggestion in Jill's voice. She must have looked as shocked as she felt, for Jill said, 'Oh, *she'd* get over it.'

Meg had expected this even less. To cover her embarrassment, she asked, 'What does he do exactly, Jill?'

'Oh, he's a chemist. One of those brilliant young scientists. He works with a big commercial firm in Ipswich. Don't ask me what they make. I don't know and I don't care. But apparently he's very good. They wanted him as professor at some university in the north – Manchester or Liverpool or somewhere. I suppose that I ought to be thankful to him for turning it down. It would have taken Evelyn even farther away. Not that he would have cared about that. He was only thinking of the money. Trust him.'

Meg said, 'My dear Jill, he's bound to think of his career. If only for Evelyn and the baby's sake.'

She answered, 'Do you think that makes it any more tolerable?'

The next week's letter brought a more pleasing item about Leonard. Jill was like a triumphant child. 'The little beast's sister's coming to stay with them,' she told Meg exultantly, 'so Evelyn's coming to stay with *me* for two nights and bringing the baby.'

Meg suddenly realized that she had never heard this baby's name: 'What's she called?' she asked.

Jill pulled a face of disgust. 'Charmian! The little beast's choice! I just call her the baby, poor thing. Evelyn says she thinks he and the sister have a lot to talk over and that they'd rather be on their own. I expect the sister mustn't be worried by the baby's crying. She's one of a kind with him, from what I saw at the wedding. ... She's pushed herself up to be some sort of fashion editress. Smart in all the wrong way. I must say that the parents were quite unassuming. He was a builder somewhere in the Midlands.'

Meg told herself as she listened that she must not let all this snobbery influence her against Jill. Andrew and she had always been snobbish, of course, but in a quite unworrying way. Meg could not have believed that hatred could have brought out such vulgarity in anyone. To deflect the unpleasing moment, she said, 'Which nights, Jill dear? I'll get a room this morning at that little hotel I was at near the station.'

'Tuesday and Wednesday,' Jill said. She gave Meg a smile of affection for accepting her move as so inevitable. Then she said, 'Meg, it would be quite wonderful if you'd come in one evening and baby-sit. Evelyn never gets to a theatre. If only we could get in to *Salad Days*! But I expect we'll find something. I shall have to spend the morning being sweet to that terrible Mr Arkwright, but I must have the two days off.'

Meg watched Jill in the next few days with fascination. It was exactly as though she were being reunited with a lover: she bought new shoes, had her hair done, filled the flat with flowers, she even for some incalculable reason bought a box of Turkish cigarettes. Then toys began to arrive for the baby – a huge and expensive doll, a Jack in the box ('Isn't it wonderful,' Jill cried. 'I didn't know you could get them still. I only hope it doesn't frighten the baby into fits') and a number of small rattling and swinging things ('To amuse her while she's here. They're all things that can be broken without its mattering'). Jill looked years younger, but she seemed also suddenly extremely shy; Meg only feared that if this shy tension persisted it might lead to some outburst with Evelyn.

Two nights before Evelyn was due, the telephone rang in Jill's bedroom. When Jill returned to the sitting room, she was holding her handkerchief to her mouth. She stood in the doorway for a moment. She seemed to be suffering from a choking fit. Meg got up from her chair, 'Jill, dear, whatever …?' but the look of real fury in Jill's eyes cut off her question. Jill, still holding up her handkerchief, turned and went out of the room. Meg heard her retching in the bathroom. She thought, what on earth can have happened? Perhaps it wasn't fury, perhaps something's happened to Evelyn or to the baby. When Jill came back, she said nothing, but picked up the *Life of the Princess Lieven* and went on reading. Only half an hour later did she look up and say:

'They're not coming. The little beast's ordered her to be there to wait on his sister.' She went to her desk, and taking out the two tickets that she had bought for the ballet, she tore them into pieces.

Meg said, 'Jill, my dear, you mustn't let yourself get so upset by it.' Jill said, 'Please, shut up.'

She went back to her book. It was not until much later when she was filling the hot-water bottles that she said anything more that evening.

'I'm sorry this should have happened while you were here, Meg.'

Meg wanted to answer that nothing had happened, but she only said, 'It's a tremendous shame, Jill. Perhaps Evelyn'll manage to get up one day soon instead.'

Jill put the kettle down on the gas ring and stared at her for a moment. 'Oh, don't be a fool, Meg,' she said.

Meg's rather stupid consolatory remark turned out in fact to have been a justifiable hope. Only a few days later Evelyn rang to say that

Leonard must attend a London dinner of the firm. He had suggested that he should drive her up to spend the evening with her mother.

'Of course that's Evelyn's story. She's frightfully loyal,' Jill said. She made it sound like a British Communist's loyalty to the Kremlin. 'She obviously had to bully him to agree to it. And even then his highness won't allow her to bring the baby. In his wonderful knowledge of babies he has decreed that it would be unsettling for her. He means, I suppose, that it would unsettle him if she cried on the way home. They've got some engaged couple of all things to sit in.'

It amazed Meg how like some old-fashioned servant Jill had sounded once she spoke on this subject, with her 'his highness' and her suggestion that the baby-sitters were certain in their concupiscence to allow the baby to burn to death unnoticed.

Meg said, 'Well, it would be rather late, Jill.'

To her surprise Jill announced, 'French children sit up until very late hours and it does *them* no harm.'

'But the baby's a bit young and she *isn't* French.'

'Trust the little beast for that. He's already informed me that speaking French is no asset these days. It was so like him to think of such things as "assets".'

Meg remembered that for all their true blue, naval background, Andrew had been a proficient linguist and Jill prided herself on her fluency in French.

Jill added, 'Of course, Evelyn's French has been absolutely wasted.'

'There's one snag,' she said later. 'I shall have to see *him*. He's calling for Evelyn here. If he gets back before we've returned from the theatre he'll just have to wait. I'm not going to have Evelyn miss a chance of a show, though I shan't be able to get tickets for the ballet again, I'm sure. Those others were pure luck.'

She got, in fact, two seats for the new version of *Charlie's Aunt*. 'It's a ridiculous show to go to without a man,' she said, 'but that's the little beast's fault. I couldn't get anything else.'

Later again she said, 'I suppose I'll have to get some whisky in for him.'

'But you've got that bottle of brandy, Jill.'

'Oh no, dear. After all he *is* a man of a sort. And it will be about nightcap time.'

Once Jill spoke of family arrangements, Meg realized that some folk-lore reigned that was quite mysterious to her.

Meg had not seen Evelyn for many years. She had turned into a replica of her father – fresh-faced, blonde, already at twenty-five putting on weight. Whereas Andrew had looked comfortable and jolly, his daughter seemed blowsy. She treated her mother with the easygoing, chaffing manner that Andrew had used with strangers, but she was very concerned that Meg should give great attention to Leonard when he arrived. She said, 'You can't think how these dinners tire him, poor pet,' and 'Be sweet to him if he looks glum, Mrs Eliot. It's so appalling that he should have to go to these silly things. But being good at your job isn't apparently enough. There's all this having to suck up to the chairman which Leonard hates.'

Jill cleverly combined a wink and a look of extreme sadness at this statement. She whispered to Meg as she left, 'I should give him the evening paper.'

Leonard, in fact, it seemed, did dislike the dinner. He arrived at the flat much earlier than Meg had expected – shortly after ten. He was as good-looking as his photograph had suggested; although Meg knew that his dark wavy hair and his flash of white teeth would only have confirmed Jill in her estimate of his commonness. It was a judgement, she also knew, that she might have made herself, but without Jill's hostility. After all the criticism that had been made of him, she was determined to show that she could get the best out of him. It was not easy at first. His babyish face wore a sulky look: he was prepared to be in a pet at the prospect of a long wait for Evelyn's return. He said, 'Oh, Lord! Really!' He had a slight twang in his voice that must have assisted Jill's dislike of him.

'I don't think they expected you to be back so early.'

He looked at his watch. 'In another ten minutes it will be the time at which Evelyn should have expected me. You tell me now that this ridiculous theatre won't be over until half an hour after that. Heaven knows how long they'll take to get back!'

Meg thought, oh, dear, it does look as though Jill may be right. She decided to take a chance.

'Well,' she said, 'you seem to be ready to take it all out on me. So there's no need to feel deprived, is there?' She laughed.

For a moment she feared that he would not accept it. Then he smiled. She thought, his smile has great charm. She imagined how Evelyn, brought up on Jill's rigid view of the right sort of man – old-fashioned even for the middle classes of her generation – must have felt liberated by a man who was so little ashamed of his showy good looks. And of his cocky, common sexiness, too, she thought.

He didn't apologize, but said, 'We'd better talk about something else.'

She smiled. 'Oh, I'm not expecting talk,' she said, 'that's outside my duties. I've given you a whisky. I understood you would read.'

Now he laughed. 'I can see you're a friend of Mrs S.'s,' he said, but he did not imply that this ruled her out. He said, 'I want to talk.'

'Oh, well in that case ...' Meg said. She paused. 'You'd better tell me why your dinner was a failure.'

He looked suddenly suspicious. 'It wasn't a failure at all,' he said. 'As a matter of fact I got in exactly the word I wanted. But it wasn't easy. That sort of thing's something I've had to learn. It takes it out of me. Evelyn knows that and she knows how to put me right again. Besides I wanted to tell her that I'd brought it off.'

Meg said, 'She's very accommodating.'

'Yes, why shouldn't she be? It's our future. I understood from Evelyn,' he said, 'that you were pretty ambitious for your husband.'

'Yes,' she said, 'too much, I think.'

'Well, Evelyn can't be too ambitious for my future. Besides she knows how to do it. I only ask for her to be there when I need her.'

Meg, thinking of Bill, knew that she must push away from this rocky shoal. She said, 'Well since she's not here you'd better tell me all about this evening's success.' She thought that in her fright she had put the suggestion too badly, no one can take off from an order like that. But Leonard Robbins could. He embarked on the whole politics of his career. He talked and she questioned for nearly half an hour. She found his certainty and determination extremely refreshing. She liked his intelligence and was amazed at his self-knowledge: she was even more pleased when now and again, she thought she had detected their limitations. She tried to accept his cocksureness because she could detect the swamps of self-doubt over which it had been constructed. If only he had a little humour, she thought, he would be a really rewarding companion. But above all she felt a sudden elation at hearing so much of a life that seemed to be moving forward. She saw herself connected for a moment with the world from which she felt so cut off. Fearing that she was making too much of the occasion, she told herself that her pleasure really came from having put herself over him.

The thought must have been communicated, for he stopped and said, 'You've got the trick all right, haven't you? I suppose I've successfully revealed myself as the cad or whatever the word is that you expected.'

She asked, 'Why should you think that?'

'I have some idea of what people are like.'

'Well, in this case you're wrong. Shall I tell you what you've made me feel? That you think you can do the job better than anyone else. And you tell yourself that, you know, because you want to have it anyway.'

He looked at her quizzically. 'You mean that I ought to be certain. Does that ever happen in real life? No, of course, I'm not *sure* that I'd be better than anybody else. But I'd be as good and I *want* it more than the others. It's not just a question of power, you know. I enjoy the work. I want to have a happy life.'

'And the others who may or may not be so competent?'

'They probably want some other things in life quite as much. At least, I hope so,' he looked a bit contemptuous. 'In any case all this about the ruthless young scientist! It's a bit corny, isn't it? I'm not so young, you know, that I don't know the answer to that. I'm perfectly aware that if you destroy others you'll probably destroy yourself.'

There was a smugness in the statement that annoyed her. She said, 'You've destroyed Jill all right.'

'Oh,' he said, 'I see what all this is about. She's destroyed herself,' he said casually. 'Do you know,' he asked after a pause, 'what Evelyn was like when I met her? I know you don't as a matter of fact. And, that being so, it shocks me a bit that you step in so merrily. She was utterly unhappy and she isn't now. She was expected to spend her life worshipping her father's memory. And Mrs S., who expected it, had never let her really know the man she was supposed to worship. Not that he could have been worth much to let it happen.'

Meg said, 'I think you don't understand what a naval officer's life is like. He was away a large part of the time.'

Leonard disregarded her. He spoke very deliberately; if there was any anger it seemed to be directed against her for needing to be told rather than against Jill of whom he was speaking. 'She did everything she could to stop the marriage. Some pretty dirty tricks too. She said, of course, that I wasn't what *he* would have liked; but she wanted to keep Evelyn for herself as a kind of doormat.'

Meg said, 'I should have thought you would have admired anyone for fighting so hard for what they wanted.'

He considered for a moment. 'That's sentimental nonsense,' he said.

'Well,' Meg said, 'and you won. Surely you can afford to be a bit magnanimous. You've told me yourself how confident you are of the success of your marriage.'

'Of course I'm confident,' he said. She thought, the trouble is that he's not quite confident of anything. 'But if she and Evelyn see each other much, we shall have her with us all the time.'

'Dear God!' Meg cried. 'If you can't manage to let Jill into Evelyn's life without fear of her swamping you! An utterly lonely and defeated woman!'

'She has her memories she's always talking about.'

At this Meg cried out angrily, 'You forget that you're talking to a widow.'

She expected him to apologize but he only said in a surprised voice, 'I thought people only said things like that in books.'

'Some books reflect reality,' she said.

'I don't read novels,' he announced. She thought she had let her chance slip away, but the irrelevance allowed him to leave his entrenchment. 'I suppose,' he said, 'that you think I should ask her down for a weekend?'

'I think you should let Evelyn bring Charmian,' she said the name and felt even more proud of getting on to terms with a man who could have called his daughter by it. 'I think you should let Evelyn bring Charmian up to see Jill.'

'She does,' he said, 'sometimes.'

'How often? When was the last time?'

'Oh, Christmas or New Year.'

'It could be *more* often.'

'No. I'd rather Mrs S. came to us. Where I can keep an eye on her.'

She was about to say, 'Have you no certainty of anything?' but she checked herself in time. 'Well, do that, then,' she said, 'but don't rush at it. I should leave it for a few weeks at any rate. And when she comes down to you, do the job properly.'

He said, 'I can manage most things if I try.'

'Yes,' she said, 'even entertaining middle-aged widows.' Even that was only half true, she thought. But he was pleased. He laughed.

'Oh, you know the trick,' he said. 'You've drawn me out. It's very annoying. Because Evelyn said you were like that. And I've let myself fall for it.'

They were both laughing, when the key sounded in the front door.

'Now behave yourself,' Meg said, as though to a child. She was pleased to see that he obviously enjoyed being spoken to so.

It proved difficult for her to disguise from Jill the elation that the evening's conversation had given to her. The preparation of Jill for any overtures from Leonard must be a lengthy business; to start it that evening might well prove a bad beginning. When, then, Jill said, 'His Imperial Highness was in a *very* gracious mood this evening,' she merely answered, 'Whisky can work wonders, dear.'

At the Garsington the girls were beginning those prickly, 'getting at each other' sorts of conversations which instantly took Meg back to her school time examinations. In those days she had been securely immunized against such panic, but now it seized upon her and was all the more tenacious because, at her age, she must not pass it on. She had not been in the habit of talking about the work much with the others, and had almost ceased to listen to their conversations; now their omission of her from their prophecies and forecasts suddenly seemed a deliberate, polite avoidance of announcing her inevitable failure. She found herself listening-in to their talk for portents and for auguries. Time, which had seemed to be mouldering away with the forgotten shavings of pencil-wood in the dusty heat beneath the Garsington's radiators, suddenly sprinted forward: the Test Day was almost upon her.

The hazards that memory offered to maturity now loomed in front of her, each day a different one: every sound or symbol she had learned, brought, by some trick of shape or assonance or rhyme or accent, an irrelevant image from her long forty years of remembered life; or, telling herself it was a game to relieve the impending tension, she fell into believing it and the lessons trickled through her head pleasingly, soothingly, leaving no trace. What had she to do with games at forty-three? Or, despairing, she remembered that she was no schoolgirl, that she was free, the fees paid, to walk out and forget the whole course, and, exulting, almost rose to do so. Above all, like some village child in a Victorian tale, she looked out of the window, saw the gold and purple of Miss Corrigan's crocuses, and longed to run pell-mell, helter skelter into the park to play. Anxiety, mourning, her own troubles, the troubles of others – among them Jill's – she squeezed and crowded away so tightly that they creaked and groaned in a 'chorus off' almost more distracting than their conscious presence. She could remember nothing as she turned out the lamp by the divan at midnight and, at a quarter past, every lesson of the course began a race round her mind that lasted until dawn.

When Miss Corrigan assured her that, accidents apart, she would pass the test, she believed her so little that she began to wonder if some material accident had been arranged – a faulty wiring of the electric typewriter, a hand crushed in the duplicating machine – that would at once protect her from ignominious failure and the principal from the charge of misleading prediction. Hearing Jill say, 'It's nice to see you looking so confident about this silly test, Meg. I think I should be scared stiff if I had to take an exam now,' she realized that her bearing lagged behind her emotions. She still appeared the confident woman that she had been before Srem Panh, and perhaps would never be again. Most daunting of all was Miss Corrigan's suggestion that she should choose from a list of vacancies for private secretaries.

'I think we can almost take your test as a formality, Mrs Eliot,' she said and she seemed to show no signs of sadistic pleasure or sudden insanity. 'There are only a few of these which will probably interest you. Most of the first jobs the girls take are naturally less responsible, but now that you have the technical requirements, I don't think that you'll lack anything for a first-class job.' She laughed. 'Except, of course, getting to know the eccentrics of the boss.' She made this sound most sinister.

Superstitiously Meg told herself that this was some practical joke list of posts with which Miss Corrigan amused herself at the expense of her more ridiculous pupils. She said, 'I think I should prefer to wait until I am sure of the certificate. In any case I need to put all my time and effort into working for the test.'

Miss Corrigan, diminutive, looked up at Meg, towering, as at the first camelopard in Europe. Meg realized that never before had anyone refused her prescribed routine. Perhaps she decided that reassurance was all that freaks lacked, for she said, 'I think, Mrs Eliot, that *your* unusual character will stand you in very good stead in the right post.'

Meg felt amused and pleased. Only afterwards she giggled, thinking that perhaps there was a threat in these words – no doubt in mental hospitals patients with secretarial qualifications were given some office work on their better days. It was her last happy glimpse of the ridiculous before the test day.

She arrived in the morning, overtired, with a headache, shivering in the bright spring sunshine that lit up the barrows of daffodils and mauve tulips at Gloucester Road station. At half past five in the evening she was told that she had passed.

Despite the throbbing in her head and a difficulty in swallowing that presaged a feverish cold, she strode the Kensington pavements feeling that modesty alone prevented her from demanding a public triumph. She knew the elation of a first victory and with it came a clearer, because a more realizable picture of the whole campaign she was fighting. She saw now Poll, Viola, Tom as battles she had both lost and won. No doubt there would be others to follow before she had lost the old world in order to find her place in the new. Only then could she hope to look back to her life with Bill, freed from the guilt that now hung around memory. The vision was absurd, illogical, superstitious; yet she knew that it was her symbol of truth.

Nevertheless, buying improbable foods and wines at Fortnum's for the celebration of her private triumph that evening, her legs wobbled under her and her throat stung so that she gulped as she gave her orders. The ageing matinée-idol faces of the assistants swam before her feverish gaze in a sea of sagging-faced, made up women with monstrous flowered hats, of tins of Kangaroo Tail soup and packets of Poppadums and Bombay Duck. She told herself it was the central heating. All the same she knew that she was in for, at least, a bad cold; yet the triumph seemed even more real for this, recalling the inevitable toothache at the birthday party or the measles rash on Christmas Eve. She returned to Victoria in a cab, laden with parcels and light in the head.

She called to Jill and, receiving no answer, presumed that she was not yet home. Then, going into the kitchen to prepare the surprise, exotic and triumphant meal, she came upon her, standing, grimmest of grenadiers, at the sink. Undaunted she cried, 'Jill, I've passed the test!' Jill went on peeling the potatoes, her fingers trembling a little. 'The test, darling, I've passed it. I'm *qualified*.' Then, 'Jill, whatever's the matter?'

Jill said, 'I think you know perfectly well, Meg. Do you mind if we don't talk about it?'

Meg thought, it's too bad, I don't have so many happinesses now. ... She said, 'I *do* think, Jill, you might show a little pleasure ...'

'Pleasure!' Jill cried. Then she stopped and stared at Meg. 'No,' she said, 'I suppose I've no right to be angry. I should have known that you were not to be trusted with any confidence, that you would act like a child. You're utterly spoilt, Meg, you always have been and, God help you, tragedy seems to have made you more irresponsible instead of less. But if you think that you can push your way into *my* life and treat me without the slightest consideration and then expect me to start clapping my hands with pleasure because you've passed some potty little shorthand test, you're very much mistaken. It's time people treated you as though you could at least be *expected* to act as a grown woman. Not that it makes any difference now as far as I'm concerned. I don't think I shall *ever* forgive you, Meg. Ever.'

Meg said, 'I don't think I know what you're talking about,' but as she said it she felt that she knew exactly what had happened.

'Don't you,' Jill said. 'If you really don't know, Meg, if you're really capable of doing something so utterly irresponsible *and* cruel without knowing, then I think you should be shut up.'

Meg felt that in one moment all the accumulated misery of Jill's life was being loosed upon her. There seemed no time to consider justice or injustice, to weigh up her own guilt or to reckon the sanity of Jill's universe; only important was to stem this flow before they were committed to an irrevocable and intolerable revelation.

She said, 'If you resent my trying to ease things between you and Leonard, I'm sorry. Obviously I went about it the wrong way or you would never have been upset like this. I intended only to improve what seemed to me a very stupid and unkind situation.'

She had thought that the bull could still be held in check, she soon realized that she was wrong – the horns broke off in her hands.

Jill said, 'You really are a child, aren't you? You think that if you admit to what you've done, everything will be all right. Well, it isn't. For five years now I've kept my feelings from that creature; even from Evelyn so that she should never guess how much she'd hurt me. And in a half hour or so while you exercise your understanding charm you've made it impossible for me to face them again ...'

Meg felt Jill's bitterness filling the small kitchen so that it had become stifling. She had a moment's vision of them both fighting one another to get out of a gas chamber. She deliberately put down the parcels, one by one, on the kitchen table. Jill's words ran on but she tried not to listen to them, she concentrated on the purchases she had made – spring chicken, real bortsch, clotted cream, Wensleydale, Niersteiner, Courvoisier, chocolate Bruxellois, and – special extravagance – an early lettuce. She told herself, I shall have my feast when this nonsense has petered out; she tried to harden herself against Jill's misery. But the words broke through – 'Have I tried to patronize you? Have I got at *your* unhappiness and made a public exhibition of

257

it? You, of all people, who know what it means to lose the one person who cares, who would defend you. Or perhaps Bill had become rather tired of being clever, charming Mrs Eliot's husband ...'

Meg walked out of the kitchen and sat on the divan. In a moment Jill appeared, Meg's purchases ridiculously and precariously piled in her arms. She dumped them loudly on the floor. The pettish dignity she assumed suddenly made all her normal dignity appear ridiculous to Meg. She said, 'Will you kindly get rid of these things?'

Meg said, 'Oh, Jill, come off it.' And immediately expected a torrent of abuse; but Jill sat down with her hands cupped between her knees – she looked like a gawky schoolgirl. When she spoke, the hysteria had gone from her voice, but she was no less angry.

She said, 'Meg, what makes you think you can run other people's lives as though they were children? Are you so sure that everything you have done in your life has been so triumphantly for the best?'

The blood beat in Meg's head now like a trapped animal. She said, 'My dear Jill, nobody's failed more than I have. And this time especially it seems. It appeared to me wrong and cruel that you and Evelyn should be cut off from each other by what was probably a sort of misunderstanding ...'

'There's no misunderstanding between me and my worthy son-in-law, I assure you. We understand each other very well. We fought a battle and he won. And he doesn't intend to let me forget it. "How about you coming down for a few days, Mrs S."' she mimicked Leonard's voice with an exaggeratedly cocky whine. '"We could bury the hatchet for the space of a weekend." Vulgar little beast! It's like talking to a commercial traveller.'

'Oh, don't be so snobbish, Jill. How can you be when it's so important to you? You talk about Evelyn's happiness and yet you won't shed a lot of prejudice for her sake. In any case Leonard's a rather interesting man.'

'So I understand. "Bring your friend along so that I can have someone to talk to while you and Evelyn are nattering." And then the little idiot's surprised because I know that you have put him up to asking me.'

'Well, what does it matter? He's a bit obtuse, but he means to do the right thing. All right, he *has* behaved badly, he *has* tried to keep you away. But after all you tried to keep him from marrying Evelyn.'

'And what would *you* have done? A man who despises everything that her own father did or believed in. *He* has decreed that the Navy is out of date. *He* and his scientific friends are to defend us now, God help us! Conceited little ass! I'd rather she'd married a conscientious objector like your brother David. At least they believe that they're acting on principles. The little beast and his friends are just concerned with grab and lining their own nests.'

Meg wanted to laugh, but she said, in an exaggeratedly serious voice to counter her desire, 'But, Jill, you must have met hundreds of people who think that naval warfare is out of date. I know you have strong feelings yourself, but you've always been so tolerant about other people's views. You've never seemed to care what they thought. I've always admired you for it.'

'Why *should* I care? We can't stop the rot now. But *they* aren't trying to marry Evelyn.'

It was the present tense now, Meg noticed. Jill was back fighting her battle, still unbeaten. Meg thought, I have blundered enough. I must disengage from this; I don't understand the insane borderland I've strayed into. She said, 'Jill, I *did* pass my test today. Please think what that means to me.' She was deliberately absurd and childish.

'Why should I? You didn't think of me. You were quite happy to play the sentimental fairy godmother and humiliate me with that little man. He's done everything he can to destroy Evelyn's admiration for Andrew. Do you understand what that means for me, Meg? It was the one thing I could do for Andrew's memory – to see that she gave him the love he wanted so much when he was alive. I was jealous, Meg, I kept her away from him. She could have been with us in Valetta or Gib or Singapore. She need never have been away at boarding school once the war was over. She could have been with him in those last years. But I *did* teach her to respect him and to know what a fine man he was. I've taken the chance that she would turn against me by telling her that it was my fault she never saw more of her father. I should have been willing if I'd lost her for *that*, but not for this little creature. He's taught her to laugh at Andrew's memory.'

'Now, Jill ...'

'He has, Meg. You don't know. I remember the Christmas after they were engaged. I'd given up fighting, though I couldn't pretend to like him. But I didn't want to drive her away. It started over some stupid little squabble. We were always having them; he was so cock-sure. This time it was some German word in one of those general knowledge tests the Sunday papers have at Christmastime. I said what a pity Andrew wasn't there, he would have known it. I was trying to take an interest in the wretched little creature's doings. He was so conceited about the thing too. Then the little beast said, "Oh, I don't think we need bring the old boy back from his watery grave just for that." I was used to him being unfeeling and vulgar, so I simply ignored it and said, "Evelyn's father was brilliant at languages. He could have been Naval Attaché at any time if he'd cared to crawl to the right people." I couldn't help it, Meg, I had to say something. Of course he knew what I was getting at. He said, in his most pompous voice, "I'm afraid, Mrs S., I don't believe in these brilliant men that get passed over." So I laughed and said, "Well, I hope you'll always be able to keep to that." "I shall, Mrs S., trust me." You've no idea how smug he can sound. But Evelyn, Meg, Evelyn laughed and said, "Leonard's not going to be in the Silent Service, Mother." She took his hand, "We'll see that *this* gem's pure rays shine where they're noticed." Then they both laughed. Meg, it was the quotation from Gray's Elegy that I'd used when I talked to her the day I went down to her school to tell her that Andrew had been drowned. They'd obviously made a joke of it. And there were a hundred other instances,' she said.

She would have gone on to them, but Meg said sharply, 'Jill, this does no good. I'm sure there were hundreds of things said on both sides that were hurtful.' She thought, I don't really believe that they actually said *those* things. It sounds so unreal, but she must have a score of such dialogues that she's worked up over and over again to keep her bitterness alive. 'He is smug. And Evelyn surely behaved badly. But you can't live on memories.'

Jill gave a withdrawn, contemptuous smile that made Meg think, she really is rather dotty.

'Can't I, Meg?' she said, 'I can't imagine what else we have to live on in the little beast's world. If you think they've any use for us you've got a lot to learn.' She stood for a moment, smiling vaguely; then she added dramatically, 'One thing we can do is not to whine. That's one of the things I shan't forget, Meg, that you've made me whine to you this evening. It won't happen again, I assure you. But you must go, Meg. As soon as you can manage. If you stay on after this we shall learn to hate one another.'

Meg lay on the divan that night, trying desperately to sleep. She felt that she had strayed into a fantasy world where she had no place.

If any stranger were to explore there, it should be a trained psychiatrist. No one else, at any rate, could help Jill, certainly she could not. She sweated and ached, every crevice of the divan bed seemed to be made of the roughest straw that chafed her body; her head was bursting, and to swallow was becoming an agony. She had taken a sleeping pill but it only added to her misery, for drowsiness pulled her down to sleep and as regularly pain and confused scraps of Jill's talk pulled her back into wakefulness. She tried once to get up to fetch herself a glass of water, but as soon as she stood upright on the floor, she became giddy and fell back on to the divan. A terror that she was going to be ill in Jill's flat seized her, that with illness she would find herself imprisoned in Jill's fantasy. And how could she say that it was fantasy? She rejected Jill's view of the world, she saw it as a surrender to death, but her affirmation had no ground of knowledge. Perhaps in a year she too would have locked tight within her some pitiful proclamation of defiance to the world, would smile to herself little knowing smiles.

She forced herself to remember her elation of the afternoon. I can't go back on my campaign now anyway, she thought, whether Jill's right about the world or not. And even if she is right, I want to know. She's never had any curiosity. Better be the cat that's killed than be like her. And then shame blotted out every other emotion; she could feel its physical suffusion, its blush above the discomfort and the burning of the fever. She saw a picture of herself, smiling and nodding and laughing and questioning, her face contorted into every grimace of charm. Lively, interested, helpful, thoughtful, loving Meg – out to do good for everyone, with no bother at all, least of all to herself. So quick at summing up, so quick with a touch of understanding here and there, so quick that there was no need to give a thought to what would happen really, so quick that she could keep the centre of her mind cosily and completely on herself and her own problems, and the centre of her heart too. Just rushing to the centre of people's lives and setting things right here and there and then off again as quick as she had come. The magic touch of a wand, no more was needed. And if Jill got hurt, well, really – she'd done her best and after all she had her own life and the test had been coming on so really she'd had no time. ... She saw herself gesturing and smiling and loving and worming confidences, and the face got older, wrinkles and lines came round the eyes and the mouth, but the smiling vivacity remained. Such a sweet, understanding, humorous, impulsive old woman. Seeing herself helping others, and seeing herself seeing herself helping others, and seeing herself seeing herself on and on. But always right at the centre herself, and at the end death. She could not tell, when the large tears began to pour down her cheeks, whether it was fright or self-disgust or self-pity or the constricting pain in her throat that had made her cry; but crying, she fell asleep.

She woke in the morning to a throat so painful that had she wanted to call to Jill she could hardly have done so. But she wanted above all to get up, go out and start life. When she moved in the bed, her limbs ached; when she pushed her legs out from the bed, they would not hold her. She sat on the edge of the bed and the tears flowed down once more. She must have sat so, shivering, for a quarter of an hour, before Jill came in.

'I think,' she said, and she wondered if her words were intelligible, it cost her so much to say them, 'that I've got a high temperature.'

Jill said, 'Get back into bed then. I suppose I'd better send for Dr Martin. Or do you have a doctor of your own?' She shook her head. So Dr Martin came.

Acute tonsillitis, he said, and, after hearing Jill's account of Meg's circumstances, delayed shock. Not in the technical sense, of course, but a nervous shock. He said to Meg, 'You mustn't feel worried by all this. There's nothing to be ashamed of about it. You've had a dreadful experience. The remarkable thing is that your will's kept you going for so long. I read the whole thing, of course, in the paper at the time. No one would have been surprised if you'd collapsed there and then. Rest is all you need. I'll give you a strong sedative. The inter-action of will and body depends on a very intricate mechanism.' If shame had shown in her face, Meg thought, it was because she knew what Jill must be thinking. He also said, 'Now there's no need to worry about jobs at the moment. Time enough for that when you're well again.' She did not dare to look at Jill. She would have liked to speak to the doctor on his own, but since this seemed impossible, she said, not looking at Jill, 'I can't be ill here. If necessary I must go to hospital.'

He smiled. 'Mrs Stokes will look after you all right. We'll see how you go along.'

She went along in much the same way. The tonsillitis diminished; with sedatives and sleeping pills she slept a good deal; but when she was awake she wept involuntarily until her whole body seemed en-feebled from the convulsions of sobbing.

On the fourth morning, Jill said, 'Meg, I've taken things into my own hands. It's not possible for you to be here in this condition. I'm not in the position to nurse you. I don't believe this flat is a good place for you. Dr Martin says that you can travel in a closed car, so I've rung David and he's coming this afternoon to take you down to Sussex. I don't know whether it's the right course, but I can't take the responsibility in case you break down completely.'

BOOK THREE

NURSERY INS AND OUTS

SLOWING up at the side of the road, David pressed the button to lower the hood. He said, 'People speak against these convertibles, but when you do get fine weather, it's so well worth it.'

Meg said, 'I think they're ideal, David.'

The traffic was heavy on the road on this hot May afternoon. The cars seemed to pass them in little groups of three or four, held up by some slow-driving family party or elderly couple out for the run.

David said, 'The trouble with a little spring weather round here is that all the residents of Seaford or Eastbourne come out of their retired holes to assure themselves that they aren't dead.'

Meg smiled, 'It's a real holiday scene, isn't it?' she said. David looked at her for a moment but she was still smiling sweetly out towards the downland.

He said, 'You get more variation here. I'm particularly fond of these chequered fields, especially where there are splashes of clover or mustard. It relieves the gauntness of those great, knobbly-kneed runs of downland.'

'Yes,' she said, 'they're quite beautiful. In the sun,' she added vaguely.

He said, 'All the same, I think we've had enough of picnics up on the Downs in these last few days.' She smiled at him as though in pleasure at their especial agreement about this. 'And there's quite a wind today,' she said. She seemed pleased to contribute. 'And the sea,' he said, 'even down at Cuckmere Haven, would be horribly crowded.'

'Yes, I don't think the seaside would be any cop.' If the slang word suggested a particular liveliness it was only by contrast with the uniform gentleness that now seemed to flatten out her speech. 'We could turn off here,' he said, 'into Alciston. It's one of the few villages round here that has not been tarted up for tourists. It's warm there even in winter. But I don't think it'll be too hot...'

She interrupted him, 'Oh, no,' she cried, 'it's so lovely to have the hot weather, David.'

'I managed to evade Else's picnic basket today. I thought we'd had enough delicatessen on our outings this week.'

'They're so good, aren't they?' she said. 'I'm amazed at how many things Else can do. And all so well. And she's really one of the kindest people I've ever met.'

He said, drawing up in front of a cottage with wooden benches and tables in the front garden, 'I'm afraid this will be no more than a farmhouse tea. No leberwurst.'

She said, 'How lovely.' He deliberately said nothing, did not even leave the car.

She said, after waiting for a minute or two, 'What an attractive garden it is, David. What are those spiky plants with the yellow flowers?'

'Crown Imperials. They're a fritillary. You get them in a lot of cottage gardens. There are some by the east wall in Gordon's garden.'

She said, 'Oh, I must go and look at them when we get back.'

At the tea table, piling strawberry jam on to her slices of bread and butter, she said as though continuing a conversation, 'I suppose you're right. I *did* always resent Father leaving us like that and probably I *did* blame it on Mother.' She frowned at the puzzle. 'I think,' she said, 'I never was able to see that they were just incompatible and that by not accepting it I only made things more difficult for her. Poor Mother!'

David said, '*I* think so.'

Meg said, 'Oh, yes, I'm sure, David.' She helped herself to two pieces of madeira cake at once.

David said, 'Those'll be rather dry, Meg. Let me ask for some more jam.'

She looked at him a moment questioningly. 'Oh, would you, David? That would be lovely. I love jam on cake. Yes, I'm sure you're right. That the only thing to think about them both is that they were as they were. Or at any rate that *we* couldn't have done anything about it. Of course, I think I was bound to think as I did then. I don't blame myself for that. That would be silly, don't you think?' She was speaking so quickly with her mouth full that David had some difficulty in understanding her. 'After all,' she went on, 'the girl sides with the father and the boy with the mother. I always thought those rules were too simple to be true, but I don't see why they shouldn't be, do you? As you say, it's far better to accept these things.'

'I don't think I ever said quite that, Meg,' he laughed.

She laughed in answer but a little strainedly. 'No. I don't suppose you did. I meant your general view of withdrawal.' She paused. 'What I mainly mean,' she went on, 'is that I really think that I can now accept Mother and why she was as she was.'

David said, frowning, 'You were bound to find it a strain living with her. You could never live like that. Any more than I could.'

She said, 'No, we couldn't, could we? All that moving about.'

'I don't think it was only that for you, Meg, you know. It was the sort of places and people she moved about in.'

'It wasn't my sort of world certainly. But they were both very restless. Father must have been driven on by something too.'

'I think *he* was ambitious, though heaven knows it came to nothing. And curious about things too,' David added judiciously.

Meg said without a moment's pause, 'Yes, I suppose that, when I *really* come to think about it, I see that he was.' She ate the remaining biscuit. 'I think *I* just want to stay put.' She laughed.

He said, waiting for the change from a pound, 'Shall we walk up into the foot of the Downs?'

'Oh, yes. That would be lovely,' she cried. She got up and set off to the gate so that he had to run to catch her up.

She said, pulling off buds from the heads of yarrow and dropping them into the high grass as they walked up the road, 'You *do* really think that I could not have managed at Jill's, David?'

He said, 'Yes, of course. I've told you so. In any case,' he laughed, 'I honestly think from the way she spoke that she wouldn't have let you stay there.'

'No, I don't mean that. I mean you *do* think that it was understandable my trying to improve things between her and Evelyn, even though I went the wrong way about it.'

'Yes. Very understandable. As you know I personally believe that one can't help people much. I'm inclined to think it's better to stand aside.'

'You *do* mean then that I should have adapted myself to Jill's attitude to Leonard ...'

'No, no,' David interrupted. 'Withdrawal doesn't mean acceptance. In fact in this case literally the opposite. You should have withdrawn yourself altogether. There's no cause to moralize about Jill Stokes's embittered attitude, but there's also no reason for living with it. What would be the sense of that?'

Meg walked beside him in silence for a few minutes. She continued to flick buds from the weeds as she walked. A tough scabious plant resisted the light pull of her finger-tips and she stopped for a moment, dragging at the whole plant. Its steady resistance seemed to rouse her from her thoughts, for she said, 'It's so difficult to give other people what one doesn't ask for oneself. Although I see that that's an egotistical approach. And not satisfactory. Just because I don't feel that my pride is a sort of guardian of Bill's memory doesn't mean that Jill truly…' She broke off, then a second later began to speak very quickly, 'I *do* think I was *bound* to feel that I should try and make some effort to come out of my grief. And then Jill's feelings about things were so much what I feared to fall into. You see the suddenness and the strangeness of Bill's death don't really make any difference to the fact. I have to adapt myself like anybody else. Only, Andrew's must have seemed the same to Jill. As you might expect, I'd never really fully thought about that. But you see Bill's death *was* an awful shock and I thought, "I won't ever be caught off my guard again. I must know what's going on in the world." It seemed so important not to sit back. I ought to have known after the fool I made of myself with Tom Pirie, but I was surprised when I talked to Jill's son-in-law. You see Bill and I lived in a very narrow circle in a way …'

David had been looking anxiously around as the words poured out over him. Now from the last farmhouse yard of the village came waddling a fat green-black Muscovy duck. He said, 'I like those creatures.'

Meg broke off immediately. 'Oh, yes,' she cried, 'they *are* delightful, aren't they? What sort of ducks are they?'

'Muscovy ducks,' he said, 'They're excellent table birds.' He waited as though expecting some comment on this phrase but none came. 'The white are particularly fine,' he added. Then, as they left the village behind, she said suddenly, 'You're very *good* at withdrawing. From conversations, I mean.'

He laughed. 'It's nice to hear a little bite in your comments again, Meg,' he said.

In her turn she laughed but nervously. 'Is it, David?' she said. 'I'm afraid I must be an awful bore nowadays. But there's so little reason for biting. Honestly, David, I shouldn't have believed that people could have been so kind as everyone has been here. Else, it goes without saying, of course. But did I tell you how good Mrs Rattray was? She'd come in to see you, I think, and she heard me crying upstairs.

I'd got up to wash my face and I broke a bottle of hand lotion. My hands were cut and everything seemed so hopeless. She was so kind and so *efficient*. She's been a nurse, hasn't she? Did I tell you how good she was, David?'

'Yes,' he said, 'you did tell me, Meg.'

'But I don't think I told you that it was she who first suggested that her husband should visit me. She said it would do me good to see men as well as women. Tim's a quite enchanting person, isn't he? He's obviously first rate at his job. And then Mrs Boniface! She's wonderful. The crown of all daily helps and yet not just a character but a person.' She searched his face as she spoke.

He said, 'I'm glad they've all been so helpful.' They had passed the small copse now and were out on the open downland. He sat down abruptly on a grassy hummock. 'Meg,' he said, 'if there were anything at Srem Panh that you felt you hadn't truly faced, you wouldn't let any silliness about money stand in the way of your taking a trip back there, would you?'

Her short, tight skirt did not allow her to spread herself on the grass with his agility. She stood over him, her shadow cutting out the sun, reminding him how cold the wind still was, and he thought how smart she always managed to look – this brownish-pink dress, for instance. Looking at her now, he could hardly identify her as she had been throughout April – with her hair seldom brushed, her face grubbily white without make-up, her dressing gown food-stained; but the breakdown had nevertheless marked her so that she looked at moments sixty and then again sometimes five or six years less than her age.

She said, 'Srem Panh? Oh no, David, there's nothing there. I've almost ceased to remember it, thanks to Andredaswood. When I look out of my window in the morning here over to the forest, I ...'

He interrupted her, 'Look, Meg,' he said, 'there could be things there that have played some part in your illness. You have spoken once or twice of your feeling above all that the unknown had so suddenly struck at you. And it was so, of course. I feel that the events that caused Bill's death lie behind you, like a cupboard full of bogies. I can understand you shutting the doors so firmly at the time. At the time you wanted to escape. But now it worries me, I confess, that you should seem so little curious about the background to his death.' She had folded herself down beside him now; her long legs tucked under her, her knees protruding below her skirt. She stared at him in distress, but he looked away and continued talking. 'Perhaps if you were only to read some books about the place. And the families of those young men – I understand so well what a horror it was to you to be able to do nothing to save them. I know that's all past, but the families might need help.' His voice died away. He saw as soon as he said it that there was nothing for her in Badai. Yet he knew he was searching for some expression of the disquiet he felt.

Meg seemed surprised at his incoherence. She waited for him to say more, picking at the straggling roots of a cinquefoil. Then she said, 'Oh, I don't think so, David. I've felt that this sudden blow from out-side was only a symbol of my ignorance of the world. That I'd been punished for living in a fool's paradise. But to say that a thing is a sym-bol surely means in a way that it's something one should dismiss once one's seen what it's a symbol of, doesn't it? It did make me feel that I shouldn't be caught again. That I should be more involved here in England. Now I don't know really. But I never thought I ought to know anything about Badai. Why should I? It was purely accidental that it all happened there. And as to the possibility that such accidents have some meaning on another level, I know little enough about the surface reality without looking further. I was upset that I could do nothing for these men, but it taught me, I must say, the limitations of my powers. That lesson ought to have made me more withdrawn if anything could. But I see I don't understand what you mean by with-drawal if it implies involvement in Badai politics.'

He saw that her smile was ironical. Once again he was pleased that she should be laughing at him and pleased, too, that his incoherence had made her speak with some certainty. He laughed. 'I was being illogical,' he said. He thought how delighted Gordon would have been with the whole occasion. 'I think you're quite right. I just wanted you to feel that there was no difficulty about money.'

'Oh, I shouldn't if I wanted it,' she said. 'But in any case Doctor Loder has been most emphatic that I should forget the whole thing as far as I can. I do consider myself lucky in having him. He's quite un-usual for a G.P., David, isn't he? He's so alive and intelligent.'

David said, 'He's all right. He couldn't have been more obtuse over Gordon's death but ...'

She looked for a few moments distressed and anxious, then she said, 'Yes, I suppose he is very limited. Everyone here seems so special to me.'

David got up. 'I think we should go back now,' he said briskly.

269

Seated in the car, he said, 'Shall we go back through Lewes and have a drink there, or round through Glynde?' Before she could refuse, he said, 'No, Meg, I want you to decide.'

Distressed, she stared at him. 'Don't you think,' she said at last, 'that with so many people about we might avoid the town and have a quiet drink at home?'

'Well. Yes, I do,' he said.

'I'm so glad,' she said. Relief at his agreement seemed to relax her. She lay back and closed her eyes.

As they were following the hairpin river road, he cried, startled by a sudden grey streak of flight, 'There goes a heron, Meg.'

She woke startled. 'Oh, yes. How fascinating!' she cried. And now she sat, looking out of the window and commenting brightly. 'Isn't that an enchanting church? Are there many Norman churches around here, David? What an attractive white house! Whose lodge gates are those, I wonder? It's so beautiful at this time of the evening, isn't it?'

He could have kicked himself for destroying her mood of calm. At last he said, 'I think your dress is very beautiful. I'd forgotten how smart you always succeed in looking, Meg.'

She stopped in the middle of a sentence extolling the size of an elm tree and looked at him. Then she laughed, 'Did you think I'd wear that old sat out tweed skirt for the rest of my life, David? Of course not. Only I couldn't really put on anything decent while I was still weeping everywhere, could I?''

He felt that he had struck a hopeful note of disagreement. He sought to improve on it. 'Would you call that dress pink or brown?' he asked.

'Or beige, I wonder?' she said still laughing and imitating his rather prissy tone. 'Do you really want to know, David? They've all come back, you know, the beiges and the dirty pinks that Mother would have worn when we were children if she'd been smarter and less determined always to wear smart black.'

He said, 'I don't remember.'

She answered, 'Oh, nonsense. You're only two years younger than I am. If I wanted to be whimsical I should ask myself what happens to all these delightful colours when they aren't in fashion. Do they live in some world of absolute values?'

'Do you want to be whimsical?'

'No. I don't think so. Except perhaps about those dirndl skirts Else wears in the evenings.' She closed her eyes again and slept. As they approached Andredaswood, he woke her.

'Meg,' he said hesitantly, 'I think we'll have to do without an expedition tomorrow.'

She was at once alarmed. 'Oh, dear God!' she said.

'Well, I really must give some attention to the nursery. You do see that.'

She answered quickly, 'Oh, yes, of course, I do see that. Yes, of course you must. I'll sit in Gordon's garden if the weather stays hot like this. Perhaps you may find you have a few moments in the afternoon and come and sit with me?'

'I'm sure I shall,' he said.

'Well, you mustn't come unless you're really able to, David. I intend to start reading Hardy through again. So I'll be quite all right. Do you think I should begin with Bathsheba or with the Albrights?' she asked as they stopped at the front door. 'I thought not *Jude* because it's not typical,' she was saying as they went into the house.

Else Bode, greeting them in the hall, asked, 'And was the country also so beautiful today, Meg?'

'Oh, yes. It was quite lovely,' Meg answered.

'There is some sadness in this middle May all the same. The first time that young Spring finds himself a little tired and cannot think why it is so.'

'Yes,' Meg said immediately. 'Yes. That is true, Else.' She seemed to search for some addition to her acquiescence. 'The leaves are perhaps losing a little of their variety.' She received Else's smile of agreement with pleasure. David started up the stairs. 'I'm fairly sure not *Tess*,' Meg said. Her voice seemed to David to follow him, trying to hold him. 'I know that to begin with Angel Clare would put me off. Or don't you feel that about *Tess*, David?'

David, driving back from the rhododendron show at Vincent Square with Tim Rattray, thought, Gordon would have made much more of this success of Tim's. It was true that Gordon had agreed heartily before his illness that this business of starting an Andredaswood series of varieties was all against their scheme of things. 'Nevertheless,' he had said, 'Tim Rattray wouldn't have come here if he hadn't been able to raise new rhododendrons, so we've only ourselves to blame if we're saddled with his successes. Besides, David, we shall get a little prestige without you soiling your hands one speck by contributing to it. I'm always pleased when your rigid ethics reveal their casuistries. It is unfortunate, of course, that Tim's additions to English horticulture should be of such extreme hideousness, but then that only ensures a greater market for them. Our moral duty at least is clear: we mustn't allow our aesthetics to get in the way of his enjoyment of his triumphs.'

Certainly today's first prize winner seemed more than ever difficult to praise. He wondered how even Gordon would have managed it. Bloom (gigantic) white flecked green, eye scarlet shading into a delicate shell pink. He had almost thought of putting his foot down at Tim's chosen name – Andredaswood Loveliness, until he had reflected that no other name could do it justice. Anyway, it was Tim's variety and Tim's the right to name it.

He said, 'I do wish you'd have let me persuade you to have that slap-up dinner at the Savoy.'

'Persuade! I almost went down on my hands and knees. The juices of that fillet steak are still in my mouth to remind me that I shall never taste it. If that's what you call persuading, your entertainment claim isn't going to worry the tax inspector much.'

David remembered all too clearly the reason why his persuasion had not been stronger. He said, 'Well as soon as you told me Eileen was expecting ...'

'Oh, Eileen's expected before,' Tim shouted to drown David's continuing, 'and she hasn't died of it.' He laughed loudly at his own joke. Then he said, 'No wonder they say sentimental old bachelors. I believe you think that the matrimonial state consists in anniversaries and special little dinners and what not. Eileen wouldn't care whether we toasted the Andredaswood Loveliness tonight or next Saturday week as long as she had the drink. I've never known anyone so ardent for the married bliss of others. You ought to try your own medicine. I've never known why you ...' He stopped. David saw with alarm that a bright pink blush had crept over Tim's cheeks and neck. People should never ask themselves questions, he thought. But they both began to speak at once.

'I should like to join you and Eileen in drinking a toast ...'

'Well, at any rate, you'll join us.'

They could laugh the moment away. Such luck doesn't happen often, David thought; there's a good chance, too, that he hasn't seen my consciousness of his embarrassment.

'I can get two bottles of champagne,' he said, 'if we stop at the house before going to your place.'

'Excellent. And you can fetch Mrs Eliot along. And the Bode if she likes.'

'I'd rather confine the occasion to you and Eileen, if you don't mind, Tim.'

'Oh, I think we ought to have Mrs Eliot. I'm sure the more she's in on any social occasion the better. Besides she's so easy on the eyes. I'd thought I'd give her a bloom or two and make some asinine speech about Andredaswood Loveliness.'

'We can have another more official party one evening this week. We can ask the staff and you can make your speech then.'

'Christ! I don't think I'd like that.'

'Why not?'

'Well, I can't keep this look of modest pride on my chivvy forever.'

'All right. But I want the chance to talk to Eileen alone this evening. I mean to the two of you.'

'Good Lord! Is this where I get the push?'

'No,' said David. 'I want to ask Eileen one or two things about my sister.'

'Oh!' They drove on in silence for twenty minutes, then Tim said, 'I don't want to barge in where I'm not wanted or anything, but I must say I think it's a frightfully bad idea to start talking about her behind her back. I'm not an expert on nervous breakdowns, but I know what moods and depressions mean. I know if any heavy depression moved down from Iceland and settled over me, nothing would make me go up the wall more than to think that people were getting together about me in corners. Anyway she's made such a terrific recovery.'

'Yes,' said David. 'Yes. She has. All the same I should like to talk to Eileen.'

'Eileen was in a children's ward. I hope you realize that.'

'Oh, it's not because she's been a nurse. It's because she's a very sensible person.'

'Ah, there of course I'm with you all along the line.'

There, when they arrived, was Eileen Rattray, half the right little wife to come home to, with all cares of house or children banished for her weary hero, and half, since John and Anne were still shouting upstairs, the kindly, efficient, no nonsense modern mother. Seeing her, David thought, what sort of sentimentalism makes me determined to denote her the one very sensible person on the place. Normally, perhaps, it was because he wanted above all to get on with Tim's wife, for a hundred mixed reasons – preventive, defensive, apologetic, identifying. This evening, however, he knew quite well why it was: she was the one person who was likely to give him the advice he wanted to hear. What fakers we all are, he thought.

They toasted Andredaswood Loveliness. Tim said, 'We ought to get some proper champagne glasses, darling. Even if it is only for the odd occasion.' He looked, as David had never seen him before, pompous as he said it, although it was clear that he intended to look composedly worldly. To David's regret, Eileen took her husband's manner quite seriously. 'Yes, darling,' she said, 'but I think you'd better choose them. I should have no idea what to get.' So much for the 'good sense' you're so determined to see in her, David told himself: he scouted the idea of 'loyalty'.

'I'm not stopping at this, you know. I'm determined to put Andredaswood on the pothunter's map, despite all David's isolation policy. With any luck I ought to push through Andredaswood Splendour and Andredaswood Daintiness next year.'

David, as he smiled his congratulations, pictured them. Green white (gigantic), eye chocolate shading to oxblood; and white flecked rosepink (gigantic), eye lilac shading to pale mauve. Even daintiness for Tim would have to be gigantic. He realized that Tim's ghastly taste only added to his attraction. He felt too that in not objecting to Andredaswood Daintiness he was performing a very satisfactory act of self-abnegation. Anyway it was all a just punishment for having agreed to maintain the pretentious name of 'Andredaswood' when they moved in.

He said, 'Eileen, I wanted to ask you how you thought Meg was getting on?'

Tim said, 'Mr Chairman may I once more register a formal protest before this unsuitable matter begins.'

David said, 'Tim thinks it's wrong for me to discuss Meg when she's not there. But after all I have to do it with the doctor and it's much more useful to talk to you.'

'I didn't say wrong. I said it might upset her if she got to hear of it.'

'Oh, no,' Eileen said, 'that's silly, darling. She won't get to hear of it. But what's the matter, David, anyway? She's made good progress for a depressive.'

'Yes,' David said doubtfully.

'I think it's amazing how she's pulled herself out of it considering what she's been through.' It was clear that Tim, for all his scruples, intended to contribute.

'Oh, depressives can help up themselves quite a lot,' Eileen said. David longed to remind her that she had after all been a children's nurse.

'Oh, yes,' David said, 'she's a person of great courage and strength of will. That's perhaps what worries me. She's content here, even happy. But it's such an acquiescent sort of contentment. There's nothing here for her. She used to have such spirit and now she's ...' he mumbled, then said, 'I wish she wasn't so anxious to please.'

'Good manners,' Tim said. 'Besides, isn't that exactly what you were asking for? You said to me the day you went up to town to fetch her that she'd stuck her neck out too much. You said she ought to detach herself more from things, take things more peacefully; or something like that. I think she's marvellous.'

Tim's reference to his illogicality somehow annoyed David very much. He said irritably, 'That's not really to the point, Tim. In any case you've misunderstood me. I don't grumble at her being more detached. Certainly not. It would be a great step forward. But she's not really. She's calmer, and that's excellent as far as it goes. But it's a negative sort of calm, or rather I feel that it's a desperate sort of calm. It's too near to apathy. Quite honestly, Eileen, I'm worried lest she should simply lapse into a feeble, contented dependence. I feel that I ought to urge her at least to *think* about getting a job. Detachment without some simple function to fulfil is an impossibility in *this* world.' He noted his emphasis with horror, but the others had not noticed it. Nevertheless he corrected himself. 'Today. The only thing is that *I* can't really be the one to suggest it.'

Eileen clearly welcomed this more practical aspect of his views. 'Yes, I see, David,' she said, 'but hers isn't a hysteric case, you know. She's a genuine depressive. Doctor Loder says so.'

Tim drank his glass of champagne off in one gulp and gave himself another. 'How do you know what Loder says?' he asked angrily.

'I think Climbers told me,' she answered casually.

'And how the hell ...?'

But David intervened, 'I'm afraid, Tim, there's an inevitability of leakage with all these women.' He smiled in turn at both of them.

'Nevertheless, Eileen, I'm not entirely content with Terence Loder's diagnosis. She's never had depressive fits before.'

Eileen laughed a little scornfully. 'I don't think I should start on a home diagnosis, David, it's liable to be as dangerous as home nursing. The truth is you're frightened that she'll stay put here, aren't you?'

'I'm very happy to have her here,' he said. 'I don't want her to be dependent on *me* that's all.'

Tim looked disgusted; but Eileen said, 'No, that's very reasonable.' She considered for a moment. 'I think, David,' she said, 'that we ought to rely on Doctor Loder's opinion. But if my opinion seems of use to you, I must say that I feel certain she's not ready to stand on her own feet yet. I'll tell you what I shall do. I'll keep an eye on the situation myself, and at the same time I'll look out for any jobs that might suit her. I think we should try to find something far enough away to give her the opportunity to live on her own but not too far in case she feels lost. The thing has to be done by stages, you know.'

David thanked her. He was furious with himself; he had sought agreement and assistance in carrying out his wishes, he had gained only interference.

David had been dreading the first week in June. Then must be held the first large cocktail party without Gordon. The two annual winter parties, smaller, indoor, but covering together the same list of guests as the June 'do' had been cancelled that year at the last moment. Gordon had fought for them but the week before the first had seen his last haemorrhage and collapse. David was determined to avoid all occasions that edged around the blank space in mourning black. He believed too that Gordon's charm alone had made their entertainments successful; he was certain that Gordon's presence, his affectionate, malicious post-mortems alone had made them tolerable. He said, 'The June party's always menaced by threats of bad weather. Not content with this, people must discuss weather prophecies for days beforehand and chatter weather platitudes at the party itself. English summer weather! What a theme! The June party becomes like reading a book of *Times* light leaders or a set of old *Punches*. In any case there are so many garden parties at this time of the year that people will be delighted to find that there is one less. It will be an advertisement for the place in itself.'

His proposal was very ill-received. Else said, 'David, I do not think it would be right for Gordon's friends to think that they are not wanted here any more. And all our old friends! They have been so good in respecting our wishes to be private, but the time has come when we must recognize their kindness. People speak always of Gordon's June party. And yours. They expect it. To cancel it would be such a selfish indulgence.'

It was as though he were Queen Victoria being told to put off her mourning. He answered coldly, 'My dear Else, we're not the royal family, you know.'

But reproachfully her large sad eyes followed him. She said, 'David, I know that you feel lost without him. I do so too. When a big oak dies, all the small trees suddenly know that they are only small trees. They feel afraid of the light from which they have always been protected. But in the end they adapt themselves to the new conditions. But because we are men and women, and not trees, we remember the big oak and we honour it. I am sorry for the sermon, but it's true, isn't it? The June party, especially this one, is in Gordon's honour, I think.'

He wanted to say, 'Fiddle-de-dee', had he not known that Gordon, in less ridiculous words, would have shared Else's feelings. 'Not for myself,' he would have said, 'but because we disregard piety at our peril.'

Climbers also was much distressed. She saw herself as pledged to certain customers – her favourite ones – on the question of the June party. Her whole success in the nursery seemed to her at stake if she did not 'keep her word' now. 'I think Colonel Fowler will be frightfully upset, David,' she said. 'He told me last week that they looked on it as the best party of the summer.' 'Poor Mrs Archer! She's arranged for a hired car. And she's not very well off.' 'I think it's the children who will be disappointed. The Glovers and the Tuckeys.'

Tim simply said, 'Oh, I think it would be rather impossible to cancel it now, David. That's the trouble with that sort of publicity. It's not needed, but once you've started it, it is an unusual thing; people would think the business was rocky if you left it off. Unless, of course, we were a much bigger sort of business than we are. I imagine that's why other nurseries wouldn't think of it.'

David longed to point out many things in answer to this; the June party was not a publicity stunt (but then, of course, since they invited their best local customers, that would not be entirely true); the 'business' that he and Gordon had built up was infinitely larger than they had ever hoped for (but this, of course, did not make it one of the big nurseries, even of south-east England); the other nurserymen did not have the personality of Gordon, or indeed of himself (but this, of course, was hardly an answer). He contented himself with saying, 'It isn't entirely, or indeed primarily, a business affair, Tim. A great percentage of the people we invite are personal friends. And those who are customers are nearly all people we've been entertained by.'

'Well you can always leave out purely personal friends if you don't want the expense.'

'It's nothing to do with the expense.' David saw no way to explain to Tim what exactly were his reasons. He said, 'I can't think of the occasion without Gordon there.' He thought that Tim concealed both impatience and a smile of amusement at this.

'Fair enough,' Tim said, 'the reasons are personal. Then don't ask any intimate friends that might upset you. Make it clear it's an entirely business party this year. Eileen will be a bit upset. You remember Gordon told her to ask any of her playmates to the three annual parties. But I'll tell her tonight to say nothing to them. I should have the nursery name printed on the invites, that'll make it quite clear.'

David thought of Else's expression if he did this. He said, 'No. Don't say anything. I haven't made up my mind yet. I'll let you know tomorrow.' He thought, every one of them is concerned with his or her own interest; but then, of course, so was he.

He looked forward to his quiet drink with Meg in the private garden at six that evening. Since a week ago, when they had given up their expeditions, he had set aside this hour and a half before dinner to be with her. There were seasons in the year when he could not have done so; he doubted if his work truly allowed him to do so now. Nevertheless he felt it a duty and he knew increasingly that the duty was a pleasure. Later, after dinner, she was always so careful not to disturb his work on 'Africa', so anxious to fit in with Else, that he was glad when she had removed her distracting self-effacingness to bed. But here in the garden she seemed so genuinely relaxed that her few exclamations of pleasure came spontaneously, and most of their conversation was of the past or of books. And their explorations of the past, David thought, were now without danger of sudden squalls or treacherous reefs beneath the smooth running waters.

They had made so many explanations to one another – of their attitudes to their parents, to each other as they had been in youth, to the caravanserai life with their mother; he had explained his pacifism, she her social ambitions – the years of estrangement really seemed to have been expiated in mutual confession. The quarrels of childhood, the battles of youth had been fought over again with a historian's detached judgement. If the victories now seemed less glorious, the defeats less ignominious, and both less decisive, cause and effect had been diagnosed in proper academic fashion and their whole relationship could now be accepted as historic stream without too much committal to its inevitability. A nice middle-road historian's position, he thought to himself with comforting irony. They had said more than once that analysis was not cure, that self-knowledge had no magic power to alter, that review of the past was not revocation; but the statements, he saw now, were probably no more than verbal safeguards, for the truth was that they did at last feel free to live together for that short evening time in a past that was dredged of conflict. A loving exchange of family snapshots Meg had called it. But they had both agreed that the evenings were no less cosy because they often mocked at the cosiness.

David admitted that his own quiet acceptance of Meg's view of their youth concealed as many reservations as did, no doubt, also her eager acquiescence in his analysis. She had said once, 'How pleased Mother would have been. She was always urging us "to agree to differ".' And he had answered, 'I don't think she could have recognized the state, Meg. Like many of her cherished maxims, it was quite beyond her scope to achieve it.'

There were parts of their lives, of course, that they had, by unspoken agreement, buried. About Gordon he was prepared to speak only superficially to her, and, because of this perhaps, she receded from the few confidences she had made about Bill. The future, too, they seldom discussed, though his suspicions of her passivity pushed now and again beneath the surface of his talk with horrid urgency. But books and the past – their own recreation of a dead world, the creations of other worlds by men now dead – mingled together in a growingly easeful communion.

So easeful, David realized, that today he felt prepared, indeed was impatient, to consult her about the party. Reflecting that to do so implied an acceptance of her own view of herself as now 'all right again', of her position at Andredaswood as 'settled', he excused himself by saying that unless he asked her for advice, he could not easily expect her to take advice from him.

Stretched almost horizontal on the bamboo chaise-longue, her face dappled with the bright sunshine and the flickering shadows of ilex eaves above, surrounded by martini, cigarettes, matches, *Jude the Obscure*, she seemed indeed a peaceful, relaxed fixture amid the fussing irritation of Nursery politics – the oracle on tap in the grove.

She listened and then said, 'But David, you must tell them that you don't intend to have the party.' She was so definite, yet her advice rested on shifting ground, for, as with Tim yet how differently, he evaded more than perfunctory mention of Gordon, and she pursued this central theme not at all. So that when he expressed a little more strongly the sentiments of the others in opposing his wish, she said, 'I see. Well, my dear, parties are always a fuss. But since it seems you must have this one to satisfy them – and they are all of them such darlings – we must make sure that everything goes well and without any bother to you. Dear God,' she smiled, 'if I know anything it's about giving parties. Leave it to me, David. It will be such a pleasure to be of some use. I promise you it will be all right.'

Such echoes of the past came from the assurance, such a conviction of freedom from anxiety, that he felt now quite free. He laughed, of course, at the superstition of his conviction. 'I don't know how you propose to do that,' he said.

'No, I don't suppose you do,' she said, 'but I wouldn't promise if I couldn't, would I?' They passed at once without his arguing further to a discussion of 'We are too many'. 'It *does* jar,' she said. 'You were right.'

'Hardy could only fall back on melodrama when his immediate vision failed him.'

'Yes,' she said doubtfully, 'I know that you academic people distrust my sort of testing of fiction by life. But I believe that that's the key. Arabella and the pigs is melodrama of a kind after all. But that I can believe. She's so like that awful woman who cooked for Mother in the Deal days. But the suicide of small children!' She shrugged her shoulders. He was conscious of sinking luxuriously back twenty years into familiar talk of Art and Life.

Meg's contribution to the party was to go to London. She came back with two new dresses and orders for lobster, chicken, and veal patties placed at Fortnum's.

'You see,' she said, 'I promised I should help over the party, David.' It was after eleven at night when she returned and she brought a strange atmosphere of rather dated sophistication into the drawing room where David and Else had been practising the Bartók. She was wearing a new hat that she had bought that day and her scent clashed with the scent of the tobacco plant coming through the window. She gave herself a whisky and soda and flopped on to the sofa. 'Oh, it's so heavenly here,' she said. 'Do go on playing.' It was, David thought, a most curiously stagey behaviour, almost as though Edith Evans had suddenly come to Andredaswood.

Else, who had up to then managed to avoid practising in Meg's presence, played shockingly. At the end she said, 'I'm afraid I shall never be happy with it, David. It's so much from the head and so little from the spirit.'

Meg, leaning over the sofa back to speak to them, asked, 'What is it?'

'The first Bartók quartet,' he told her.

'It's quite beyond me. I shouldn't know if Else was playing the right notes or the wrong ones.'

Not Edith Evans, David thought, Kay Hammond. He looked to see the expression on her face. It was clear that she had said it with a certain malice, yet it was also clear that she was too pleased with life to think that Else or anyone else could be offended. There was nothing in such a mood, either general or particular, that should have pleased him, yet he found himself delighted that she was there, longing for Else to go to bed. He deflected the conversation from Else's playing.

'The new hat is nice,' he said.

'I'm glad you didn't say what Viola said, "*Silly* but nice",' Meg answered. 'She has some sort of idea that a new hat should advertise a woman's frivolous side, whatever that may be. Part I suppose of women's duty to attract men that Viola's so keen on.' She laughed.

'You saw Viola?'

'Evidently, David darling. I gave her lunch. I asked Tom, but he didn't come. I'll get him next time I go up though, I'm determined to lay all those ghosts. I had Poll out to dinner. We laughed so much she upset the wine.'

Else gave him a knowing look that said, Hysteria, Watch out, but he only asked with a malicious giggle, 'What about Jill?'

'All right,' Meg said, 'I know. I shirked my Waterloo. But I'll ask her next time. It's quite all right, David, now, you see, because I can treat *them*. I realize now that all the trouble happened because they were in a position to patronize me. I suppose it's rather moral sucks to me that I couldn't take it. But I couldn't. Oh, it's so marvellous being down here and spending nothing and then being able to go to London and do things properly. You are an angel, David.'

David, seeing Else's expression change, thought, if the next phase of Meg's behaviour is to be like this, we're in for a lot of trouble.

'We are all very tired, I think,' Else said, 'and ready for bed.'

'I'm not,' Meg said, 'but, for goodness' sake, don't worry about me.'

After Else had gone, David thought that at least he should suggest to Meg the effect she had produced on Else.

He said, 'Your mood's very euphoric.'

'Euphoric? I don't think so. Unless that means having had a few drinks.'

Unwilling to produce a hostile reaction, unwilling perhaps to destroy her gaiety, he left aside what he had intended to say. He compromised by saying, 'Don't in helping me about the party, tread too much on the others' territory. Else and Mrs B. are so used to running this sort of thing here.' He knew as he said it that, though the speech seemed relevant to what he had intended to tell her, it wasn't so.

She said, laughing, 'Oh, don't fuss about your old party, David. I said I'd help and I shall. But I'm not going to wait or wash up, if that's what you're worried about. I like it down here far too much to do those sorts of things.' She smiled at him and, soon after, fell asleep on the sofa.

In fact, she was of the greatest help when the party took place. She looked her exotic best, and although this reminded David of her precarious nervous balance, it seemed to assure his guests that his sister, at any rate, had her feet securely planted on some good, worldly ground. She talked to everyone, amused them, and made them talk. David could see that though their neighbours and customers had been charmed by Gordon into accepting an eccentric household, they were very pleased to be charmed by Meg without any need to forget their prejudice. He was a little alarmed by some of the remarks he overheard her making – 'No, I don't know a *thing* about gardening, I'm afraid, but they all work so frightfully hard here that I'm sure it's good for them to have someone about who just sits all day'; and, 'Yes, I adore it. I hated it when I lived near here as a girl, but then I was always having to *do* things. What I hadn't realized was that Sussex was such a wonderful place to be idle in.' There were those, of course, besides David who were worried by such remarks. It was not, could not be, in view of their active daily lives, their picture of life in Sussex. But Meg got away with it, he could see, even with the women. They felt, he imagined, as he did, the communication of her energetic pleasure, although on occasion he heard Gordon's voice in one of his favourite phrases, 'I say, dear, aren't you living it up a bit much.' But how could he say what was 'much' for Meg? She seemed fully in control of her mood.

There were, David noticed, two women who perhaps were not entirely with her. Else gave him many little looks of conspiratorial alarm. He heard her once in conversation with someone speak in uncharacteristically sharp tones. 'Yes, you are quite right. Like a humming bird. What a charming idea! It is unfortunate really that Mr Parker has decided to close down the stove house. Mrs Eliot should have tropical plants for her background.' Eileen Rattray, too, clearly insisted on a clinical view, for at Meg's remark to some guests, 'Heaven knows what delicious things they feed me on here! Lotuses, I think, I'm getting so fat and lazy,' she said, 'We must find some rehabilitation exercises for you, Mrs Eliot.'

Even with Else and Eileen however, David was amused to see that, whether by design or by accident, Meg effaced a good deal of the bad impression she had made, by singling out for special attention among the guests, of all improbable people – the Rogersons. Or perhaps not improbable for when Meg declared her wish to know more of the world around her she was surely sincere. And the Rogersons were probably a less known factor to her than all the wealthy stockbrokers, retired service officers, and horsey, doggy old maids, or indeed than the odd stage star or successful country tweed television personality. Again, too, she might well have cultivated them to please him because, as Else had told her, Fred Rogerson was the only other local who had been in the Friends' Ambulance Unit besides himself and Gordon. She was hardly to know that, despite this bond, he didn't really much like either Fred or Joan Rogerson. Fred with his quiet, pipe smoking, pacifist Labour assurance had exactly the sort of personality that increasingly impressed him as aggressive in a manner the more dangerous because there was no consciousness; Joan, the hiking, canvassing companion turned wife, had a minority-dedicated heart that not even devotion could mute to her husband's still, small beat of peace. He knew that the Rogersons thought him off-beat, unrealistic, smug; he thought them smug and unrealistic and sincere, and evaded them more than the colonels and stockbrokers whose unrealistic, sincere aggression touched nothing in him.

But for Eileen Rattray, who, before the babies came, had taught first aid with Fred as headmaster at the glass and steel Comprehensive

Secondary School, the Rogersons were the nearest thing to sensible, normal people this side of Crawley New Town. She was not with them politically – thought them children playing in a game for professional crooks – but hygienically, domestically, artistically, and, above all, socially she was with them body and soul.

Poor Eileen, David thought, she had been so unlucky in the circumstances of her life; in an England teeming with her kind, she had first to associate with the peasant backwardness of Irish Catholic nurses and then with the difficult problem of the Sussex *rentiers*. The Rogersons were her first breath of reality since she had left home. That Meg got on so well with them was clearly a bulls-eye score with Eileen.

With Else, too. In general, the Rogersons, like the Rattrays, represented too much the materialism of the modern world for Else; only fools put their faith in washing machines, glass and steel, and a Comprehensive School. There was, of course, music, but then they were undiscriminating; and child art, but David remembered only too well how deficient she had found them in piety towards the Vienna School. And then had come Nuclear Disarmament, and the Rogersons – silly children with their caloried school meals and their school recognized skiffle groups (it's valid, it's a community expression) – because somehow spiritually one with the trees and the rivers – good people. With her, too, Meg's success with the Rogersons was a redemption, although Else's eye, he could see, was a little more sceptical than Eileen's.

Afterwards in the large kitchen they gathered together for that mixture of 'helping hands' and 'finishing up drink and food, and gossip, which was Mrs Boniface's part of the day. They went there by no prearrangement, but singly or in pairs as the dwindling party made it possible. It had been one of Gordon's high times in the Andredaswood routine, when, the last sadly to bid the last guest good-bye, he would rush in, scarcely keeping up his pretended relief that the party was over. Nor was it for him, because then came his famous 'moment of relaxation', a barely disguised mounting dénouement to his evening of charming and pleasing and enjoying and contact-making.

David remembered how he had snapped once, 'the star's dress rehearsal, Gordon, in reverse – just old friends and the servants!' He had always felt that he should disapprove of such a riot of self-expression. But Gordon had only answered, 'Much the best time for a dress rehearsal. One gives a better performance to the servants and the event itself isn't spoilt by dismal predictions. The White Queen and I, dear David, always dress rehearse in reverse.' And then because, as always on party days, he ceased to bother, he had added, 'As a matter of fact the White Queen and I do *everything* in reverse.'

In any case, it had always been impossible to withhold oneself from Gordon's will for success on those occasions. He knew his audience, a few old friends who could be trusted not to make too much of skits on the neighbours, Mrs Boniface, with Mr B. wonderingly in tow, the hired helps (friends and kindred spirits of Mrs B.), Else, Climbers, latterly the Rattrays – a mixed collection which therefore gave Gordon a greater challenge. He never failed. Even David had found himself roped in, his few rather dry humorous observations of the party expanded and broadened by Gordon so that everyone should feel that Mr Parker was almost as amusing as Mr Paget. It was extraordinary how Climbers had always thought that he must resent that 'almost' and had taken such pains to assure him that Gordon was the comedian, but he the wit. Insecure herself, she could only feel affection for others by supposing them equally insecure. In fact, of course, he had never been happier than when following Gordon's lead.

This evening he was only too well aware that he was no star, nor even an understudy. The few little absurdities or pieces of gossip that he retained from the party remained obstinately dried up in his own personal idiom. No current seemed to run between him and all these people he knew so well to change his little store of observations into flashes, let alone into any pyrotechnic display. Only one blinding flash seemed to have filled the room, stunning all of them into silence – the sudden recognition that Gordon was dead. It had pierced through all the protective insulation that they had wrapped around them since that day when they had first learned of the operation's failure. He sensed that to each at that moment Gordon's absence stood for all their deprivations and lost hopes in life. But their despairs were only a smudgy penumbra to his own desperate conviction that, through all the years of his association with Gordon, he had deprived himself, deprived them both, of what could have been a transforming friendship and had twisted it by his obsessive guilt into a copy-book lesson of moral maxims. He knew that, in fact, it had been more than that, but at this moment he could feel only its failure in what might have been.

He roused himself to exchange a health with Mr Boniface. Mrs B., he noted, had also come to from her depressed trance and was trying to brighten things a bit with a cockney joke. He remembered that Meg had not been told of the kitchen party and he did not regret it: she would only have underlined Gordon's absence the more.

And then – there she was, making the most definite of entrances at the kitchen door. He recalled how once they had both laughed at their mother's comment on a play – 'Such a badly constructed play, David. And such a waste of Marie Tempest. She was on when the curtain went up. In all good plays the star comes on last.'

It was clear, he thought, that Meg had learnt that lesson. And as the evening went on he had to admit that star she was. She seemed to start with such a disadvantage – no local jokes, no certainty of her audience; but she turned her ignorance into an asset. She confused local personalities in the most comical manner; she assured her audience that she had heard things said that were most improbable from mouths that were even more so; she asked questions in such openly sly mock innocence, that it was apparent not only that she enjoyed her performance, but that she had been genuinely interested in all the people she had met, and not with that dead and rapturous acceptance that she showed towards the members of the household. She made her audience laugh and chatter; she banished Gordon's ghost. She could not, of course, give what Gordon had given; her performance was not a tried, beloved old turn. But she had advantages. It was, if no more, a change, to have the star a woman. Knowing less of her audience, she gave them all a chance, bores included, to do their turns and, when called upon, they rose to the occasion. And then she was tragic Mrs Eliot, beautiful and brave, who had stepped out of the pages of the newspaper as a very human heroine.

All sorts of malice filled David's mind as he felt her success underlining the transience of Gordon's hold on their loyalties; but he couldn't sustain the mood – she so patently wanted only to enjoy herself and to see that they did so too. She tried to bring him in and he resisted. At once she let it go and started a cross talk with Mrs B. which only came to an end because they were both giggling so much. Then as suddenly she was sitting quietly by Else's side.

'Those friends of yours, the Rogersons,' he could hear her ask, 'when am I going to see them again?'

'You find them especially funny?' Else spoke in a tone suitable for reproving an over excited child, but, David thought, there's a note which suggests that patience may soon be exhausted and love with-drawn.

'Funny? I suppose so. Yes. As most people are. But I found them extremely interesting. I think I should like them. I don't believe in making up my mind too quickly. But nor, I should imagine, do they!'

It was exactly the right note, David thought; and yet, looking at her as she talked to Else, he could see a new note of independence. She had chosen to appease Else, but with none of the absolute and mechanical acquiescence of the last weeks. She was genuinely interested in the Rogersons, and if that could help Else to accept the rest of her behaviour, she was prepared to stress it.

'They are really Eileen Rattray's friends,' Else said. She was used to more mollifying than this before she was prepared to abandon her moods.

Meg said, 'Oh, come, Else. Surely you're not going to discourage me from knowing them. They would do me so much *good*.' Her voice carried a slight note of open mocking.

David wondered for a moment if she was a little drunk; but she was not, only elated, and even the elation seemed under control.

Else said, 'I don't know whether they will have time to do you good. They are very busy people.'

'Well, I'll do *them* good, then. There's nothing that relaxes busy people so much as a drone to entertain them.'

'And you like being a drone?'

David, turning to listen to Mr Boniface's electrician cousin on the way the Americans in their war films conveniently forget who in the hour of isolation ..., could only vaguely hear Meg's reply, but though the words were fragmentary, the tone told that she was replying with friendliness. 'Letting things roll over me. ... David's influence perhaps – so much to learn if you've been spoilt.' Then she gave a laugh. 'Besides, drones have to work very hard in order to please.' She was charm-pleading a little now.

'It's lucky to have such convenient theories,' Else said, but she laughed and put her hand on Meg's arm. She's been won over, David thought.

Then surprisingly Meg said, 'Yes, isn't it?' Her drawl was a direct rejection. 'I shall have to get Eileen Rattray to take me to the Roger-sons', I can see. They have such a high opinion of her usefulness.' She paused. 'The Rogersons and Eileen,' she said, 'they fascinate me. They're part of the England I don't know. I don't imagine I'm going to find it all that easy to adapt myself. But I dare say if you can, Else ... After all, I have *some* common roots.'

It was, David thought, an unkind and bad piece of pettishness; yet somewhere in the tone there were echoes that made him feel loving, protective towards her, even as he disapproved. 'No, I never made the Italian landings,' he said. Meg was coming towards him now. And something tired and puzzled in her pouting look recalled suddenly their mother when she felt that the 'world was really too difficult'. He knew then what had softened his annoyance with Meg.

She stood smiling for a few minutes while Mr Boniface's cousin described fighting near Padua with the Eighth Army. 'Of course, there was precious little resistance by then and the locals were all out to show they were on our side. I liked them myself,' he told Meg as though she was notoriously chauvinistic. 'But not the priests. You've only got to see some of the poverty to make your mind up about that. Everything goes to *la chiesa*, you know. I learnt a bit of the language. The superstition's appalling. In my opinion that's why they were no good at all as soldiers.' He offered the views judicially. 'They never would have been in it at all, you know, if the Germans hadn't forced them.'

When he had moved away, Meg said, 'Dear God! What tact! Talking to you, David, about army life.' There was an edge to her voice that was intended to provoke. He tried to speak lightly, but he knew that he was irritated.

'Dear Meg,' he said, 'I rather pride myself on the fact that they know that I was an objector and that they don't care. Perhaps they don't,' he added, 'as much as you do.'

There was a moment's silence, then he said, 'In any case your *own* tact can desert you.'

She looked up at him angrily. 'I can't stand people who paw me,' she said. Tears came into her eyes. 'I'm sorry,' she said. 'I should have managed Else better. I did so mean to be of help to you today.'

Her face, tired and anxious again, recalled their mother's. He thought, now I've seen the likeness once, I shall see it all the time. And, of course, it was there – petulance, provocation, pathos – mother's three p's that had always produced their response in him. I must watch out, he thought. Nevertheless he said soothingly, 'You *have* helped, Meg, enormously. You've been a terrific success. I'm tired. That's all it is. I ought to have warned you about the kitchen party. But they'll be gone soon.'

She looked round the room. 'Oh, my dear, it's flat.'

'Let it be flat. They'll go home the sooner.'

'No, David, don't. I can't bear to end on failure. I have such a fight to hold depression back these days. Help me to make it all end with a bang.'

He felt annoyed that he had not guessed her feelings before, that she had been forced to explain them. He said sharply, 'Don't you want to ask Eileen Rattray to take you to see the Rogersons? You told Else you would do so.'

'Oh, don't David,' she said. 'Please let's make it end well.' And off she plunged to entertain the audience with a grand finale. She drew him in to make a duet of it. Together they brought the house down. Deliberately, he could see, she reverted to old patterns, to those times when, in moods of sudden closeness, they had set out to liven up some living-dead party of their mother's. They 'did' Aunt Lily and her dogs, and the day the coach party arrived drunk at mother's tea-room, and the time that mother sent the funeral wreath to the bride, and, rather daringly, Uncle Eustace's 'little bit of fluff'. Then she began to guy her own girlhood and to draw him in – she made him 'do' David with Miss Murray her headmistress, and David winning the chamber pot at the fête, and David in mother's *tableaux vivants* as 'When did you last see your Father?' (rich in ironic memories, this last, for both of them) – but if she teased him a bit maliciously, it was with such caressing malice that the ragging was more like a flirtation than a 'send up'. There won't be a dry eye in the house soon, he thought, seeking to detach himself. Yet he knew that he was pleased and happy.

Sure enough, Climbers came up to him as she was leaving. 'I say, Mrs Eliot was terrific tonight, wasn't she? Anyone could tell you were brother and sister just from the way you can both make people laugh. All the same, you're the real wit, David. She's more of a comedian really.'

Tim said, 'Best evening we've had for years, David.' But Eileen said, 'It was fun enough for us, but I was a bit worried about your sister. Of course, she's bound to be up and down like that. All one can do is to flatten out the bumps as much as possible. I doubt if this sort of thing helps much, though, David. However, when I told the Rogersons she was a depressive, they couldn't believe it; and they're very sensible. They *liked* her.'

It was all he could do, David thought, to like Eileen sometimes.

Yet only Else really distressed him, leaving him with guts troubled and anxious for the future. She said, smiling, 'We've been like children this evening. That is quite good for once.'

He answered, 'I'm happy to see Meg throw her depression off so completely.'

'Oh, yes. Children can do that.' Then she looked at him sadly, 'I don't think *you* are a child, David. For you, tragedy and some small mishap are not the same thing. I hope you won't try to make them so. We can hurt ourselves so much by pretending, like children, that we don't feel.'

It was a mercy, David thought, that Meg was not by at that moment. She looked at once so elated and so exhausted. When they were left alone, she said, 'David, please take me out for the day tomorrow.'

He said, 'My dear, Collihole's exhibiting roses in ten days' time. You don't realize that I run this place as a business.'

'Collihole! Roses!' she answered. 'I realize that the others run it for you. Under your direction. And quite right too. Please take me out for the day.'

'But you're exhausted already.'

'Exhausted, yes, but not depressed. And I believe I can move on now to a quieter happiness. But just for tomorrow I could be so depressed.'

He said, 'Very well, Meg. We'll go quietly somewhere to the Downs.'

'No, no, David. I must slow down gradually. Let's go to Brighton and quiz people from the terrace of the Metropole. We'll play Observations.' When he had finally agreed, she asked, '*You* want to go, David, don't you?'

'Yes, yes. But let me say things for myself.' She looked so hurt that he took her hand. 'You've made this awful day quite all right for me,' he said. He wondered whether Gordon would have giggled or been sad for him; yet he knew that whatever might have been Gordon's reactions, his own feelings of anxiety were only feeble irritations that hardly disturbed even the surface of his growing pleasure in her regained company.

David ordered a dry sherry.

'How prim!' Meg said, 'I want something absurd to mark an unusual occasion.'

'Unusual? Surely nothing can be *usual* in this holiday period of your life.'

She raised her eyebrows. 'Holiday?'

'Well,' he corrected, 'let's say like the Americans, "intermission".'

He had bathed in her chatter as they drove to Brighton, but with the nagging thought that he must speak to her about the future. Now he approached it, aware that he was less concerned to persuade her into any plan than he was to get his lecture over and enjoy the rest of the day unhampered by conscience. However, she ignored his implication.

'I like every day to be rare now. Like American steaks.'

He thought, her gaiety is forced, she would never phrase-make like that if it were not so. She went through the list of fancy-named cocktails. 'No,' she said, 'they'll all taste like bath salts.' She settled for the mildly rare – a White Lady. Looking out through the glass front of the hotel bar she indicated a thin, elegant old Jew, discreetly rich, with sensitive oriental features, tired and worldly. 'Look,' she said, 'the day's got him for a moment.'

David, looking, saw the old man pause for a second and, letting his family walk ahead, gaze a little bewilderedly nowhere in particular as the mild south-east breeze and the bright sunshine played upon his yellowy parchment, cigar-scented old body on this last day of May. 'Something,' David said smiling, 'of the old wisdom of his people has pushed for a moment through the money bags and the family marriages and the loving purchase of the little Boudin that is yet an investment.'

'No, no,' Meg cried, 'the deep wisdom of his people is a much more routine thing that comes to him at solemn family moments, or alone at midnight when he pads upstairs to bed in the great family house. ... Well, that's probably gone long ago anyway. But this moment is something deeper. A sudden realization that the whole natural order of things is growing and pushing and decaying and sunning itself all around him all the time and that he has no contact with it.'

'Can the natural order of things sun itself?'

'You know perfectly well what I mean, David. The smallest weeds and insects. And the largest.'

They were both laughing; it was one of the favourite games of their adolescence – the parodying of stock type novels. And yet he guessed her to share in his feeling that whatever they said today would be important to both of them.

'Even that old man,' she said, 'must once have been a small boy for whom caterpillars were monsters and bindweed a jungle. He remembers that.'

'Oh dear!' David said, 'I can't continue that sort of novel. In any case his pantheistic imaginings won't liberate him from the prison of a rich man's authority. You share Else's pathetic fallacy about Nature's power to heal.'

'Oh, David,' Meg cried, 'you've forgotten the rules of the game. You've drawn a moral conclusion.'

He had not forgotten the rules of Observations – to invent histories and thoughts for the people they saw, but to make no judgements; but the habit of censuring was too strongly with him now. He said, 'You broke the rule first, when you said, "Even that old man". If that wasn't an implied moral judgement …'

'I suppose I did,' she said. She pointed to the wife and daughter now richly ensconced in the back of the Bentley, chattering, their made-up faces stupidly discontented, their smart hats nodding. 'They've had no intimations,' she said, 'and we need make no comment on the fact.'

'No,' he said, 'their heads are full of the trip to New York, and cousin Myra's wedding, and the records of *My Fair Lady*. Fair?' He smiled happily at her.

'Fair enough,' she said, 'though I think we're out of practice. Boudins and *My Fair Lady*! they don't really fit together.'

'No,' he said, 'it's all right. The women folk lag behind in culture. They always have done.'

The conversation seemed a happy serial stretching back and back in repeat to his fifteenth year or so – the War, Gordon, the nursery seemed a hardly real intervening time. Later as they sat over their coffee he said, 'You've taken me back too much, Meg. It's absurd, I've been feeling as though the world lay before me. It's not the time for dreaming about pearls in unopened oysters. If there are pearls, then the more people leave them alone for a century or two the better.' But he realized as he said it, that this was only what he believed, not what he felt. He felt as though he was about to plan a hundred different lives from which to choose when manhood at last came to him. It was an absurdity, not even true to the youth that Meg had recalled, for his dreams as an adolescent had been most carefully circumscribed.

Meg said, 'And I feel more like the chattering ladies. Let the day care for itself. No, that's not fair to myself. But as though all the burden of putting dreams into practice had been lifted from me.'

Perhaps, David thought, it was exactly because he, knowing his own feelings, could not use this proffered chance to question or to advise her on her future, that she seemed impelled to meet the criticism that he had not made.

She said, 'You *must* accept my present frivolity, David. I'm resting. My determinations are not scattered and my curiosity hasn't died on me, they're simply in abeyance. Meanwhile you must let me drone a bit.'

When he said nothing, letting his glance drift from the lobsters and chicken piled on the raised cold table to the ornate chandeliers and then to a sad, lipstick-smudged, flat-footed old waitress, she went on a little fiercely, 'You haven't altered, David, you still don't listen when you don't choose to. But I think you've found some sort of peace in this negation you're seeking. At any rate your view of life's affected me. It may seem simple frivolity, the way I'm being now, but it is an attempt to get away from imposing myself everywhere. As I did on Bill, as I made such a fool of myself doing with Tom and Jill. You can't escape all responsibility for my present mood.'

He said, 'Meg, the last thing I am, you know, is a hot gospeller. It's the essence of the way I live that it's my own. But if you can get something from it, of course, I'm glad.'

It didn't seem entirely to satisfy her. She said, 'But you *do* think, don't you, that we've found some link again that exists between us?'

'I don't know about "again",' he answered. 'We've found a link, certainly, but whether it was there before, I really don't know.'

'Well, whatever,' she said, 'I feel that we can be together much or only a little but always with profit. So long as we're absolutely honest. That's why I've not hidden my present mood of easy laziness.'

He would not answer the appeal in her voice for fear of committing himself to an approbation he might have to withdraw, but, 'Honesty with each other. Certainly,' he said, 'to that at any rate we can commit ourselves. In fact, we must.'

After luncheon they did all the sights. Only at the Pavilion was there any note of disharmony. Music greeted them from every corner as, with the crowd of sightseers, they made their way amid pink and green chinoiserie wallpapers and beneath great golden dragon chandeliers.

'The Haffner,' he said.

'Yes, it's a pleasant idea to have this relayed music,' she remarked.

'No, it isn't,' he said. 'Music should be listened to. Not pumped out as a phoney means of invoking the gracious living of the past.'

His fierceness made her say, laughing, 'Oh dear, I've got it wrong, haven't I? It's a pest about music when you're around, David. It was just the same when we were young. I always liked going to concerts and to opera, but it wasn't really until I'd married Bill that I could indulge myself. You'd always inhibited me by making me feel that one had no right to enjoy music in ignorance.'

'I never intended to. It's not even what I think.'

'Well, you must let me listen to the quartet. I heard so much about it at the party yesterday. Why haven't you met since I came to Andredaswood?'

'Oh, Gordon's death. One thing and another. We're losing our cellist.' He didn't want to talk about it. Only two days before he had received Mary Gardner's letter of resignation – she was extremely sorry but she didn't see her way to playing any more with Else.

Meg said, 'Oh! Well, I look forward to it in the autumn. Anyhow you might let me sit in, when you and Else practise, without looking so unhappy.'

'It wasn't that, Meg. Else gets nervous and she's not a good player to start with.'

'I rather thought not.'

His desire for her sympathy was stronger than his instinct not to involve Meg in the Else–Mary Gardner fracas. He said, 'As a matter of fact that's why the cellist is leaving us. She quite rightly feels that she's too good to play with Else.'

'But can't you get someone better than Else for second violinist?'

'I think we could but ...'

She looked at him in amazement. 'But this is something you *care* about, David.'

He was determined not to retract. 'You must see the kitchen,' he said. 'It's the best room in the place and beautifully set out. These gargantuan Regency meals.' He strode ahead.

Later in one of the bedrooms he drew her attention to two Meissen jugs. 'They're good, aren't they?' he asked.

'Yes,' she said, 'quite lovely.' But she hardly looked at them.

In the next room there were Chelsea figures. 'David, I'm sorry,' she said, 'I'd like to go. I can't bear looking at the porcelain. I didn't realize how much I minded selling my collection.'

They soon recovered their gaiety on the pier. They went to Madame Nora, the fortune teller, and David asked if her parrot was psychic; he carried on such a straight-faced absurd conversation about the bird's powers that Meg had to go out in a fit of giggles. They put pennies into innumerable slot machines; Meg was fascinated by the peep shows of girls undressing. 'This one must be nineteen-twenty-two,' she said. 'I can tell by the drawers.' She spent a long time going from one to another until an elderly man in a macintosh began to follow her and pinched her thigh. Laughing wildly, she made David take her on the dodge'em cars. He proved a poor driver and when she took over she was little better; they were bumped into breathlessness. When they got off, the gipsy-looking, tattooed-chested proprietor said to David, 'I'll take you round next time,' and winked. It was part proposition, part send up.

David was not sure whether Meg had heard, but at tea, under the noise of a selection from *The Boy Friend*, she said, 'Do I take notice of your conquests, David, or not?'

He had often, when they were young, imagined her broaching this subject of his sexual interests and had hoped so much that, if it must happen, she would not choose the wrong words. Now he only wondered how he could convey to her, so that she would believe it, that he had for so many years had no sexual life at all. If he could convince her of this unlikely truth, she would perhaps henceforth leave the subject alone.

He said, 'The answer is that you don't, Meg. And in any case you won't have to. That man was sending me up – making fun of me. And even if he hadn't been – well, that kind of thing happens almost never now, I'm glad to say.'

She asked, 'Why glad to say? I'm always pleased at passes. Well, not perhaps pinches from men in macintoshes. But from handsome gipsies, dear God!'

He said nothing.

'Don't look so prim,' she said. And then, 'I'm afraid I've offended you, my dear. I'm not trying to pry, you know. But after all these years its ridiculous for me not to be able to mention it.'

'There's nothing to mention. I don't have a sex life.'

'Sex life! What an expression!' She began to laugh, then her face softened; she put her hand on his arm. 'I'm sorry, David. I've been incredibly tactless. I'm a bit out of my depth. Of course, I know exactly what you feel. I never wanted anyone else when Bill was alive and I don't suppose now that I ever shall.'

He said, 'I never had sexual relations with Gordon after the first few months that we knew each other.'

She said, 'David! My dear, why ever not?'

'Gordon was a Christian, Meg. It was a mortal sin for him.'

She put the milk jug down on the table so abruptly that milk spilt on her dress. Wiping the skirt, she looked down and said, 'But surely he couldn't expect you to remain faithful ...'

'I didn't want anyone else,' he interrupted, and as she was about to speak, he said, 'No, he wasn't to blame, Meg. Not at all. He thought I was crazy not to have other affairs, although in the end he accepted it. He had them himself. He was naturally very promiscuous. That was in a way easier, from the religious point of view, than any permanent relationship. But long before I'd met him I'd known that for me it didn't work. It was too much of an act of personal assertion, too much of a piece of personal defiance ...' His voice tailed away.

She said, 'Oh, those bloody laws, you mean.'

'Yes,' he said, 'that and so much else. I sometimes think that even if I'd loved women, I wouldn't have been equal to it.'

'Oh, nonsense,' she said. Then after a pause, 'Well, I know so little about it. Probably for people like yourself the emotional is always more important than the physical.'

He didn't know whether she said it as a sop to her own feelings, or to his, or whether in fact she believed it.

Smiling, she said, 'I'm afraid I always liked sex with Bill, David. Loved it very much,' she added.

He said with complete sincerity, 'I'm very glad, Meg.'

For the rest of the day, as Gordon would have said, Meg 'lived it up'. But although David could feel that she was driving herself to make the day a success, it did not alter the fact that he enjoyed himself hugely. Only once or twice he was disturbed to see her looking at him with a maternal sadness. He thought, however, we've come through so many difficulties in the past weeks, she'll succeed in accepting this about me also. As long as we leave well alone.

There were others, however, he soon discovered who did not think that it was well and who, therefore, had decided most firmly not to leave it alone. Only two days after their trip to Brighton. David received a telephone call from Eileen Rattray.

'The gods are on our side,' she said.

It was so much a phrase that came uneasily from her that he knew at once that she must have prepared it carefully. He felt an immediate hostility, a need to be on his guard.

'Oh!' he said, 'which gods?' Certainly, he thought, his gods and Eileen's were not the same.

It was the sort of whimsical conversation that he knew her to be unaccustomed to; but clearly she was anxious to adapt herself. She made a noise that, over the telephone at any rate, was insufficiently like a laugh to serve even for politeness.

'In this case, the Rogersons,' she said, and continued rapidly enough to prevent interruption, 'Miss Snaith's overwhelmed with work and Fred Rogerson's got permission from the Education Committee to take on another secretary for his own personal correspondence. For the rest of the term at any rate. And once the job's created, you know how these things are, it could become a sort of permanency.' She came to a pause, evidently waiting for his whoop of joy, but he felt immediately angry at the intrusion. He said only, 'Oh, I'm so glad. He's obviously badly overworked.' Though really, he thought, it's this Miss Snaith who's getting the relief, but as I've never heard of her before I can't comment on that. His annoyance lent him some of Meg's frivolity. He said, 'I don't know Miss Snaith, but it's nice for her, too.'

Eileen Rattray must have sensed his hostility, for she said in an aggressively honest voice, 'You'll make a great mistake, David, if you don't encourage your sister to acquire some interest outside herself pretty soon.' She must have felt that this was a doubtful tone. She went on persuasively. 'You said it yourself, David. And I ought to have known you were right. After all, you're with her all the time. Anyhow I said I'd keep a watch out and I have. I can tell you now, I was more worried at the party than I let on. Convalescence, you know, can produce its own neurosis. People are more awake to that nowadays than they were a few years back.'

'Ah,' he said, 'get them on their feet. Yes, I read about that in the paper.' But this irony was a self-indulgent evasion. 'It's really a question for Meg and the Rogersons,' he said, and, hearing her about to speak, he added, 'Oh, the doctor's all in favour, I'm pretty sure.'

He allowed her to take in his disapproval of this lobbying. Then he

said, 'Ah! Of course, Meg's had no experience. I suppose Fred Rogerson realizes that.'

'Oh, yes. After all it's only for six weeks as a start. And they like
each other. It's ideal, really.'

'Well then, I suggest Fred Rogerson speaks to Meg. Or if you're
acting as his agent, you could.'

'I imagine she's bound to find a lot of excuses. It's not her fault.
She's been ill and she's unwilling to face the fact that she's well again.
It's a fairly usual pattern but it mustn't be allowed to get fixed.
Couldn't you prepare the ground?'

'No,' David answered. 'I couldn't, Eileen. You may be right in
what you say. For myself, I'm not so sure as I was. I think Meg knows
where she's going, but she's taking a rest. In any case, I'm the last
person to question her decisions. But you put it to her. It would be
kind of you to do so.'

'I was only trying to be kind in the first place, David.'

'But, of course. And I'm grateful to you.'

He wondered, when she had rung off, whether he had behaved
badly; on the whole, he thought not. Meg will be able to deal with
her, he decided, and for reasons he did not wish to examine too closely,
he knew that by 'deal with' he meant 'refuse'.

Eileen Rattray, however, was only the advance guard. The main
attack took place that evening.

Over the years David and Gordon had discovered the habit of
communal silence. At first an artificial approach to inner quietude, a
protest against random talk, aimless reading, or music played to fill
up stillness, their silence had become a real reservoir of strength, even,
they felt, a communication that was something more than personal.
That it was more they had come especially to believe, because Else,
in so many other ways a distracting and devitalizing person, had
the power, when she sat with them in their silences, of contributing a
positive sense of peace and order. It seemed, moreover, to come from
some source deeper than her everyday, clamant, sentimental egotism.
In this silence, when the intelligent and the unselfconscious were
often 'all at sea', Else, so absurd, so driven by uncertainty into pretension, was absolutely without thought of her surroundings, of
others or of herself, entirely still from a core of unselfness that her
egotism had never been able to dissolve.

For Meg, David had been all too aware, these times of silence that
came so naturally to him and to Else, were an agony. Her desperate

attempts to disregard them, to avoid laughter, to join with them, had been one of the aspects of her early adjustment to the house that had most distressed him, perhaps above all her attempts to join with them which had so underlined her neurotic desire to please. In the last fortnight, however, he had noticed a change. She could genuinely disregard their silence, reading without covert glances, or moving, if she needed, without elaborate hushedness. On occasion even he noted that she also sat still and silent, and her face, when she did so, seemed to him truly relieved of the strain that had marked her, even in her gaiety, right back to their childhood. It gave him great happiness to think that he might have brought her some true peace if only for a half hour or so. He truly felt, as he had told her, that his disciplines were not to be preached, but if he had communicated some part of the inner quiet that, despite all his moral anxieties and all the tension of his repressed desires, lay within him, the severe limits he had imposed upon his life seemed to be vindicated. To reach one person and to still them seemed to him more than he had hoped for in so hopeless a world.

This evening Meg sat silent. She had found for herself, as he believed people must, a naturally relaxed posture. Her dark eyes had stopped their constant, restless moving, she apparently even found no need for her endless jerky cigarette smoking. She was truly, he believed, at peace.

It was Else who broke the silence; and immediately David realized how strong her hostility must have become; how great the misery of her jealousy, that she should be driven to destroy what was certainly her greatest and perhaps now her only bond with him.

She said, 'Meg.' He saw Meg look up startled and also tense against Else's unaccustomed use of her Christian name. 'Meg, I think that David is not being fair to you. No, David, please! I wish to speak quite freely to Meg about this. Eileen Rattray has told him today of some interesting work near here that is offered to you. And he has refused to speak to you about it.'

David said, as calmly as he was able, 'Else, this is all very foolish, you know.'

But Meg wanted him to be silent. 'But now *you* can tell me about it, Else,' she said.

David could only guess at what anger she felt, for her tone to Else was entirely friendly. Only a flickering smile and a very slightly puzzled frown suggested that she didn't understand why such tension had gathered around the subject of a prospective job for her. Once again David could not believe that she did not know why.

Else was certainly disarmed. 'I really think it's a marvellous chance,' she said. She told of the Rogersons' offer. 'You will be doing something so good. He is such a fine man and so badly overworked. He needs an intelligent sympathetic person to work for him. And then he too can help you. He has such great energy.'

Meg smiled. 'You think I need energy, Else? Perhaps I do. I don't feel it myself. I'm rather glad to have a rest from energy.' Then she said, as it seemed to David without any overtones. 'I don't know whether I should take it, Does Eileen think it's a good idea too?'

'Yes,' said Else, 'everybody does who cares for you, I am sure. There is a time, you know, when someone like you who has been ill must resume her life. And you were so sure that you wished to take up secretarial work. You spent so much time on the course. Too much, perhaps. You made yourself ill. But now I am sure you are ready to begin again. It's difficult for you, I know, to take this step. That is why David should urge you.'

'I'm not going to urge anything,' David said. 'It's entirely for Meg to decide. I didn't tell you about it, Meg, because I didn't want to influence. I thought it was up to Fred Rogerson to tell you himself. Or Eileen since she'd broached it to me.' He wanted desperately to tell her that she need not consider taking it if she didn't wish to, but he somehow feared to be responsible for urging her not to. I can't commit myself to asking for her presence here as a full-time member of the household, he thought, it would be wrong. But he knew that fear was stronger than belief in non-interference as a motive in his withdrawal.

She said, 'I see. I wonder what Dr Loder would say.'

'I think,' Else said, 'that he would certainly agree.'

Again Meg said, 'I see.' Then she added, 'Of course doctors always talk more to other people than to their patients; one must expect it.'

He could detect no note of sarcasm in her voice.

'It would be a job that would allow me to go on living here. I shouldn't take any other kind.'

There seemed no threat to Else in her words. She appeared simply to be speaking her thoughts aloud. 'I don't think, Else,' she said, 'that you should have expected David to urge me. Of course what he said would influence me greatly. As it would you. We are here because of him, and if we push him into disposing of us, he might have to say things that would make us very unhappy.'

'I came here because of Gordon.'

'Yes, of course you did. But Gordon's dead now.' Meg's tone was without any cruelty. She seemed simply to be announcing from far away a rather irrelevant fact. 'But why didn't Mr Rogerson ask me himself?'

'He wanted the ground to be prepared. He would not have liked to be refused.'

Meg looked surprised and interested. 'Dear God! Not like to be refused? Such a fine man. I'm not being sarcastic, Else; I too get the impression of a fine man. But not to want to be refused! That really is interesting, David. It almost persuades me to take the job.'

David could not look at Else, he was too angry with her. He gave himself to considering the loneliness that must be driving her. I must, he thought, find an acceptance of her; I owe that at least to Gordon.

Meg broke the silence. 'You've all made it very difficult for me, Else,' she said, 'by the way you've arranged this. You, Eileen, the doctor, all think I should take a job. I'm bound, you know, to feel against it. But I'm trying not to be influenced by that, but simply to decide whether I want to. I think, on the whole, it's worth trying. At any rate, if I don't try it, I might miss something interesting. And I shall be here still. That's the main thing.'

Else smiled. 'If you insist on taking our interest like that, you must do so. The important thing is to help you out of this inertia.'

'Oh, I'm not really mistaking your motives,' Meg said. 'I think you'll be glad to see the back of me during the day. Why shouldn't you? But I'm sure you also feel that I need to be shaken out of my lethargy. And I'm sure that Eileen thinks everybody should be occupied with a useful task.'

David thought, My God! She's travelled a long way since she thought everyone here was so 'enchanting'; or perhaps she still thinks so, she makes all these statements about them so completely without sarcasm, as though they were facts that she happily accepted. Something disturbingly simple about her whole behaviour made him wonder if she were not a more childlike person than he had always supposed. He said, 'You *do* feel that you're qualified to take on the job, Meg?'

She laughed. 'Well, really, David,' she cried, 'you opt out of all this. And why not? But then, when you contribute, it's to doubt my competence. Yes,' she went on, 'I think I can manage. I might be quite good. At any rate, we can see. I'll go and ring Rogerson now.'

Later David got Meg a whisky and soda to take up to her bedroom. She had said, soon after she recovered from the first days of her breakdown, 'Do you mind, David, getting whisky in for me? Now that I'm in a proper house again instead of hotels and other people's rooms, I can't bear the idea of not having a nightcap. It was one of Bill's strictest habits.' Tonight, when she took her drink, she said, 'It was nice having Bill to protect me from people. I don't care how bad for me it was, it was still very nice.'

David said, 'Meg, you don't have to take this job with Fred Rogerson.'

She smiled. 'Don't I, David?' she asked. 'No, I suppose I don't. But I shall. I've agreed now, and I think I shall find it interesting. Besides, I shall still be here and that's all that matters to me at the moment. Although I'm afraid I'm not managing it very well.'

As far as David could tell, Meg greatly enjoyed working for Fred Rogerson. She left Andredaswood every morning in the Rover at a little after eight and was back most evenings before six. His attention, however, was given very closely during June to the nursery. He knew that he had been neglecting it and, if he realized with a certain amusement that the staff managed very happily without him, he felt a certain dislike for the idea of recognizing himself as a sleeping proprietor. He told himself, and he knew that there was enough truth in the view to make it tenable, that if the Nursery staff could get on without him, they got on better when he showed a full interest, Climbers, it was true, her affection secured by Eileen's using her as a baby-sitter and proxy 'aunt' for the children, had developed a dogged attachment to Tim. It was an attachment perhaps a little more maternal than that she had for David, and certainly not without patronage, but Tim, under his wife's management, was now rather proud of his capacity to deal with 'the old thing'. Each indeed began to act as interpreter of the other to David. Climbers clearly saw herself as one who understood the younger generation and the new class.

'I shouldn't take too much notice of Tim's abruptness, David,' she said, 'it's only a part of the sort of upbringing he's had, you know,' and 'I know how you feel, David. We liked things done in a certain way, didn't we? But these young people have a kind of directness that's jolly good really.' And on occasion Tim would say, 'Oh, I shouldn't worry too much with what looks like the muddle of Climbers' sales returns. It used to send me up the wall, but I've found she has her own ways and methods and I've given up arguing. She was usually right in the end.'

All this David took with amused detachment; but there came a day when Climbers and Tim approached him together in the little office. Collihole, they said, was given too free a hand with the shrub roses. 'We haven't the facilities here or the experience,' Tim said, 'to make all these experiments with hybridizing. He's wasting time repeating work that's being done, and far better, in specialized rose nurseries. Some of the graftings he's made are ridiculous. Work done ages ago by Korde in Germany.'

'Yes,' Climbers chimed in, 'it's quite quite true, David. Tim's been showing me a lot of articles in the Rose Annuals.'

'We can't do more here,' Tim said, 'than supply tried favourites.'

David felt angry. 'You have a free hand with the rhododendrons,' he said to Tim.

'I know what I'm doing,' was the answer.

He reminded Climbers of Collihole's long and loyal service.

'Oh, yes, David. He's a wonderful chap. But he's a bit of a stick in the mud.'

He forbade them to interfere; they had to accept, but he could see that they didn't like it.

David had always spoken a little sarcastically of the shrub roses because of the 'chic' aura that hung around the demand for them. Yet, as he knew, when the shrubs, the hardy herbs, and the annuals had all become routine bores to him, the shrub roses still retained his affection and interest. He now gave his full time to working with Collihole, and his trust in the rake-thin, glassy-eyed old man was confirmed by the number of prizes that they won at the June show.

On top of this, the new electrical machinery was installed in one of the houses to generate a moist heat for forcing on rootings. Tim was enthusiastic and grateful to David for allowing the expenditure.

'We can advance everything by at least two weeks,' he said.

David knew that Tim would master the working of the machinery and its potentialities far more quickly than he would. Nevertheless he set about studying it himself and towards the end of July felt able to meet Tim in discussion of its value and its future uses. Tim, perhaps, proved a little less on the spot in these discussions, since his mastery had already been completed for some weeks and his interest diverted to a new colour reproduction process which might allow them to insert two illustrated pages in their annual catalogue. David noted his own perseverance and excused any misgivings he felt by telling himself that he must either be competent at the Martha tasks of his life or relinquish them. There for the moment he let his inner debate rest.

Preoccupation and fatigue, then, allowed him to do little more than note the success of Meg's acceptance of the job with Fred Rogerson – a success which, in any case, was brought to him daily by Else's proud reports of Meg's evident but less irresponsible happiness and of Fred Rogerson's complete satisfaction.

June had given him further reason to delight in Meg's presence. The nearness of Glyndebourne had been one of the chief factors that had decided the purchase of Andredaswood. For him and for Gordon the June season was the crown of the year. They disliked the chic atmosphere but easily forgot it in their pleasure at the performances. Else, on the other hand, found it impossible not to think the smartness was in some way an evidence of a certain falseness, shallowness, or unseriousness, which her spiritual integrity demanded that she should detect. Things could be done on this lavish scale, she seemed to imply, on the Continent; but the essence of *English* musical culture was its simplicity, almost its amateurishness. If they remarked on the great Continental singers or conductors who appeared there, she smiled in a way that suggested she knew with what embarrassment they saw their talents subordinated to English shallowness. She loved to say, 'So all the snobs have had their spectacle. The opera was beautifully arranged to enhance the decor.' She made this joke every year.

Meg, then, was a welcome companion. He suspected that he estimated her appreciation and her knowledge more highly than was justified because she always seemed to ask the questions that he found worth answering and to minimize the faults that he thought inconsiderable. Her enthusiasm was unashamed and he decided that it was not sentimental to find this refreshing. Also she took the social aspect of Glyndebourne for granted with an entirely neutral acceptance, and made him, perhaps for the first time, entirely at ease with it.

June, then, when it brought them together, did so entirely and satisfactorily. July kept them largely apart. As the end of term approached she began to return later in the evenings, often staying for dinner with the Rogersons. She even went to Fred Rogerson's house on two Sundays to cope with arrears of work. When David *did* see her, she was full of talk of the school and of Fred and Joan. Fred, she told him, was a different person as soon as he got down to school affairs.

'Different from what?' he asked.

'Well,' she said, 'I'm afraid I can't take all his political and "local culture" activities very seriously. It's fascinating to me because, never having met that sort of professional progressive, it was that aspect that made me interested in him. But he's largely a fool in such things, David, or perhaps I should say very conventional – only I'm not used to the convention. He's what I imagine Tory people mean by a typical *New Statesman* reader. But the truth is he's not really interested; he does it all out of habit. Don't tell Else I said so. Joan's quite different. Her emotions dominate her intelligence, but she cares about it all, and in so much of it, I think, she's right. But he *doesn't*. And as a result, he's unbearably pompous in things outside the school and, of course, Joan's admiration for him doesn't help. In fact, he's like that a bit with all adults because he feels at a disadvantage. But as soon as there's anything to do with the girls or the boys, he becomes a very impressive person indeed, I think ...'

David thought that this view of Fred Rogerson's virtues, if somewhat a stereotype of those of a good schoolmaster, was probably true, but as he had no interest whatever in the school, it did not alter his view that the Rogersons were slightly tiresome bores. He was interested and a little moved to see the ardour with which Meg came to what were, after all, somewhat trite conclusions. She's like a child in her ardours, he thought, and realized that it was the mixture of simplicity and sophistication in her that he liked. He was pleased to know that she was there, talking with enthusiasm about her new life; he heard her with amusement once or twice trying to fuse her admiration for Fred Rogerson with Else's, although their reasons for liking him were entirely opposed; but, on the whole, he ceased to do more than pretend to listen. Indeed, once or twice the pretence was not well maintained, for Meg said, 'Oh dear, David, I didn't think secondary-modern schools were going to bore you so much,' and again, 'It's not fair. I should listen if you told me all about that old electrical mistmaker, but you're so unselfish, you never do.'

It seemed to him, however, that the value of Meg's presence there was made surer by the fact that he still welcomed it when their interests diverged.

When term ended, Else gave him to understand that Meg would

go on with Fred Rogerson in the autumn; and Eileen told him that Fred had secured the agreement of the Education Committee to the establishment of a second secretary. Meg said nothing that suggested she would not continue; indeed she talked of the events of the winter term – the school play, for instance – as matters of interest to her. She made the suggestion that she should take a holiday in London for the last two weeks of August, but the plan came to nothing because on August 10th Else received a telephone call from Birmingham to say that Gordon's mother had had a stroke. There were nurses, there was recovery of movement and of speech to be expected; but still there was need of Else. She left an hour later. She was in tears. 'I have always taken Ada for granted,' she said, 'and I know what being taken for granted means.'

Meg agreed to give up her London plan and take over Else's work in her absence. Else left a careful list of what had to be done. David, going over it with Meg, was appalled at how much there was and how much he and Gordon had come to accept it. Else kept house for them, shopped, did much of the cooking, and yet two days a week managed to act as secretary and wages clerk for the nursery. Every job she did was carefully ordered by the most exact system of time tables and cash books. He thought of the irony of her parting words: she supposed that he and Gordon took her personality for granted, when in fact, they had lavished much care and thought on understanding her and accommodating their lives to her edged character; yet this mass of work which they had so selfishly disregarded, she did without considering that anyone need be grateful to her.

After the first week of doing Else's jobs, Meg said, 'I really don't know how she fills in her time, David. Of course, all these little books she keeps spin things out. But even so ...'

He said, 'But Meg, I was appalled at what she does. And the little books are surely models of neatness and exactitude.'

'Of course, they are,' she answered, laughing. 'They're the sort of things a little girl would invent when playing at "keeping houses". I'm sure it's something Freudian, only I don't know the name for it.'

He asked her earnestly, 'Well, do keep them up to date, please, Meg. It's Else's job and she mustn't be made to feel you don't regard it seriously.'

She looked for a moment as though she would object, then she said, 'Of course, if you say so, David. The dear little books shall be my only concern. After all, as you say, it's her affair if she likes to spend all day on this sort of thing. I never thought, David, I'd be a locum tenens. Do you remember how Mother loved that expression? She must have had a series of absentee doctors, she was forever calling in locum tenenses or whatever the plural is. It was one of my mystery words as a child. And now I'm locum tenens for Else Bode. Well, well! Secondary-modern schools, locum tenenses, wages clerk, there's no end to what life holds in store.'

He saw all the same that she was enjoying herself. And he, too, enjoyed her housekeeping. It was not only that the food was better, he had expected that; it was also that she was more obtrusive than Else; she frequently discussed household affairs with him and he thoroughly enjoyed the discussions. Poor Else! She prided herself on her unobtrusive management of the house. Mrs Boniface was enthusiastic about the new regime. 'I must say it's nice to have things done with a bit of life. And someone who tells you what they like and what they don't like before it's done and not after.'

David said with that sort of mock solemnity which is meant to be taken seriously, 'Mrs Boniface, Miss Bode will be coming back in a few weeks, you know.'

She winked at him. 'Oh, don't you worry, Miss Bode and me get on all right. I just said it was nice to have a change.'

As to Meg's efficiency with the Nursery correspondence, both Climbers and Tom said that inevitably Meg's being professional made an enormous difference.

David had been more moved than he expected when he had heard that Mrs Paget's twisted old oak tree had been struck down. He was anxious, in any case, to hear that, since death was not yet to release her, she should be mistress once more of her eccentric, purposeful movements. But now her quick recovery seemed to him even more urgent, so that Else could return before opposition to her rule had hardened into partisan lines. Perhaps what he feared most was his own defection. He mistrusted the strength of his loyalty against the pressure of his wishes. Knowing that his very recognition of this self-mistrust was a step towards its realization, he hoped that Else would return very soon.

Mrs Paget recovered enough to 'get about' by the first week in September and Else returned. Her loneliness assuaged by having been of use, she was at her best; and faced by this best the consciences of all at Andredaswood were roused to make her welcome. Meg had kept faithfully to her promise over the little books. Else, reassured by this attention to her totems, felt her suspicions of Meg fading. Everything, David thought, was well: loyalty had been saved.

Meg went to London for the last week of the holidays. The Rogersons too were away at a summer school until two days before term. It was exactly then that Meg, returning to Andredaswood, announced that she would not be returning to the school. Fred Rogerson, she said, did not want her.

The outcry against the Rogersons was loud and immediate. David said little, wishing only that he had exerted his influence to prevent Meg from taking a job before she was ready, to have saved her a humiliation that might well retard the recovery of her self-confidence. For all the honeyed words that had been spoken, he had no doubt that she had proved unequal to the job. The vacillation and evasion with which Fred Rogerson had dismissed her was all that he could truly blame, and these did not surprise him. Else was strongest in her condemnation. All the idealism she had found in the Rogersons was forgotten, she saw once more only their shallow materialism. She remembered above all a picnic on a summer afternoon of especial beauty when Fred had discoursed to them on the paramount importance of the teachers' new wage claim. Eileen was almost as distressed. 'The truth is,' she said, 'that Fred's got more and more tied up with these political summer schools and things and he's letting the school go to pot.' She remembered suddenly a number of complaints that various parents had been making in the last months. All this they said to David. No one liked to speak to Meg about it, because behind her calm acceptance of the rebuff and her refusal to say more than that Fred Rogerson presumably knew what he needed, they sensed that her self-esteem had been badly wounded. Silence seemed best.

In the second week in September Eileen telephoned to David and asked him to come over that afternoon. He entered the toy- and nappy-strewn contemporary sitting-room to find Eileen looking like a schoolboy unfairly punished, Tim trying to look grave, and Else, the more severe for the mannish felt hat she wore when visiting, looking like a schoolmistress who's been 'let down'.

Tim offered a drink as one who feels that, despite a death in the house, the duties of host must be observed; but Eileen brushed such concessions aside.

'We don't want to make a mountain out of a molehill, David,' she said, 'but Mrs Eliot's behaved pretty badly.'

Tim said, 'But look here, darling, she's been very ill, you know.'

Else said, 'All this is for David to decide. It is a matter only for him.'

Then what are you doing here? David thought. He felt disgusted and very angry at their interference in Meg's affairs, whatever might be the cause.

He said, 'Look, Eileen, all of you. This sort of thing has got to stop. Meg's affairs are entirely her own concern. If you've got some objection to something she's done, you must speak to her.'

'I'm sorry, David,' Eileen said with an offhand, no nonsense laugh, 'I'm afraid this is very much our concern. Certainly mine. I won't speak for anybody else. Else and I got her the job with Fred Rogerson, and she's let us down very badly.'

Tim's attempt at gravity had broken down into plain embarrassed gloom.

Else said in an artificially soft voice, 'David, surely you must see that it would be a very bad thing if I or Eileen were to talk to your sister about this business. I think maybe she is ill. There is certainly something not open in her conduct over this that seems not quite healthy.'

He said, 'I think you're both talking a lot of nonsense. But now that I'm here, you'd better tell me what it's all about.'

Eileen made it as a public announcement. 'Mrs Eliot has let us think that Fred Rogerson promised to keep her on next term and then withdrew his promise at a moment's notice. She made us think very badly of old friends and to say so to a number of people. In fact, we now learn that he was only too glad to keep her on and that she refused.'

Tim intervened. 'I think you must take into account, darling, that Mrs E. didn't want to work late in the evenings and ...'

David said angrily, 'I don't want to hear any more about this, taking into account or no taking into account. It has nothing to do with any of you. Nothing to do with anybody but Meg.'

Else said, 'Oh, David!' as though reproving an excited child.

'You seem to have no consideration for us whatever,' Eileen cried, 'I'm sorry, Else may be right and one of us speaking to Mrs Eliot may well upset her. But I'm afraid I can't help that. If you won't say anything to her, I shall demand some explanation from her.'

David banged his fist on the mica-topped table in front of him so that its little contemporary steel-tube legs rattled. 'You will not say a word to her about this. It's your own fault if you've gossiped about the Rogersons. Do you understand?' he shouted. 'You'll leave my sister alone.'

He got up and walked from the room. As he left, he could see astonishment at his show of anger in all their faces, but happily it was an astonished alarm that would keep them silent. And well they might be amazed, he thought. He had not lost his temper in this way for ten or fifteen years. That he had done so now depressed him more than any other aspect of the affair.

To address Meg in almost monosyllabic speech was Else's only protest after David's show of anger. To David's distress, Meg showed no surprise; it was clear that she was fully aware of the cause. David tried to avoid any moral judgement on her behaviour. Such blame as had attached to the Rogersons had been largely contributed by their friends, Else and Eileen; Meg had said that it was Fred's own affair. If the blame had been bruited abroad, that was entirely the fault of gossiping, with which he had no sympathy. Meg had been reticent with all of them, even with him; there was no reason why she should not be. Only one thing struck him painfully: he was certain that she was aware of his increased sympathy for her as a result of the supposed snub, and she had welcomed, almost encouraged it. It was behaviour so contrary to all she had said. Their relationship must be one hundred per cent, guaranteed all mutual honesty, she had said so herself; that was its justification. Yet, the word formed in his mind, he thought, that may be the *justification* for my purchasing it, but its value is something quite different. I don't even know what, but nothing to do with mutual honesty. The suggestion that the metaphor aroused of his comparative wealth and her indigence, the realization that he had left his apartness for a relationship that held him by motives he couldn't define, that did not stand on the sureties of complete openness that had been his familiar ground with Gordon, all combined to alarm him. At least, he thought, if I can't retreat, I mustn't commit myself further; yet his hurt feelings would not allow him to leave her disingenuous treatment of him unexplored.

Else went to her bed early. Putting aside Sir Harry Johnston's amateurish and therefore obscure remarks on East African Flora, he said, 'What do you intend to do now, Meg?' As soon as he had asked it, he knew that, in evading the subject of their relationship, he had asked a question that on all grounds he believed should not be his business.

'I don't know, David. Should I intend to do something?'

'You had the idea so firmly in your head before you were ill.'

'Oh, yes. I haven't lost it. But for the moment, judging by my failure with Fred Rogerson, I'm not ready to go ahead with it.'

'But Meg dear.' He knew that his voice sounded like a well-adjusted parent's in dealing with a child's lies. 'That just isn't true. Fred Rogerson was very anxious to have you back.'

'Not anxious enough to go without my services in the evenings.'

'But Meg, you can't always hope to impose your will ...'

'I don't expect to. He's quite right to insist on what he wants. I said so at the time. But if I'd been really good, he'd have taken me on my own terms.'

He thought to say that practice alone wóuld give her such a power; yet the idea of someone he loved wanting the power to dictate her own terms seemed so repellent that he decided again that she must be more mentally ill than appeared. Indeed, looking at her she suddenly seemed to him tired, the skin round her eyes drawn and lined. He said, 'I do see that evening work was too much to ask of you so soon.'

She said quite simply, 'I was losing contact with *you*, David. I can't do that. I depend on you for the sense of peace you've given me. There are no more nightmares now. Bill is with me as he used to be. I've lost all that pressing need to atone for my guilt towards him. And the guilt I felt towards Mother. You've freed me from all that, David. I never realized how it preyed on me.' She sighed deeply. 'It's a wretched dilemma,' she said, 'I need you and anything else I do takes me away. My interest is easily stimulated. I was fascinated by that school and Fred Rogerson's set up. But it was pulling me away from here. I thought perhaps that just to work the routine hours would be a compromise, but Fred Rogerson wouldn't have it and he was probably quite right. Even for me. It's all or nothing, you know, if you do anything well. But for the moment I need what *you* can give me, David, most of all. Am I in your way?'

'No, of course not, Meg. It's only that Else and Eileen ...'

'Oh, that,' Meg cried. 'I'm afraid I don't care, David. They pushed me into the job. It's nothing to do with them. Besides, they were only annoyed because it had been their idea and it didn't work. But I'll manage with them, David. Don't worry.'

There was much he wanted to say, but after all, he thought, they had intruded abominably, and he remained silent.

She said, 'I wish I could think you liked having me here.'

He said, 'I do, Meg, you know that.' He thought, she ought not to press me like this.

'I think you do,' she said. 'It isn't the money, is it, David? Gordon left you well off, I thought.'

'Oh yes,' he answered, 'Gordon didn't get the family business. God knows what he'd have done with it,' As he said it and laughed, a wave of his love for Gordon swept through him and enfolded Meg, because now he could talk to her about Gordon. 'But he was the old man's favourite of the two sons. He left him quite rich. And Gordon was very careful.' He laughed again, thinking of Gordon's foibles and how much he had loved them.

She said, 'Well, so are you, David. You must have been a pair of cheeseparers.' Her voice was affectionate. 'Not like my poor Bill,' she added, 'or me. Well then,' she said, 'it's all right for the moment.' She sounded like a condemned woman reprieved. She got up and poured out her whisky. 'I shall go to bed. I'm horribly tired.' At the door she turned to him. 'We said that we would be quite honest with each other, David. You do honestly want me to stay?'

Her eyes, begging, trying to hide their anxiety for fear of displeasing, were their mother's. I let *her* down, David thought, for 'principles'. Not again. 'Yes, Meg, quite honestly,' he said. His voice sounded in his ears like a stage performance of sincerity. It was not altogether fair, he thought, because in so many ways he *did* desperately want her to stay. But she must have been listening to the words alone, for she broke into a delighted smile and was gone to her room.

As far as David could tell, Meg did try her best with Else and Eileen; or, at any rate, she tried very hard.

It was not very difficult to overcome Eileen's hostility, or, at least, to neutralize it. Her intervention had been a piece of professional pride, the sudden action of a woman who every now and again came to the surface from the sea of her house and children, and, when she did so, suddenly resented being considered only a housewife and mother. Meg apologized. 'Eileen wasn't very gracious,' she said. 'Usually when people apologize, that's the end of that. Or so I thought. But she told me rather sharply that if she had her way, she'd set me down to a week's hard scrubbing of floors. However, she seems all right now.'

And so, of course, David reflected she would be. The fact once established that Meg couldn't come the gracious lady over her by apologies, she would return to the world of Omo and Crumbly Crust and babies' nappies. It was a world that David usually revered, but after Eileen's recent tiresome behaviour he suffered doubts about its simple virtues. As for himself, she told him once that she had always thought him weak but now she thought him spineless; and, after that, their straight-from-the-shoulder chaffing, uneasy, friendly relationship returned to its normal course.

Else was altogether a different problem. It would have required Meg to have tried more than her 'best', let alone 'very hard', to have appeased her. David, guessing at the depths of wounded feelings and the immensity of the isolation she was enduring behind her near silence, made one painful effort to reach and assist her – painful because it inevitably disregarded the reticences by which they had, for so many years, successfully converted mutual irritation into mutual affection; painful too, because it seemed one more step away from his general practice of non-attachment.

It was not easy now to gain her attention, and he was driven to make his advances leaning uncomfortably against the airing cupboard door while she checked and counted laundry.

'Else,' he said, 'I've always thought, considering how we were brought together by chance and with no real interests in common, that we have reason to be proud of the friendship we've built up.'

She said, 'David, we shall need to buy more pillowcases. Shall I get them, or will Mrs Eliot?'

He said, 'I know you find Meg's being here a strain. But I don't really understand why. We have our *own* friendship, but we've never pretended it was a deep one. You loved Gordon and so did I. I hoped that you were staying on here because it was the house in which you had been with him, the place where his memory is strongest for you and in which you'll therefore be most happy.'

She said, 'Gordon's memory is always with me, thank you, David.'

'Of course it is, Else. Only perhaps you and I know what a remarkable person he was.'

'You know that, do you, David?' There was real spite in her voice as she asked the question, then she apologized. 'No, I'm sorry. I should not have said that. We should not be having this conversation.'

'I think we must. Listen, Else, surely if you and I could live in the same house with the person we loved and not be jealous of each other, we can manage now. I don't like to say it, but it seems a poor compliment to Gordon that you should feel so bitter and lonely when he left so much that is permanent.'

'You are right. You should not like to say it. It is not true. I am practical. I don't think that a house should be burdened with two mistresses.'

'But Meg won't be here forever. You understood so well that I should ask her here when she fell ill. You were so good to her. I can't turn her away until she's ready to go. Else, surely you have enough affection for me to understand that she's my sister; I have a whole past in common with her.'

She threw down a pile of sheets on to the floor. 'Yes, you have her love. As you had Gordon's love. And I have nobody. Is that what you want to tell me?'

Rubbing his back against the door handle to bring back sensation to his body, numbed by pressure against the wood, he said, 'Else, this is impossible. I can't talk to you if you *will* see it like that. All I can repeat is that Meg won't be staying here.'

'No?'

'No. Not even if I wanted her to do so, I'm afraid. She's a person who has too much interest in life.'

'And you think I have no interests? There are other interests than people, you know. People don't concern me very much, David. I have only to go into the garden or the forest or on to the Downs to fill myself with a power that is much stronger than people.'

He thought, I only wish she'd do it, but he said, 'Else, will you try to think of this place as your home where you can be at peace?'

She answered, 'It is my home, David. Gordon wished it to be.' She refused him even a smile as she carried a pile of towels – he felt that she had purposely made it an absurdly large pile – to distribute in the bedrooms.

It wasn't to be her home for long. David never quite straightened out what eventually decided her to leave. He believed that, although Meg did all she could to improve the situation, Mrs Boniface had by then decided finally to transfer her allegiance. Much as he liked Mrs B. he had little doubt that the least attractive motives had swayed her – snobbery, hostility to a foreigner, being on the winning side. He also guessed that once she had made up her mind, she had not made life easy for Else.

Early in October he received a letter from Else sent by post. It was, he thought, a typical manifestation of her hugged isolation.

'My dear David,' she wrote, 'You have been so kind to let me stay at Andredaswood after the first shock of Gordon's death. Now is the time for me to leave. There is no sense in having two women to run the house. And if you love your sister, you will know that she needs occupation. All that she can do here is what I do. I am sure nobody doubts that she will do it better. I am so very grateful for your friendship. I shall hope to leave in one or two weeks.'

He managed to see her once more on her own. 'I've said nothing to anyone about your letter,' he told her. Then deliberately he tried, by recalling events of their life with Gordon, to break down the cold hostility with which she protected her unhappiness. He succeeded only too well, for she burst into tears. Now, he thought, she will surely find it possible to relax into some acceptance. But when she recovered herself, she said, still sobbing, 'I don't want to go, David, you know that. If you can send your sister away, I shall stay.'

He answered very coldly. 'I'm afraid that's impossible, Else.' Then, ashamed of his hardness, he said, 'But where are you going to? You must go to Mrs Paget. She needs you now. And anyway she has always told me that she would be glad to have you there.'

'No, David,' she said, 'I have lived too much in other people's houses. I think that the worst thing that Hitler did to me was to make me able only to live in other people's lives. Now I must begin to live on my own.'

He looked at her and thought, she's not only old, but she's without relation to anything outside this place. We've preserved her in lovable eccentricity, Gordon and I, until she couldn't possibly fend for herself. He said, 'At least let Mrs Paget know you're leaving, Else, or let me write to her.'

She said, 'No, David, please! I must ask you not to do so.' She was determined. After all, he thought, there are eccentric old women working and living in their isolation in the most incongruous communities; and people, even the most conventional, cope with them and are kind to them. Immediately he felt ashamed of his thoughts. Else, for all her absurdity, had devotion, courage, and a sort of self-sufficiency – she was no object of patronizing kindness. It's only I, he thought, who give her these wounds that she so morbidly nourishes. Away from here she'll be all right. Nevertheless, he wished that she were different, so that he might not feel glad to see her go.

He told Meg of Else's decision that night. She seemed so unconcerned that he said angrily, 'I genuinely believe, Meg, that if you asked her to stay, she would do so.'

She looked away from him and said, 'I'm sorry, David, I can't. It would be an impossible footing for either of us to live on. I can't see why she was ever here.'

'Because she was a very old friend of Gordon's,' he said. 'She came as a refugee to the Pagets' when Gordon was still at the University. She was with them all through the war. When we bought this place and needed a housekeeper, she was the obvious person. She's been extraordinarily kind to both of us. Does that explain it?'

She said soothingly, 'Yes, of course. But she belongs to the Pagets really. I expect that now Mrs Paget's had this stroke, she'll be glad to have her there. These indomitable old women will never admit to needing anyone, but when it's arranged for them ...' Her voice had, David thought, that note of worked-up interest that one uses in speaking of friends of friends.

He said, 'Else refuses to go there. She's determined to go off on her own. God knows what she'll do!'

Suddenly Meg's manner changed. She turned on him, her voice excited, rapid. 'Oh, no, David,' she cried, 'she can't possibly do that. Poor old thing! She'd be utterly lost. Oh, no, you must write to Mrs Paget and tell her what's happening.'

'Else's forbidden me to do that.'

'Forbidden? What do you mean?'

'Just that. Forbidden.'

'Well, it's nonsense. She needn't know you've written. Tell Mrs Paget to say nothing.'

'I can't possibly do that.'

'Why not? If you don't, I shall. You can't let that wretched woman's pride hurt her like that.'

'On the contrary, Meg, I can't humiliate her by disregarding her own wishes. Surely that's fundamental in one's treatment of any human being. No, Meg, if we can't find a way to keep her here, we can't soothe our consciences by treating her like a child.'

Meg looked at him searchingly. He could not tell what she was thinking. 'Well, it's none of my affair,' she said. He could not feel that this was a quite fair statement of the situation, but he said no more.

In fact, as it later appeared, she also recognized her involvement. Three days before she was due to leave, Else received a letter from Mrs Paget.

'Oh, David, listen, please,' she said, as she read it. 'She writes to ask if you can spare me from here. The recovery, she says, is good, but not so good that she can do all herself. She writes, "I suppose I must admit that old age has at last put me out of work, but I believe, Else, that if I had another pair of hands and another pair of feet I could still keep at it. And there is so much to do here. The man who's organizing the Nuclear Disarmament Campaign is a fool. I suppose David would think it very selfish if I asked you to come and be my extra hands and feet".' She was so excited that the letter shook in her hand, then she pulled herself together and assumed a severe, judicial look. 'I suppose that I ought to do what she asks,' she said.

'I suppose you ought too, Else.' David could hardly keep from smiling. He could tell without looking at Meg that she had written and that she was now putting on a special face that he knew from their youth, a face of triumph. There seemed no sense in reproving her when Else, all happiness, had gone from the room. He only said, 'All right. You know best.' Nevertheless he was troubled by the divergence in their views of ends and means.

In the weeks after Else's departure, however, there seemed to be no divergence between them. October was bright with sunshine. The nursery, all dahlias and michaelmas daisies, looked gaily garish with that ordered, commercial colourfulness which, hardly beautiful, yet banished the natural melancholy of the season by its obvious show; banished a little, too, the remembrance of the year before, of the first alarms of Gordon's illness and, David judged from Meg's ease, of Srem Panh also. Working together was such a constant delight. Meg was full of ideas for this and that, ready to argue for them, and when they proved impracticable to relinquish them with laughter. David, in fact, seemed to hear nothing but laughter or voices rising and falling, shouting each other down in discussion or argument that was yet never angry – his own, Meg's, Tim's, Climbers', Mrs B.'s, even Collihole's; they were all brought in and they all loved it. Meg seemed to be able to live within their world and yet in a way outside it. There was a morning when Climbers asked them to look at her dahlia display set out at the entrance of the nursery to enable visitors to make their choice without touring the garden. He knew from experience what to expect – jars of dahlias set out in groups of pompons, collarettes, cactus, and so on, all ranged within their groups from giant to dwarf, and by a colour range adapted crudely from the spectrum so that purples faded genteelly into mauves and orange destroyed both scarlet and saffron; the whole display was set out against a back-cloth of sky-blue velvet somewhat torn. Meg took one look at the display and said in a sort of Beatrice Lillie voice, 'But *lovely*, Climbers!' and then burst into peals of laughter.

Miraculously Climbers was not at all offended, they all laughed together and the whole display was changed under Meg's direction. Climbers' only protest was to say, 'Of course, blue used to be the colour, you know, Mrs Eliot,' and even then she giggled at her own remark.

Later, David was even more delighted when Meg said, laughing, 'Don't imagine that you'll sell more because they look better on display. You'll probably sell less.' He had thought exactly the same thing.

Yet, for all the laughter and talk, Meg managed the house and the nursery correspondence quickly and well. David's only fear was that, when the order season was over, she would find too little to occupy her energies. He also wondered now and again what she made of the comparatively small amount of work that really demanded his attention. On occasion, too, when he was left alone to meditate, he was disturbed to reflect how short a while ago he had supposed her entirely alien to the way of life he was seeking. She was not different from what she had been. Yet he did not feel that she had deflected him from his course in anything that was essential; he remained as resolute, he hoped, in his love of life and in his withdrawal from it, he accepted the minute progress and the constant failures of his self mastery, and he still sought strength to do better. Above all, he still felt an inner quietude that never, he hoped, allowed him smugly to forget the wind that howled in the desert world outside. If he was strengthened in his progress by the conviction that he had given some sense of peace to her, he did not allow himself to speculate on what the nature of her peace was, or to seek to mould it to his own. But that she had found some peace, he was convinced, and that it should be expressed in such a life of gusts and energy did not make him sceptical, for in this she recalled to him always Gordon.

Nor could he consider her liveliness to be a less hopeful expression of a growing inner strength because unlike Gordon's it was not founded on religious belief; to have done so would have made nonsense of his own agnostic discipline. He could only decide that sorrow, defeat, an acute sense of personal loss – personal experience, in short, of man's universal tragic predicament – had given her a new grace, a new sweetness that yet still expressed themselves through her old high spirits and energy. He felt, above all, though they never talked of it, that she had known, as he had, absolute despair and had not allowed it to turn to hatred.

Meg, oddly it seemed to him, was the only one of them all now and again to recall Else in conversation. She asked questions about her background, her views on this or that, whether she had ever had a lover or even been in love. 'She was an interesting person,' she said. 'Circumstances were against my getting to know her. I don't know that a year ago I could have accepted that, but I've learnt so much about the limitations imposed by time and place.' She was quick, however, to point out to David that he could now build up a good quartet. 'You must write to that Miss Thing the cellist at once, David,' she said, and kept him up to it.

Mary Gardner replied that she was now playing with a quartet in Lewes, but she was not entirely happy with them and, after certain promised performances in the Christmas season, she would be glad to start with David again; meanwhile they could look out for a new second violinist.

Meg immediately began to urge him to practise regularly again. But in the weeks that followed, he did not play the violin often. Meg's encouragement of him led her to speak of her own interest in music. He discovered at once such a mixture of real feeling and of technical ignorance; of prejudices, some of which agreed pleasingly with his own, others of which he longed to demolish. In no time he found himself explaining, by illustration from records and at the piano, some of the difficulties she found, introducing her to some of the pleasures he most regretted that she had been denied. Successive evenings were passed in this way until Meg, perhaps feeling that they could no longer regard each occasion as arising independently, began to refer ironically to 'musical appreciation, a speciality'. Irony for both of them, as they openly agreed, was the high-road to acceptance and now they began to plan a short course.

'It'll help to keep you going until Mrs Thing's ready with her cello. You need some sort of compulsion, you know, David. As for me – well, at least I shall have some idea of what I'm listening to. And then I shall be less ashamed to listen.'

David was not so happy, indeed at first appalled, when Meg announced that Climbers would like to be in on it. 'She's tone deaf, Meg dear,' he said. But Meg insisted. 'You've no right to condemn people in that way. In any case, we need someone from outside, otherwise we shall skip the parts that bore us. And,' she added, laughing, 'we don't want our life to get too cosily brother and sister. It wouldn't be quite decent.'

Climbers, as David expected, embarrassed them the first two evenings by her own embarrassed gratitude, but Meg, by attacking her fiercely, brought out an independence that David had never suspected. Climbers' presence, indeed, seemed only to bring him closer to Meg. Gradually, too, he found that teaching the slower witted, if it had not the same excitement as feeding a ready intelligence, had its own satisfactory triumphs.

When he told this to Meg, she said, 'Well, there you are, David, you wouldn't go on with being a teacher.'

'A *teacher*?' The word had no association with his past.

'Fellow or whatever it was.'

'Oh, there was no teaching about that, Meg. It was purely a research fellowship.'

'Research on what? I could never see, David, what you could research about Richardson. I never got through *Grandison*. But I've read all *Clarissa*, believe it or not. And, of course, *Pamela*. *Clarissa*'s very exciting once you get used to the pace. But I mean there they are. There isn't much more to say, is there?'

He told her of the later novels of sensibility, of the Continental analyses of virtue and of seduction, of the epistolary form in France and Germany.

She said, 'But most of that must be well known, isn't it?'

'There are details to be filled in,' he answered, laughing. 'That was the trouble, Meg. I was collecting the crumbs more untidy scholars had dropped on the floor.'

She said, 'Yes, I *do* see. Well, anyway,' she announced, 'I've seen Richardson's *bones* and I'm sure you haven't. Yes, truly I have. He was buried in one of those bombed churches. Bill and I had to go round them with some American friends. And the sexton showed us Richardson's coffin which had burst open. So you see.'

He was glad that his own estimation of the research work he had given up was so confirmed by her frivolity. When, after the war, he had refused to return to the University, he had thought with guilt how much Meg would have given to have had that career when she was a girl. Of course, by that time she had been married and the point was in all senses academic; all the same, her acceptance now seemed to absolve him from all those advantages that as a boy he had enjoyed over her – advantages which their mother had seen as the natural order, and Meg, then, as a monstrous system. She had said that he had removed past guilts for her; now she was doing the same for him.

That Meg herself was conscious of no longer feeling the jealousy of her youth was apparent to him a few evenings later. He had been discussing questions of rhythm in music with them, and Climbers, as she made one of those many half exits from the room which inevitably preceded her final departure for home (if her bed-sitting room at old Mrs Turner's could be called that), said, 'I suppose you don't approve of jazz, David?' He wondered if such irrelevance meant that she had misunderstood all he had been saying that evening, and again what, in Climbers' strange, unrelated world, 'jazz' meant. He said, 'I don't think about it much.'

Meg said, 'Bill and I used to go dancing a lot at one time. But I suppose that isn't jazz. Is that a word that's used now, anyway?'

But Climbers had a different motive, 'It's only,' she said, 'that I think it's rather bad of Eileen telling Tim he's got to give up that jazz band of his.'

Meg said, 'But, Climbers, are you sure? It's absolutely monstrous!'

David said, 'But they've always had such a live-and-let-live attitude!'

For some reason Climbers seemed to think that this phrase had a salacious overtone, for she let out a loud guffaw and then blushed scarlet. 'Oh, I know,' she said, 'and Eileen's frightfully good, really. But I suppose she *does* get left an awful lot on her own. And they aren't just tiny babies any more. But in any case I'm always willing to sit in. But I suppose that's just it, now that she can go out more, she wants Tim to go with her. Anyway, she's awfully against jazz.' She made the word seem more and more mysterious every time that she used it. 'And then she says it makes Tim neglect his work. That's what I think is so frightfully unfair. Nobody works harder than Tim, I'm sure.' The transference from Eileen to Tim was clearly quite complete. 'And I wondered if *you* would say something, David, because Tim cares about the jazz so much. But, of course if you're against it ...'

'I'm neither for or against it, Climbers,' David said. Then, realizing how pompous this sounded, he said, 'Well, yes, I suppose I am against it as I am against Siberian wallflowers or mice. It never occurs to me to encourage them. But I certainly shouldn't discourage Tim from doing something that gives him pleasure. On the other hand, I shan't

321

interfere between him and Eileen. If he wants to play in the jazz band very much he'll get his way. No, not even that, because Tim's a good and unselfish person. But certainly I won't interfere.'

'I thought you'd say that, David. And I expect you're right. But it does seem a shame. What do you think, Mrs Eliot?'

Meg said slowly, 'Well, if it *does* interfere with his work ... But no, of course it's – disgraceful. I wish Eileen wouldn't keep on turning out worse than I thought her. But David's quite right. He couldn't interfere. Nor should you, Climbers. Take my word for it. I've done such a lot of interfering for people's good, and it's been disastrous. I should be just the same now if it weren't for David. I'm a natural Emma, but luckily David's Knightly and Mr Woodhouse rolled into one.' She laughed with surprise when she had said it.

After Climbers' final departure, Meg said, 'It used to be Maggie Tulliver, you know. But there was as much rivalry in my love for you, David, then, as in Maggie's for Tom. And now you're Knightly and Mr Woodhouse. I hope it's not too Freudian.'

They both laughed. Afterwards it occurred to him as strange that he should feel so unworried at her assertion of dependence on him. Yet if Emma depended on Knightly and on her father, they, after all, remained with their own lives of masculine privacy uninvaded. Whereas in the past, in their youth, he had felt all the time that assertion of Meg's to control, to prove that he was not necessarily her superior because he was the boy, to use her control of him as a signal of victory – the most cruel that there could be – to wave in the face of their mother. Amusedly, he thought, in any case there's an irony implicit in what she said and she knows it – Knightly was a prig and Mr Woodhouse a vegetable. He was well aware that there was something of both in him. As long, it seemed to him, as there was that degree of detachment in her 'dependence' on him, their happy relationship was surely also free from danger.

Only once in those last months of the year did Meg behave in a way that irritated David. The occasion was annoying enough, for it was entirely of her own making. Suddenly it seemed that Meg had decided that it was an absurdity to burden themselves with two parties in the New Year; one of them must be held in the fortnight before Christmas. Useless for David to urge that the pressure of winter deliveries was even further swelled then by the supplying of Christmas potted plants; she merely said, 'There may be a rush, David, but there's nothing in this nursery you can't delegate.'

It was the first time she had mentioned David's own work. She was, he could see, watching his reaction with a quizzical smile that was ready to vanish at any sign of resentment. For a moment he did resent it. He had fashioned his own life, he had only his own conscience to satisfy; for Meg to walk in halfway through the performance and judge the line of the play was inadmissible criticism. Yet if he was really satisfied with the amount of Martha tasks that he contributed to life, he surely ought not to mind others judging it with a certain mockery. It should be enough for him that Gordon, who had known the breaking work of those first five years of the nursery should have approved his acceptance of the lightened load of these last years, should indeed have left him enough money to continue to accept it. He and Gordon had always detested worship of work as one of the most assertive and corroding of human passions. But for this very reason Gordon would have found any bullfrog swelling of resentment at Meg's amusement peculiarly ridiculous. So now he laughed.

'Do you remember,' he asked, 'how Mother delighted to find that things would just cover a sixpence? I suppose my labours would hardly cover that.'

'Oh, no, David, you do quite enough work to cover half-a-crown. But you've still enough time to give a party. Anyway, two parties spread out like that are far less exhausting than two in the same week. And people will expect it just before Christmas. Anyone would think that I hadn't proved a success at the summer party. I shall be able to run the whole affair this time with Mrs B. You'll hardly know a thing about it until it's over.' She piled up the reasons.

David felt disturbed lest beneath her easy happiness at Andredas-wood there might be some pressing boredom. He asked, 'Is life proving distressingly dull for you here, Meg?'

She said, 'Oh, David, don't make such a thing about it. No. I just would like to show myself off a bit. I'm bound to be a backslider now and again.'

They laughed. And so the party was given.

Meg was as good as her word; the arrangements were excellent. On the morning of the party day, Mary Gardner rang up and asked did David mind if she brought the Grant-Pritchards, she thought it would be good business anyway for David to meet them. Not at all, David said, but who would they be? Michael Grant-Pritchard! Mary exclaimed, but surely David had heard of him; he was that M.P. who'd been so strong in pressing the Government about the Trade

Union danger. David said that the Trade Union danger had not threatened Andredaswood closely so far.... There was an agreed irony in any conversation he held with Mary Gardner that did not concern music. No doubt, he said, Mary's husband had felt it more seriously. Mary laughed but then spoke in her serious, responsible voice. People who didn't live in the clouds had reason to know how dangerous all these restrictive practices and things were. Anyway Michael Grant-Pritchard, who was a brilliant lawyer, was one of *the* coming men and the sooner David knew about him the better, especially as he was buying 'Oblongs' now that the Phipsons were going to live near Cape Town. David would certainly like Frederica Grant-Pritchard, she was so very quiet; in any case he must, for she had all sorts of ideas about the garden at 'Oblongs'. The garden at 'Oblongs', David said, was a creation of Miss Jekyll's, and while he was not wholly in accord with Miss Jekyll's horticultural aesthetic, she had been one of our great gardeners; the Phipsons had already done enough to ruin her creation by their neglect, he did not propose to assist Mrs Grant-Pritchard in completing the ruin of a great garden by her ideas, whatever *they* might be. But Mary Gardner only replied with one of the principal articles of her creed. 'My dear David,' she said, 'money is money.'

Frederica Grant-Pritchard proved to be a rather big woman in her late thirties. She seemed, at first, shy and undistinguished, likely to be a bore. Her shyness was, however, a quality that predisposed David in her favour, and when it turned out that her 'ideas' were simply a desire to restore the garden at 'Oblongs' to Miss Jekyll's original design he was quite won over. She had taken great trouble to read all Miss Jekyll's books, and, if David found it rather strange at this time to meet someone from a sophisticated world who seemed unaware that herbaceous borders and wild gardens and iris walks were not the perfection of gardening, he was only too ready to sink his criticism before such genuine, if naïve, enthusiasm. Looking at her swelling white neck and bosom, her rather prominent blue eyes, fresh complexion and red hair, he thought sadly that had she lived in the age of Rubens, she would have been a great beauty. To have discovered this made him feel that somehow she was his own creation, whose shyness and ordinariness must be warmed and cherished by him. He would have talked to her for much longer, but that to be noticed by the host was clearly an ordeal for her.

'All your other guests,' she said, and then blushed for fear she had seemed to remind him of his social duty. They were fully agreed, however, that he was to assist her professionally in her garden scheme. 'I expect I shall be here quite a lot,' she said. 'Michael doesn't find me much help in London. So we bought this house.'

Her husband's constituency, it seemed, was in North London so that what with his constituency and with the House, he was not likely to be much at 'Oblongs'. Frederica Grant-Pritchard seemed quite relieved at this – 'He might get bored,' she said – and David, looking at her husband, felt no distress.

Michael Grant-Pritchard looked all that David had expected – tall, dark, with greying side hair, too charming, too distinguished, and a great deal too assured. What or whether he was all that could be deduced from his appearance, David had no intention of finding out; he instinctively kept away from such embodiments of self-assertion as notable people must inevitably be. Mr Grant-Pritchard made only one contribution to his wife's plans for the garden. 'Don't let her exclude roses altogether, will you? I'm simple enough to think that a garden's not a garden at all unless it has roses. The old-fashioned sort, you know, that have got some scent.'

The belief that modern roses lacked scent was one of the common delusions that David found most tedious, so he merely smiled in answer to this affability. He had no doubt, anyway, that left to his uninstructed taste, Michael Grant-Pritchard would prefer roses of the largest size and of the most vulgarly 'delicate' shade regardless of their scent.

Even if David had wished to improve his knowledge of Michael Grant-Pritchard, he would not have found it easy. Meg and the distinguished visitor talked to one another throughout almost the entire party. David, Mary Gardner, Tim, even Climbers, brought up various people to be introduced to Michael Grant-Pritchard; they were one and all politely but firmly shaken off. Frederica, with an awful sudden brightness, produced, David thought, not only by shyness but by a real fear of her husband, said, in the manner of a totally different woman, a bright, domineering middle-class wife, 'Now, Michael, that's quite enough, you know. You're monopolizing Mrs Eliot.'

'Frederica,' he said to Meg, 'always *observes* things at parties. And this time, darling, your observation's quite correct.'

David, overhearing this, wondered that Meg should continue talking to someone who was so crudely bullying to his wife. True, Meg, hearing only this inept intervention of Frederica Grant-Pritchard's, might well have presumed her to be a silly, tactless woman but even so ... He was annoyed enough to say directly to Meg, 'I think the party wants a little supervision,' but she looked round the room and answered quite simply, 'Oh, I don't think so, David. They all look quite happy.'

It wasn't even true. There was no doubt that Michael Grant-Pritchard had offended the greater number of his new neighbours by ignoring them, and Meg had quite lost the good opinion she had won in the summer. Climbers, like a scout on the losing side in a battle, kept bringing reports of people who were leaving 'rather hurt' by Mrs Eliot's failure to talk to them. Eileen and the Rogersons were disgusted that she should make such a fuss of a man whose politics stank. Even Tim said, 'I didn't know Mrs E. had parliamentary aspirations. She's certainly got *him* thinking she's the best.'

Yet there was no element of flirtation in Meg's manner with Michael Grant-Pritchard; nor, David had to admit, in his to her, though it was easy to imagine the sickening sort of womanizer he was. There was a good deal of gaiety and laughter in their conversation, it was true, spotlit perhaps the more as the rest of the party fell into an increasingly deadened sense of being unnoticed; but, in the main, they seemed to be discussing solemnly, or rather, Meg almost greedily asking questions and putting up objections as he held forth. Once or twice, indeed, they seemed to be in violent disagreement. Meg's voice rose above the subdued chatter, saying, 'I think that's a lot of high-flown talk to keep your conscience quiet'; and he later suddenly boomed in a tone hardly decorated even with politeness, 'I'm afraid you simply don't know what you're talking about.'

Suddenly, as the party was almost ended, they seemed tacitly to agree to break up their conversation and mingle with the other guests. For the remaining ten minutes Michael Grant-Pritchard gave an exhibition of his charm working at full pressure, and Meg, too, was at the top of her social form. With a certain pleasure, David noted that they were both too late to repair the effect they had created.

He was as puzzled about Michael Grant-Pritchard's motives for behaving so 'badly' as he was about Meg's, but a good deal less concerned. He supposed, perhaps, that the man for some reason was in a bad temper with his wife, to whom he had certainly caused acute embarrassment. Then, too, these were not his constituents, nor indeed people who particularly 'mattered'; perhaps he had bought 'Oblongs' with the intention of working off the contempt and dislike for human beings that his careerism normally forbade him to express. It was said that ambitious, successful people never failed in charm even with the dustman, for fear of offending potentially useful people; but David reflected that this might well be a groundless platitude; he knew nothing about the psychology of careerism and cared less. Probably, he thought, Meg had seemed the only *mondaine* person present, although really this was not true. It was impossible to say what the man's motives had been. He had known Bill in the course of business, it seemed, but they had not been close colleagues; and Michael Grant-Pritchard was certainly not likely to be governed by sentiment or by any compassion for Meg's tragic loss of her husband. It was really most likely that he had used Meg as a weapon in some complicated marital battle. As he left, he had said to her, 'I shall hold you to your promise,' and although Frederica Grant-Pritchard did not look particularly distressed at this, she was no doubt intended to be inflamed into some fire of jealousy. David felt that he had seldom met a man that he disliked so much, and he hoped never to have to consider him again.

Meg's motives he had to consider. She continued to be entertaining and charming on the adjournment to the kitchen, but only Mrs Boniface, unaware of the party's failure, responded. The others were listless and resentful. It seemed that Meg realized that she had gone too far to recover them, for suddenly, with no more than a perfunctory smile, she left the kitchen.

After what he judged a decent interval of five minutes, he followed her into the drawing room. She was crouched in front of the huge fireplace, trying, with puffs of the bellows, to hold in glow the wood that yet obstinately paled into white ash. She stopped as soon as he came in. All the glasses and dishes and ashtrays had been removed, but the room still wore a desolate battlefield air. He said, 'There's no point in keeping the fire alive. We can't sit in here. Let's go to the morning room. We can have the electric fire there.'

She answered, 'We'd better not sit together, David. I feel so guilty that I shall probably say something unkind.'

He said, 'Oh, it isn't important.'

'I'm afraid it is. That's one of the prices one pays for the gentleness and peace of this house. Things that are only misdemeanours appear crimes.'

'I think that's unfair. Nobody's suggested it's a crime.'

'No, I'm sorry, David. I'm only trying to excuse myself by attacking first.'

'Well, there's no need. It was annoying that you insisted on this party and then failed to do anything to entertain people. It's also a bit odd that you should want to talk to that ghastly man for so long.'

'Yes, he is pretty frightful, isn't he? Bill always said he was. But he's very interesting, David. He was a poorer lawyer than Bill. Bill always said so. And he himself admitted it this evening. Not much poorer, you know. A clever man, but just not first class. But he's been more of a success.'

'A success? Meg, do you really mind about that?'

'Mind? No. Well, only in this way – that he's happier than Bill was. After all, Bill aimed at being a success and I did so for him. And we slipped up. Oh, I know Bill *was* successful, but I also know, we all do, that it couldn't have lasted. He was too desperate. That man said Bill didn't care enough. I suppose he meant care about making a career.'

'But Grant-Pritchard's happiness is only self-satisfaction, and satisfaction of greed for power at that. Anyway, I should think his happiness, as you call it, is only skin deep. Look at the abominable way he treats his wife.'

'Does he? I didn't notice. He's pretty thick-skinned, David, so that if his happiness *is* only skin deep ...' She left it in mid-air and after a moment's silence, 'We came quite to like each other, I think. Not *really* like, of course, for me at any rate, because he's so awful; but when you've been very rude to someone ... I don't know why he didn't walk away, and perhaps I liked him because he didn't. I expect nobody, no *woman* anyway, who was a stranger, had been rude to him before, and that took his breath away long enough to make him stay and listen.'

'What on earth did you say to him, then?' David asked. He wanted to hear no more about it all; yet he could see that she expected the question.

'Well, he came up and condoled about Bill. That was all right, he had to. But then he started in an awful flowery way to talk about Bill's heroism in this drab age. I remembered how Bill had despised him and I saw him sitting there, successful and purring, and Bill was dead. I was very angry. I said, "You know very well that you despise Bill for having got killed in such a chance way. You don't think it heroism, nor was it. But if it had been, *you* wouldn't have been capable of recognizing it!" To give him his due, he admitted the insincerity.'

He was very rude back. He said, "I imagine Bill Eliot must have been starved of love to have thrown his life away like that". It was quite untrue, but it was a fair retort to my rudeness. He was very frank all the time. Maybe he felt able to be so with me since I don't "matter" in his sense of the word. A sort of indulgence of honesty. Or maybe it's simply a line he shoots, I don't know. Some of it sounded terribly phoney. For example, he said that one has only a right to be ruthless in life if you've really understood the person whom you're sacrificing. To the point of love, he said. I think he knew that I thought it repulsive, but he's a man who must make a violent impression. I told him that it was melodramatic nonsense. But he obviously has a lot of personal ethics like that which he half believes in. It was the same when he talked about his attack on the Trade Unions. Oh yes, we talked about that. He admitted that he'd made himself spokesman largely to please the industrialists and also to make his mark in his party, but he also thinks that it's a rallying point for what he calls the responsible elements in the country. "A sense of responsibility, and particularly a sense of something to fight for, is the only thing that can save the intelligent middle classes in this country," he said, "and an intelligent middle class is the only future a country like England has in the modern world."'

David said, 'He sounds a rather nasty sort of tough windbag. They go together, I think, more often than is supposed. But you must have met up-and-coming men of all parties again and again in London.'

'I suppose so. *He* certainly came to Lord North Street once or twice. But most people who came to the house, whether I liked them or not, were just part of the setting for my life with Bill. It was only obviously unhappy people I thought of looking into.'

'I must say I should prefer to look into people like Grant-Pritchard in novels. I'm sure Michael Grant-Pritchard can be found in many a modern novel without meeting him.'

'Probably, but I like to do both. I couldn't be interested in novels if I wasn't interested in the real people.'

'A narrow conception of the art of the novel,' David said dryly, 'that would receive short shrift from any good modern critic.' Then, as disposing of the Grant-Pritchards, he added, 'Well, I'm glad that I concentrated on *Mrs* Grant-Pritchard. She's quite nice and she has good ideas about her garden. I'm going to help her to restore it to its original form.'

'In *that* case, David, I think it's just as well that I did monopolize him. I'm sure he only thinks of her as someone to contradict. He'd have undone all her plans and yours into the bargain. Plus, of course, the fact, or so he told me, that she brought him a good deal of money.'

'Meg, he sounds revolting.'

'Yes, I'm afraid he is quite unpleasant. He's almost certainly mean, which is unattractive. He shares his secretary with some other M.P.s, although he could obviously afford one of his own. He asked me if I would go over and do some work for him when he's moved into this new house.'

'Was that the promise he mentioned?'

'Yes. Of course, I've no intention of doing so. He simply wants secretarial service on the cheap. He'd be a dreadful bully as an employer anyway, I suspect.'

There, with the additional promise from Meg that she would do her best to repair any bad impression made upon the customers of Andredaswood, they left the disastrous party.

David thought for a while that night about Meg's behaviour. There were many disturbing motives that he could imagine – disturbing, that was, to him – but in the end he decided that it was all due to the sudden appearance on the scene of someone connected with Bill. He had hoped that her torments and regrets about her married life had now faded before the happiness that she had undoubtedly known; that Bill's memory had finally ceased to fret and to hurt her, had become instead a source of strength. No doubt it was asking too much; guilt or regret inevitably smouldered here and there. Perhaps the little fire that Michael Grant-Pritchard had lit for that hour or so would be the last of it.

Certainly the winter months were a time of great happiness. He felt sometimes amazed that he could so completely share his life with anyone – particularly a woman, particularly, perhaps, his sister Meg – without feeling invaded or exhausted or swallowed up. He felt himself none of these things; she had the extraordinary power, it seemed, of needing someone and yet leaving them whole. Nor did she fret him at all to do this or that. He had felt that she was disturbed lest 'musical appreciation – a speciality' might, much though she clearly enjoyed it, be keeping him from playing seriously again. He was not altogether sorry when Mary Gardner's husband got pleurisy and, on recovery, took Mary off to Madeira; the question of the quartet was postponed until the spring. There was nothing then which he and Meg could not, did not share in that mild, sunny, early spring-like winter.

In February, it was true, she did make a change in his life, but it was one for which he was grateful. One morning a letter came from the publishers asking whether and when 'Africa' could be expected. He had contrived a desultory research for the book, but now he must face giving the larger part of his evenings to it. When he mentioned the letter to Meg, he feared that she would urge once again how much of the work in the nursery could be done without his supervision, that he could, in fact, work on 'Africa' by day as well. Yet now that she was so much involved with the nursery work, so that he could discuss any part of it with her, he was even more reluctant to admit that it did not demand his full attention. Instead she asked, 'What made you and Gordon write those books?'

'Money originally,' he said. 'When we started the nursery Gordon's father was still alive and it was quite a struggle to keep going.'

'I see. I don't mean that I don't think they deserve their success. But ... well *you* wouldn't read them, would you? They're nice Christmas books, or books to put in guests' bedrooms.'

He said, 'Thank you.'

She said, 'Well, they are, aren't they? Gordon's photographs are first rate, and the illustrations you've chosen are pleasing. It's all *pleasing*, and I can imagine a lot of the reading you've done for the books must have been fascinating. But, David!'

He explained to her how completely aware he and Gordon had been of the minor, bedside nature of the series, and yet how, for him, anxious to produce nothing that could add to all the personal voices that were leading mankind to boiling point, their very insipidity was their value; they pretended to nothing. At first she could not understand at all.

'Well, nice as they are, David, those sort of elegantly served up pieces of history and geography seem to me as pretentious as books *can* be. And I'm sure a very pretentious sort of people buy them.'

He tried then to explain how that sort of chic was not pretentious as she feared, since it laid no claim to authority, no assertion of importance. Anyone might see that the books were at best written to make needed money, at worst as a pleasing hobby.

She said, 'I see. Yes, yes. I do see.' Then she announced, 'David, I've been reading your doctoral thesis.'

'Good God,' he said, 'where on earth did you find it?'

'It was among all those books in Else's room.'

'Oh Lord! It must be fabulously boring.'

'Some of it's boring, yes, though academically excellent, I'm sure. But there are passages that fascinated me. Expecially one arising from *Pamela* about the sexual excitement attaching to lower-class people – servants and so on – in the eighteenth century. And the degree to which the subject has to be purified or sentimentalized in novels, at that time even. I should have thought that the nineteenth century would provide even better material.'

'But of course. It's one of Thackeray's chief warnings, and Trollope and Samuel Butler follow him up. And Dickens is obsessed with it from Little Nell to Lizzie Hexham. It's got two strands – the deflowering of virgins and the corrupting of oneself with harlots.'

'I should love to work those patterns out.'

'Well, why don't you?'

'Oh, David, I haven't the training for that sort of thing, but if *you* were to work on it, I'd like to help.'

He looked at her gravely. 'If this is a subtle attempt to get me back to the University, it's no good, Meg. Firstly, this kind of theme wouldn't do in the modern literary academic world. It smells far too much of sociology and Freud. Secondly, I've been too long out of that world to get back, at my age. Thirdly, I don't *want* to go back to it.'

She laughed. 'I can see you might think that was what I was up to, but I'm not, David. Quite honestly, I thought possibly of some articles and eventually, perhaps, a book very little more respectable than your Garden Flowers in their Homes series; but a good deal more interesting to me, and, I believe, to you. But it wouldn't make any greater assertions than your 'Africa' will, if you publish it.'

'Yes, it would. Assertions literary, sociological and possibly intellectual. Very assertive,' he laughed.

But she did not respond to his laughter. 'Oh, well,' she said, and sighed. The sigh sounded so remote from him that he said immediately, 'If you'll work on it with me, Meg, I'll certainly consider it. I'll write to the publishers today to say, "No Africa" and then we can start. After all, it will only mean re-reading a great number of books that I shall be glad to read again. If it works out, then I'll see about writing some of it up. A good book couldn't appear for a long while. The time for writing here is inevitably so limited.'

'Inevitably? There's no earthly reason, David, why you shouldn't hand over the nursery to Tim whenever you want. Certainly for as long as you needed to write a book.'

'Oh yes there is, Meg.' He tried to make this sound as definite as he could.

She asked, 'David, why are you so entrenched in your attitude about the nursery? You're not basically interested in gardening. You went into it because of Gordon.'

He said, 'That's not true, Meg. And, even if it were, that would be the first of reasons for my continuing with it.'

There was silence for a moment, then she said, 'I'm sorry, David. I shouldn't have said that. I hadn't truly understood how you felt about it.'

And now they were brought even closer. David suggested that they should start with the minor eighteenth-century novelists – 'to get over the boring part first.'

Fat little calf-bound volumes of Coventry and Johnstone, Mackenzie and Mrs Robinson began to arrive from the London Library. With all the exchange of comment and analysis that passed between him and Meg, these stilted, shallow novels proved enthralling. It was difficult even to fit in 'music appreciation' for which Climbers was clamouring – she had suddenly and improbably decided that she wanted to know about the development of Church music (shades of Gordon, David thought). It was often very late when they went to bed.

Yet in the day-time, David worked as he had not done for a year or two. He felt somehow impelled to prove to himself that the nursery needed him. He supervised sterilizing of soil and of boxes, preparation of houses, seed preparation, temperature regulation for the forcing of annuals. He spent hours with Collihole discussing the renewal of grafting stock, methods of layering, and new pest controls. He even poked his nose into Tim's hybridization experiments and once or twice nearly got it bitten off. He found peculiar delight in the vulgarity of a Homes and Gardens type of display house which Climbers thought would give an up-to-date look to the entrance of the nursery. And all these things he discussed again with Meg. He found pleasure in the affairs of the nursery; he knew that the enthusiasm of the pioneer years with Gordon had gone for ever, but this gave the work its proper measure of remoteness. When at last he got to bed in the early hours of the morning, he lay meditating on the mystery of man's supreme value and of his utter insignificance which demanded in turn the mysterious power to love and to remain apart. He allowed himself to hope that elsewhere people, Robinson Crusoe like, were building up little island cultures of work and pleasure deliberately kept simple, and of loneliness accepted; little islands that might, if chaos were by some improbable chance not yet come, give human activity a new, slow-burning start. Above all, he tried to fight back to the limit of its critical usefulness his natural rage of irony that, playing around these simple, defenceless ideas, might consume and destroy the truth that he surely believed to be within them.

He drove over twice in those warm March days to 'Oblongs' where even the year's exceptional sunshine could reveal no more than a neglected mockery of Miss Jekyll's wild garden of daffodils, muscari, and anemones. Upon each visit he liked Frederica Grant-Pritchard the more. He discovered in her a turn of sentimentalism combined with self-mockery that peculiarly appealed to him as she argued for a complete restoration of the garden of 1905 with no 'improvements', no later species or varieties, only renewal – and then at the next moment agreed ruefully that this would be an affectation of puristic traditionalism, more charming perhaps, more idiosyncratic, but no less pretentious than the re-creation of the parterres and formal walks that once must have ornamented the house, reputed to have been designed by a pupil of Burleigh.

'*That* piece of grandiose snobbery,' he said, 'at any rate was knocked on the head when its Edwardian owner gave it its early Tudor new look and found somewhere the rather bogus old farm-house name of "Oblongs".'

Meg did not accompany him on these visits.

Easter came rather early, and with it the sudden announcement by Meg that she would, after all, be doing odd secretarial jobs for Michael Grant-Pritchard during the recess. David was too annoyed, and, he had to admit to himself, too afraid of what this meant for the future, to make any comment. Meg offered some explanation unasked. 'It's only that I'm not having him say that I made a promise and didn't keep it. Yes, and after all, two hours wasn't very long; there's a little more I want to find out about his whole mystique.' She laughed nervously.

'That's all right,' David said. 'You'll try to fit it in with what's needed here, won't you?'

At this she seemed to lose her nervousness. She smiled mischievously. 'Yes, David, I will try,' she said.

It had to be admitted that at no time during the fortnight that followed did she allow either the housekeeping or the nursery correspondence to be neglected. Only the evenings' musical discussions and the novel reading suffered as she whizzed backwards and forwards from 'Oblongs' in the Rover at every sort of hour by Michael Grant-Pritchard's request. She reported in those days a good deal of the things he had said and her deductions from them.

'It's a whole pocket of English life,' she explained once or twice, 'that I've simply left unexplored under my very nose. And a very important pocket.'

David truly succeeded in not hearing most of what she said and in quickly forgetting the rest. Only once did she rouse his anger. 'Mr Grant-Pritchard,' she used this form of name habitually and ironically, 'is very broadminded, David. He thinks you ought to have a boy friend.'

David knew that he sounded like 'retired colonel' from the past pages of *Punch*, as he said, 'I'd be very glad, Meg, if you would not discuss me with him. And if you must, don't think it necessary to repeat his comments to me. I've no wish to hear them.'

His evident annoyance surprised and disturbed her. 'David,' she cried, 'I only thought it was rather funny. The *impertinence* of his broadmindedness, I mean.'

'Perhaps,' David answered, trying to recover his temper, 'he'll evidence it in the House when the subject comes up for general discussion.'

'Oh, he wouldn't say such a thing in public,' she said. 'He believes that these controversial issues that cut across party lines are liable to get an M.P. into more trouble than they're worth. No, it's just that he's horrified by any sexual self-denial, or for that matter, sexual indulgence – they distract a man from his central aims.'

David, his sudden anger cooled, allowed the rest of her comments to go unheard.

It was Michael Grant-Pritchard himself who succeeded in seriously upsetting David during that fortnight. They met, by chance it seemed, in the hall of Andredaswood where Grant-Pritchard, passing by in the car, had come to bring Meg some correspondence.

'Oh, I'm glad to see you, Parker,' he said. 'I was intending to ring you up. I'm a bit at sea about this garden scheme of yours.'

'Of your wife's.'

'Yes, she's really found herself an interest, hasn't she? I suppose it's all right, but I can't help thinking that all this Edwardian garden-making's a bit out of keeping with the house. It's by a pupil of Burleigh's, you know. The proportions are beautiful.'

David spoke as sweetly as he was able. 'The interior is very fine,' he said. 'I'm less happy about the early Tudor exterior.'

'Yes, that's a frightful bit of nonsense. I suppose it's got a charm *as* such. I must see if I can get Betjeman down to say whether it's amusing or not. But these great herbaceous borders! They always strike me as suburbia on a large scale. I think if you have a really good house, you should go all out for the formal garden these days.'

'Oh yes,' David said, 'I think Miss Mitford would agree that it was more U.'

Michael-Grant Pritchard gave what David imagined was his charming, boyish chuckle. 'That's exactly where I got the idea from,' he said. He dismissed the subject with a smile. He waited until David had turned to mount the stairs, then he said, 'Your sister's a phenomenally good secretary.'

David turned round to face him, but gave no more than a perfunctory smile.

'She's that rare thing,' Grant-Pritchard went on, 'an intelligent woman who can also do dogsbody work quickly and well. She'd have no difficulty with research and, of course, she's got all the social gifts. She's the perfect private secretary in fact. I must tell you that I've been advising her to leave this place altogether. She's completely wasted here.'

It was only as he heard this said that David knew what utter desolation Meg's absence would mean for him, had indeed meant on the evenings during that fortnight when she had been at 'Oblongs'. He managed with difficulty to say, 'Wasted is a relative word, surely.'

'Oh yes,' Michael Grant-Pritchard was more arrogantly drawling than usual, 'I'm using it so. Her exceptional talents are wasted in relation to a backwater like this.'

Meg was not home until after eleven that night. David had determined to say nothing to her, but so great was his anxiety, that the question burst from him as soon as she came in.

She looked at him in distress. 'Oh, David!' she cried, 'of course I'm not taking any notice of what he says. As a matter of fact, it was the most impertinent suggestion. Apparently I'm so good that even Mr Grant-Pritchard considers relinquishing his share in his present secretary. He's pretty certain he could find some other M.P.s to share in the expense of my services. And since I'm such a pinko he might even be able to get a Labour chap to join with them just to please me.

Ha, ha, ha! When he's uncertain of my reaction, David, he treats me to little jokes suitable for a niece of twelve.'

David, as he heard this out-of-hand rejection, first calmed into stillness and then trembled with happy excitement. He laughed aloud and Meg, pleased, echoed the laughter. Then she added, 'But I wish you weren't so upset by a thing like this. David. It isn't right.'

She continued with her journeys to 'Oblongs' but they gave David few qualms now. Indeed, he hardly noticed when she was at home one whole day until she said, 'Mr Grant-Pritchard's given me three days' well-earned holiday. He used those words!'

It was on the second of these days that Frederica Grant-Pritchard suddenly appeared at Andredaswood to see David. She looked, David thought, tired and older; her plump pink and white flesh seemed mottled, and her blue eyes protruded more than usual through her heavy eyelids now red rimmed.

She said, rather breathlessly, 'I'm afraid it isn't going to be any good. I'm so sorry I've given you all that trouble. Michael's got quite different ideas now – terraces and long avenues of beech hedge. I think there are to be fountains. It'll all be enormously expensive. But much more in keeping with the house, of course.'

David said only, 'With the sham early Tudor?'

'Oh, well, I think Michael's having the façade restored.'

'It will be expensive.'

'Yes. But, of course, it'll repay us if we have to entertain a lot. If Michael's made a junior minister, you know.' She looked so desperately at him that he made no further comment. 'Of course, you're to do it for us,' she said, 'Michael's most insistent on that. You'll find him full of ideas when you work with him.'

He did not wish to distress her further, so he kept back his rejection. 'Well, we'll leave that until you're ready to start, shall we?'

'Yes,' she said, 'it might be some time yet. Michael won't be back again before the House sits, and then in the summer recess he's leading a study party to the Ruhr. He feels we've so much to learn from them. Oh,' she added with a little cry of remembrance, 'will you tell your sister that he's gone? I don't think he had time to tell her himself. I expect she'll be only too pleased. He's been overworking her monstrously.'

David told Meg with a certain relish. He had expected her to be surprised or, at least, angry, but she seemed only amused.

337

'Oh dear, I can just see him thinking that not to give me notice would serve me right for refusing his moth-eaten offer.'

'Such lack of self-control can hardly be helpful in his career,' David said.

'Oh, dear God! He wouldn't allow himself such childish indulgence with anyone that mattered,' she said. 'Scenes from the private life of a great man. That's what we've been privileged to see, David. And very interesting it's been. I shouldn't be a bit surprised if he wasn't trying to cheat me out of my wages as well. He probably thinks I'm too much of a lady to write and ask for them. But he's wrong.'

David told her of the changes of plan for the garden at 'Oblongs'.

'Oh, dear,' she said, 'that means a loss of money to you. But I *do* see you couldn't work with him.'

'I'm mainly sorry for *her*.'

'Yes, I suppose I ought to feel more for her. But, you see, after all, David, like Mother, she has an adoring son to fight for her. He's only fourteen but I've seen the way he looks at her and at *him*.'

David felt, that evening, as though he had been playing one of the race games they had possessed as children – there it had been – four spaces ahead the Wicked Tory Wizard, land on him and you must go back to the beginning; but he had thrown five and was clear. Nevertheless, for a day or two Meg seemed abstracted and depressed, so that in the end he said to her, 'We agreed to be honest with each other, Meg. Do you regret not taking that man's offer?'

She smiled and said, 'Good heavens, no! It's unsettled me a little, but I'm happy to see you happy. No, that's like Mother. I'm truly happy, especially if we could get started with those articles.'

To David it seemed only fair to help Meg to adapt herself after the 'nervous attack of Grant-Pritchard', as he now called it to himself. He waited until the next day when in the office they were checking accounts, then he said to Tim in her presence, 'Do you think you could take over for a few months, Tim, if I wanted to have time off? I'm thinking of writing a book, not a gardening one.'

Tim said immediately, 'Good Lord, yes. Any time you like,' so that even Meg laughed and cried, 'Do be more tactful, Tim.' But she was clearly delighted.

The next day Tim said, 'Eileen was as pleased as Punch that you were considering handing things over to me for a while.' There was something in his tone that made David raise his eyebrows. There were ambitions in the simple Rattrays that he had not divined. This he told Meg, but she said only, 'Well, why not? He really cares about the work.'

He smiled a little grimly, and she said quickly, 'In any case, you can rely on him for a few months. It's as well, really, that she *did* veto the dance band.'

He said dryly, 'In fact, everything is for the best in the best of all possible worlds. Nevertheless, the hand-over will have to be made by easy stages.'

'Not too easy, David,' she said.

The exhilarating weather of April with its lively south-east breezes and bright sunshine turned to a boggy, sodden May. The wind still blew, but in south-westerly squalls that brought, in the first days, showers and eventually a ceaseless, dampening, fine rain, alternating with torrents and gales that beat down the azaleas, broke the stoutest tulips and left the rhododendron bushes with sodden blooms. Despite the south-west wind, it turned cold, with frost at nights and one or two hailstorms. All gardeners and farmers were in distress. Tim lived to protect the blooms of his new hybrids. Mr Boniface was forever saying to Meg that they, being townspeople, suffered more from bad weather in the country than the natives; yet, for the first time she had some differences with her over the need for fires. But Meg won her way and fires there were. Over them she and David crouched, happily absorbed in their reading and note taking.

They had enlarged their scheme to take in evidence from periodicals and from diaries and memoirs. Even the additional number of books they could get from the London Library by making Meg a country member would not now suffice, and they scoured Sussex, Kent, and Hampshire for booksellers with sets of periodicals. These days spent in book-hunting became a pleasant activity in themselves. They drove through cloud-menaced downland, across marshes swept with rain, and along gale-blown sea fronts, remarking only, with a mock eighteenth-century phrase or two which they now often exchanged, on the grandeur of nature in her ruder aspects and more horrid moods. They ran from the car to the shelter of hotels and ate bad luncheons amid strange, washed-up people and laughed delightedly over both.

A part of each morning for Meg was spent in making lists of desiderata for second-hand booksellers, and in checking booksellers' catalogues. The bibliography was clearly going to be fun. David's quiet self, looking on, approved it all – Meg's pleasure, his own. Now and again a crisis in the weather-battered nursery called him out and he went, always with one eye on Meg for her approval; but Tim was clearly in full control and the interruptions were few.

David had now agreed with Mary Gardner and the Wing Commander that they should postpone the resumption of practising together until they had fully considered on various local candidates for the place of second violinist; to practise regularly with anyone and then finally to choose someone else would provoke embarrassment. Mary Gardner, indeed, was not satisfied with any of the violinists who offered themselves and declared her intention of looking beyond their immediate acquaintance during the summer. David agreed to do the same. As to 'musical appreciation – a speciality', this had now reduced itself to one evening a week of record playing – a relief from reading and a chance to lessen Climbers' loneliness. He and Meg were, therefore, able to give themselves up entirely to the novels. David read and took occasional notes; Meg read and prepared an ever-extending bibliography.

David could not remember such a time of relaxation and he saw from Meg's fresh, smooth face in the mornings, and the disappearance of the hungry look in her eyes, that she knew this peace in her night-time solitude as well as in their day-time communion. They were both a little startled when those around them commented on the departure of so disastrous a May and on the better auguries of June's first week of blazing sunshine.

A mild winter followed by a wet May had, however, brought every kind of pest and blight upon the vegetable world. A violent quarrel broke out between Tim and Collihole at the loss of a number of rose bushes from blackspot. Tim insisted that Collihole, intent on the graftings that were in any case blind avenue work already carried out elsewhere, had neglected elementary precautions. Collihole, furious, said that he was blamed for the inevitable effects of weather. Tim insisted on a complete reorganization of the rose culture. Collihole came in fury and appealed to David; he would give notice if ... Tim, consulted, declared that the man's departure was long overdue. It seemed to David that he must intervene; if he explained the changes Tim wished for, carefully and with great care for Collihole's pride, he would accept them and stay. Meg asked, 'Why, David? Is it fair to Tim? Surely if the man's as foolish as that, he should go.'

David replied with an attack on such root and branch attitudes to human beings, 'Collihole has bees in his bonnet. We've probably indulged him to let them buzz too much. But he's done excellent work for us.' He tried to meet her a little. 'Gordon and I ran things on paternalistic lines, Meg. Perhaps we were wrong, but you can't mould people to that pattern and then throw them overboard because they conform to it.'

She did what he could not remember happening since they had been adolescents; she rubbed the back of her hand against his cheek. She said, 'I don't *want* to hurt you, David, you know.'

He cried, 'Hurt! My dear Meg, I truly believe that it's you who saved me from a hopeless bitterness after Gordon's death. But let me do this my own way.'

She answered very softly, 'Of course. Of course.'

It was almost now the longest day of the year and David thought perhaps the happiest evening of his life. It had been a difficult day. The heat was intense. Nothing in the nursery seemed quite unimpaired by ravages of one kind or another. Collihole had been excessively obtuse, almost playing the simple gardener to test how far David would bear with him. Tim, too, was sulking like a tough little boy. It seemed to David that unconsciously they were playing in rivalry upon his sexual feelings. The women, also, had hardly been more helpful. Climbers ran to and fro, gruffly urging Tim's rights and Collihole's hurt feelings, in a desperate effort to show that she shared in David's divided emotions. Eileen rang up and, in an extra matter-of-fact voice that suggested hysteria, informed David that perhaps he didn't realize that Tim regarded this as the test of how much he was valued, and perhaps also he didn't realize that, for all his hearty manner, Tim's self-confidence hung by a thread. Mrs Boniface announced that new brooms swept clean but that they soon wore out; she would not have credited, she said, the affection that an ordinary chap like Collihole could command in the nusery and in the village. There was no doubt that the quarrel had produced strong emotions among all the nursery staff, but David suspected that not a little of the passion was born of the sudden intense heat and the strain of the damage done by the rains. He made it his aim to pacify, listen, sympathize, encourage, and yet to remain withdrawn. He had, he believed, that day made much progress; there was beneath the appearance of intransigence and caballing a new spirit of respect for each other's virtues in both Tim and Collihole.

By evening, however, he was utterly exhausted. It was then that

Meg's comforts seemed dearest to him. Not most important but very valuable were the material comforts she offered: a good and cooling gin fizz in the private garden, dinner of cold duck and orange salad, preceded by a pâté made from the giblets, and followed by fresh strawberry shortcake. After the meal they sat in the morning room, because here, with windows and doors open, came the scent of the climbing pelargonia from the Victorian greenhouse on the one side and the scent of the tobacco plants from the window beds on the other. They drank iced hock and soda. They listened with Climbers, tranquil and entranced, to his favourite recording of *Trovatore* with Milanov as Leonora. When Climbers left they still had an hour or two to give to their reading.

He was deep in the second volume of Godwin's *St Leon*. The book, as he read, seemed to speak particularly to him. Godwin's sense of the corruption caused by ambition, by self-assertion and, above all, by the use of absolute power for high moral ends, was his own article of faith. As he read the passages that told of St Leon's tranquil, simple home in the Alpine sweetness, he found tears in his eyes as he expected the coming of that offer of the philosopher's stone that would corrupt St Leon, bringing power and ruin in its wake. If only St Leon could accept the inevitable destructive forces of nature – the hailstones that reduced simple peasants to beggars overnight – and not seek the power to master the universe; if he could learn to ride the storm instead of fighting it. ...

Meg, perhaps less deeply absorbed in checking *The New Monthly Magazine* book advertisements for obscure and forgotten novels of the seventeen-eighties, said suddenly, 'I wonder if this theme will provide a whole *book*, David?'

Absorbed in *St Leon*, he said abstractedly, 'Perhaps hardly that. But I shouldn't be surprised if it didn't make quite a fascinating article.' She made no comment. As he read on in *St Leon* he found himself in greater opposition to Godwin, though no less admiring. Godwin's ultimate pessimism about man's fate irritated him. It was born, of course, of a Calvinist upbringing – there was always a vengeful God withholding grace in the background, and suffering in having to withhold it, he thought with disgust. A masochistic God must produce a masochistic creature, no doubt. Then he thought how much he shared of Godwin's masochistic pessimism; but I don't go with it that far all the same, he decided. Perhaps if women in Godwin's books – St Leon's wife, for example – had been less sweetly simple, had had more of Meg's vitality and surprisingness, there would have been a less self-punishing determinism about the novels.

He said, 'Reading Godwin, Meg, makes me wish that abridgements were not impossibilities. It's true that a few people knew *Caleb Williams*; but the importance of his other novels for the world today is so striking.'

She said, 'I didn't find much in *Fleetwood* that threw light on *our* theme.'

He said, 'No, you're quite right. I was just thinking his failure to depict anything like a sexual relationship is central to the weakness of his books. It's a reflection, I'm afraid, of his own private life – an escape from the too rending memory of Mary Woolstonecraft. It makes him a minor novelist. But within his obsessive limits, he's great.'

She said, 'Yes, I don't know what *we* can do with him, do you?'

He answered, laughing at the utilitarian implications of the phrase he used, 'No, *we* shan't *get* anything out of him.'

He went back to his reading. It was only some time later that he was conscious of her closing a volume with a snap of the cover.

'July, seventeen-eighty-seven finished, David,' she said. 'I'll make a note of that for you.'

'Good,' he said.

He heard the hiss of a syphon and, reaching his arm over the back of his chair, he sought her hand to say good-night. But her voice came from the doorway. 'Good-night, David,' she said. 'Don't stay up too late, you may have a hard day ahead of you.'

For a moment his mind went to Collihole and Tim. 'Oh, Lord, so I may,' he replied, but he heard the contentment in his own sigh. The door had shut and she was gone to bed.

He read on, needing to see with horror St Leon fall to temptation before he could leave the book. When he got up from his chair the clock told half past one. He was conscious of the chatter and succeeding high trills of the nightingales in the copse at the garden's end. As a rule the bird song was monotonous and tedious to his ear, but this evening it seemed to carry him away in pleasure over into the wood and on through to the forest. He thought, as he stood by the open window, of Meg perhaps awake in her room, listening with joy to the same song. It was then that he decided that this was the happiest evening of his life. He rejected the obsessive self-punishing voice that said it would soon be the only real kind of pleasure that man can know – nostalgic memory. He said firmly to himself, 'It's only *one* of a long chain of such evenings to come.'

When Meg came down to breakfast the next morning, she was wearing a hat. David took in no details of its shape, no details of her suit – except that the colour which fuzzed and swam before his eyes was a sort of sickly biscuit. Immediately he saw the hat, he thought, I have known this for some time, she's going. And yet this knowledge was only a voice among many in his consciousness, and all the others fused together from various memories to tell him that he had never thought of her leaving, that there was no reason why she should leave, that she was not, in fact, leaving, that there was nothing strange about her appearance save the hat. His vision steadied, ceased to revolve before him, and what came foremost to his now clear gaze was her eyes – they seemed not birdlike and bright as usual, but round like a lemur's, staring in a sort of dotty surprise. She said, 'David, I'm going this morning.'

His mouth filled with bile and his stomach heaved nervously. He heard himself saying, like someone fencing on the stage, 'I thought the Tunbridge Wells trip was *tomorrow*.'

She said slowly, 'I'm going from Andredaswood, David.'

He spoke pleadingly, again hearing himself as though on the stage, 'Look, if you'll give me two days to settle the Collihole business, I'll come with you if you'd like that. We could take the Gothic novels to the Rhineland. That would be rather amusing.'

She sat down as though exhausted already with the scene to come. 'You know that I mean that I'm going from here for ever.'

The stagey, dramatic note of that last word made him giggle, and at the sound, she turned away as though she could not bear to see how much she would hurt him. She said, 'David, you must have seen how I've felt in this last week. I *must* go to London, get a job, live on my own. For my own sake, and for yours.'

The sane part of his mind insisted to David that he *had* known, and yet he could remember nothing but the conviction that she would stay, that their happiness was complete and final. He felt that the voice was trying to rob him of the right to feel badly treated. He said, 'It's that bloody man Grant-Pritchard who's got at you.'

'Oh, David, whatever sort of fantastic picture of our relationship have you built up? I haven't thought of the man again. Oh, that's not true. I've often thought of the implications of his existence and of people like him. I wrote to him, too, and got my money and a thumping good reference. But as for his influencing me! Really! Oh, please don't make it difficult for me by refusing to understand. I've behaved badly enough.'

'Meg,' he said, 'you've not behaved badly to me at all. You've made all the difference to my life. I've told you so. I think, if you ask me, not that you're behaving *badly* now, but just crazily. I don't speak only about the happiness you've given me, but about your own happiness here. You've said how happy you are; and even if you hadn't said so, I've seen it for myself.'

'Happiness?' She queried the word. 'Of course I've been happy here. I could go on being happy for some time if I gave no thought to what it meant. I'm to blame. I came here and fed on the calm you gave me and refused to give it up. But I was ill, David, you must grant me that. What I don't understand is how you can confuse the real living peace that *was* in you, for all your unhappiness, all your tight discipline and self-repression, with the vegetable ease, the creeping lethargy that's gradually paralysing you now that you're what you call happy.'

He shook his head, and she said, 'No, you're quite right. Now that you are happy. Oh, I'm not against happiness. Dear God, no. But how long will this last? This compromise, for that's what it is, David. You give me calm, I give you happiness. You pretend to change things to the way that I want them for you. Yes, it is *for* you, as it was *for* Bill. That's the way I destroy people, I suppose. And *I* pretend that I accept your pretence. I've tried to fool myself because I've wanted to be with you so much, but last night it came home to me too forcibly. You've given up the frets, the irksome things that pressed up on you – that Africa book; Else; probably you'll gradually give up the nursery. But you won't start the quartet again – why? Because it's more cosy sitting with me reading all the books we read when we were young; and if I like to believe that out of it something constructive will come, a book worth writing, well, I'll gradually learn that it won't. Oh, you may not think that consciously; but that's how it's going. And it's all my fault. I've just misunderstood. All the things I've tried to relieve you of – the nursery work that had no interest for you, playing in a poor quartet because of a woman you had nothing in common with, working on a book you despised. Yes, and no doubt living with a man you loved whom you never touched. All this self-denial and self-discipline which seemed futile to me was what made you apart, withdrawn – what gave you that calm that saved me when I was lost. And now slowly but surely the calm is turning into plain self-indulgent apathy, the irksome disciplines into pleasing triviality. And you just don't notice it, David, that's what I can't understand. I've tried not to, but the sentimental, cosy futility of last night decided me.'

He said slowly, 'You only decided this last night! I see, Meg, you'll go away for a while, but you'll come back.'

She made no answer, and he went on, asking, 'Where will you go? You know how it was before.'

She said, 'Oh God, David, do you think I want to go back to that loneliness. But I can face it now, and that's because of the help you've given me. Surely that I can take on loneliness again shows you how important I think it is for us to break this up.'

He said, 'Meg, I haven't made many plans for myself in my life, but don't you see how horribly lonely I am going to be?'

She answered slowly, 'Indeed I do, David. It's an agony to me to think that you will be so and to believe that if I wanted to, I could change it. Your loneliness is your strength, David. And anyhow, what does it mean? You will be alone. I will be alone. Were we any less so really when Bill and Gordon were alive? No, that's casuistry. But all the same, for you, David, I know that loneliness and self-denial have made you somebody of strength, and I will not destroy it. Nor, David – let me be honest – will I destroy myself. You feel that apart, cut off from the world, you can live a life that, by not harming, helps the world. I've wanted to persuade myself into it because it soothed me; but for me the only way I can feel of use is to keep my curiosity, to be with people – yes, even awful people like Michael Grant-Pritchard. It's no denial of your truth, but for me the only sense is to assert one's faith in people by living among them. I'm quite a silly person, David, really.'

She looked at him wearily. 'I can't produce more than platitudes, David, but don't let's hurt ourselves more than we need; we're only such very unimportant specks among millions. I love this place, David, and you more than I could have believed. When time's passed a bit, I'll come for a visit. But don't expect letters, I don't write. But I'll let you know that all's well.'

He said, 'This is only a sudden impulse, Meg. You'll come back.'

She was silent, then she said very lightly, 'I've flown in this, that, and the other direction, David, so that it's very reasonable you should think so.' She had made preparation enough, however, for a taxi to

346

come, and for her luggage to be sent on after her. She kissed him on the cheek. 'Don't come to the station,' she said and was gone.

It was only ten days later that a letter arrived. 'I've taken a job with two psycho-analysts – husband and wife, a very roly-poly, chuckling *gemütlich* middle-aged German and a funny, slightly common, intelligent, good-looking English wife who wears jeans. She's years younger than him, she seems almost a girl. It will be interesting to see the witchdoctoring and voodoo from behind the scenes. And I've found a room near Regent's Park that really isn't at all bad, with a sort of Victorian landlady that I would not have believed existed. She's a Baptist and never goes further than Baker Street or Swiss Cottage. She talked about having crossed the water five or six years ago to see a sister in Kennington! And all this is a little street behind that expense account world of Abbey Road.' There were four pages of interesting things she had seen or heard.

David's nursery seemed to envelop him into a mist where every sound or sight in Andredaswood came with the shock of an object walked into blindly.

No letter came then for many weeks. David's loneliness, his unhappiness grew into unbearable tensions and insomnia. He spent much of his energy fighting a wish to hate and to blame her. One afternoon he heard Tim singing, 'I'm a little boy that's lost in a wood, misunderstood. Won't you be good and watch, watch over me,' his eyes filled with tears. It was a turning point. Such nauseating self-pity drove him at any rate to a determined course of self-control, so that gradually the unhappiness became a numbed pain. He remembered Gordon more and more, though Meg not less, yet he felt that Meg had perhaps only filled in the void that Gordon had left.

In this mood, he began to think again of 'Africa'; he wrote to the publisher. They had found as yet no substitute author and he agreed to resume work on the book. He could not really tell whether this was because Gordon's memory pulled him to it, or whether it was to escape from the misery that he felt in reading the Gothic novels without Meg beside him. He involved himself again completely in the nursery affairs. Tim was inevitably disappointed, and Eileen angry, but, it seemed, she found it easier to blame it all on Meg. Indeed the feeling they all had that Meg had treated him badly – and his obvious misery confirmed it – made his return to the nursery easier. When he mentioned that Meg was working for a psychiatrist, Climbers said,

347

'I should think that might do her a lot of good, shouldn't you, David?' and Tim said quite simply, 'I miss her.'

He received another long letter from Meg at Christmas. She was leaving the psychiatrists, she said, but on very good terms. 'It's been quite fascinating. They're inclined to be godlike in their attitude to everybody, but it's understandable really if you saw the ghastly wrecks they've helped. They have eighty per cent success! They've been very kind to me and I've met a lot of fascinating people through them. But I can't accept their attitude to their two children; and as my motivation is all too obvious, and anyway, they're hardly likely to listen to me, we discussed it all and agreed it was better that I should leave. They've given me a wonderful reference. I'm going to work with Helen Rampton, the Labour M.P. I thought a woman out for a career would be interesting. She seems an edgy, unsatisfied sort of woman with a strange and pleasing directness. I think we shall get on well together. She's involved these days with what she calls "the old people scandal"; I seem to be back with "Aid to the Elderly" but from a rather more interesting vantage point. Funnily enough I got the job through some friends of Bill's who used often to come to Lord North Street. I never knew them well, but I've seen a good deal of some of our nicer friends of those days.'

Then suddenly the writing changed. 'David, I should dearly love to come to Andredaswood for Christmas, but I just can't. I'm not free yet nor, I suspect, are you.' There was a postscript. 'I haven't been able to keep away from ceramics. David, there's a quite perfect very small object, what they call a chamber candlestick – Bow with a blue underglaze. Would you buy it for three hundred and fifty pounds? Why should you? It's only that I should love to buy again *and* I should like to think of it at Andredaswood.'

David agreed. When it arrived, he thought it quite lovely. He hoped its presence might draw Meg down there again. Else Bode, who had returned to take over the housekeeping, thought it 'unreal'. Mrs Paget, who had now come to live at Andredaswood so that Else could look after her, wondered what Gordon would say about the expenditure of so much money on a candlestick. A second stroke had left her still mobile, but with her mind impaired.

In the early spring, David got a letter from Hong Kong. Meg had gone there as secretary to a Labour delegation examining the social services of the Crown Colonies. 'I can't tell you how interesting work with Helen Rampton has been. She's a desperately sad woman in many ways; she hasn't got quite what's required ever to become a minister, and she knows it. Yet it hasn't made her ungenerous. She's been extraordinarily kind to me. This trip, of course, has been a lifetime's chance. I was terrified of what would happen when we went to Srem Panh, because I miss Bill so dreadfully still, and always shall. But we only stopped at the airport and it meant nothing. Nothing at all. My memories now of Bill are happy ones. And what I didn't do for him I shall have always to suffer for. Something that could have been upsetting but in the end was only comic happened at Nairobi. An old American woman got on the plane for Colombo. She was that old globe-trotting Christian Scientist I told you about that was on the plane to Srem Panh with Bill and me. I thought she hadn't recognized me but she had. As we got off she said with such an archness it was almost obscene, "Love's a great healer, dear." I suppose she thought that I'd married again, but as I was sitting next to Ronald Shuffler, the Trade Union man, who's seventy-five and fifteen stone, it wasn't very flattering.'

Towards the end of the letter she wrote, 'As a matter of fact, I think I shall make a change when I get back. I know the political chatter now. I should like to see something of the industrial side of things. Old Shuffler suggested that I got a job as secretary to a personnel officer at some big works in the London area. It seems a good idea. At any rate in a few years at least, the modern world won't be able to take me by surprise so easily again.'

There came other letters from Meg in her new job during the summer and autumn months. David was always aware that in the back of his mind he knew that she would return; and being so aware, he ceased to feel the possibility as a very real one.

BY THE SAME AUTHOR

The Old Men at the Zoo

'Each new novel by him is an adventure, opening up strange perspectives of the heart and mind to the reader's alerted and alarmed inspection' – *Sunday Times*

In the offices of London Zoo Simon Carter, the new Secretary, is enmeshed in power games with his colleagues. Into this disciplined, civilized atmosphere breaks the cataclysm of atomic war. As the novel develops into a chilling imaginative vision of the apocalypse, blending myth, symbolism and fantasy, Angus Wilson emerges as one of the most influential political satirists of the twentieth century.

No Laughing Matter

This exhilarating, panoramic novel charts the fortunes of the Matthews family, a group of unconventional, middle-class Londoners, from the First World War to the 1960s. Theatrical, a brilliant mixture of parody and pastiche, it explores history as farce and superbly captures the complexity of family relationships and tensions.

'*No Laughing Matter* draws its strength not from its cunning technique but from its unerring sense of what made England tick between the two world wars ... His ears missed nothing, not a single nuance. They captured, time and time again, the sound of the way we live now' – Paul Bailey in the *Observer*

Hemlock and After

For Bernard Sands, the novelist, great liberal and humanist, the setting up of a writer's colony at Vardon hall is to be the climax of his distinguished career. But Bernard has influential enemies, and life is further complicated by his wife's mysterious illness and his own homosexual affairs. Writing with dazzling originality and insight in this, his first novel, Angus Wilson ensures that Bernard's liberal ideas, public and private, are put to the test.

'A very remarkable achievement ... Mr Wilson is one of the most gifted and original writers of his generation' – Jocelyn Brooke

Anglo-Saxon Attitudes

In *Anglo-Saxon Attitudes* – considered by many to be Angus Wilson's masterpiece – a gripping detective story of archaeological fakery combines with the portrait of a man compelled to face the truth about himself and his marriage, family and professional life.

'Angus Wilson's brilliant and ambitious novel is about the conscience as it worries two generations of a middle-class family ... And here lies the great originality of Mr Wilson as a novelist and the richness of the book. Its moral seriousness is matched by the comic explosions of our tradition' – V. S. Pritchett in the *New Statesman*

The Wild Gardens: or Speaking of Writing

The Wild Garden is both an autobiographical essay on the creative process and a remarkable personal account of the circumstances surrounding the nervous crisis that impelled Angus Wilson to become a first-time writer at the age of thirty-six.

'*The Wild Garden* is, quite simply, one of the finest accounts of the creative process by a recent writer that I know. Here Angus Wilson looks at the springs of writings in a way that all writers can recognise, and all readers can appreciate as a way into the brilliant, discovering imagination that lay behind his major novels' – Malcolm Bradbury

and forthcoming:

As If By Magic
Late Call
Setting the World on Fire
Collected Stories